Joyce,
Thank you for all your
support!

S. Overton
4/16/22

MW00610866

The Mortal Gate

by

Seth Overton

Copyright © 2021 Seth Overton
All rights reserved. No part of this book may be reproduced in
any form on or by electronic or mechanical means, including
information storage and retrieval systems, without permission in
writing from the author, except by a reviewer who may quote
brief passages in a review.

ISBN: 978-0-578-34383-9

To Bethany, for there is no obstacle too great that we cannot overcome.

CONTENTS

Afterword
About the Author
About Party Up Publishing

ACKNOWLEDGMENTS

To my wife, Bethany, who gave me the push to follow my dream. If it wasn't for her, this would just be another notebook collecting dust.

To my family back home, who never stopped supporting me.

To Andy Norley, my editor, for his hard work and keen eye during the writing process.

To Cecelia Schrock, my cover artist, for her endless creativity and imagination to bring my cover to life.

And finally, to you. The readers. Thank you for following my characters on their journey of action, adventure, and self-discovery. You helped me give life to this story, and I am forever grateful.

Thank you.

CHAPTER 1

The view through the scope is starting to get shaky. Keeping the retinal view steady for the perfect shot is always a daunting task, but it's necessary for those who had the patience to wait for their prey. The trigger is picking up condensation from how long my index finger had been resting on it. But it's time to be vigilant. The sounds of approaching footsteps cause me to stir but couldn't be cause for hasty action. All sides are covered, save for the one directly in front of my position. The only place the target could approach, knowing that they weren't alone here. The footsteps slow down to a walk. Just a couple more seconds. The target goes into a sprint again. Through the 'scope, the target finally shows their face.

"Bang."

The trigger is squeezed and it's a direct hit. But the target isn't done yet, hanging on for dear life. I quickly reload my rifle to end it. Gazing through the 'scope, I find the target, frantically but fruitlessly trying to escape. I squeeze the trigger sending one last round into the target's head. Finally, it's done. "#1 Victory Royale" flashes on the screen.

I can hear the last player cursing and insulting my mom, but that didn't matter. It only made me chuckle as I gained all the awards from the battle royale. After months of practice, this game has become less of a challenge and more of an endeavor to see how many twelve-year-old kids I can piss off.

"You probably live in your mom's basement!"
"You're probably 40 years old."
"You've never gotten laid if you're this good at *Fortnite.*"
"Get off your fat, lazy ass and do something with your life, you pathetic waste of human life!"

That last one is my favorite. It's amazing to see what lengths these kids will go to make themselves feel better. I live in an apartment in Salt Lake City with a roommate, paying $400 a month for my half. I am 20 years old going to the University of Utah for video game design; go figure. I am not a virgin, but it's been a few years since...that. I am, in my opinion, a slender built guy, although I'm not the biggest fan of the freckles under my eyes.

I take the headphones off of my head and set my controller down, rubbing my eyes and looking at the time on my phone. It's 11:38 A.M., meaning I've been gaming for about six straight hours and class starts in twenty minutes. "Christ." I leave my small bedroom and into the hall that separated my room from my roommate's, who was out of the apartment at class, before going to the bathroom at the end of the hall. I close the door after turning the light on and look at myself in the mirror. My dirty blonde hair is matted down from how long I wore my headphones, and there are dark circles under my dark green eyes. I turn on the faucet and cup some water in my hands before splashing my face with it. Some droplets land on my dark gray oversized tee, which didn't bother me much because I often wore it for bed. Running my hands through the towel I had, I wipe the remaining drops of water on my gym shorts before leaving the bathroom to my room to get ready for class.

When I get to my room, my 'phone is lighting up on the nightstand near my bed. The 'phone shows a missed call and a message from a guy that I met at a game shop in North SLC called "The Cache". His name is Riley, a major gamer like me, but more into tabletop games like *Dungeons & Dragons* and *Magic: The Gathering,* while I stick to console games like *Mass Effect* or *Call of Duty.*

Riley was texting me about a game tournament happening at The Cache and wanting me to get into it. He knew how much of a gamer I was, hardly ever backing down from a challenge that I could face. But in truth, I don't find any challenge in tabletop gaming because I know how Riley thinks during his campaigns. He's predictable and it takes all the fun out of challenging myself. I don't see myself as conceited or self-absorbed, just kind of good at reading people.

I reply with a "Maybe" before putting my phone away and shuffling through my closet for clean clothes. The best I can find was an Xbox One shirt, blue and gray flannel to throw over it, a pair of dark cargo shorts, and my best pair of shoes that have lasted me for a couple of years now. Once I'm dressed, I quickly leave my apartment and run down the stairs that lead to the parking lot, where my bike is locked up at the rack. Quickly taking the chain off, I mount my bike and take off down the street towards campus.

In Salt Lake City, I live in a complex that's about six blocks away from campus, which is a big ass campus for those who have never visited "The U". Nearly 33,000 students, five different schools of study, and a *very* open campus with a lot of foot traffic that was not kind to those of us that rode bikes around. Don't get me wrong, I can drive a car well, but in a place that has so many people and such crazy traffic everywhere, I can't help but feel safer on foot or on a bike.

I ride my ten-speed down the bike lanes on the streets on the way to campus, getting honked at every other car or so. It doesn't bother me much since I always have my headphones in and hooked up to my phone to drown out the endless noise of the city. Reality is a giant clusterfuck of noise and endless conflict at every turn. Violence, death, lies, deceit, and it all just simply sucks. That's why I turned to video games and electronic living, really. It's an escape. The best kind. One that allows us to be whomever, wherever, and whenever we want to be in time and space. An escape where we make our decisions based on how we feel, and we learn the consequences of them without hurting anyone. If, somehow, people could learn to make decisions like those and put them into reality, the world would be less fucked up. At least, in my opinion it would.

I maneuver around some of the cars and bystanders before getting onto the campus itself, getting yelled at by some as I pass by. Sometimes it makes me laugh, other times it just makes me roll my eyes. Campus security often didn't like those who rode bikes or skateboards on campus, but it has hardly ever stopped us. I pull up to the Entertainment Arts and Master Gaming Studio building, where most of my classes and studies undertook. My entire future is in this building, and I love every damn minute of being here.

"Yo, Connor!"

I look behind me with a small smile, glancing at who called out. Mark Yong, a guy I frequently see in the building, and we've become friends and we hang out at the campus social while we wait for our next classes. He's an Asian-American that is going to school for the musical entertainment industry, producing and generating music through different kinds of electronic instruments. Mark is about two inches taller than me, has softer features in the face, and short black hair. In terms of style and appearance, he looks like a kid on Halloween going to a rave. Today, he's wearing a bright blue muscle shirt with Steve Aoki's signature silhouette on it, along with loose-fit shorts, shin-high socks, and sandals. Around his neck are a set of bright white 'Beats' that he wore all the time. Locking arms with him is a young woman, African American, lovely features that compliment her angular face, brown eyes, full lips, and long black hair with red highlights. She's about my height, but healthily slim wearing a white tank top and cut-off shorts, also wearing sandals. Danica, Mark's girlfriend.

They both approach me, with Mark delivering a half-power punch to my shoulder that I returned. "Dude, you look like beaten shit." Danica tries to stifle her laugh, but a small hic-cough still came out of her.

I sigh and stare Mark down, "Dude, you look like a douchebag."

Someone walking by us made a spit-take sound at my comment, which makes me smile in victory while Mark simply just flips me off. Danica pats us both on the shoulder, "You two idiots have fun. I gotta go. See ya." She kisses Mark before walking away, leaving him and I to walk into the building together.

"Plans for Spring Break back home?"

I almost forgot that Spring break is coming up in about a week. "Not really. Probably just hang back here and see if Riley needs any extra hands at The Cache. I could use the extra money for rent. Dennis is getting sloppy with his half."

"Dude you need to get out more," Mark scolds. "Get the hell away from the video games for a while and get a girl or something. Look, this weekend, just come hang out with Dani and me. We'll get some people together, get some drinks in us, have some fun."

I stop in front of the computer labs that I had all of my training and classes in to make my quick exit, "Maybe another time. Gotta go."

The lab is huge. It has nearly thirty computers that are built specifically for programming and game design. Each computer came loaded with two gigahertz of processing power with some damn good RAM, HDMI outputs, and enough system cooling to air out a sauna to keep from system overloads with the amount of programming we do every day.

My computer station is in the far back corner of the lab for me to work in a more private part of the lab. Everyone in the class was responsible for a huge project by the end of the semester, which was creating a startup for anything of their choosing. From my position in the lab, I got a firsthand look at some of the projects the others were doing, and when I say they are rip-offs of every major startup that has been made, I don't joke. I have seen "the next best sandbox title, a revolutionary new MMORPG, and my personal favorite, "the greatest game since *Mario*". The gaming and movie industries have really slipped up on originality, which is why I am trying to create a much more unique style of gaming for a time that looks to find an escape.

"Mr. Wright?" My eyes shoot up from my station and look to the instructor, Professor Torres.

"Yes, sir?"

Professor Torres's expression went from concerned to amused, "Don't give me that 'sir' junk, Connor. Remember, it's Mister T."

That was cringy to hear, a man trying to get everyone to call him by a famous actor's stage name. But he's in charge of giving me my future passing grade to do what I've wanted to do my whole life.

"Yes sir, Mister T."

"That's better," he jokes. At least, I hope he's joking. "So, how goes your work on... what did you call your project again?"

"*Soulscape,* and it's coming together nicely. I think it'll be something to remember."

Professor Torres smiles and gives me a thumbs up before moving on. I look back to the screen and begin working on the programming and mechanics of the startup. This startup, *Soulscape,* was everything I have been building up to on my journey to become a designer and developer. A chance for me, and others that would become interested, to finally escape what they thought was a shitty, empty world.

CHAPTER 2

"Okay everyone, shut down your programs and make sure everything is cleaned up from your stations," Torres announces. The time was up for this class period, and so was another day of frustrating bug fixes and coding. I hate that I can get so easily upset when something this big doesn't go the way I want it to. That's probably the one real lesson from my dad that I'll always hear in my head; "Patience is key. Take your time and it'll all work out." Easier said than done if you ask me.

I gather my things and am out of the door before "Mister T" could try and inspire me any further, deciding to go to the lobby of the building to wait for Mark to get out of his class. I make for one of the vending machines in the lobby to get me a drink just to kill time. The halls are starting to fill with other students leaving the classrooms all fighting to get out of the building. My pockets jingle as I fumble around for some change to put in the machine.

"Christ, a dollar fifty for a can?" I mumble to myself as I deposit the quarters and push the buttons for a Dr. Pepper. The vending machine whirs and clicks, but nothing happens. So, I press it again. And again. Nothing. I shuffle around for more quarters when the sound of a firm hand slaps the side of the machine, scaring the hell out of me.

"Relax. This thing sucks and needs some encouragement at times."

I look to the voice to thank them, but everything in my head suddenly shuts off. The hand belongs to a girl. A college girl. A very grungy, hot college girl. She's got her dark brown hair in a high ponytail where a lock of hair on either side of her head hanging down to frame her face. Her eyes are a light brown that seem to pop with the eyeliner she has on. She's wearing a red and black flannel button-up that was not buttoned, a 'Panic! at the Disco' shirt underneath of it, faded tight jeans with a pre-made tear in the left leg, and finished with a pair of aged blue and black All-Stars.

"Hey, my eyes are up here, weirdo."

Her comment sends me into a frenzy of mentally kicking myself. *Goddammit, get it together! She's talking to you!* I blink rapidly and take the can of soda she's holding for me to take.

"Right. Sorry. Thanks for the help."

"Sure," she says as her hand returns to the solo strap of her backpack that is slung over her shoulder. She turns to leave, and in that moment it feels like the force of the world reached into my stupid mind and pulled out, "I'm Connor!"

My words flood and echo in the walls of the lobby, as bystanders and onlookers pause to watch me stumble and freeze. Even the girl stops and turns in amusement with a cocked eyebrow. Everything in me told me to just turn and run, by my damn legs betrayed me and glued to the floor. The laughs and stares from everyone around me are enough to send me straight into online classes, in the comfort of my own sanctuary. The girl lets out a dry chuckle before she exits the lobby, leaving me to my embarrassment. I don't even wait for Mark to come and meet me; I just leave and don't look back.

I suck at talking to girls. Period. It is sad, pathetic, and I know it. The last successful encounter I've had with a girl was back in my junior year of high school at the Sadie Hawkins dance. Jessie Creed asked me to go, and I said yes. Jessie was nice, but not exactly my type. She was chipper and a bit of a teacher's pet, always getting into people's business. But she was the one who asked me, which was a shocker to me since I never really made myself noticeable. We went to the dance, I danced a couple of slow songs with her, she kissed me and declared us a couple. Everything else that came with being a teenage couple lasted the two of us a solid… three weeks. Memories, eh?

I unlock my bike from the rack and pull it free before I feel my phone go off in my pocket. I pull it out to see another message from Riley reading, *Store, ASAP*. After that mess in the lobby, I could use a good distraction. Odds are that Mark already heard about it and is ready to rip into me about how badly I suck at interacting with women.

I respond with *OMW.*

I mount my bike and put on my headphones, playing some 90's alternative rock from Spotify, before riding away from the studio building. 'The Cache' was settled at the Lower Avenues, about six blocks from campus, conveniently enough. Riley figured the location close to campus may attract some of the nerds that look for a game haven away from their own home, which actually sounds like a good idea if the store wasn't smashed between a coffee shop and a clothing store that got more business than The Cache.

Salt Lake City has bike lanes all over, which absolutely no one enforces or recognizes. Friggin'. Ever. So, just to have some fun, I tend to ride from the sidewalks to a little bit out of the bicycle lane just to piss some people off. I've had a few close calls before, but it only cost me a new bike to learn my lesson on South Temple. It takes about ten minutes for me to arrive at the store. The outside looks almost like an opened treasure chest in a weird brown and gold color combination. In the window, they had some cardboard cutouts of *Magic: The Gathering* characters and *Dungeons & Dragons* posters. But the shop is just a bit smaller on the business street than the other shops nearby, which killed quite a bit of business. The shop sells an abundance of gaming cards, RPG manuals for players and game masters, tabletop game model kits, dice, and even some comic books.

I lock my bike up outside of the store before walking inside to find Riley. As I enter, I look around at the inhabitants of this quaint little nerd hideaway that are all sitting at different tables, playing different games, and talking. It's amazing to me, how close most of these guys all resemble the kind of nerds you would see in a sitcom or a movie; all dressed in some sort of cartoon tee shirt, a choice of either cargo shorts or sweatpants, cheap reading glasses, and disheveled bed-hair. Then you have the nerds like me who try to look somewhat normal. Most days.

"Con-Man! You made it!"

I look past one of the *Yu-Gi-Oh* tables and see Riley rolling past his customers right towards me. Yeah, rolling. Riley is in a wheelchair. He uses his condition to his advantage a lot, and it was hilarious to watch.

He rolls up to me and holds up a fist, so I hold mine up and connected with his. "Hey, Riley. How's it going?"

"Nuh uh," peering through his glasses. "It's D-Day. Today, I am Genathet, the Dungeon Master of 'The Cache'!"

I roll my eyes hard at his proud proclamation. It was "D-Day", which made Riley fall into his alter ego that he made for each *Dungeons & Dragons* campaign he ran. He would even deck out his wheelchair to look remarkably close to the Iron Throne from the show just to "get into character".

"I'm not calling you that while I'm not in character. So, you said to get here ASAP. What's going on? One of your players drop?"

"No! I found something that's gonna to blow your freakin' mind and completely rock the game world. Follow me." He turns around in his chair and rolls to the back of the store. I follow him while stealing glances of everyone that was gaming at the tables we passed by. It did somewhat make me smile to see that while so many people are either lying, cheating, or stealing their way through this crappy life, there are these people who have found a way to ignore it and create better lives of their own.

Riley opens a door to his back room where he has his inventory delivered to, "It's something that showed up in one of my regular deliveries." He reaches into one of the boxes and pulls out a small flat device that resembles an iPad, putting it on one of the unopened boxes.

I raise an eyebrow and look at Riley, "Wow. This really *is* 2020, isn't it? Portable electronic devices."

"Shut up and watch." He touches the center of the device. It lights up and starts playing this awesome and strange music. The lights swirl around on the face of the device, forming an image of a man's face. It looks familiar. Distinguished features, lightly shaved face, slicked back blond hair, dark blue eyes.

"Is that…"

"Dominic Dawson," Riley nods with a smirk. "The chairman of SnoWire Interactive. It gets better, keep watching."

The image gives a soft smile as it looks at the two of us and began to talk. "Hello, loyal customer and fellow gamer. My name is Dominic Dawson, CEO and Head Developer of SnoWire Interactive. You've found a specially placed message meant specifically for *you*. I am offering you an opportunity that you will find very interesting. We at SnoWire have been hard at work on a newly designed and efficient gaming experience, and we want you to be the first to test our new product. Should you accept our offer, this device comes with an acceptance input that will allow us to send the product to the address of your choice within seven business days. Accepting this offer will compensate you, handsomely, with beta testing fees for testing our product. All information and requirements on the product will be found in this device. I, and all of us here at SnoWire, eagerly await your response. Thank you." The simulated message ended with the head disappearing.

Riley chuckles and crosses his arms, "So? What do you think?"

"I think… it's a pyramid scheme. And you're getting hella scammed."

He swats me in the leg. "Come on, man! That was Dominic-freakin-Dawson! And he wants *me* to test a new SnoWire product! I've read into the details, and I need people to help test it!"

"Riley, this doesn't sound right. Why would a multimillion-dollar company send a small game shop an opportunity like this? They're saved for the bigger ones. No offense."

Offense is definitely taken as he picks up the device and scrolls through the material before pushing it at my face. "Read that. If that doesn't interest you, then I'll back off."

I sigh and look at the page he pulled up on the device. As I'm reading, the page explains the benefits of beta testing the product the company would send. The benefits include no charge on the shipping of the equipment, full rights of discovered flaws and bugs to repair, and student financial aid to testers enrolled in college. My eyes grow big at the last benefit, seeing that I can get fully compensated for college courses.

"Holy. Shit."

Riley smiles triumphantly, "So you're in?"

I nod, "Hell yeah I am. Wait... it says the product requires five participants to operate."

Riley grabs the device from my hands. "Five?? That can't be right... 'This new product requires five participants to operate properly and to immerse the players in an adaptive experience.' Always with the fine print bullshit. You're the only one I can think of that is qualified in my friend circle to find bugs and understand the math behind it. I don't trust anyone in the store enough to take this seriously."

I cross my arms as Riley reads over the material. If this beta test is solely for the purposes of product testing and consumer reviews, maybe adding some fresh eyes and gaming noobs could work to our advantage. "Wait... I think I can get us some recruits. What do you have to do to get the equipment?"

"I need to input my information and they'll notify me in a day."

"Do it. I'll take care of the rest."

CHAPTER 3

A couple of days pass until I finally get a message from Riley, saying he successfully got the beta testing approval, and the equipment will be sent to him in four business days. That's how long I have to find three other players for this thing. Based on the information that he sent me, this thing is supposed to be revolutionary gamer technology that will reinvent the whole industry. Apparently, the requirement of five players ensures that it can support a number of players simultaneously without crashing or overloading the system requirements, a little like MMORPG servers.

Lost in my train of thought, I hear my phone getting blown up with texts. Mark keeps hounding me about a party that he wants me to come to tonight with him and Danica. Any other day, I would've blown it off for some gaming or some down time for my project. But I plan to use this chance to corner Mark into teaming up with me and Riley on this thing because he's a sucker for money. The biggest problem I have with partying in college is that everyone expects you to never be without a drink or a person to socialize with… or seduce. Just how the modern age has been destroying the confidence and self-esteem of everyone my age. But I need to swallow my pride on this one, regardless of my views on society, for a few reasons: One, it would do me some good to actually try and be social. Two, the only real friend I have besides Riley is Mark and he has tried to get me to "liven up" as he puts it.

Three, also in the view of Mark, is that I need to get better at interacting with women.

I wait until around 6:00 before starting to get myself looking relatively normal for the first party I have gone to since high school. There's a single mirror in my room that I use to observe the clothes I have, trying to find anything that didn't scream "virgin", or an extra from *Revenge of the Nerds*. I pull out a *Stranger Things* tee shirt and wear it underneath a gray, long sleeve button-up, a pair of faded jeans and my best pair of shoes. Admittedly, it doesn't look any better than what I normally wear, but they're clean and actually make me feel good.

A ding comes from my phone, showing a message from Riley. *It's done. Your turn.*

I smile to myself, pocket my phone and head out of my room. In the kitchen, I see Dennis making a pot of ramen noodles while wearing his headphones and listening to music. As I walk by, I gave him a pat on the shoulder to show that I'm leaving, so he gives me a wave in response before I walk out the front door.

Not knowing if I was going to be drinking, I decide not to take my bike and to just walk to the party. It's being held at one of the local frat houses, only a few blocks from campus and about the same distance away from my place. I text Mark that I am on my way, but he hasn't responded yet. If anything, he was either already there or picking up Danica, which could make it hard for me to ask him about the whole game situation. Danica was nice enough, but she didn't really support his nerdy side. She's very outgoing, loves to be social, and is always in the gym. He won't admit it, but Mark does like the experience of being in a gaming group like ours. Mark used to think that the whole idea of tabletop gaming was just a bunch of fat, four-eyed nerds that had speech impediments and never left their mom's basements. But, after the second campaign day he attended, he became "Sokar, the Goliath Barbarian". It was pretty fun for a while, until he met Danica, who herself attended one of the games at his request but thought the two of them should spend more time together in an environment that didn't involve weird voices and role-playing scenarios. After a few weeks of them dating, Mark convinced Danica that I wasn't a complete nerd, and the three of us started hanging out together, just not in D&D campaigns.

After walking for about ten minutes, and some sore calves, I make it to the frat house, loaded with people and loud, blaring music. Guys in bro-tanks and gym shorts, girls in tube tops and skirts, everyone with drinks in hand, like something out of an 80's film. I push my way past as many people as I can while avoiding eye-contact, attracting glances of all kinds my way before I run into someone and spill their drink on the floor.

"Whoa! watch it!"

"Shit… I'm so—" I look up from the floor and see a girl. The same girl I saw on campus yesterday. Her hair isn't up high this time but draped around her face and framed beautifully. She's in a black tank top with a pair of dark jeans and black open heels. I rip my eyes from her outfit and look at her face, "I-I'm sorry. I didn't see you."

"I think you saw what you wanted to. Wait a minute, you're the guy from the vending machine!" I can't help but stammer before she speaks again, "Well? Gonna get me another drink, or what?"

I blink a bit before nodding, "Y-yeah. My bad. Umm, kitchen, I guess?" She nods at me with impatience. Pushing through the crowd, we get to the kitchen and see a huge assortment of liquor, beer, and a keg.

"What's your poison?" My lame attempt to sound cool.

"How about one of those beers?"

I nod and walk over to one of the many coolers, grabbing a beer before having my wrist held tight and yanked up. "Who the hell are you?"

I'm face-to-face with one of the frat guys holding my wrist along with two of his buddies backing him up.

"He asked you a question." One of them leans in and sneers at me. *A walking cliché.*

"I'm getting a beer," I respond. "It is a party, isn't it?"

They laugh while the head frat guy's grip tightens on my wrist. "Yeah, but you're not a Sigma. So, unless you're a chick in disguise, which you clearly ain't, you need to get the hell out."

"Hey, baby! You got my drink?" Mystery Girl runs straight up into my arms and takes the beer from my hand. She then looks at the frat boys with a disgusted look, "You guys got a problem?"

They all look dumbfounded at the two of us, until the big one lets my wrist go. "You two?"

"Connor." Mark and Danica come up behind the girl and I, looking to the frat guys. It's now a standoff between us and them. Mark steps in front of me and stares them down, "Why don't you guys go enjoy the party. We'll go and do the same."

A couple of moments pass until we all go our separate ways. The girl separates from me and laughs. "That was fun! Almost a full-on fight."

I can't even respond as I try to calm down, so Mark speaks for me. "Thanks for your help. What's your name?"

"Krissy," she smiles while popping the tab on her beer and taking a giant gulp. This impresses us all, even Danica laughs.

"I'm Mark, and this is Danica." She waves in response while I stand silently. Mark reaches over and puts a hand on my shoulder, "I see you already met Connor."

"For the second time. First time was funny back on campus, watching you make an ass of yourself. Good to meet you."

I smile through the embarrassment, feeling judgement coming from the others. That's when I remember what I came here to do. "Mark, can I talk to you for a moment?"

"Sure. Let's go outside away from the noise."

I nod and follow him through the crowd with Krissy and Danica bringing up the rear. Before I can even protest, Danica sent me a glare that read "Not a chance." It's always hard to convince her to give Mark and I a moment. Her, I understand, but why is Krissy tagging along? We make it to the back door that leads outside. There are tables for beer-pong, a large firepit in the center of the patio, and a bunch of groups circled around each other. Mark leads us away from the noise to a table near the pool for us to all sit down. The girls begin talking to each other, getting introductions and gossip out of the way while I sit close to Mark.

"So, what's up? Need a pick-me-up for your date?"

"What? What are – You know what, never mind. Look, I need you back in the game."

Danica must have the ears of a cat because she immediately directs her attention to our conversation. "What game? Mark?"

He instantly backs away, "Hold up, alright? Connor, you know I don't do that anymore…"

"What's going on here?" Krissy chimed in, to which Danica answered the question with the most annoyed tone of voice. "These two used to play some game that is meant for kids. Dunce and Dragons or something?"

"*Dungeons and Dragons*!" I correct, sounding nerdier and more offended than I wanted to.

Krissy's eyebrows shoot up before drinking awkwardly from her beer.

"Besides, this is something different," I begin explaining. "It's some new, immersive virtual reality game that Riley got selected for beta testing. It's from SnoWire."

That grabs his attention, which makes me smirk. I knew that would get him. No matter how much he denies it, or the amount time he spends with Danica, he's a nerd like me and knows quality. "Wait… SnoWire Interactive?"

"With a message from Dominic Dawson, himself. He's offering beta testing to a group of five people for their new experimental project called *The Mortal Gate*."

Mark is genuinely curious at this point, but then Danica pulls on his sleeve "No! Mark, you promised me you'd stop. You need to focus on graduating so we can get out of here. Not wasting time playing make-believe."

"Dani! It's not just about the game. It's about affording the rest of college. Dawson is offering the beta testers full compensation to all participants. Riley is giving us the chance, and I'm not doing it without Mark." I shift my attention to him, "Don't you wanna get the money you need to afford your sound equipment? Rent out a sound studio? I need you, man."

That shuts everyone up almost immediately. Mark looks from me to Danica, then back to me, "How much are we talking?"

"Five thousand a head."

I feel the daggers Danica is shooting into the side of my head from her eyes.

I ignore her staring and hold out my hand for Mark, "One more?"

Taking a deep breath, he nods firmly and takes it. "One more." We smile to each other before feeling a hand slap on top of our clasped hands. We both look into the eyes of a scorned woman. "Fine. But you're not doing it without me."

Even Mark is caught off guard, "Babe, seriously? You hate video games."

She is seething, which makes me scared to even try to take my hand back. "Damn right, I'm serious. One, you broke a promise, so you're in deep shit. Two, it's worth a lot of money and I could use it. Three, I'm going to make sure that this is the last one."

We sit there in a stupor before I shrug, "I mean, she's got a point. Plus, she doesn't need to be experienced to beta test. It'll be a fresh experience for everyone involved."

Mark sighs deeply in defeat, "Fine. So, it's us and Riley. Who's the last one?"

Shit. I pause a second before looking at Krissy, sitting silently, drinking her beer. She looks at the three of us staring at her.

"What? Did I spill something on myself?"

CHAPTER 4

It's been about a week since the party, and it hasn't been a fun one. Danica was constantly ripping into Mark, who decided to take it out on me for doing what I had done. But they agreed to the game as long as they got what they were promised. In that week, Krissy cornered me on campus to give me hell about convincing her to join, which wasn't easy to endure. Even with the money promised, she thought it was a waste of time and overall childish. But eventually she caved, and I'm pretty sure it was Dani who helped us out by saying ever-so supportively, "Don't leave me alone with these idiots." When I told Riley that I had gotten our troops, his response was immediate and explosive.

"HELL YEAH!" was his exact text.

He gave me specific instructions that we were to meet at a location that was not 'The Cache', which surprised me. I asked him about it, and he kept giving me absolutely nothing in return.

It was now the following Saturday, and I got a group text that Riley sent to everyone, giving us some weird instructions: *5:00 P.M. Warehouse District. 19402, Walker Rd. BYOB.*

I give a "thumbs up" emoji as a response, believing, I was the only one responding. But, to my surprise, Krissy actually got back to the group message.

Snacks too, or I'm not coming.

Heh, I like her. Krissy was not the kind of girl I thought she'd be, which is cliche for me to think about in the first place. But she is pretty badass in my book.

I gather some essentials that I think we'll need for the campaign and put them into a duffle; food, character sheets, and a couple half-bottles of alcohol I had stashed away from Dennis so he wouldn't take it. After I pack it all up, I make my way out of the apartment and ride off to the meeting spot. The warehouse district is a solid half-hour bike ride from my place, but I hate the transit busses and didn't want to leave my bike at the apartment for it to be taken. For my evening bike ride, it was actually quite a tour to go on alone since I hardly ever leave my room. The view is pretty cool to see, plus I get to ride by the sculptures and buildings that are always on display. My view on the world may be pretty shitty, but there are things that I like about it. People, on the other hand, not so much.

My calves are practically on fire by the time I finally pull up to the address in the warehouse district that Riley instructed. So, I hop off my bike and start searching for the spot. I look at my phone, seeing that it was 5:13 and I had missed messages from Riley spazzing out on me being late. I roll my eyes and pocket my phone, continuing my way towards the meeting place. As it comes into view, so does Riley pacing around in his wheelchair.

"Hey, Riley!"

He whips his head around and throws his hands in the air out of frustration. "You are impossible! All of you are impossible! I said *five o' clock.*"

I sigh and lean my bike against the wall, locking my front wheel. "Oh, shut up. You're lucky the others even agreed to this. Mark and Danica have been arguing all damn week and taking it out on me at the same time."

"Ugh, fine. At least they agreed."

About five minutes after our little spat, we hear a car coming around the corner. It's Mark's crappy Nissan pulling into the drive of the building and parking. Danica climbs out of the passenger side, followed by Krissy from the back.

Mark walks up to the two of us groaning, "They wouldn't shut up about how much they are *not* looking forward to this."

"Doesn't matter because the boys are back in the game!" He holds up his fists for us to bump, to which Mark and I look at each other before shrugging and bumping them. He's smiling like a lunatic, turning his chair towards the door of the building behind him, "Onward!"

I can hear Danica audibly groan as Mark takes her by the hand and pulls her in after Riley. Krissy nudges my shoulder, "Better have brought that food, nerd."

I hold up my bag and pat it with assurance, "All over it."

Inside, the building was practically hollow, aside from a few crates and some loose items lying around. "Riley? Are you going to murder us?"

"I know one of the warehouse workers here. He let me borrow this space for today for $80."

"Wow, cleaned out the register at 'The Cache', did ya?" Dani and I snort almost simultaneously.

Riley pauses his pushing to flip us off. He leads us to an open space with a waist-high crate that had a black box on top of it.

"Yeah, this looks like the plot of a *Taken* movie..."

Riley quickly pushes himself to the makeshift table he'd set up, turns around, throws his arms open and exclaims, "Welcome, adventurers, to *The Mortal Gate!*"

We all approach the crate and look at the black box, which did indeed bear the title, *The Mortal Gate*. The box art displayed a stone archway with five glistening slots around its frame with a starry night in a mountainous background.

Mark looks at the setup, then at Riley, "What's 'The Mortal Gate'?"

"I'm so glad you asked, my friend!" He clears his throat and begins reading from the back of the box:

"Welcome, Vanguards of the Realm! You have been called to aid the people of Albistair, who are in terror of an occupying dark force of knights known as the Crimson Order, led by the mysterious and tyrannical Archon. This enigmatic force has ravaged the land in search of the Mortal Gate; a great source of unknown power that could either restore peace to the realm or destroy everyone and everything. It is your duty to stop the Archon and reach the Mortal Gate first. Define your roles, work together as a team, and become the heroes, or villains, you want to become!"

I look around the room, seeing a different assortment of reactions to our little group. Mark's dorky side came out, looking genuinely interested in this enigmatic story. Danica is looking absolutely weirded out or disgusted, I can't tell which. Krissy, on the other hand, is stoic with a raised eyebrow. Riley scans around for reactions after putting the box down, "Well?"

"It sounds so dorky."

"Babe, it's for a lot of money."

"But is it worth it to be this...nerdy?"

Mark, Riley, and I all said at the same time, "Yes."

Danica groans but gets a supportive hand on the shoulder from Krissy. "Don't worry, chica. You and I can muscle through this with these geeks. Plus, we have drinks and food, so we're square." Realizing she's outnumbered, Danica sighs deeply in defeat.

Riley starts giggling and unloads the box that had the game inside. Everyone gathered around the table that the game would be set up on, giving me a chance to talk to Krissy.

"Thanks. It wouldn't work out if we didn't have Dani and Mark."

She leans in close and sneers at me, "If this whole doesn't work out, I'm kicking your ass. Got it?"

Admittedly, I'm both scared and impressed with how aggressive she's being. But I didn't blame her for being annoyed. All of us were taking an empty chance on Riley's ambition, thinking that it would help us get through college easier.

Riley finally gets the box opened and empties the contents, and it was quite underwhelming. It consisted of a rolled up black placemat, a package of odd-looking gloves, and metal circlets. Mark and Riley unroll the mat, almost the size of the table that we're using, and nothing was on it at all.

"The hell is this?" Mark looks on the underside, which was the exact same.

Krissy takes the package of gloves and inspects at them closely. "It feels like there's wiring inside these things."

I take one of the metal circlets and look closely. It almost resembles a crown with padded wiring and sensor-looking pads on the inside of them. "These must be some sort of new VR headsets or something."

"There aren't even any written instructions in the box." says Mark, as he and Riley fumble through the box looking for any sort of written directions.

While the others are fumbling and arguing in a state of confusion, I look at the headset inquisitively and put it on my head. The second it rests around my head, part of the placemat lights up and projects a digital message, much like the message from Dominic Dawson. The others hear the glittering sounds coming from the placemat, surround the table, reading the projected message: *"Player One Crest Interface linked. Please synchronize interface gloves."*

I look to the others with my mouth hanging open in shock, "This... this is leading edge tech, right here..."

"Quick, put the gloves on!"

I react quickly and look to Krissy, taking a pair of gloves from her. I shove my fingers into the gloves and strap the Velcro around my wrists. Not entirely sure what to do, I hover my hands over the mat and wait.

"Player One, synchronized. Please wait for remaining players."

I look around to everyone, who all have different reactions to what is happening. "Come on guys, we're in it now. Let's do this."

Without hesitation, Riley grabs a Crest and a pair of gloves, syncing up to the interface.

"Player Two, synchronized."

It takes a few moments for Mark to be the next one to sync, then Danica, and finally Krissy.

Once we are all synced up to the system, the lights begin swirling and project a colorful twisting graphic. We look to the center of the pad, and a strange music starts erupting from it.

"Everyone else seeing this?"

Before I can respond, a screen of dialogue forms in front of my face. I look around to see everyone having the same thing happening to them. I start reading the text from the holographic screen aloud, *"Welcome, Vanguards of the*

Realm. Before you can begin your adventure, the gods must assess your worth. What kind of adventurer do you wish to become?" Then, a list of titles appears in place of the dialogue: Fighter, Mage, Rogue, Cleric, Ranger. Each one has a short description as to what they were.

I looked to the Ranger class and reached up to select it, but then it disappeared. "What the hell? Did anyone else lose the Ranger class?"

"I didn't." I looked over to Krissy's holo-screen, and the words "FIGHTER" were floating in front of her.

"Seems that we only have one of each to choose from." Riley quickly picks MAGE.

Danica, looking weirded out, chooses one without even looking. "ROGUE."

Mark and I race to get the Ranger, but in vain on my end. "CLERIC" appears in front of me, while Mark's read "RANGER".

The screen begins shifting around and starts giving us more choices to create our characters, based on given choices for us to decide. It takes me about fifteen minutes to create my character and have the game generate their overall appearance. Once I finish, the profile I made got sent to the center of the game mat, along with everyone else's when they finished. The game's voice returns once we finish, *"The gods have heard the call of the citizens of*

Albistair and have decided that you shall answer their call. Place your hands on your assigned stations."

Riley is the first one to place his hands on the mat, which turn blue around his hands, showing he is locked in. I follow his example, then the others follow suit. The whole game mat starts to light up in a digital blue color. *"Prepare for your adventure. The game will begin... in 5..."* When the voice announced the number "5", Krissy's Crest lights up, her eyes go blank, and she passes out.

"Krissy?! Krissy are you--"

"4..." Danica is suddenly knocked out.

Mark freaks out and is about to stand.

"3..."

When Mark blanks out, Riley and I look at each other. "Connor...?"

"2..."

I'm trying to take my hands off, but they won't budge. It feels like they're magnetized to the mat. I feel this strange humming in my head and the hair on the back of my neck standing straight.

"1... enjoy the adventure." My vision goes black.

CHAPTER 5

The smell of fresh cooked meat and sounds of chirping help to force my eyes open and adjust from the sudden darkness. I let out a groan and put my hand to my face, dragging it from my forehead down to my mouth before I feel a sharp prick in my palm.

"Ow!"

I pause. My voice sounds lower than usual. I look to where I felt the prick in my palm and freeze. My hand... this isn't my hand. *This. Isn't. My. Fucking. Hand!* My palm is a pale cream color, rough and calloused all the way up to the fingertips. At the edge of my fingertips, I see dark, pointed, claw-like nails coming from behind them. I turn it around to see the top of it in a light green skin color. The skin looks rough and strong. I look to my other hand, exactly the same. I bring both hands to my mouth and find two teeth, sharpened, protruding from my bottom jaw.

"What the..." I quickly look around my surroundings, trying to get a sense of where I am. It's a small room with wooden walls, rotting and old. The room is bare, except for a large trunk at the foot of the bed, a table to the right of the room, and a small mirror laying on it. The only other item in the room is the bed I'd been lying on. It has a straw mattress, which is hard and flat, but allows me to see what I'm wearing. My pants are a pair of torn cloth trousers that are ripped on the legs and expose my calves, my feet are in some makeshift leather wraps, and my shirt is dark gray with a coarse weave with the top three buttons undone. I quickly get up and go to the table where the mirror is, grabbing it and facing it towards myself. What I see in it is like something out of a dream… or nightmare.

The face looking back at me in the mirror isn't my real face. The face is green. *Green.* The same color of green that's on my hands. My cheeks have faded black splotches on them. My hair is no longer dirt blonde and shaggy, but black and shaved on the sides, long enough to be pulled back and tied into a short braid. My ears are pointed with pale ridges on the inside, and the tips have gold rings pierced into them. The color of my eyes is now gold with light brown around the edges. My eyes scan down towards my mouth; two white fangs from my bottom row of teeth are poking out of it passing my upper lip. I open wide, seeing that some of my teeth are sharp while the rest are dull.

"I'm… I'm an Orc…" My voice is still slightly deeper than normal, but that's the least of my current problems. I'm no longer me. I'm something else.

A scream comes from outside of the room I'm in. A woman's scream. I throw the mirror down and rush out the door. Outside the room I woke up in, it's empty and dank with an old, abandoned house smell. It came complete with creaky, wooden floors, a dusty old fireplace, and shabby wooden windows.

"Hello? Anyone there?"

A second later, another door nearby swings open, and someone comes out. Or rather... some*thing*. A tall, dark, furry creature walks out of the room with a horrified look on its face. It's as if a pitch-black cat had been stretched into the size of a person and taught to walk on its hind legs. It has piercing green eyes with vertical pupils, a silver hoop in one of its pointed ears, and a metal choker around its neck. It's wearing a white shirt that was laced up the sides, dark green pants that were high-waisted, and nothing else. The freakiest thing is that this creature had a tail that was whipping around wildly behind it.

This thing looks at me and screams, "Get away from me!"

I hold my hands up in defense, "Wa-wa-wait! I'm not gonna hurt you! Who are you??"

"Who the hell are you?! Where am I?! Where's Mark?!" It's a female, judging from its voice and, admittedly, its physique.

"I... wait... Danica??"

She looks at me with wide eyes. "How do you know my name? What are you??"

"Dani, it's me! Connor!"

She blinks and steps up to me carefully, "Connor? Why do you –"

Another door opens near us, making us both jump and look. Out comes a man, broad in frame with long blonde hair, sporting a leather harness on his chest. Seemingly normal looking at first, but everything below the belt is pure insanity. His lower torso is the body of a horse. A full-on, dark brown back and legs of a horse. The horse-man is struggling to walk out, fumbling around before standing tall. Tall enough to smack the top of his head on the ceiling of this shack.

"Ow! What the f--" He rubs his head while looking down seeing his legs... all four of them.

"I... I can stand?!" The horse-man rakes a hand through his hair, showing his face. While it's not one that I recognize, his statement about standing gives him away almost immediately.

"Riley??"

He looks me and Danica. He isn't scared or confused, but shocked. "Orc... Tabaxi..." He looks down at himself, "Centaur... holy shit... I can walk..."

"Riley... you can stand because you have *horse legs*!"

Danica was barely keeping herself together. "You....
You did this to me!" She grabs her tail and holds it up, "I
have a *fucking tail*!" She let's go and rushes at him.

I get in between her and Riley, "He's half of a damn
horse, Dani! You think we did this on purpose?!"

Riley was doing circles around himself chuckling,
which does nothing for my defense.

"Anyone out there?!" Another voice comes from
another door nearby. "Someone, open the door!!" It' a
guy's voice, which could only mean that it's coming from
Mark.

"Mark? Hold on!" I run over to the door where the
voice is coming from and open it. Inside is a silver-blue
skinned thing with wispy sea-foam green hair, glaring at
me with these deep and dark eyes. I take the opportunity to
scan him up and down, seeing that his hair barely covers
those fish-fin like flaps where his ears should be. The
clothes he's wearing are rags that look damp and just barely
fit, but just enough to expose his arms and legs, all of
which sport the same fin-like things on his head

. "M-Mark? Is that you?"

He gives me a look of confusion. Or is it anger?
"W-What the fuck are you?! What happened to me?!"

"Mark... It's me, Connor."

"Holy shit! Mark is a Triton!!" Riley yells out almost too excitedly. I look behind to see him and Danica gawking at us. I'm pretty sure Dani was spazzing out as her paw-like hands move to cover her mouth. I look back at Mark and reach out to him, "Mark... it's okay. We're all here."

He looks at everyone frantically, then stops at Danica's cat-like form. "Dani? I-is that really you?"

Danica doesn't move at all. The moment is interrupted by another door opening. All eyes turn and stare. It's a woman dressed in some shoddy leather and cloth with bright red skin, bright yellow eyes, snow white hair that drapes around a set of scaly horns coming out of her forehead, a tail twitching back and forth behind her, and fanged teeth. She steps out holding her arm, making sounds of aching pain, "God... what happened?"

Mark and I say it at the same time. "Tiefling!?"

She looks up and gawks at us. "What... what is this?! What are you things?!"

It has to be Krissy. The only one missing from the five of us.

"Krissy... It's going to be okay." She must've been really freaked out, because she launches out and punches me in the nose, knocking me onto the floor.

46

"Ow! Shit!" I cover my face on the ground. Riley trots over to give me a hand up. He helps me to my feet while I wipe my nose, seeing blood streaked on it. Actual blood. I could feel its warmth and stickiness on my hand.

"Can someone please tell me what the hell is happening right now??" Krissy looks at everyone before looking at herself. She couldn't have seemed any more scared. She touched the edge of her clawed fingers, ran her hands down her sides, then yelped as her spear-tipped tail flashed in front of her face. "Why do I have a tail?!"

Riley seems all too eager to explain, "Guys... I think we are *in* the game..." Everyone looks at him as if he's nuts. But, then again, we are looking at a half-horse, half-nerd, so I think crazier things have happened.

"What's that supposed to mean?"

"It means that the technology that was made to create a fully immersive experience, through the equipment we had to put on to interact with the game, must have pulled our conscious minds into a state of augmented reality, where we have embodied the characters that we created at the beginning of the game."

Nothing. Total, utter silence.

Mark must've understood because he begins explaining it to Danica, who is still blank in the face. "That nerd-speak means we are actually inside the game and have been turned into the characters we made."

"No... no we're not. There's gotta be a better explanation. We must've gotten shocked or something... and are in a coma?"

"Together experiencing the same comatose dream? Riley's right. We're inside *The Mortal Gate*."

"But I didn't choose this." Mark looks at himself, twisting his arms and observing his finned appendages, "I didn't choose a fish-man... I chose a human, I swear."

Krissy nods frantically, "So did I."

"I think we all did. Well... I'm sure Riley picked his Centaur."

"Actually, I didn't. I chose human, too. In a new game, I always go for humans because I don't know what kind of things will be in it, and human races are the best guinea pig decisions."

I rub the back of my neck, "So... the game just Russian Roulette-ed our races? No humans, just... these?"

While looking around at the others, I try to get into the headspace of a gamer to understand our current situation. Curious, I go back in the room I woke up in and see a brown leather bag hanging from a chair at the table. A satchel. I pick it up and open it. Inside is a small leather-bound book with an insignia on the cover in the shape of an archway. At first, after opening it, the pages are blank and empty. I flip through it cover to cover, but still nothing. I flip back to the first page and watch as the page begins to fill up with text and pictures. At the top, it reads "Character Logbook".

"Guys!" I run back to the others and show them the book. "I think we each have our own resource guides." I watch as the page finishes filling with information, then I begin to read from it out loud:

"The Vanguard's Logbook of Zarimm, the Orc Warpriest. The healer class of Mortal Gate that beckons their vengeful gods to either buff and heal their companions or invoke powerful curses upon their enemies. Though not the most combat efficient, Warpriests hold the ears of the gods and can cause massive effects and damage in the battlefield while protecting their companions. Warpriests can wield daggers and/or staves, so long as they are blessed by their patron god(s). At the start of the game, Warpriests must select a single patron god to worship and obtain their blessings, starting with simple invocations until leveled higher."

After I finish reading from the Logbook, everyone goes back to the rooms they woke up in and grab their own satchels. They return and start reading from their own books. Riley, who chose the Mage class, is now Amocus, the Centaur Stormlord, who can choose to master one of three elements of magic: fire, ice, or lightning. Mark chose to become a Ranger class and is now Konvos, the Triton Totemist, that utilizes animal companions and polearm weapons like spears or tridents. Danica, who chose Rogue at random, is given the tribal name of Night Silk, a Tabaxi Gambler that uses luck and intuition to achieve her goals. Then, there's Krissy, who is now known as Nevine, the Tiefling Outrider that is a master tactician and the dominant fighting class of all of us.

"*Night Silk??* What kind of name is that? I sound like a fucking stripper."

Mark tries comforting her, "Babe, Tabaxi are supposed to be tribal and have names that describe them. In fact, I'm sure you would actually just go by 'Silk'."

Persuasion check failed, Mark. She looks as if she's about to tear his head off, which she can do whether we were here or in the real world. But thankfully, Riley intervenes at the appropriate time. "Guys, relax! Remember, this is a beta test. There's probably a system moderator that's tracking our progress and will let us know when our job's done. This is what we signed up for."

"I didn't sign up to become a she-devil!" Krissy yells with her pointed tail whipping around behind her.

"Well, I didn't sign up to be a fish-man either, but Riley's right. We signed on for the stuff we get after. So, let's ride this out and see what happens."

I nod, "I agree. First, let's see if we get any starter gear. Check the rooms you woke up in and see if you have any weapons, armor, rations, things like that."

We break and go back to our rooms to search for any gear. In my room, I look behind the door and see a large staff in the corner. It's a crudely shaped staff made out of wood with faint red marks from top to bottom. I look at them closer and realize that the marks are some form of Orcish runes. At the top of the staff is a dense bulb of crude wood with a jagged blade shoved into it to make a melee weapon. I take another look into my logbook and find a list of Orcish gods and goddesses that can give patronage to me as a Warpriest. The only one that seems most prevalent than the others is the god of vengeance and strength, Olagog.

I meet the others back in the open room, seeing different things in their hands. Mark is holding a rusty harpoon, but I also notice he's wearing some sort of fish amulet that he wasn't before.

"Apparently as a Totemist, I have these relics that give me control or communication with that animal," he explains half-enthused.

Danica has a pouch of smoke pellets hanging from her belt and a pack of antique-looking cards in her hand. Or paw, in this case. According to her logbook, they're "Trick Cards" that served some sort of arcane purpose, depending on the card.

Krissy joins us next with a hunting axe holstered at her side, as well as a map, a red phial and a fancy looking horn she found in her satchel.

Riley is the last to reveal his starting gear, which consists of one phial of magic elixir and one of health while wearing a blue crystalline stone around his neck. "I chose lightning magic! I'm gonna be a galloping storm!"

His response doesn't get the reaction I think he wanted. Feeling the tension in the room as thick as fog, I start to think we're still taking in the fact that we're all these different creatures. I look towards the front door of the windowless shack we were in, take a deep breath and approach it. I hold the knob of the door for a moment before looking behind me. "Come on guys… I think the first level is outside this door."

CHAPTER 6

Sunlight pours into the windowless shack the moment I open the door, causing me to shield my eyes with my large hand. I step out and feel my boots crunch on dead leaves as I lower my hand from the sun's rays and look out in awe. The landscape around us is vast and vibrant in color; nothing like what I thought it would be. There are a lot of games out there with amazing landscapes and environments, but this all seems so real. The trees are all in different colors and shapes, the ground is patched with vibrant green grass and fallen leaves, and the air feels brisk and soft. I can *feel* the air brush against my skin and smell the fragrance of nature carried by the wind. I reach down and pick up a leaf, feeling it crunch and crumble in my fingers.

I turn to see everyone walk out from the shack into the sunlight and take in the sight of their new bodies. Riley is much taller now that he isn't being restricted by a low ceiling. Or a wheelchair, for that matter. His build is muscular, unlike his actual pudgy and greasy build in the real world, his long blond hair fell down to the middle of his back, and his skin tone is fair. His horse half is chestnut brown, strong and broad with four legs and a black tail. Krissy's crimson red skin was more visible, but her most noticeable feature is her bright yellow eyes that look like they could pierce into a person's soul. Her pointed tail slowly sways back and forth behind her, and the horns on her head are black, which makes her appearance more menacing. Mark steps around the two of them from out of the shack, his blue skin almost glistening in the sunlight. His eyes are like ocean jewels that must have darkened in the shade of the shack. The barbed fins on his arms and legs were of different color, faint red and yellow. His build actually reflect his real appearance, only with a little more muscle. Danica's full appearance is kind of adorable, but I'm not gonna say that to her face. Her black fur is short and fine, which made me think of Binx from *Hocus Pocus,* if he was female and human sized. She has emerald cat eyes and is about my height, around six feet tall. Like Krissy, she has a tail that swayed behind her, though more erratic than the former. Her hands and feet resemble the paws of a cat, but her hands look slightly elongated for gripping.

"I know this may not be the best time, but you all look pretty badass."

Riley is smiling like a kid in a candy store with his hands balled into fists and resting on his hips like a superhero. Danica wraps her arms around herself insecurely, prompting Mark to try and comfort her, but she recoils away from him.

"What's wrong?"

"What's wrong?I I'm a freak! I'm a fucking cat! Look at the rest of you!" Her ears flatten back, and her fur stands on end in anger.

Mark's eyes get wide. "Babe, it isn't real. It's just a game. Once we're done, you'll be back to your hot self again"

Oh, you idiot.

Before anyone else can say or do anything, a sound comes from a path that leads into the woods. It sounds like a strange kind of chittering accompanied by rustling and crunching leaves.

"What's that noise?" Riley trots towards the path and the sounds to investigate.

"Riley, what are you doing?" Krissy hisses at him. He holds up his hand for her to be quiet as he listens in.

From down the path, the sounds get louder until like a stampede of large animals is moving closer to our spot. Instinctively, I grab the staff I'd slung on my back and hold it defensively. Everyone else, besides myself and Riley, steps back cautiously. From the path, three horrifically giant spiders charge forward into view. These are meaty, hairy, black spiders with giant legs, drooling pincers, and four sets of piercing red eyes. Once in view, they spread out to trap us against the shack, twitching their limbs and snapping their pincers at us with high pitched chitters. Danica is screaming and Mark jumps in front of her, instinctively holding out his spear. Krissy joins Riley and I in a stand-off against the spiders.

"Giant spiders? How basic can this get?"

"Well, if this game is as immersive as it seems, we may have a challenge."

Krissy pulls her axe from her belt holster and holds it with both hands, "So, nerds... how do we beat these things?"

One of the spiders charges with a screech. Krissy lunges forward in response, bringing her axe in a side-chopping motion. The blade cuts through one of its arms, causing it to stumble back defensively, leaning on its good side to stay stable.

"Holy shit, nice hit!"

"Go for the carapace!" We look back at Mark, his eyes shining a pale yellow like the totem around his neck. "The spider's weak point is its carapace!"

I scan the bladed head of my staff, then the runes painted on the grip. I can't explain how I know to do this, but it's almost like a voice in my head is giving me instructions. I grip the staff with both hands and mimic the voice in my head, *"Granav alnej ukavrengavh!"* The air around me starts swirling and glowing white around me, making me feel a burst of sudden strength. One of the other spiders lunges out to grab me, but I hold up my staff to defend myself. The weight of the monster is on top of me, but I hardly struggle against it. I'm somehow holding up the beast against my weapon, using all my strength to push against the spider and force it away from me. It falls over on its back next to the one that Krissy attacked.

"This is pretty intense gaming! It really feels like I'm exhausted."

"Stop talking and kill these things!" Danica screams.

Her command startles us, pulling our attention from the oncoming attack that was from the spiders. By the time I turn around, all three spiders lunge out at us, screeching. I freeze, bracing for dear life when a blast of electricity knocks them all back. I look where it came from and see the outstretched hands of Riley are crackling with electricity. "Stormlord, bitches!!"

Blinded by his pride, one of the spiders quickly recovers and lashes out, clamping its pincers onto Riley's horse leg. He lets out a loud cry and collapses to the ground, pounding his fists on the beast trying to get it off of him.

"Riley!" I run over to help him, take up the bladed end of my staff and stab at the spider's midsection, causing it to screech in pain and fall to the ground. *Right in the carapace, just like Mark said!*

The other spiders soon rush in for the attack, only to be met with Krissy yelling loudly and swinging her axe with skill and aggression. The one she injured before wildly rushes in for the kill, but Krissy's attacks cut up the spider's legs and cause it to crumple down to the ground. The last spider standing made an advance on Mark and Danica, who were trying to get away from it. Mark tries using his spear to keep the spider back, but it knocks his weapon away and rears back, lifting four of its eight legs in a show of aggression. I rush over and jab at its leg with the blade of my staff, causing it to recoil. From his position, Riley fires a shock blast at its midsection, causing it to curl up and die.

I rush to his side where he's laid out on the ground, one of his legs bleeding from the attack. "Riley! Are you okay?" He nods and grunts at the same time. He's actually able to feel the pain in his leg. Not a good sign.

"How can he feel that?" Krissy walks up behind me covered in a pale green ooze. Spider guts. "I thought this was virtual reality or some shit."

I shake my head, being just as confused and worried as she was. "This is intense… those Crests we put on to start the game must have some sort of nerve receptors that make our brains think we are actually hurt."

"You mean if we take them off, we can get out of this?" Danica stands up with hope in her voice. "How do we get out? I want out."

Mark starts feeling around on his head, "Maybe… if we try to reach for the Crests… we can pull them off… Dammit, where is it??"

I try something different and comb around in the logbook, seeing if there was some sort of instruction manual on how to exit the game. All there was in the pages, was my character description, plus one more page that was filled out. It describes the spider attack, showing how the group won against the monsters. The game is narrating our actions as we progress.

I look back at Riley and watch him take out a red phial from his satchel, chug it back and wait. We all waited. The wounds on Riley's body lightly glow red and close, cleaning and healing themselves. "Holy shit," I whisper in shock while Krissy helped him back up to his… hooves?

"That… it felt so real…"

Mark grunts out loudly, "I can't feel the fucking headgear. How do we get out of this??"

"Easy… look, maybe it's like a milestone game. Maybe we need to find a checkpoint or a save point before we can actually log out for a break or something."

I feel deep scratches cut through my arm. I yelp and hold it with my other hand while getting yelled at. "I don't want to wait! I want *out*!"

"Dani, relax! We'll get out of here. We just need to find one of the save points and try from there." That's when I get an idea. "Krissy, you had a map. Show it to us."

Krissy reaches in her satchel to grab the map, unfolding it in front of us. It's huge. It shows every corner of the game's world, Albistair. There are multiple regions with odd names and different landscapes, snowy mountains, desert canyons, swampy dredges and more. "Look here." She points at a spot on the map, showing a bright blue circle.

"Take a step towards the path, Krissy." Raising an eyebrow, she humors me and walks ahead. I follow curiously, and sure enough, the blue circle moved towards the forest.

"That's how we know where we are. It's a living map that tracks our current location. It must be some sort of relic or magic item."

She inspects the map closer and points, "Look here. It says 'Merrin's Tavern'. Is that important?"

In clear lettering and an outline of a building, the part she points at looks to be the only logical destination for us to go. "Okay… Guys, we're going to the Tavern. Pick yourselves up and let's head down the path."

"You mean the path where huge fucking spiders came from? Great idea." Mark never ceases to make his sarcasm and point very clear for all of us.

"He's got a point. Look, there's another one through the thick trees that can cut us through to the tavern quicker." Her clawed finger points to the alternate path, slightly slimmer and out of the way.

"That normally means that stuff is either more dangerous or difficult," Riley points out. "I vote we take the Spider Path." It was a two-to-two vote. I look back at Danica, who is already shaken up, but I want to try and make this easier on her. "Dani? Which one do you want to take? We'll follow your lead."

She looks up at us, her face a mixture of fear and irritation as she looks to the forest, then to the path. Her nose and ears twitch, while her eyes dart back and forth. Then, she points to the forest, "We should go that way." I nod in response and lightly pat her shoulder supportively.

Hopefully the spiders were our biggest problem.

CHAPTER 7

The walk in the forest is a sight to see. So many beautiful colors of trees and plants that I've never seen before outside of internet searches. But the part that really gets me is the smell. The overwhelming smell of flowers, the sap of the trees, the fog of the forest's atmosphere. I watch the others walk ahead before I pull Riley aside to get his attention.

"Riley... this is all a little too real, right?"

"What do you mean?"

I match pace with him so we can keep out of earshot from the others, "Look, I know you've noticed. When that spider attacked, it hurt. A lot. I felt its full weight against me. You were bleeding from getting bitten."

"Yeah? But maybe it's just how intense the technology is."

I gesture to my nose, "But then why am I smelling everything?" I pick up a nearby flower to make my point, "I can smell this clear as day. It smells sweet and intense. There's no way any kind of virtual interface can make us smell this, like it's real."

Riley takes the flower and smells it. "Maybe it can. The human brain just needs to think of a scent, and it turns that thought into action. Like an itch."

"Riley, seriously," I grab him by the arm. "I think this is more than what we paid for..."

"Hey, you two coming or what?" Mark waves us down trying to get us to catch up with him and the girls. Riley drops the flower and trots on, leaving me frustrated that he wasn't seeing what I am. Krissy is still trying to comfort Danica, still shaken up about what happened to us at the cabin.

Mark waits for me ahead and pulls me aside, "She's really freaking out. I don't know what to say or do." He was looking at his hands while he talked to me. "This is weird, right? Why would the game make us into races that we didn't choose?"

Riley hears his question and gestures to his horse half, "I'm pretty satisfied with this. This is the first time I've walked since I was four."

I remember him telling me about what put him in the chair in the first place. When he was four, he was on a road trip with his mom coming back from an amusement park when a semi driver clipped their car. His mom broke her arm and shattered two of her ribs, but he got his legs crushed in the door when it caved in from how they were hit. They were in the hospital for three months when the doctors told them that his legs were shattered, and he would be confined to a wheelchair. Since then, he turned his condition into his own mobile throne and attempted to embrace it. Most days, he's a charismatic guy and tries to see the upside of everything. But other days, he only sees things from the view of his chair.

The question came back in my mind after my stroll down memory lane, "Maybe… maybe it's not designed to give us what we want. Like a critical role? Some sort of randomizer based on chance?"

Mark groans softly, holding his hands on his neck, "Dude, I don't like this. This game is freaking me out."

I put my bear-paw of a hand on his shoulder to try and comfort him, "It'll be okay. We just have to get to the save point and then we can get out of this."

Fingers crossed that's true.

My train of thought is interrupted when Danica screams. Ahead is a man standing in our path with an axe in his hands: a big, bulky, bald guy with an eyepatch over his left eye, wearing leather and fur armor. He smirks, revealing a mouth of probably only five total teeth in it. I don't know if it was my character's senses or my own, but I can smell this guy clear as day. The smell of stale alcohol and dirty sweat almost makes me gag.

"Well, well," he chuckles through his teeth as he grips his axe tighter. "Looks like we have some lost travelers, boys."

When he says the word "boys", chuckling and metal scraping sounds come from around us in the trees and bushes. From all directions, about eight more leather-clad men with weapons surround us, sneering, and growling as they close in. Mark stepped in front of Danica while Krissy, Riley and I stand in a circle around them.

"Bandits. Usually low-level brute enemies. This'll be a piece of cake."

"Who ya callin 'low-level brutes', ya horse-legged freak?!" One of the bandits is brandishing a dagger in each of his hands and points one of them at Riley.

"Listen, we don't want any trouble. We're just trying to get to the Tavern."

All the bandits start laughing. "Quiet!" the one-eyed brute in front yells over the laughter. Clearly, this guy is in charge because they all stop. "Take the horse and cat alive! Their pelts and materials will fetch a nice price. Kill the rest!"

In that moment, a switch flips in Mark. The barbed fins on his arms and legs flare open, and his eyes stare down One-Eye. "Like hell you will!!!" He pulls his harpoon from behind him and lunges forward at the bandit, who parries with his axe. The battle begins.

With a unanimous yell, the bandits swarm us all in one wave. I pull my staff out quickly to defend myself against a sword attack, blocking it. I struggle against the sword, blade lodged in my staff, and glare down at the bandit in rage. Something must have spooked him because his confidence looks shaken. "You damned half-breed beasts! Why won't your kind just die?!" I muster what strength I have and shove forward, throwing the bandit back against a tree, knocking him out.

"Connor!!"

Krissy is parrying off against a couple of bandits with her axe, but she's struggling. Their attacks are wild and unplanned but determined. I rush over to try and help but feel a stinging pain in my shoulder at the same time. I cripple to the ground with the head of an arrow pierced through my left shoulder, dripping with greenish-black ooze. Blood. My blood. Looking behind me, a bandit with a bow is pulling another arrow from his quiver and knocking it back in my direction. I see Danica huddled under a tree, getting threatened by two other bandits. Her pouch of pellets dangling from her belt gives me an idea.

"Danica! Use a smoke pellet!! Now!!"

Danica's eyes don't move from her attackers while she fumbles with her satchel, pulling out a little black ball and chucking it at them. The pellet hits one of the bandits and explodes on impact, causing the area around her to be screened in smoke.

"Don't lose the cat!" Loud coughing and blade swinging follow the command.

The archer that shot me aims his arrow towards the smoke and releases, giving me the time to pull the arrow out of my shoulder with a roar of pain. My blood drips onto my staff and causes the runes on it to shimmer. I suddenly hear a hoarse voice in my head yelling something I can't make out entirely. "*Dam ul daum! Dam ul daum!*"

My attention is pulled over to Mark slashing and prodding at One-Eye, who is blocking and striking back at him. "You won't survive this, you damn fish!" Mark doesn't even flinch as he keeps attacking and yelling.

I hear yelling in another direction, to which I see Riley kicking at some of the bandits with his horse legs. Then, he holds his hands toward one of the bandits and shoots a shock blast at him, sending him flying.

"*Blood for blood!*" I hear in my head. "*Invoke me! Make them suffer!*"

I shudder, gripping my head tightly. "This isn't real… this isn't real… this isn't REAL!" The pain in my shoulder, the voice in my head, the clashing of weapons all start weighing me down and make me feel engulfed in a place of no escape.

"Leave us alone!!"

I open my eyes and see Danica, standing in a threatening stance. Next to her stands… another Danica. And another Danica. A whole bunch of Danicas. The bandits all look to the army of the same Tabaxi and hold their weapons up to them, trembling slightly. The green cat-like eyes of the Danicas fiercely glare at the bandits, flashing their extracted claws from their hands and feet, then baring their fanged teeth at them. It's like a pack of standing panthers eyeing at their prey.

"Leave us alone, or I will rip you to shreds while you watch," they threaten in an echo. The bandits all look at each other, then at the army of Danicas before running into the woods out of sight.

In a flash, the fight is over. Mark is huffing and holding his arm, bleeding blue through his fingers. Krissy helps Riley up onto his hooves, both looking like absolute hell. My attention focuses on the Danicas, who all slowly phase out in a magic blur until only one of them is left.

"Danica?"

She holds up a card in her paw of a hand, "I think I found out what the cards do…"

I walk to her and take the card. On the face of it is a silhouette of a person split into three. Atop the card, like something from a tarot deck, is a phrase written in a weird language I can't read. "What does it say?"

"It says, 'Mirror's Deceit'. Like some kind of magic photocopier." Danica's eyes flash over to Mark, still huddled over holding his arm. She dashes over to his side to help him up, "Mark? Are you okay?"

Mark nods as he holds his bleeding arm, "I'm great. Feel like a friggin' fish on a hook..."

I snort. I can't hold it back, but I snort. In that moment, everyone joins in the laugh. The first time we've laughed since this game started.

After coming down from the joke, I walk over to Mark and look at his wound. *Wait a second.* I take my logbook out and look through the pages, opening to a page on Warpriest spells and blessings. "Okay... *mikog lutaum.*" My staff's grip pricks my hand, making the runes glow slightly red. His wound warmed in my hand and began to shimmer lightly. I pull away and the wound is gone.

He stood up and looked at me in confusion, rotating his shoulder. "What the hell was that?"

"I'm a Warpriest. I use spells and cantrips from my patron god to do things. In this case, heal battle wounds." I get pushed away by Danica as she hugs him close. She's terrified of what happened. Everyone is. They want answers to what was happening to us. I have no answers. Thoughts, but no answers. "Let's find the Tavern. Maybe we'll get answers there."

CHAPTER 8

We continue our walk through the dense forest that was on Krissy's map. Meanwhile, I'm wracking through all the thoughts racing through my head about what was happening to us. This "game" isn't what I expected. We can feel pain. We can feel, hear, smell and taste everything in this world. The bandits acted and reacted too real to be traditional Non-Playable Characters. Their anger and obvious hate towards us seem just as real.

"You okay, Greenie?"

Krissy pulls me from my train of thought. I take this moment to observe her Tiefling form, seeing that there's hardly any difference from how she really looks here. Aside from the red skin, horns, and tail, she looks almost the same as she does in real life. Strong, young, and beautiful.

She snaps her fingers in front of my face.

"Sorry. Um, this... this just isn't what I expected."

"Why? Because you look like Shrek's illegitimate love child? You could look like half a donkey, like Riley."

I chuckle at what she says and grab the back of my neck. "Not what I meant. Look... we didn't sign up for this. Dawson's invitation didn't say we were going to be stuck in this damn game. Let alone that swords and arrows can hurt us, or that the animals can actually bite us."

Krissy stops mid walk and swats me in the back of the head. "Suck it up, Shrek. Yeah, we're stuck, but it's not going to be forever, right? You're supposed to be the guy that knows all about this nerd stuff, otherwise we have to listen to Riley's annoying rambling."

"Hey!"

We both look to Mark waving us down. We slate the conversation and catch up to him when he is pointing to an opening. Through it, we see a gathering of people outside of a cabin-sized building with lit windows and music coming from inside.

"That must be Merrin's Tavern."

"Looks like a cabin."

"More like a dump."

"Who are those people outside?"

"NPCs most likely." Krissy and Danica stare blankly at Riley. "Non-Playable Characters. Programs in the game that either serve no purpose at all, give quests, and side quests, or become fightable foes. Like those bandits from the forest."

"This can be our chance to get some answers. Hopefully, the Tavern will give us a chance to choose if we want to stop the game and leave. If it does, great, we're out. If not…"

The silence comes off as unsettling, so we start walking towards the Tavern. Some of the people outside see us approach and gasp. A few bystanders start talking to each other looking at us, others run from the Tavern quickly.

"What's their problem?"

"Must be programmed to run from or gossip about newcomers."

"Or maybe it's because they're all human. And we're not."

Everyone looked down at themselves, then at the people outside of the Tavern, seeing I'm right. We're the only non-humans in the area.

"Well… this just got awkward."

"Speak for yourself," Danica scowls.

I raise an eyebrow, only to understand it too late. Those outside of the Tavern kept quiet and to themselves as Danica opens the door and marches inside. I try waving to those outside, but they look even more uncomfortable than before. Once inside, the whole tavern went silent, like an Old West saloon scene. Just like outside, the people inside are all humans. There are a couple of humans by the fireplace with instruments in their hands, most likely bards playing the music we heard outside. Around the different tables, groups of people with food, drinks, coins, and weapons stare at us. A group of men stand up with weapons drawn and eyes fixed but are stopped by a dagger flying across their faces and into a nearby post.

"No fighting in my Tavern," a woman's voice rings from behind the bar. We all look to see a woman with blue skin, white hair, red eyes, and webbed fingers that pointed at the humans angrily. She's a Triton, like Mark. "Take a seat. I will be with you soon."

I look at the men that stood up, all the way until we got to our seats. "Anyone else think this is weird?"

Krissy nods. "Fucking freaks. What did we do to them?"

"You exist," the Triton woman says as she approaches our table. "We all exist. Humans never have liked us. Since they are so… fragile and ordinary. What can I get you all? Maybe a Marsh Mist for the Triton?" She looks at Mark with a smile. I hear a low growl coming from Danica, knowing this was about to set some shit off.

"Um, could you just get us what you think we'll like?" I insist. She shrugs and leaves the table.

74

"Why are we still here? We're supposed to get out of this stupid game. Where's that 'save point', genius?"

Riley and I look to each other with concern, but Mark steps into the rescue "Maybe there's a tutorial or extra thing we have to do to get to a point of saving. Let's wait till the woman gets back."

Awkwardly, we all sit and wait, looking around the Tavern. A lot of the humans were just staring, either with worry or anger. "Damn… why are they acting like this?"

"The lady said it was because we existed," Krissy points out. "See how she was the only one not human in here? It's like we're diseased or something."

She was right. I notice a couple of tables nearby clear out and either leave or move further away from us.

"It's weird for NPCs to be so… real."

"You noticed that too?"

Danica and Krissy look confused, so Mark tries explaining. "Non-Playable Characters only have a few lines and points of action to follow in their programming. Especially if they are docile and only meant to give life to the landscape or give a quest or something. Riley? Connor? Tell me I'm wrong."

I sigh deeply, "He's right… look, even if this is augmented reality, we shouldn't be able to feel all these things." I instantly shut my mouth when the Triton woman comes back with a wooden tray of copper mugs, handing them out one by one. "Bog Grog all around. On the house."

"Um, excuse me?" She looks at me with an eyebrow raised. "Look, my friends and I are looking for the save point, so we can log out. Is there one here? Or maybe at another Tavern?"

The Triton woman looks at me blankly with an awkward silence before she turns and goes back behind the bar without uttering another word.

"The hell was that?"

I look at my drink, getting lost in thought. The way everyone is looking at us, how the Triton woman talked and acted, even how the last few hours have gone. That's when a crash comes down on our table, making us all jump. A dagger stabbed into the table, and a gruff looking guy holding it, backed up by about four others.

"You freaks. Why won't you just leave the rest of us alone? The whole of Albistair is burning because of what you and your kind brought upon us." He digs his dagger out of the table, snarling and clearly aching for a fight.

The rest of us sit back in silence, but Riley speaks up. "What is happening to Albistair? It's the main quest, right?"

"Do not dare try and insult us. You hell-borne monsters brought on the plague of the--"

The door of the Tavern flies open, causing everyone to look. Marching inside are five armed knights in dark red tinted armor, blackened weapons, and matching emblems on their chests. The emblem is some sort of black sun with pointed rays circling it. Everyone in the Tavern stays silent as a sixth one marches in. Unlike the others, this one is wearing a cape made of some sort of animal flowing behind him and holding his helmet to his side. He's a human with tanned skin, thick facial hair, and a very menacing look on his face. He scans the inside of the Tavern until his eyes fix on us, then makes a b-line to our table.

"Does there seem to be a problem here?" His voice is deep and scratchy, but in a menacing, villainous way.

The one who stabbed our table points at us, "These monsters are being taught a lesson. It is the will of the Archon to rid our land of these beasts!" His followers yell in agreement.

The knight responds by drawing his sword and swatting the knife out of the bandit's grasp before holding the blade at his throat.

"You do not speak for the Archon." This makes the thug back away, along with his buddies. The knight looks down to the five of us while sheathing his blade, "As for you. I do not recall ever seeing you here before. Where do you come from?"

We all look at each other and then back at him. I remember when we started the game that our names and backstories were written out for us. I stand up slowly, watching his men grab hold of their blades.

"I am called Zarimm. I come from the Green Marsh. My companions and I are adventurers, traveling the land." Everyone looks at me weirdly, but this is the only thing I can think of to make us not look like absolute strangers to their ways. *Who says being a nerd doesn't pay off?*

The knight gives me a once-over, "What business does an Orc have outside of their tribe? On one of your kind's pillaging raids?"

"Is there a reason you are harassing my customers, Captain?" The Triton woman approaches our table with her arms crossed. The tension is so thick you could cut it and serve it on a plate, but she doesn't back down. "You know the laws. Taverns are neutral places of security and repose. Even ones ran by non-humans."

The captain is glaring daggers at the woman, but he gives a simple nod. "Watch yourselves, travelers. Albistair does not take kindly to those who disrupt the peace." The captain whips around towards the door, his animal-skin cape flying behind him, and marches out with his men.

Waiting until the soldiers left, the Triton woman wags her finger. "Come with me and keep your mouths shut."

I didn't even take the time to check on the others before I went to follow her. As far as I'm concerned, this woman is the only one willing to talk to us and possibly give us answers. I hear footsteps trailing after me as I follow her behind the bar of the Tavern and into some sort of storage room. Once inside, the woman shuts the door and lights a lantern to illuminate the room. It looks like something out of a crime drama series with papers stuck to the walls and books spilled open everywhere.

"It is obvious that you all are strangers to this land, otherwise you would be wise not to provoke any trouble for the rest of us. Especially from the Crimson Order."

As if everything up to this point isn't already confusing enough, I can't begin to understand what this NPC was trying to tell us. "Look, there must be a place where we can save and log out of this damn game. A temple? A shrine? A friggin' campfire?"

"Those words… your mannerisms… your ignorance of our laws… perhaps you were taken from your lands by the Mortal Gate," she puzzles.

In the dim light of the room, I look to everyone else after she said the game's title. Riley looks too excited. "I think we're about to get our first story-mission quest!"

Mark smacked him upside the head. "What are you talking about, lady?"

"My name is Merrin. You and your companions must have entered from the Mortal Gate. It explains why the Order is suddenly on high alert and bolstering their efforts. This is… not good news."

I see how aggravated the others are getting, so I try to speed things along. "You're right. We're not from around here. Tell us everything you can, so we can understand."

Merrin's large blue eyes look to me sullenly. "Very well."

"It all happened years many before my birth, when Albistair was in a state of prosperity and grace. A land that was a true wonder of beauty, where humans were the majority but held respect for non-humans. Our kind maintained a level of trust with humans after we taught them magic, shared our trades and borders, even encouraged marital unions. But it all ended, and tensions grew with the first wave of a plague that ravaged Albistair in the form of the terrorghasts."

She ominously points toward a portrait on the wall with a rough sketch of a horrifying creature. Three dead eyes in very narrow sockets, a short nose resting just above a long mouth filled with rows upon rows of small, jagged teeth and a slimy tongue. Small slits where the ears should be on the side of its huge, thin head, which itself is covered in web-like fans. The body is long and slender built with two long arms on either side of its broad shoulders, attached to bony claws with twelve curvy fingers in total. Its legs are wide and stand straight with two crooked feet. The skin looks decayed and slimy from head to toe. One final detail that makes itself attentive is a long, fanned tail that extends over its head.

"The terrorghasts were birthed from a trench that tore open the earth on the night of the Violet Moon, a night where raw magic becomes volatile and unpredictable. We have come to know this trench as the Chasm. Like a ghastly plague, they poured out from its maw sweeping over the land and began destroying everything in their path. That is when blame was cast in every direction on who let loose the beasts, with most of it falling to non-humans and their natural affinities to magic. Wars raged between everyone, even amid this plague. Until the Archon arrived, that is."

"What does this have to do with our situation? We weren't around when all of this happened."

Merrin directs our attention to another illustration on the wall, showing a very intricately drawn archway sitting on an empty path. The pillars look like cobblestone with large round bases under each side. The imposts of the pillars look like blooming flowers, bridged together with a smooth crown that has carved rings that stop at two prongs, separated by a smooth haunch. Along the face of the stone arch, there are five spots drawn to catch our attention. Each spot had a different symbol drawn into them as they framed the arch perfectly.

"The Mortal Gate. A magical phenomenon our most brilliant scholars and mages have scarce knowledge and understanding of. It is said to be a doorway to worlds unlike our own. Some believe it leads to the realm of the gods, others believe that it is a door to the Underworld. What we do know is that it is only activated and accessed by the Keystones," she explains as she runs her finger along the five symbols on the face of the archway. "According to the oldest recordings, the Gate once opened and let the gods into the world, allowing them to shape the realm and colonize Albistair."

I'm trying to put this all together in my head with the little I could comprehend. If Merrin is right, that means the "gods" must've been alpha testers tasked with laying out the groundwork of the game. Which can only mean that the Mortal Gate is our exit out of the game itself.

That's when Riley spoke again in his excited tone. "Who's the Archon? What's he like?"

Damn, I want to clamp his mouth shut.

Merrin's face shifted in discomfort. "The Archon is the reason humans are distrusting of us. He and the Crimson Order have acted as the governing force of Albistair that promises the destruction of the terrorghasts, and we in return give him our undying support and loyalty. They arrived two years after the Chasm opened and took immediate action against the threat. In that time, humans came to believe that non-humans caused the event, causing many to take a personal vendetta against us all. So, the Archon initiated a decree that no unlawful persecution against any of the races is to be condoned. But, like the elitist organization of prideful enforcers that they are, the Order instills constant fear among the non-human races."

Looking back to the picture of the Mortal Gate, Merrin lightly brushes it with her fingers and sighs deeply before continuing. "The humans believe that accessing the Mortal Gate can rid the realm of the terrorghasts... but there are those that believe the Archon wishes to obtain the power of the Gate and acquire godhood to subject all races to his rule."

Riley taps me on the arm, "That must be the main objective of the game. Maybe if we stop the Archon, we can win the game and get out."

"But I don't want to do this stupid game," Danica hisses. "I want to get out and go home!"

"You cannot leave." Everyone stares at Merrin.

"What the hell do you mean we can't?"

"The Keystones that open the Mortal Gate have been lost for years and the Gate itself has mysteriously disappeared," she explained. "Before the Chasm was opened under the Violet Moon, one of the scholars tasked with studying the Gate was witness to a strange occurrence. The Gate erupted in some magical expulsion of energy that scattered the Keystones all over the land. There have been countless expeditions to try and find them, but every one of them ended in tragedy."

Mark gives an aggravated breath before leaning against the wall, and I honestly can't blame him. This whole thing was messed up. We need to get out of this game. There's no telling what kind of physical or psychological damage the equipment is doing to us in the real world. I look back to Merrin for one final question, "Where do we start looking?"

Everyone looks at me like I'm out of my mind, except for Merrin who looks surprised and relieved all at once. She opens a shelf from her desk, pulls out a rolled-up parchment and holds it out for me to take. "I think you are who we have been waiting for. The Vanguards of the Realm, warriors and adventurers sent through the Mortal Gate by the gods who will cleanse Albistair from these dark times and deliver us from the chaos. Take this map. It holds clues and notes of the suspected sightings of the Keystones. But you are not yet strong enough to take on the beasts that plague these lands. You need to improve, grow, and acquire better protection."

I tilt my head confused, but then it clicked. We're still in blood-soaked rags from fighting the spiders and bandits. "We need to level up."

CHAPTER 9

We walk out of the Tavern without making eye contact with anyone else to avoid problems after our secret meeting. All the things Merrin told us makes this world seem even more real and dangerous. She was seriously afraid of those monsters and whoever this Archon guy was. Why would SnoWire create this world of fear that can literally hurt its players? Do they not care about the potential lawsuits they can get slapped with?

"Hey! Earth to Connor!"

I snap back to the moment. "Sorry…"

Mark runs his fingers through his seaweed-green hair, "This is great. No answers. No way out. I'm so going to sue Dawson and his whole fucking company for this shit."

"Take it easy, Fish-Boy. We did get answers! We need to keep playing and win, then we're out! Easy!"

Krissy and Danica stand off to the side of our conversation but chime in at Riley's comment. "See, that's not gonna fly with me. I don't want to intentionally look for things to fight. Not after that crazy mess we dealt with."

"I don't think we have a choice." The others look at me annoyed. "Guys… were you not in there just now?

Those NPCs *believe* all of this is real. We got attacked by crazies, giant bugs, and people that hate what we are. We can't take our gear off to get out, there are no saving points. We. Are. STUCK. Trapped."

No one tries arguing with me. We stand there in silence for a solid minute, realizing that this is worse than what we thought. This game is no longer a game. It's real, and we were in real danger.

I pull out the Player's Logbook from my satchel and flip through it to find any hints on levelling up. So far, it's logged everything we've encountered after the spider attack from the cabin to this moment in time. It's crazy to see that every action and encounter we've had fill up the book like a regular codex from any other game. Currently I'm a level one Warpriest with only a couple of invocations to my character's patron god. Flipping through the pages, I see some sort of progress bar that looks like a phial that was half filled with a gold substance.

"Looks like I'm almost out of the beginning level. The rest of you may be at the same point. Looks like we need to keep exploring and beat some enemies to get to higher levels."

"So, you're saying we have to *look* for trouble to get better? Just to get out of this game?"

"It's the basic rule for RPGs," Riley explains. "Dungeoneering, raids, random incursions, and side quests help to level up characters, depending on their stats and involvement in the game. By rights, Danica would be the highest level of us because of what she did against the bandits."

Danica's ears perk up. "Wait, what?"

Riley trots up to her and takes her satchel, pulling out her Logbook.

"Whoa, check this out." Like something out of a fantasy movie, Riley reaches into the page of the book and pulls out the phial of shimmering gold liquid.

"What is that?"

"Drink it." She widens her eyes at me like I'm nuts, but Riley got where I was going and insisted. Danica hesitantly takes the phial into her paw, pops the cork, and drinks it slowly. When she finishes, her body starts to shine in a swirling halo, making us to take a step back and watch. Nothing happens to her, physically, but when the shimmer goes away she seems a little different. She's standing more confidently and relaxed.

Mark blinks before asking, "You okay, babe?"

"I… I don't know. I feel pretty good…and strong. What happened to me?"

"Must be how we level up," Riley deduces proudly. "The books keep track of our progress, fill up the level meter, then we take it like a buffing potion. Nothing physically changes, but our stats must increase." Riley opens Danica's book and shows us her character statistics. Night Silk is now a level two Gambler, increasing her intuition and charisma from +1's to +3's, while her strength, speed and constitution slightly raise to +2's.

"So that's how this works. Like character sheets in *D&D*, the more experience we attribute, the better our stats and skills are in the long run. As a Gambler, Danica relies on stealth and persuasion to increase her abilities. Each of us has a role to play within the group."

Mark listens closely before snapping his head towards me, "Show me that map that Merrin gave you." Curiously, I give it to Mark, who unrolls it from its tie. The map isn't as detailed as the one that Krissy had, but it focuses on one spot. The waypoint was made to the east of Merrin's Tavern in some place called the "Ordowell Bowels", a place that looked swampy, dank, and thick with forestry.

"Looks like our first quest is here in the Ordowell Bowels."

The mention of the name makes Krissy's face scrunch, "Sounds like a shitty place."

Her pun almost makes me snort. "Guys, we can't go there yet. We need to get better gear. Luckily, there's a place that can help us out." I point past the Tavern to a small town not far from it. From my experience, towns and settlements have gear and sutlers hat we can visit. I look at everyone in their ratty clothes, "We got lucky with the spiders and bandits. But what happens when we face something worse? Without the right gear, we're screwed."

The others look offended at first, but slowly start to nod in agreement. Krissy wasn't fully sold. "What if they don't sell to us? You saw what happened in the Tavern. Looking like this, we're hated."

"It's a risk we have to take, Krissy. I don't want us to lose. Who knows what will happen if we do?"

. "I agree. Let's see what we can get. When I last checked my satchel, I think I saw that I have about 50 gold coins. Maybe that's the starting amount that we have."

Riley nods, holding his satchel up. "Same here. May not be much, but it should be enough for at least one or two things from the right vendor."

Finally agreeing, our little group heads for the town. The sun is slowly setting on the landscape, which is a wonder all by itself. The sun is setting with a hue of green, yellow, and orange over the horizon. I admit, the developers had some wild imaginations to create this place. I start seeing the buildings in town lighting torches outside of the doors and along the path leading to it. The townsfolk all look human, from what I can see, which is kind of alarming. If it's anything like the Tavern, we may have some trouble on our hands. We pass the town's border gate and see common folk going about their business and preparing for the night. A couple of townsfolk see us and immediately run into their houses slamming the doors, but everyone else just simply either turns away from or glances at us.

"There." Riley raises a finger to a building with a sign hanging from a post with a picture of a hammer and anvil. "Must be the blacksmith. Who wants a better weapon?"

"I think it should be Krissy." She turns to me with her eyebrow raised. "You're the fighter of the group. Outriders have a higher need for melee weapons than the other classes, and yours is... rusty."

Krissy looks to her axe and shrugs, "Fine. What about you guys?"

"I'll go in too," Mark volunteers. "I may be a Totemist, but I'm still a Ranger class. If I get better equipment, I can be better in a fight."

"I think the rest of us will do better at a magic shop. Maybe we can get more potions and better items. Who knows what we'll face out there?"

I nod, "Meet back out here when we're all done. Don't go far, don't start any fights."

"Jeez, you're worse than my mother. Come on, Dory," Krissy says to Mark, not giving him the chance to snap back before she walks in. Riley, Danica, and I go into town a little further to try and find a magic shop while taking in the sights. It's a simple town, nothing too fancy to write home about, but almost comforting to walk through. Quiet, content, the crackling of lit torches, the rustle of trees shaking, and some small talk among the townsfolk that are outside.

"This place is as uncomfortable as it was back at the Tavern."

"Over there. Magic shop."

While Riley makes a beeline to the shop with Danica in tow, I notice a book shop further towards the town's square. "Guys, go on in. I have a different thing in mind to buy."

My stroll towards the bookshop is interrupted when I feel a thud against my foot. A small red ball rolled into my foot. I look around to find the owner and see a small human boy, frozen in place. He looks at me while keeping his distance, puzzled and scared. I kneel to pick the ball up and hold it to him.

"Here you go." The boy looks at me a little worried and backs away. I don't get why the game would make us hated by everyone. To be less Orcish, I put my weapon aside and sit on the ground with the toy in my hand.

"My name is Zarimm, what's yours?"

The boy looks at me and waves, "My name is Jarell. You have funny teeth."

"Heh, nice to meet you, Jarell. My teeth are funny because I'm an Orc." I toss it back to the boy. He catches it and smiles, passing it back to me.

"Jarell!" A woman runs straight to him mid-catch, grabs him by the arm and pulls him away. "You stay away from my son, you filthy creature!"

I immediately stand up with my hands up defensively, "I wasn't hurting to your son, lady. I'm just giving him his toy back." The woman doesn't even acknowledge my comment before she turns Jarell away from me and runs off. This whole thing has me reeling. I've seen racism in plots of fantasy games before, but this is intense. I turn my attention to the bookstore and reflect on that encounter. I need to know more about this world and look up its history. Opening the door to the store, I walk in to see stacks and stacks of books and parchment scrolls filling the store wall-to-wall.

"Holy shit." I approach one of the bookshelves nearby running my fingers along the spines of the books, and it feels so real. The texture of the cloth and leather-bound books are so intricate and detailed. Threads of some of the books stick out, showing age through cracks and tears. The scrolls are dry and feel fragile to the touch, but their aging and delicacy is amazing.

"May I help you?" I turn around to see an elderly human woman about two feet shorter than me, gray hair braided down her back, thin spectacles hanging off her nose, wearing a purple robe that was decorated on the hems with gold-laced symbols along the edges.

"Oh, sorry. I didn't see you there."

She smiles up at me and fixes her glasses, "Please, dear. I have not had many visitors come into my store lately, so it is nice to have someone interested in books instead of blades or potions. Call me Vittoria."

I smile and nod respectfully, "I'm Connor... I mean, Zarimm. Nice to meet you, Vittoria."

"It has been a while since I have had a native of Daraktar in my shop. So, what are you looking for, young man?"

"Well... I am looking for a history on Albistair. As far back as you can go," I request. She must've been surprised by what I asked, because she squints at me through her glasses like she's studying me. "Huh... I will have to look at our deeper sections. History is not favored in this town."

She waddles her way to the back of the shop before returning with three books in her hands. "Here are some that should be of use. Unfortunately, they only go back to 1038 RE, but should be of some use to you. Why does history of the realm interest you if I might ask?"

I try to find the right words to say without offending her as she hands me the books. "Honestly, you're the first human who hasn't treated me like I'm diseased since I got here. I just want to know why."

She looks at me over her glasses before taking them off, "Dearie... you will not find the answers you seek in any history books. Life in Albistair has just been... unsettling for centuries. Since the events of the Violet Moon, no race has ever trusted the other to be forthright or honorable, human, or otherwise. Luckily for you, I do not turn away scholars, no matter their race." In a moment of pity, Vittoria pats my hand that's holding the top of the books. "It is not history that creates our future, but what we decide in the present. No charge for the books, dearie."

I frown slightly before I turn and leave the store. I open my satchel and put the books inside, watching them get swallowed into a black hole. "Pocket dimensions... classic."

In my moment of distraction, a gust of wind sweeps, by big enough to blow out all the torches on the main road in town. "That's never a good sign." I reach behind me and take out my staff. The town is almost in complete darkness as the crescent moon in the sky was shrouded by some clouds. The winds start to die down, but the whistling wind would've been better than what I hear in that instant. What I hear could've been mistaken for a flock of pterodactyls from the *Jurassic Park*; light, raspy screeches that are slowly getting louder, going from light screeches to a more guttural, scratching cry. I can't tell where they're coming from, but they were getting closer really fast. I hold my staff firmly in my hands, slowly turning where I think the sounds are coming from. I suddenly fall to my knees and shut my ears tightly, dropping my staff and my guard. The voice from the forest is in my head again.

"Okak re Stuzar!

I clench hard before I could make out what the voice was saying, now in English: *"You are weak!"*

The screeching sounds get louder while I'm trying to fight off the voice in my head.

"You are too weak to evoke your full power. You will die."

"Fuck off!!" I yell to the sky above me in rage before a shadow streaks through the barely lit night sky. I quickly get to my feet taking my staff back into my hands, shuffling around to find what was stalking the night. My feet are swept from under me, sending me flat on my face with a loud thud. I roll onto my back and am now face-to-face with the ugliest thing I've ever seen but recognize it immediately. It's a terrorghast. It looks exactly like what Merrin had shown us a drawing of, but still did almost no justice to how disgusting and terrifying this thing really is. Its three eyes are a piercing, pale yellow that shakes me to my core. Its mouth opens to show a long, prehensile, forked tongue slobbering over its bottom rows of jagged teeth. Its breath smells like decaying flesh and rotten eggs, making me gag. *Can this body vomit?* I try to wiggle my arms free, but they're pinned down by its massive claws digging into my wrists.

The terrorghast opens its mouth wide and leans closer to my head, but then gets thrown off me with a great force, screeching in pain. Leaning up, I look to the monster as it writhes around on the ground, pierced by brass spear in its back.

"Get up, Connor!"

I look to my other side and see Mark, all fanned out in a combat stance, with the others right behind him. Krissy is holding two iron axes in her hands and wearing new leather armor that covered her chest and shoulders, wraps on her wrists, and leather pants. Riley replaced his lightning amulet with a jeweled leather bangle on his left wrist that is shining electric blue, keeping his focus in shock magic. Danica's clothes are the same as before, but she now has multicolored phials attached to her belt and is holding two green phials in her paws while standing behind Mark.

After admiring their upgrades, I quickly get up with my staff in hand and stand in combat position.

"What the fuck is that thing??"

"It's a terrorghast! Like Merrin showed us!"

The monster gets back up onto its ghastly feet and screeches aggressively, with Mark's weapon still stuck in its back. It charges at us so quickly that it blows right through us, knocking us all into different directions. I grunt and try getting up, still hearing the rough voice in my head repeating, "*You are weak.*"

I shake the voice off and scan around me, "Anyone got eyes on it??"

"Lost it after getting tossed like a ragdoll!"

A loud clanking sound rings out next to where Mark is standing. He looks next to him to see his new spear, the tip dripping with gray sticky liquid. Slowly looking up, the terrorghast pounces down on him. He struggles against it as he quickly grabs his weapon and shoves the shaft into its jaw.

"Someone kill this thing!"

Everyone freezes, not sure what to do or how to keep from hurting Mark in the process. Thinking quickly, I do the only thing I knew how to. I aim my staff at Mark and shout, *"Granav alnej ukavrengavh!"* In my head, I hear the English translation: *Grant me Strength.* The blade of my staff glows white as it shoots a beam engulfing him in a dim white halo. His struggle lessens a little bit against it, giving me time to strategize. *Okay Connor... this is a video game... your wheelhouse...that's a high-level monster... it's strong, but it can be killed.*

"Riley, get its attention! Dani, when it's away from Mark, hit it with something that hurts! Krissy, when it staggers, give it everything you've got!" I may not do much with combat, but I know how to strategize. The others take an extra beat before Riley leaps into action, galloping forward and aiming his new weapon at the beast.

"Storm Bolt!" He thrusts his fist forward and the jewel ignites blue, shooting a ball of lightning at the terrorghast. The bolt hits it in the back, causing it to stagger away from Mark, who quickly shuffles back towards the rest of the group. The beast roars at the galloping centaur, rearing back trying to keep its focus on him. Riley fires a couple more Storm Bolts at the beast, but it's too fast. Its fanned tail whips at his horse legs and knocks him into a nearby wall. It slides into a halt, glares at him, and charges again only to be stopped by the sound of glass shattering and a pale green cloud.

"Stay back! It's poison!" Danica pulls another phial from her belt and launches it. I watch as the beast tries to swipe its way out of the poison cloud, screeching, and coughing.

"Circle around it! Don't let it get the drop on you!"
I hold my staff out in attack position, dagger-end pointing towards the cloud. Mark finally gets back up with his fish fins fanned out. Krissy stands in front of Riley, who is still grounded from the attack, holding her axes in her hands with her piercing yellow eyes locked onto the monster. The cloud slowly fades out and the beast roars out, drooling a thick purple ooze from its jaws. The loud scream staggers us, like when a monster rolls Intimidation against adventurers in any RPG I've ever played. "Hold," I say softly. "Hold... hold... NOW!"

Krissy yells out like an Amazon warrior as she runs forward and jumps into the air, bringing her axes down in a slashing motion. The terrorghast looks up and reaches with its long arms to swipe out at her, not noticing Mark cocking his spear back in a javelin pose and hurling it forward strong and hard right at its midsection. As it grabs at one of Krissy's arms, it misses the incoming spear that is now sticking into its ribs, causing it to drop her to the ground. Now free, she spins around and slashes at one of its legs, crippling it down to the ground. Wounded and cornered, the monster lifts its head to see me standing in front of it with my dagger-headed staff pointed at its head. "Eat iron, you ugly shit." I thrust my weapon into its mouth with enough force to make it pop out of the back of its head.

The terrorghast gags loudly as it's choking on what I can only assume as its blood, coming out thick and gray and slimy. I hold tightly to my staff, step on the jaw, and pull it from the monster's head, stepping back to watch how the beast dies. It wriggles around turning on its back, flopping and gagging before a purple shimmer begins to erupt from inside its chest. The shimmer glows brighter before the whole body is enveloped in it before disintegrating into the air. The only thing left behind is a few different colored spheres glowing on the ground. I approach them and pick up a green sphere, holding it up to get a better look at it. As I'm holding it, a dim light broke through and showed a dark leather tunic hovering inside.

"Wow... I think these are gear drops." I look over to Riley, who is back on his legs and limping from being attacked. I think for a moment, then toss the sphere to him, "You could probably use that." He looks at the sphere and then to me before squeezing the sphere in his hand. It breaks and sends green dust around his body before it disappears, showing him wearing a new tunic; dark, leather, strapped on him in a way that made him look like a superhero. He smiles, "Thanks! This is freaking amazing."

Before I can talk him up, I hear yelling coming from behind us. A mob of angry citizens with torches are yelling angrily as they march toward us. Danica stands behind Mark again, Krissy grips her weapons standing between Riley and me in front of the two of them. Before the mob got closer, I quickly grab the other spheres and put them in my satchel.

The mob stops, keeping a short distance from us while they yell, "Beasts! Freaks! You've doomed us all!"

Krissy is confused. "We saved your town! Why the hell are you mad at us?!"

One angry human steps forward with a torch, "You killed one of the Chasm beasts! That one was a scout! They travel in hordes! The rest of its horde will come to destroy us all because of you!"

A tomato is thrown from the mob and smacks Riley right in the chest. "You beasts are the reason all of this has happened! You blighted creatures! Why won't you just leave us humans alone!"

I see Jarell in the crowd, holding tightly to his mother's side. I put my staff into the strap of my back before taking a step forward. The whole mob takes a cautious step back.

"We don't know why this is all happening, but we didn't start this. My friends and I are going to stop those things, one way or another," I promise, looking straight at Jarell. It doesn't help to settle the crowd at all, but it's the best I could do.

I turn away from the crowd, "Let's go guys... we're done here." We walk away from the mob and away from the town. I can't stop thinking about Jarell and Vittoria, the only humans that have been kind so far. With the books I got, I'm going to make it my personal business to find out where this all started.

CHAPTER 10

The journey out of town is awkward and quiet with no one saying anything. The fact we made it out of that fight is miraculous on its own. Merrin's description of the terrorghasts didn't live up to the actual thing, which kind of scares me even more because of the townsfolk saying they come in hordes. If just one took all of us to take it down, what would happen if we met a horde of them?

"Krissy, how far is it until we get to the Ordowell Bowels?"

Krissy looks to her map, "Looks like it's about another ten miles of walking. It's going to be a long ass walk, guys."

I heard a huge sigh coming from everyone and couldn't help but chuckle slightly. "Well, seems like a good time to get our steps in, eh?"

No one laughs.

"I read the Logbook a little more and it says we can actually 'sleep away hours'. Like taking long rests in a tabletop game."

"God, you're such a nerd," Danica groans as she walks past us, making Krissy snort.

Before I can comment, Mark starts shushing us to be quiet. "Do you hear that? Is there a town or something nearby?"

My eyebrow shoot up at him. "Dude, you okay?"

"Can you seriously not hear those voices? It's like they're getting louder."

Krissy scans the map everywhere and shakes her head, "There aren't any towns nearby. The nearest thing to us is a river that we need to cross."

"Jesus, the voices won't stop!" He groans and holds his ears. *Does he have a voice like me?* Something grabs my attention: The amulet around his neck was shimmering slightly.

"Mark... what does a Totemist do again?"

"What? A-a Totemist channels animals based on the acquired level, taking on their traits, commanding them, even—" That's when he looks at me with the same look of realization I have before we say it together, "Talking to them."

Krissy and Danica look at us confused, but Riley is in awe.

"The river must have fish in it, meaning you can hear them talking as if they're people. Let's go to the river and see if you can tell what they're saying."

I think this is the first time that I've seen Mark really get excited since we got into this mess. Riley is racing to catch up with Mark, leaving me with Danica and Krissy.

"How do you do that?"

"Do what?"

"Make people feel better. You've been doing it since before we started all this crap. You've somehow managed to keep everyone cool about everything."

I don't know if it would be obvious to her or Danica, but I feel my face heat up. But that's quickly ruined when Danica decides to put in her two cents.

"Are you shitting me right now? It's his fault we are in this place. If not for him, Mark and I wouldn't be in this fucking mess. Now he's hearing *fish voices*, Connor! This is all your fault," she spits at me. She marches off after Mark, leaving me to stand there in silence with Krissy.

"Dude, where did that come from?"

"Don't worry about it. Let's just... let's just go to the river."

"Why are you being such a pushover? Why did you let her yell at you like that?"

"Because she has a point." I take a deep breath, "Look, they're in this because of me. Even you. Riley and I would've done this whole thing ourselves if we didn't need five people. Mark used to game with us, but Danica didn't like it. I wanted to get my friend back, but he comes as a package deal. Then, you were at the party and—"

I feel a hard hand hit me upside the head, interrupting my speech. "Would you stop? It's not cute to lay down and take all the shit that's being thrown at you! It's not like at that frat party. So, suck it up and grow a pair, you idiot."

Why is everyone hitting me?! I follow after her into the tree line that went towards the river. When we break through the trees, the river comes into view and leaves me dumbfounded. This game knows how to blow minds. It's enormous and colorful by every stretch of the imagination. The water is crystal blue and almost see-through. The riverbanks are almost every shade of green that it could possibly be, sprouting a few amazingly colored flowers.

I walk up to the others standing at the edge of the riverbank, minus Mark.

"Hey, where's—" A huge splash erupts from the river like a geyser. From the water comes a Triton with a loud yell, doing a flip mid-air with a loud "YEAH!" and diving back in. I can't stop myself from laughing at the trick, watching him have fun and forget about our current situation. Danica, on the other hand, is steaming pissed while watching him. But I wasn't about to let that ruin the fun he's having in this moment. I set my gear and satchel to the side, take a running start, and jump into the river. The water is cold, but oddly relaxing at the same time.

I swim back up to the surface of the water and let out a laugh, looking to the others. "Come on! Gonna jump in or what?"

Danica stood with her arms crossed and ears pointed back. I can tell Riley was hesitant because even he didn't know if Centaurs could swim, but then he gallops forward and leaps into the water, causing a huge splash. I look around for him in the aftermath and see him surface a little wildly, making me do a horror laugh. The water settles a little bit to the point that I could see his horse legs kicking underneath, which made me laugh harder and struggle to keep myself above water.

"Cannonball!" I look up to see a red demon girl leaping in the air and curl into a ball before hitting the water. The water explodes and splashes us all. She rises from under the water, whipping her white hair back out of her face and smiling. For the first time, aside from Danica, we were all having fun.

Mark is swimming circles around us, laughing and smiling. "Holy crap… I never knew being a different species would be this fun."

"Did you try to talk to any fish?"

His face lights up, "Holy shit I forgot! Hold on, let me see." He dives into the water, slightly out of sight. I try looking, to see what he was doing, but only see a small golden glimmer coming from where he dove down. A few moments pass and he came back up with wide eyes.

"What? Did you find Nemo?" Krissy asks, making Riley laugh.

"We gotta go, *now*!" Mark swims past us to the riverbank where Danica is sitting.

Before I can ask what he's talking about, I hear Krissy scream and turn around to see what was happening. Upriver, something was tearing through the water and coming right at us. Almost like how a shark charges at its prey, this thing has three barbed fins sticking out of the water that are jagged and dark green. It slowly starts to emerge, revealing a long, scaled, green body like that of a crocodile.

"Move!" Mark yells out as it moves closer. We swim as fast as we can away from the beast, but it's too late. The shape leaps out from the water in its full form. It's a giant crocodile like I have never seen before; six legs with three long claws on each scaled foot, three rows of barbed fins on its broad body that trail all the way down to its tail, and a long crocodile jaw with jagged teeth. The monster looks at us midair with its devilish red eyes and wide-open mouth before plunging back into the water.

I swim as fast as I can away from where it plunged, gripping onto the soil of the bank to pull myself up. I'm suddenly thrust up onto the ground by Danica grabbing my damp shirt with her claws. We look at each other and nod before I reach out to grab my staff.

"Riley, get out of there!"

I turn and look to the Centaur struggling to get out. The monster is darting towards him opening its jaws, but then it suddenly starts thrashing around in the water. On its back is Krissy, holding on like a bull-rider to its back and hacking at it with one of her axes. But none of her hacks break through its scaled back and only make it angry as it bucks around in the water trying to throw her off. This gives Riley time to climb out of the water and flop onto the ground.

One giant thrust upward from the beast throws Krissy off its back and into the river. It turns around and dives down after her, gripping one of her legs in its jaws and pulling her down.

111

"Krissy!" I grip my staff and am about to plunge in after her, but Danica holds me back. "Let me go! I can help her!"

"No, you can't!" She digs her claws into my shoulders to keep me back from the river. I grunt in the pain, but then shove her aside, run forward and dive into the water. I scan around to find her and see her stuck in the jaws of the monster, which was trying to keep her down and drown her. Blood is coming from her leg where it's biting down as she struggles to hold her breath.

In a moment of pure adrenaline, I grip my staff with both hands and attempt to call on some sort of help from my patron god. *'Okay you fucking voice! I invoke you! Help me!'*

My staff's red runes start to glow bright, surrounding my whole weapon in a dim red aura. As if it were possessed, the staff pulls me forward toward the monster dagger-end first and plunges into the soft underbelly of the monster. It opens its jaws, releasing Krissy's leg, and swims away from us. I grab her by the arm and swim up to the top of the river. I gasp loudly as I hold her close and side-paddle to the edge of the river.

"It's coming back around!" Riley yells out. I look behind me and see the monster's barbs sticking out of the water coming right at us. The only thing I think to do is to keep Krissy behind me and hold my staff forward in hopes of jabbing it. As it resurfaces with jaws wide open, it hisses out and thrashes around as an arrow strikes it in the eye. I blink the water out of my eyes and look to see where it came from. On the riverbank, I catch a glimpse of an archer aiming a bow at the monster, wearing a green and brown hooded tunic with leather bracers on their wrists and has the body of a horse. A Centaur like Riley. Behind him, five more charge out of the tree line with arrows fixed onto the monster, releasing all at the same time. Some of the arrows bounce off the monster's back, but a few manage to get lodged into its underbelly.

The archers keep up their attack until Mark yells out with his arms up, "Stop! It's screaming for you to stop!"

The attack stops as the beast thrashes around and climbs onto the riverbank, falling flat on its stomach. Mark pushes past everyone and approaches it slowly until he's within arm's reach of it.

"Mark, get away from it!" Danica yells at him, but he doesn't stop. I watch while holding Krissy in my free arm, trying to keep us both above water. Mark slowly kneels next to it, watching as its breathing becomes slower and softer. The chain of his totem is glowing dimly as he puts his hand on the top of its head. At first, it snapped its jaws at him, but then it starts humming softly with fewer breaths. Silence finally falls and Mark stands up slowly, unsheathing his spear, hovering the bladed tip over the wound on the side of its belly where I stabbed it, and thrusts forward. The beast hisses out in pain before dropping dead on the ground. He pulls his spear from the beast and stands silently over the corpse.

I feel a pair of hands lift me by the arm to pull me and Krissy out of the water. I look up to see two of the Centaurs peering down at us both as they pull us onto the riverbank. I look down at Krissy's motionless body and panic, "Krissy, wake up!" I'm shaking her shoulders to try and wake her, but it's not working.

"Connor, use your skills! You're a Warpriest. Try to heal her!"

"My patron god is a war god, Riley! Not a healer!"

"Just try, dammit!"

I growl lowly and look at her, knowing if I don't do something, she could die in the game. If she dies here, what happens to her in the real world? I reach into my satchel for my Logbook and look for anything I can use. As a Warpriest, I have a cantrip called "Spare the Dying", but it requires a lot of my willpower. Shaking off any doubt, I hold my staff in one hand and put the other hand on her wounds.

"*Ukpare avhe Dyaumn.*" The cantrip invocation causes red tendrils to seep into her wounds, her body starts to shake a bit before her eyes shoot open and she turns to vomit out the water she inhaled in the river.

After coughing up the rest of it, Krissy looks up at me with wide eyes and heavy breathing. "Th-thank you…"

I nod hesitantly and gently squeeze her arm before glancing up at the Centaurs that saved us. They're brooding off to the side, casting judgmental glances at us and the creature while talking quietly to each other.

One of the two that pulled us out of the water steps forward. His face is grizzly and square-jawed with a thick short beard under the hood he wore. "Who are you? Why are you here?"

"We are trying to get to the Ordowell Bowels. We stopped here to rest before that… thing attacked."

"You stepped into the hunting grounds of a murkodile," one of the other Centaurs informs us as she joins the leader. "They are extremely territorial, as you should know."

Riley trots up to our side, "Sorry… we're not exactly from around here. But thank you for your help. It's good to see fellow Centaurs."

They glance at Riley strangely, "This was an unnecessary conflict, young colt. Or has your tribe denounced the teachings of the gods?"

Riley blinks at the comment, looking a little offended. Honestly, I can't blame him. The way they talk to him sounds very condescending. On the other hand, it's better treatment than what we've been getting lately.

"You have disrupted the creature's habitat with your presence, causing it to act aggressively and attack you and your... companions."

"Dude, you're being a bit of a dick right now," Riley spits back. "I thought centaurs were supposed to be noble hunters."

"They're right." Mark and Danica join up with the rest of us. "I heard it. It's thoughts. It thought we were destroying its hunting grounds and attacked. I could hear it speak and scream... and die."

Jesus Christ. He used his ability as a Totemist to hear what the murkodile was saying, maybe even feel its pain. He looks like a serious mess with empty eyes. Danica pats his shoulder lightly, "It's okay, baby. It wasn't real... none of this is real."

"It felt real, Danica! It felt very fucking real!" His fins fan out in anger. All of us stand in silence as he looks only at Danica in a full-on rage. She jumps in surprise and her ears flatten back. "I could hear its dying screams. It begged me to kill it because it was in so much pain. Why the hell is this happening?"

It was such a cryptic silence that we're all standing in until one of the Centaurs approaches him slowly and puts a hand on his shoulder. "Totemists are the world's greatest empaths of nature's inhabitants. We cannot always protect it, but we can ensure that the cycle continues. Life takes what it needs, but also gives what it believes is owed."

Mark looks up at him visibly calmer, even making his fins close. The leader gives us a pitiful look, seeing that we were pretty shaken up. "Come with us. Our *harras* is not far from here. You can recuperate there, then we will discuss your intrusion in the forest. Put the Tiefling on the back of Nara. She is too weak to walk."

Standing up, I carefully scoop Krissy up in my arms, having hers wrap around my neck. The one called Nara walks over and helps me to settle her onto her back. Nara trots next to the lead centaur as they lead us into the forest.

The walk is eerie and quiet as we're ushered by our saviors. The tension between Danica and Mark is so thick that there's practically fog forming around them. Riley is busy talking with one of the other Centaurs like they're long-lost relatives, which to me is a bit surprising after what happened at the river. My focus is on Krissy, gently resting on the back of Nara rocking back and forth. I can't believe that Danica almost made me leave her to be killed by the murkodile. What's worse is that I'm supposed to be the cleric of the group and I choked. A *healer*. Instead, I'm an orc Warpriest that is devoted to an Orcish god of war and vengeance. I've hardly had the chance to level up or get any good items because of the mayhem we've been put through. Too much is happening at once, and no progress has been made since we got thrown into this thing. Hopefully, when we sit down with the centaurs, we can find the Ordowell Bowels and make the first real step to completing the game.

Our walk seems to be coming to an end when I finally start to hear voices coming from ahead of us. Looking past the escorting Centaurs, I see huts and tents that spread out quite a bit in the forest. Outside those makeshift homes are dozens of Centaurs of all sizes and colors, young and old. It's insanely cool to see. They start watching and observing us as we are ushered further into their camp, some in shock and others in disgust. It's as if most of these Centaurs had never seen any of our kind before, aside from Riley.

"We have an open hut for your party to rest," the lead Centaur offers and points to the hut. "Once you have recuperated, I wish to have you join us at our council gathering in the center of the camp." Danica and I help Krissy off Nara's back, keeping her arms around our necks for support.

Thankfully, the opening is tall enough for Riley to enter. The inside of the hut is decorated quite well for being unused; two candles lit in each of the four windows, a few hay nests on the floor, even a chest that reminds me of stash chests you would see in most role-playing games. Danica and I help to lay Krissy onto one of the piles of hay for her to rest on, while Mark secludes himself into one of the corners of the hut.

I sit near the door, looking out into the camp, while Riley joins me. "You okay man?"

I sigh loudly and lean back against the wooden wall, "Yeah, I guess so. It's just… nuts."

"We really haven't had the chance to sit down and talk, have we?" His horse tail is wagging lightly behind him, which makes me chuckle a bit.

He returns the chuckle when he sees what I'm laughing at. "I still can't believe I can walk. It's been awesome having legs that work."

"But… you know you're not *really walking*, right?"

His mouth drops slightly. I don't want to be that guy that destroys my friend's fantasy, but this is all in our heads. SnoWire is at fault here, messing with us all like this. Especially Riley, giving him the chance to walk again by making him a Centaur.

He runs a hand through his hair and sigh deeply, "Yeah, I know… but it's nice to feel this again. I mean, I can literally feel every step I take. I can feel the grass and water around my hooves, and I lost all feeling in my feet twelve years ago. So, I don't really care if this is all in my head. It feels very real, and I love it."

119

My heart sinks as he explains his sensations to me. This was messed up, letting Riley feel all of this like it was happening. It's not enough for him to know that it isn't real because he's accepted it as being real here and now.

"What about you? How are you dealing with this? You're a badass Orc that tore into two monsters. That's gotta feel good, right?"

I look to my green, clawed hands before looking back at him. "It's not what I thought it would be. I mean, like this, I'm strong. I've never acted strong before this, let alone felt strong. So… I guess I know what you mean when you say it feels great." In all honesty, I believe everything I say. Like this, I feel powerful and necessary for the group. I quickly recall the party that I went to so I could recruit Mark and the girls, remembering how weak and intimidated I was when those frat guys confronted me. Not at all how I am now in this game. Is that what Dawson wanted for his players?

I look at the others in their sorry states. "We need to get morale back up… any ideas?"

Riley scuffs his beard for a moment, then his face lights up as he reaches into my satchel, shuffling around through it, until he grabs something and pulls it from the bag. He holds up the gear drop orbs that we got from the terrorghast.

"Guys, catch," he tosses one differently colored orb to each of them and hands the last one to me. He gives me a pat on the shoulder and smiles, "You gave me the one with this tunic. See what you got, man."

I smile in gratitude as I squeeze the orb in my hand, watching it burst red and surround me in red glittering dust. I feel something forming in my hand in place of the orb, something sturdy and strong and bound in leather. The dust slowly disappears and reveals an intricately carved bone dagger about half the length of my forearm in size with red orcish runes inscribed on the blade. Personally, I would've preferred a piece of armor, but maybe this would be better than the staff. I look to see what everyone else got from the drops. Danica's provided her with a new stack of Trick Cards that are violet and gold, different from her starter brown and yellow deck. Mark's ratty shirt is replaced with a brass shoulder pauldron strapped on his left shoulder with leather and across his chest like Aquaman. Krissy's drop is a hooded tunic that looked sturdier and stronger than what she was wearing before and is black in color.

"Well, looks like we got some useful stuff. Maybe it'll come in handy as we progress through the quest."

"Stop," Danica hisses. "Just stop trying to make this okay, Connor. You can't make this better."

My buttons have been pressed. I shoot up to my feet and glare at her with fists clenched, "What the fuck is your problem?! You've done nothing but rip into me for God knows how long since we've been in this game!"

She blinks rapidly before getting up on her feet, "Don't you fucking talk to me like that! This is all your fault! Mark and I would be comfy at my place right now thinking about our future, but you came in with your nerd shit that he didn't want to be involved with in the first place!"

"Since when do you speak for him?! Mark is a grown-ass man that can speak for himself! You don't speak for any of us, you psycho! You almost let Krissy get killed by the murkodile because you tried telling me what to do!"

"No, I didn't!" she quickly replies before everyone audibly gasps. Krissy looks up at her in shock, "What?"

Danica starts stammering in a panic, "Y-you were in the water... that thing was massive... I thought if you weren't in the game anymore, you could pull the rest of us out. Krissy I'm sorry."

"You fucking should be," I snap. "I was about to jump in after her to help, and *you* held me back and told me I couldn't help her."

"Shut up!" Mark jolts up from his huddled position. We all look at him in shock as he grips his hands into fists before pointing one finger at Danica angrily, "*You* need to quit trying to control everything! You almost got one of us killed, and we don't know what happens if we die in the game!"

He swings around and aims his finger at me, "And *you* don't get to be angry at her because I don't hang out with you as much anymore! Neither of you speak for me!" His rage-filled rant calms down when he looks at Krissy with watery eyes, "I'm sorry that happened to you. I didn't react fast enough when I heard the murkodile coming. I didn't know what was happening and I feel responsible. I'm sorry."

Taking a long, drawn-out breath, he sits back down and leans against the wall, falling silent like the rest of us. Riley stands up to break the tension, "Listen, those Centaurs are expecting us to be out there soon. So, let's just stow this for another time when we aren't within earshot of a bunch of dangerous, bow-and-arrow wielding horse people. Okay?"

I grasp the back of my neck with both hands defeated, especially from being stumped with what Mark said. I turn and leave the hut to go and find the council meeting spot we were instructed to find. I can't be in that room anymore. I sheathe the bone dagger in my belt and saunter through the camp, seeing different eyes follow me while I walk. It occurs to me that most of these Centaurs have never seen an Orc before, which makes this whole plot much thicker. I need answers, and hopefully these people have some for me.

CHAPTER 11

I turn gaze ahead to the council fire. It's a large stone circle, save for an open gap with hoof prints leading in and out of it, with a fire sitting dead center in it. Standing around the pyre are three centaurs, proud and stern from the looks of it. One on the far left is an older male, bald headed with a burly gray goatee around his mouth that's been braided about half an inch down. He's wearing a forest green robe that's closed tightly around his waist with a brown embroidered sash. On the far right is the one who brought us here, standing with arms crossed and still wearing his warrior's tunic while his bow is holstered across his back and chest. Between them stands a slightly younger female Centaur wearing a wood-brown cloak with gold trims and a gold sash closing the cloak around her torso. The trio look to be whispering quietly with each other as more centaurs join the council meeting in the outer circle. Once I come into view, they all grow quiet until there is complete silence, and all eyes are on me. I walk further into the circle until I stop in front of the fire across from the head three, all looking at me intensely.

"This is the Orc from the river?" The female asks aloud. The one that saved us nods in response, looking at me with a softer look than before. She nods and speaks directly to me, "I am Corene, chieftain of this *harras*. You have already met Sebaros, our lead hunter. And this is Andrysus, our druid priest."

Both men nod to me, Sebaros slightly smiling more than Andrysus. I gently return the nod, "I am... Zarimm. I am the Warpriest of my companions." I hear a few murmurs coming from the crowd around me, even spot a couple of eyes glaring in uncertainty.

"An Orc Warpriest," the one called Andrysus sneers with disgust in his voice, "a beast that prays to gods of war, blood and destruction. And we allowed it into our midst?"

I hear some scoffs and chuckles, along with some murmurs that sound both approving and disapproving of the druid's comment. "With all due respect," I say, "what horsefly crawled up your ass and died?" Silence, again.

Andrysus' face is as red as beetroot. He's about to speak, but Corene's hand shoots up to stop him. "Enough. We have convened this council to assess the appropriate action to take with him and his companions. Not to lower ourselves to petty squabbles." Her eyes look past me, prompting me to turn around and see the others coming to join me. They all look very uncomfortable as they approach, but it's not like I'm feeling any less comfy here.

Corene walks around the fire to meet us, "Now that we have convened and recovered, explain what you are doing here."

"Plain and simple; we are going to the Ordowell Bowels to try and find one of the Keystones that can open the Mortal Gate and save Albistair," Riley blurts with a nerdy smile and crosses his arms. Everyone watching the meeting starts going nuts with overlapping conversations and yelling. Even Andrysus is disturbed by this, holding up his arms towards the crowd.

"Silence! Silence, all!" He glares at us with a real hateful look, "You creatures have no business trespassing in those lands! Nor do you have any cause to collect the Keystones that will inevitably be the destruction of us all!"

"Andrysus, still yourself," Corene orders calmly. Like a loyal dog, Andrysus stood back silently but kept his glare on us. Corene looks at us with a new face of interest and curiosity, "Tell us everything. Start at the beginning. Please."

CHAPTER 12

It takes us about twenty minutes to tell Corene and the other Centaurs our story and why we need to get the Keystones. In that time, there were countless murmurs and whispers around us, but I can't tell if they're good or bad. Corene, Andrysus and Sebaros convene with each other after we finish our story, keeping us out of earshot.

"Why are they taking so long?" Danica scowls as she paces around us. Krissy grabs her by the arm and pulls her into a stop. She turns her back to the fire, where the head Centaurs are taking their positions again. Andrysus looks absolutely pissed, but Corene and Sebaros look at us, stoic, and stern.

Sebaros trots around the fire to our left, "We understand that you are looking for the Keystones. However, we find it hard to believe that you could possibly be the Vanguards of the Realm, as legends foretell. But there is only one way to prove your story true. We will allow you to enter the Bowels and find the Keystone."

This surprises me. "Wait... you want us to find the Keystone? Just like that?"

"It is more complicated than that," Corene explains. "Our *harras* is one of only a few left in Albistair. The Archon's armies have restricted and banished us from our ancestral grounds, waging wars on our people. We need something that can help us against his assaults."

I'm a little confused at first, but Mark steps up to the rescue, "So there's something in the Bowels that you want us to get. Right?"

A quest. We were getting a side quest. The nerd in me is now at full attention, but I need to keep that under control. Sebaros nods and steps forward, "The Ordowell Bowels are filled with dangers and are protected by dangerous and powerful magic. We believe that the magic in the Bowels can help protect our *harras* from the Archon's legions."

"What does the Archon have against Centaurs?" I think this is the first time Riley looked worried since being here. Even Corene looks worried, but I don't think it was for the same reasons.

Andrysus smugly walks around the fire, opposite from Sebaros, "The Archon is not what he seems. No one knows his identity, nor does the realm's history provide evidence of his existence. The man is always hiding behind his mask but holds influence and approval over all the human populaces. Since the events of the Violet Moon that tore open the Chasm, humans have believed all non-humans conspired to use magic to eradicate them. No one ever believed such things until the Chasm vomited out the terrorghasts and the Mortal Gate disappeared. So, we must find a way to protect ourselves before our kind becomes extinct. The Ordowell Bowels may just have what we need. If you are what you say you are, you will find the magic that protects it and bring it to us."

"Wait, why would we do that? We can just go into the Bowels and find the Keystone and move on to find another one."

Corene shakes her head, "It is not as simple as that. The Bowels have kept the Archon's men out because of that magic. It created a phenomenon that has devoured all who enter the Bowels. We have come to call them mistwraiths, creatures made of possessed mist that makes them untouchable and invulnerable." Corene turns around to face Andrysus, gesturing his attention to the fire. The druid reaches into a sack he has tied to his waist, pulls out a handful of green sand and tosses it into the fire. The fire changes colors and gives off a mirage-like smoke. In the smoke, an image takes shape that looks like it is lunging out at us all. It had an oblong shaped head with no eyes, nose, or ears, but it also had a long, open mouth that extended down its neck like the mouth of a cavern. Its body was very long, thin, and spindly, lunging forward and reaching out with four arms, each having three long clawed fingers. It's lower torso disappeared into a fade, not showing its feet or the rest of its legs.

"These creatures fade into the mists of the swamp, stalking those who enter it without being seen, like perfect predators. When they attack, the mists solidify, and they strike with their sharp claws. The bodies of their victims emit a steam into the swamp's air, which they feed on to thicken the mists and become stronger," Andrysus explains with a small air of arrogance about him.

This couldn't have gotten any worse for us. We are being challenged to find an artifact that we need to get out of the game, while also fighting off chasm and mist monsters.

"So, we get you this magic that is protecting the swamp, what do we get out of it? It seems like we're walking straight into the hornet's nest with a high chance of death." I swear I can see a vein popping from Andrysus' head from what Krissy said, but she makes a solid point.

Sebaros nods, seeing her point like I did. "I understand. But we can guarantee a safe entrance into the Bowels. There is another way in that my hunters have scouted in previous excursions that were, otherwise, unsuccessful. We can get you into the swamp safely, and you will be able to get out of it once you find the source of the magic. You do this for us, you will safely obtain the Keystone and we can help lead you to another one's possible location. That is our promise."

I raise my eyebrows and look to the others for their thoughts. Krissy and Riley nod at me, Danica is keeping her gaze away from mine, and Mark steps up to my side looking at Sebaros. "We're in," he says sternly. "We get you the source of the magic, we get the Keystone, and you help us after that."

Andrysus looks suspiciously pissed off, but Corene smiles softly and approaches us with her hand out. I take her hand in mine and we shake, "Let's get started."

We take time to go over the layout of the Ordowell Bowels that Sebaros had drawn in his hunting lodge, which is an awesome setup. The interior has decorative tapestry of green and purple along the walls with a few animal pelts in between them, a few ceremonial weapons on wall mounts, and a shrine-looking table against a far wall that has an idol sitting on it. This idol was chiseled out of wood in the likeness of a powerful looking Centaur.

"What is that?" Sebaros looks at the idol and approaches it, "This is Iroas. He is the Centaur god of victory, one which we praise in our hunts and battles."

He turns his attention back to the table the map is on, which the rest of us circle around. The map shows an intricate layout of Albistair, more detailed than the one that Krissy has with her. He pulls an arrow from his quiver and uses it to point out positions on the map for us, "The Ordowell Bowels are here, roughly half a day's ride northeast of our encampment. The swamp is small, but that gives the mistwraiths more control over the area. The thick forestry keeps much sunlight out of it, which does not help with visibility. However, there is a cavern right here that goes underground and into the borders of the swamp. Now, we believe that the source of the magic is somewhere in the center here, but the mists create senses of misdirection and can cause you to get lost. Your only hope to find it is to try and thin out the mists, gain your bearings and find the center. With your combined traits, it should be enough."

"Should be?" Krissy blurts out with a dry laugh. "We hardly have a handle on any of this shit. We've gotten lucky so far to stay alive."

"I wouldn't call it luck," I argue. Krissy gives me the stink-eye in confusion. "Look, if it were luck, I would say that at least one of us would have died already. In every game I've played, everything is based on how you think and react to situations. Choosing the right things to say, the right course of action, even who to trust. If we've managed to stay alive this long, I think it's because we actually know what we're doing and how we want this to end."

Riley smiles and pats my shoulder, "He's right. I've been in a wheelchair for a long time, but I'm running like I've been doing it my whole life. We all have something to help us get out of this. Krissy, you're a total badass. I've never seen anyone fight like that. Danica, I hardly know you, but you're quick on your toes and have the most amount of luck with your class traits. Mark, I know you have been dealing with a lot, but dude, you are the bravest one here after facing down the terrorghast." His gaze turns to me, "And you. You've been helping and leading us the whole way. There's no way we can't win. So, let's fight some fog monsters and get this shit done."

Not gonna lie, I'm getting serious goosebumps on my green skin from his little pep-talk. The others are speechless themselves, which shocks me. After a moment, I look sternly at Sebaros, "Let's do this. First, we need to stock up. Do you have anyone that makes or sells healing potions?"

The hunter nods, "There's an herbalist lodge near the entrance of the camp. Look for Nara, she leads the healers."

I nod in return, then look over to Riley, "Go grab what you can. See if you can get anything else that could help us in the Bowels."

"Sweet! I've been waiting for a chance to talk to her. She's hot, for a horse girl." He trots out of the lodge, ignoring the snort that came from Krissy.

I compose myself and put my finger to the map on the table, "See if your map has these coordinates. Mark the Bowels on yours and we'll see if we can predict where we move on the map."

She nods and grabs the map from her satchel. Holding it over the table map, hers begins changing like some sort of update. The map highlights both the cavern and the Bowels, even creating a swirling cloud over the swamp. "Holy shit, that's cool."

I nod with a chuckle, "Okay, then. Let's do an equipment check, see what we have and what we can do to better prepare for what's ahead. Dani? Mark?"

The two of them barely glance up at us, still sitting silent and angry. In this state, they're not going to do well against a bunch of fog monsters. "You know what? You two sit this one out. Stay here until we come back with the Keystone."

"That is not wise," Sebaros says abruptly. "The mistwraiths are strong and have unknown numbers. You could be overtaken, separated, or killed on the spot."

"Hold up, Seabiscuit." Mark gets up from his seat, walking right up to me and pushing a finger into my chest, "Who the hell are you to tell me what to do, you fucking troll?!"

I smack his hand away from my chest and he looks at me in shock. "You and the cat are the ones who want to get out of this game the most, and now you're bitching about who gets to be in charge? If you wanna have any say in what we do, then quit moping and get involved. That goes double for *her*."

The room goes completely silent for a few moments during an intense stare down between us. "Fine, I'm in. But I'm calling the shots for this one," Mark demands. I give a silent sign of agreement, not backing down. He and I are friends, but this is the biggest fight we've had. Who knows how long we've both wanted to tear into each other? He brings his attention back to Sebaros, "Are you the one taking us to the swamp?"

"I am. But, only as far as the cavern. I cannot endanger the *harras* by venturing with you into the Bowels."

"We get it. It's more than what we can ask you, and we appreciate it. Thankyou."

He bows his head in response, "I will meet you at the south entrance of the camp. We must get to the cavern entrance before dusk." He trots out of the lodge for us to prepare. For the next ten minutes, we do an equipment check of our supplies. Aside from the new stuff we got from the terrorghast and murkodile drops, we don't have much. Luckily, we all gained enough experience to get some improvements on our stats and abilities. I reach into the page of my Logbook and pull out my experience potion, holding it up with everyone else's like a toast, and shoot it back. Just like with Danica, I get surrounded with a golden halo that lasts a couple of seconds but makes me feel stronger. In my new level, I gain +2 in my Wisdom and Strength skills, giving me better Blessings for myself and my ceremonial dagger. Mark's Intelligence is raised +4, while his Dexterity is raised +1, giving him more knowledge of his Totemist abilities and increasing movement speed. Krissy gains +3 for her Constitution and Strength skills. Once our levels and gear are in order, we exit the lodge to go and find, Sebaros and Riley, so we could head to the Bowels. A lot of the centaurs around are looking at us like they still don't trust us, showing just how informed and tight knit these people were.

I see Riley talking with Sebaros at the rendezvous, but I also notice how red Riley's face is as we got closer. "What's with that look on your face?"

Before he has the chance to speak, Sebaros explains with humor and no hesitation, "Young Amocus was asking me questions about possible courtship with Nara." Krissy and Danica's faces twist like they were smelling something bad, but Mark spits while trying to hold a laugh and failing. Riley's face may be bearded, but it can't cover the redness that was growing on it.

Something catches my attention with how Sebaros called Riley by his character's name. At least, that's how I heard him. "Sebaros? I don't think we had the chance to get formalities from everyone. Our languages are different, so if I say that his name is Mark, what do you hear?"

The Centaur cocks up an eyebrow in confusion. "Konvos, like you just said a moment ago."

"And Danica?"

"Night Silk. A rather traditional name for her people."

"Krissy?"

"Nevine. A rather unique and pretty name for a Tiefling if that isn't too bold to say. Is this some strange custom of yours, Zarimm?"

I shake my head clearing my throat, "Sorry. Just doing a little experiment. Let's get going."

Not arguing on the request, Sebaros leads us away from the encampment and our journey to the Bowels began. The journey gives me time to put a few things together in my head about how this game and world operates. The NPCs are so close to looking, sounding, and acting like living people, even to the point of addressing the five of us by our character names and treating us like the races we look like. They react to the events of the world as they unfold like a proper RPG is supposed to, showing real-time consequential actions and conversations. Now, all of this is pretty cool to me, but thing that freaks me out the most is how easily the human citizens resort to fear and aggression when anything and anyone different crosses their path. It all seems to be the fault of this Archon character. This big bad guy is making humans fear all non-human races, while maintaining some sort of control in Albistair, like it's the friggin' Galactic Empire. This makes me realize the one real truth in this world of realistic irony; before we can escape, we're probably gonna to have to face this guy in an epic, final boss fight.

CHAPTER 13

The trek to the Bowels is, for the most part, long and silent, the only noise, being the occasional pointing out of landmarks by Sebaros. After a few more minutes of traveling, we reach the end of a path, climbing a hill that dips down very steeply and overlooks a clouded-over swamp of dank and dark trees that we can barely see through the heavy mists that swirl around like a small hurricane. Sebaros points, "The Ordowell Bowels. To the west is the cavern that will gain you access to its borders unnoticed by the wraiths. Follow this footpath, and you will see the cavern entrance. I will return with healers and escorts when you have succeeded. May Iroas grant you victory this night."

I glance at Mark, who looks a little nervous before following the path to the cavern. We follow after him quietly, but I can't tear my eyes away from how creepy and eerie the Bowels look. It was like something out of a horror movie; not exactly comforting. The mists are swirling and twisting around it in an orchestrated circle, as if there's a dome over it and it couldn't escape. The color of the mist was less comforting as it was a ghastly grey color with small crackles of blue light, like a thunderstorm.

"Look, there's the cavern." My eyes follow his finger, pointing to where the hill becomes less grassy pointing where the hill became less grassy and rockier. The path led to the mouth of a cavern, the kind that reminds me of my parents telling me to stay away from when we went on camping trips in the mountains.

"Okay, Mark, what's our next move?"

He grumbles lightly as we reach the cavern entrance. "It looks pitch black inside. Anyone got a light?"

"What are you talking about?" Danica said as she crossed her arms and peered into the dark entrance. "I can see just fine. Maybe your stupid fish-brain is going blind."

That's when it hits me and I get excited, "Danica, you're a cat-person! Tabaxi must have racial traits to see at night or in dark places. You can't see color, but you can make out shades of gray."

She blinks at me then back at the cavern, peering inside in surprise, "Whoa... that's pretty cool, actually."

"That still leaves the rest of us."

"Easy, I've got this." Krissy reaches in her satchel and grabs a stick of wood. On the end of it is a cloth wrapped into a ball. Reaching back in her bag, she pulls out a tinderbox from her equipment and strikes it against the cloth, causing a spark that lights up the cloth end to make the torch light. She smirks and joins Danica at her side, "Shall we?" They both smirk at each other and lead the way. I can see Mark clench his jaw before exhaling through his nose and walk in after the girls, followed by myself and Riley.

"It smells so rank in here," Danica says through her paw that's covering her nose and mouth. Unfortunately, I smell exactly what she's talking about. *Barf*. It's damp and dank like the inside of a wet sock.

"Keep your eyes open. We don't know if any of those wraiths are in here."

"Seabiscuit said there wouldn't be any until we got into the swamp," Mark scowls.

"His name is Sebaros. What the hell is your problem? You're in the lead, like you wanted, yet you're still being a dick."

In the dim firelight, Mark spins around with his fins flared, "Because I hate all of this right now, Riley. You two clowns are having the time of your life, but some of us are not. So would you just shut up until we get this over with?"

A loud crackling noise echoes from behind us, stopping the argument. The torch doesn't let us see much from where we entered, but it clearly shows the shock in Danica's face. After a moment, her eyes go wide and her ears twitch slightly, "Run... NOW!"

She darts past us and grabs Mark by the hand, pulling him with her. The crackling becomes louder and closer. Dust and rocks began falling around me, and then it clicks; the cavern is collapsing on us. We run away from the noise as fast as we can, trying not to trip or fall as dust and rocks began to rain down on us more.

"Don't stop!" I yell. We dart and jump around a couple of corners as the debris starts coming down faster. I watch Danica and Mark running ahead of me before completely dropping out of sight. I skid my feet to slow down to a stop, but Krissy runs into my back, and we tumble forward into darkness. Our yells echo out in the cavern until we crash in a pool of water. Flailing around under water, I look up to see Riley's horse half crashing down over me and pushing me deeper into the pool.

I struggle to make it to the surface of the water and gasp for air, quickly looking around to find the others. "Guys?! Where are—" I'm suddenly pulled under the water, causing me to panic. *This is my nightmare!* I'm tugged down lower until I'm face-to-face with Mark, pulling me to eye level and pointing below us. I look down to see a small greenish glow coming from underneath us, watching the silhouettes of everyone else swimming towards it. I follow him to the glow, which turns out to be glowing plants that light up the pool like guiding lights. He swims after the others, gesturing for us to follow him through the drowned cavern. Riley is really worrying me with all six of his limbs floundering for him to keep swimming, but he's pushing through. Mark suddenly swims upward as a rock wall comes into view, the further we go. Mark and Danica breach the surface of the water

144

above us into another tunnel. The rest of us follow shortly after, catching our breaths, and crawling onto the rocky surface.

I roll onto my back gasping loudly to catch my breath. I hear the others doing the same until it came to a dead silence. Riley broke it in the only way he knew how, "Anyone get a real… *Temple Run* vibe from that?" We just glare at him, making him hold his hands up in surrender.

"Look, there's a light. Maybe it's an exit." I dust myself off and follow Mark towards it, hearing the others close behind me. The light gets brighter and leads us to another cavern opening, giving me a small thread of hope. Instead, we walk out into a horror movie setting; gray and dismal skies barely visible, through the thickening fog and mist, decaying trees decorated with moss and broken limbs litter the ground, and murky waters, which reflect the gray color of the area.

"The Ordowell Bowels," I say out loud.

"This place is creepy." Danica's ears flatten. She moves a bit closer to Mark and takes his arm as he scans the area, mainly looking to the little pools of water.

"Mark? What are you thinking?"

He points to the pools, "I think there are some fish in the waters. With any luck, I can use my Totem to see if they know where the Keystone is."

This would be the first time that I see him properly using his special abilities without complaining, so it seems like the best option for us right now. I nod, "Good idea. Go for it." He straightens himself up before walking down the slope that we're on. We follow closely behind, going deeper into the mists of the swamp. I look behind us to see if I could still see where we came out from, but it begins to disappear in the thickening mist the further away we walk until it's completely gone.

Well, this is comforting.

CHAPTER 14

I watch as Mark looks over the pools of water, I assume looking for the most populated one. He kneels and touches the water with a single finger, making his Totem glow slightly. The rest of us stand back and wait for him to tell us what his little friends knew. I can't stop myself from staring off into the swamp and the mists. Every time I turn my head, I swear I can see shapes forming and moving quickly out of sight, making me jumpy and uneasy.

"Hey," Krissy nudges me in the shoulder, drawing me out of my trance. "You good?"

"Yeah... I'm alright." In my peripherals, I see another shape moving in the distance. *This can't be good.*

She snaps her fingers in my face, "Hey. Where are you right now?"

"I don't like this... at all," I say in a shaky voice. "I feel like we're being watched. It's not like the terrorghast. Or even the murkodile. These things? They could be breathing down our necks right now, and we wouldn't know... how the hell do we fight that?"

She takes my hand in hers and gives it a squeeze, "Connor, look at me. You can't lose your grip now, you got that? Mark may be on point for this one, but we've been following you the whole time. You have a grip on all this fantasy stuff and we're all flying blind. We'll watch your back, but you need to watch ours. Okay?"

Taking a few deep breaths, I answer with a nod. I turn my attention back to Mark still in a state of focus with his finger in the water. I see dark shapes circling where his finger poked the water, guessing they're some sort of fish. A few moments later, he stands back up and looks into the mists.

"They say there's a hum of powerful magic coming from that direction," he explains and points west. "They're not sure, but it seems to be upsetting the ecosystem here."

We look west and grow silent. It's thick and haunting that way; enough to make me more uneasy than what I was seeing before. Every alarm in my head is telling me to not be stupid and just get out, but we don't have a choice in the matter.

I take a deep breath and draw my dagger, "Let's do this, then."

My gesture to muscle-up doesn't get an applause or anything, just cocked eyebrows, and strange looks. Mark leads us in the direction that he was told by the fish, which is weird enough all by itself. Danica's ears are twitching in different directions every so often, showing just how sensitive her senses are. She seemed to be a bit more on edge than the rest of us, which starts putting me on edge.

"Dani? What do you hear?"

"It sounds like gurgling... or creaking? I can't tell... but it's creeping me out."

"Doesn't anyone have a move or something that can clear this crap up?"

All eyes fall on Riley shaking his head. "I'm a Stormlord... none of my magic can clear the air. I disperse energy. All of my spells are attack moves."

"I'm trying to hear more fish," Mark says from the front, "but they're being quiet." That's an even worse sign.

I grip my dagger more firmly before feeling a prick in my hand. I looked at my palm and see my blood stemming out onto the hilt of the dagger like what my staff did before my equipment change. I thought it was just a splinter or something before, but now I'm pretty sure it's how my equipment works. My patron god must know that something is coming.

That's when the mist starts to get thicker. I start losing sight of Danica and Mark in front of me. "Guys?" I look behind me for Riley or Krissy but can't see them. I lose sight of everyone and start hearing the sounds Danica was talking about, gurgling, and creaking coming from every direction around me. We're being ambushed.

"Guys! The mistwraiths are here!" It's like yelling into a tunnel as I hear my own echo. I spin around with my dagger in front of me, slicing through the mist trying to see ahead. The more I cut through the mist, the thicker it returned. Panic starts to set in.

Suddenly, a sharp pain in my shoulder throws me back onto the ground and makes me yell out loud in pain. I put my hand on my shoulder for a moment and feel warmth coming from it. I pull my hand away and see my blood. Something attacked me, but from where? I'm frantically spinning and looking around but don't nothing, which is the scariest thing I could think of in this moment. I get back up to my feet and hold my dagger in front of my face, gripping it tightly. "Okay, patron god... Let's do this your way... I invoke your strength and blessing into my weapon... help me to destroy my enemies..."

At first, nothing. The voice is quiet. *Now, of all times, you choose to keep your mouth shut??* But the blood on my dagger's hilt suddenly starts to glow dimly red. "*I am Olagog, god of vengeance and strength. You must prove your worth in my service. Destroy one of the mistwraiths, alone without my aide. Only then will I give you full blessings as my Warpriest,*" the voice demands.

My eyes grow wide, "How the fuck can I do that?! I can't see them! And they're made of fucking water and air!" Nothing. Utter silence. I growl in frustration and slash at the mists around me, which does nothing but fan the mists away like smoke and reform thicker. I begin to hear groaning and gurgling again all around me, making me tense up. *If I can't see when they were attacking, how could I possibly kill one?* I need to think of what these things could possibly be weak against. I fumble in my satchel for tools that could be useful, trying to ignore the increasing monster sounds closing in around me. In my satchel, besides feeling the hardback covers of the books I got from the town, I find a tinderbox of my own. That's when it hits me: heat and fire. That could be the one thing that could at least stop the mists from thickening more. It's a long shot, but it's better than waiting to be eaten alive. I had everything in the tinderbox that I needed, but I need wood to light it and I'm in a swamp.

"Fuck... I need dry wood... in a goddamn swamp." I can't see anything around me, but I also can't just stand here anymore. I put the tinderbox back in my satchel, grip my dagger firmly and start walking, occasionally swinging my dagger in front of me to try and fan away some of the mist. The gurgling sounds aren't as frequent anymore, but they're still there, as if the monsters were stalking behind me from a distance. Trying to find even a single tree feels like I'm walking in circles, until a shadow appeared in the mist. It's tall but is getting smaller and darker the closer I got. The mist breaks away and reveals the shadow to be a small willow tree with damp, dark bark. I put my hands all over the trunk trying to find a dry spot. The gurgling in the mist began to pick up again. I'm running out of time. Trying to think quickly, I looked to the ratty cloth shirt that I'm still wearing from the beginning of the game. I look to one of the branches of the tree and get an idea; I tear a strip of cloth off and tie it around the head of the branch tightly. I reach back into my satchel and grab the tinderbox, taking out the starter and try to light the cloth on fire. I feel sweat running down my face as I rush to light my makeshift torch. A few more tries and the shirt finally catches fire and started to burn. I stand up with my back against the tree and wait for the firelight to grow, holding my knife tightly in my free hand. The shirt dried some of the bark just enough to light it on fire, causing the heat and light to burn brighter, but that's when things turn for the worst.

There is just enough heat to dissolve enough of the mist to start revealing shapes in it that shake me to the core. The shapes are long, thin, hunched over, and in huge numbers. The shapes become more visible, and for a moment, I see a face in the mist break through. The face is empty like Slenderman, except for a gaping hole in the lower half that's filled with tiny sharp teeth. The head lurches forward opening its mouth wider, letting out a raspy gurgled roar, to send chills straight down my spine. The body begins to move closer and two long arms push out of the mist like they were locked inside of it, followed by two spindly legs. The monster struggles against the mist and pushes through in its full, horrific form, letting out another roar from its black hole of a mouth.

I gulp and try to move away, but my back was already pinned against the tree. The mistwraith doesn't charge at me but instead skulks forward with two long steps forward and arms stretched outright. I cock back my dagger and swing forward at it, but the blade fazes straight through

152

its arm. I spin into the swing with enough force to expose my back to it, allowing it to slash at me with its claws and leave three long gashes in my back.

"GAH!" I buckle down to the base of the tree, feeling the stinging pain of the cuts on my back. The mistwraith roars above me, holding up its arms for another attack. Leaning against the tree, I grab the torch I made and blindly swing it behind me, not expecting to hit anything but air. With the swing, I feel a heavy thud as it hits against something solid that wailed in pain. I look back and see that I managed to hit the mistwraith with my torch in its arm, causing the pale-white limb to darken and crack. The beast recoils and grabs its injured arm, taking its focus off me in that instant. I muster up a burst of adrenaline, hold up the torch and charge at it with my very own battle cry.

"Suck on this!"

With a rising thrust, I swing the torch against the head of the monster with everything I had. The heat of my torch causes its head to become solid and crackle from the strike, leaving it weak and stunned. I swing again, this time at one of its legs to bring it down. Its leg cracks and crumbles, making its whole body drop down to the damp ground. I look down over it, keeping the torch close to its body so it doesn't try to go ghost on me. I move the heat of the torch to its head, making it turn solid. It had no eyes still, which is kind of a relief. I twist my dagger around, raise it over the head and plunge it into its head. Its body starts to flail and thrash around, letting out gurgled screams until it lays still on the ground. Letting out a few final groans, it starts to flake and fade away in the air of the swamp, disappearing and leaving behind a gear drop orb like the terrorghast at the village.

I take in a few deep breaths and approach the orb, picking it up and crushing it in my hand before being surrounded by red dust. When it settles, I'm now wearing a dark gray, sleeveless leather Warpriest garb with an iron collar, decorated with red painted runes and a symbol on the chest to represent my character's devotion to Olagog that looks like a brush-drawn hand with an eye in the palm.

Before I can admire my new gear any further, I hear another blood-curdling roar from behind me. I turn around to see what it is, but then the world goes black.

CHAPTER 15

The veins in my head are throbbing heavily and my ears are ringing. I hear muffled noises that I can't fully understand. I feel like I'm dangling off the ground, swaying back and forth. My eyes feel heavy and couldn't open. The muffled noises grow louder and slowly became clearer.

"Connor, wake up!"

My eyes flutter and finally open. When they came all the way open, all I can see are dark images and outlines. Wherever I am, it's super dark and smells like a sewer. I notice that my arms are lifted over my head, so I look at my feet to see them trapped in some rocks. I'm hanging upside down.

"Connor! Over here!"

I whip my head around to see a pair of yellow eyes in the dark. I try to find the head they belong to, but the most noticeable thing I can make out are the horns.

"Krissy??"

"Fuck, I'm glad you're alive," she says with a sigh of relief.

"Are you okay? What happened to you?" I try to get an idea of where we're hanging from, but I can't make too much out as far as our surroundings.

"That mist separated us, and I couldn't see shit. I called out to you guys, but no one answered, so I just kept moving. I kept hearing something like a cat drowning in water and the mist got thicker. I swung my axes all over, but I got jumped. I woke up here with a bunch of those things around me. I have no idea how long I've been here. They dragged you in a while ago and stuck you to the ceiling. You've been out for a long time."

I groan trying to reach for my feet, but I can't reach. I grunt and fell back into suspension. "I don't get it... why didn't they kill us? They're supposed to be primal monsters..."

"Maybe they're like wendigos," Krissy guesses. She must've taken my silence as confusion because she continued with, "Like *Supernatural*? The monster thing that has a whole lair of bodies to eat and stuff?"

That doesn't make this any better. "Sebaros didn't say anything about what they did with their prey. Just that they're made from some sort of magic."

"Do you think it's the Keystone?" she asks. "Maybe it made all of this stuff happen?"

In that moment, it didn't occur to me that the Keystones could actually contain power to do things other than unlock the Gate. She may be onto something.

"One thing's for certain. We're not going to find out by just hanging here. We need to get out and find the others."

"You're a genius, Sherlock. Any ideas?" she scoffs. "My weapons fell to the ground, and I can't reach my feet."

I look around to see if I can see any more of our surroundings. It's still too dark for me to see anything, so I try reaching around myself to see if I was close to anything.

"Krissy, are you close to anything? The wall or a pillar or something?"

I hear rustling around and grunting, as well as some rocks falling to the ground. "Wait... ugh... I think... Yeah, there's a wall here. I'll try to reach it."

I keep trying to reach for my feet, coming close a couple of times, before hearing a familiar roar coming close. "Krissy... hurry up..."

I hear her struggling through her panicked breathing. The air of the cavern started getting cooler. The sounds got louder and closer. A small glint of light appears that gives a little more visibility to where we were. It was a dank cave, but the floor below is littered with bones. Horse and human bones…Centaur bones. Dozens of them scattered on the ground, some broken and shattered, others still whole.

I finally get a glimpse of Krissy. She's trying to cling to the rock wall to reach up and free herself, but her feet were very much stuck in the ceiling like mine. Her eyes fix on the light coming into the cave, and they grew big. I look in the same direction and see heavy mists rolling in, followed by gurgling roars. The mist starts forming the shapes of the mistwraiths, three of them, breaking through the barrier and becoming physical. The long-bodied creatures creep toward Krissy with their claws outstretched and surround her from all sides. One creeps behind her and aggressively grabs her tail, which makes her yell out in pain and twist around, swinging an arm at the beast to swipe at it. And it worked!

I'm shocked and confused at how she's able to hit the mistwraith. Then I think about what the Centaur council said about the monsters and how they feed. They must need to be physically whole to feed on a victim, and that was the chance to hurt them. Not just creating heat. The creature she hit lashes back at her and claws the arm that she hit it with, causing blood to fall and mist to rise from the wound. Krissy screams in pain while the monsters lean into the misting wound and began to feed from it, sucking the mist into their gaping mouths.

"Hey, you ugly fucks! You want a full meal?? Try someone that killed one of you!" I shout. All three of them twist their bodies toward me with a snarl and stalk towards me.

"Connor, no!" Krissy pleads.

I think I'm hyperventilating at this point because I can't catch my breath seeing them start to circle around me. "It's okay…" I watch them get closer before feeling their claws tear into my arm, back, and chest. I clench my teeth and try to keep from yelling in pain. I look to see what they were doing, sucking up the mist from my wounds. I can feel the burning pain of the cuts digging into my skin. These things were taking their sweet time with me, slowly and painfully draining everything they could get. I hear Krissy yelling for the monsters to stop, but they ignore her cries. I look to the one closest and see it drawing its claw back, ready to plunge it into my chest. But that's when the bronze tip of a fishing spear pierced its chest, making the monster screech in pain. The other two shuffle and sprint towards where it came from but are shot back by two bolts of lightning that launch them into the walls.

"Dani! Get them down! We'll hold the wraiths off!"

Danica comes sprinting in after Mark and Riley charge at the mistwraiths. "Hold on, Connor!"

My eyes flutter rapidly trying to stay open. I point to Krissy, "No…Get her first… use her axes to loosen the rocks…"

"Goddamn you're stubborn." She runs over to pick up the axes and scales the rock wall with her cat-like claws to get a better angle at her feet. I hear grunts, clangs, and blasts of fighting behind me coming from the others.

"We've gotta go!"

Mark sprints over and uses his spear to chip the rocks away from my feet. After a few hits, I crash down to the ground with a loud grunt.

"Riley! Get Connor on your back! Dani and I will get Krissy! Go to the spot!"

I try pushing myself onto my feet before a pair of burly hands yank me up off the ground. Riley throws me over his horse back and sprints out of the cave. He looks behind him and fires two more bolts of lightning while I try to hold onto consciousness.

"It's getting too close!"

"Hang on!" I hear Danica yell. The next thing I hear is the sound of glass shattering and mistwraiths shrieking. I don't know what she did, but it seemed to buy us some time because Riley pulls a hard-right turn and gallops hard before I black out again.

CHAPTER 16

My eyes flutter back open to see everyone circled around me. Krissy, Danica, and Riley look relieved that I'm awake, but Mark looks annoyed.

"Jesus, we thought you were dead for a moment," Riley laughs dryly. "You are heavy as shit, you know that, right?"

I try to give him a shot back, but a sharp pain in my chest takes it away from me. That pain is replaced by a blow to my head from Krissy, "I hate you. Why did you do that, you idiot??"

"Enough, let him breathe," Mark says in my defense. He comes to my side with his hand out, "You okay?"

I look to his finned hand, then to him before clasping his hand with my own and nodding in response. "Yeah... thanks for saving my ass. You did good."

Mark nods back. After our truce, I take the chance to look around and see where they brought me. The walls around us are faded stone bricks and lit by small oil lanterns. The stone walls are littered with vegetation from the swamp, so it must be very old. On top of the walls are some torn and tattered banners with some sort of symbol on them. The ground I'm lying on is wet and had multiple ruts in the shape of horseshoes.

"Where are we?"

"From what we can tell, this place might have been some sort of temple or church. That symbol on the banners was the same one carved into that figurine back at Sebaros' hut."

"It also seems to be the only place that isn't crawling with those things."

I cock up an eyebrow, "What?"

Danica walks around to my left and points out of a nearby doorway. I wince standing up from the ground and walk to see what she was pointing to. Looking out the opening, I see a huge swirling wall of mist that stopped just a couple of feet from the path that led into the temple, and in the mist are dozens of shapes of the mistwraiths.

"Why? That doesn't make any sense... what's so special about this place?"

"That's what we asked when we found this place," Mark says. "When the mist separated us, I kept hearing the fish voices directing me here. One of those things almost broke through and got me until I ran inside. I waited for them to try and get in, but they didn't. Just hovered around outside like it was barred. I heard more voices telling me where Danica and Riley were. I found Dani getting chased up a tree by one that broke through. I tried helping, but those things are strong. Dani was able to make these fire flasks and buy us some time. Once I got her back here, I went to find Riley. He got cornered at a mud pit and almost sank, so I used my spear to pull him out before two wraiths could get their claws on him."

I'm impressed. "Nice work." I gesture for a fist bump.

He shakes his head and pushes my fist down, "No. I trapped us in here, man. We can't get out of this place without those things getting at us. We're screwed and it's my fault."

A moment of silence takes hold of us. We look back out the door where the wall of mist was stalking and waiting. "No... this is not how this game ends. Not with us getting 'dementor-ed' by these things. There's gotta be more to this temple. A back door... a cellar tunnel... something. All dungeon setting levels have at least one or more exits. If we're lucky, there's another way out of this. So, pick your asses up and help me look."

I grab a nearby lantern hanging from the wall and look around until I spot a hallway to the left of where we entered. "There. That's where we start. Mark?"

He looks at me with no expression before taking the lantern from me, "Let's win this thing."

I smirk and nod, taking my dagger and follow him into the hallway while the others filed in behind us. The hallway corridor is winding and sharp at every turn until it opens into a large, open space that's too dark to see.

"Danica, can you see anything?"

She joins him and looks ahead, suddenly holding her mouth. "Oh God…guys… this isn't a good place…"

I try seeing in the light of the lantern Mark is holding. In the light, I scan around and notice a giant metal bowl sitting on a stone pedestal. I walk up to it and put my fingers in the bowl, feeling a cold sticky liquid in it, bring it to my nose and recognize the smell. "Oil… Mark, give me the lantern." Handing it to me, I open the hatch and put it towards the oil bowl. The heat ignites the oil, and the flame travel down a long oil trail, slowly lighting up the room. It's humongous, littered with tapestries, jeweled frames, rusted tools, and huge statues of Iroas, the Centaur god. It's a monastery dedicated to him, and it's amazing. Then my eyes fall to the lower level and what I see makes my heart stop: Decayed and rotten corpses and bones of centaurs.

"Gods…" Riley whispers softly.

"What the hell happened here?" Krissy's voice is shaking.

My eyes scan around the room and over the bodies that look like they're still decomposing on the floor. The smell is not as strong and obvious to us as it probably is to Danica, who is retching in the background. At that far end of the room where the oil trails end sits some sort of altar; tall, stone, and decorated with idols and offerings along the base. At the top of the altar is a pedestal, and on it sits a jagged, glowing blue stone.

"Look...the Keystone..." I utter. Everyone looks to me confused before I point to it. The stone is shimmering lowly on top of the pedestal.

I walk down the steps leading into the pit of corpses, but a hand grabs my shoulder.

"Wait. What if it's a trap?"

"We have to risk it," I argue. "The Keystone is right there. It's one step closer to getting out of this."

Mark sighs, "Fine. I'll do it. Watch my back."

My attempt to argue falls on deaf ears as he walks past me down the stairs toward the altar. He may be right about this being a trap, just like any other dungeon-based game where either a boss fight or ambush happens before achieving the goal, but he wants to be in charge here. He steps slowly reaching the lower level of the temple and we all watch as he slowly and carefully steps around and over the bodies and bones littering the floor. I catch him burying his face in the crook of his arm. *I bet it smells like a morgue down there.* While he's tiptoeing around toward the altar, I walk down the steps a little to get a better look at the bodies to see if there was any clue as to how the centaurs died. I feel my stomach turn at some of the bodies that look like they'd been torn apart, but others that seem more whole look like they've been sucked dry. Whatever did this was large, strong and could drain a person into a friggin' prune.

My focus goes back to Mark, who is finally at the steps of the altar and climbing towards the relic. The weird thing about the altar is that the closer he got to it, the brighter the Keystone started to glow. It's pulsing a blue glow at an in-and-out rhythm, like it was coming to life. He reaches out to take it in his hand, but it suddenly bursts out a large wave of blue energy that blows me against the stairs, causing me to roll down into the pit of dead bodies. I groan from hitting the floor and open my eyes to check on the others only to see a bunch of glowing blue shapes taking form around the room. I stand back up watching shapes taking form of centaurs gathered around the altar. At the top of the altar, one Centaur shape stands next to the pedestal that the stone was placed on.

"My beloved kin," the shape calls out in a distorted voice. "Iroas has given us a gift! He has bestowed upon us the magic of this Keystone to protect our kind from the clutches of the Archon! With my knowledge and the power of the Keystone, we shall uplift our kind into a future of security and strength!"

The other shapes yell and applaud in approval. The voice of the first shape sounds fuzzy and weird, but a bit familiar. The one near the Keystone faces it, raises their arms, and begins chanting some strange prayer or spell in a weird language. The other phantom shapes start to chant with them, raising their arms in unison. The stone pulses and hums in response to the chanting. As everything grew louder, something pours out of the Keystone and takes shape in front of the crowd of worshippers. It was large, had six giant limbs, and seemed transparent even in this projection. As the thing takes form, the centaurs all become silent and look up at it. A few moments of silence pass before the altar centaur rose his arms and spoke, "Behold! Iroas has sent us his avatar to protect us and strike fear into—"

He's cut short as the large figure lashes out and strikes down one of the worshippers and causes mass panic with the others. Screams and shouts of pain flooded the room, as the large beast lashes out and strikes down everyone near it. The figure at the altar backed up hesitantly, ran behind the altar and disappeared. One of the scared centaurs yelled after them, "*Andrysus!*" The blue figures suddenly fade away and the room turned back to normal.

I stand up in shock, "The Keystone made the mistwraiths... and it was Andrysus that caused all this..."

"The Keystone must've shown us an echo. A memory of what happened here. That thing has some very intense magic."

While Riley is fawning over magic, I'm steaming in anger before a heavy wind gust rushes past my ears. I quickly turn to Mark and the Keystone, which is pulsing again. In front of the altar, a flood of fog and mist pours into the room and begins to take shape. The fog and mist start becoming solid into a tall, monstrous form of a mistwraith that's different from the ones we've faced before. It has six limbs, two arms and four legs, the face is warped and twisted with four electric blue eyes, and it's tall enough to almost touch the ceiling of the room.

This... alpha wraith lets out a loud screech that made my ears ring. The only thing I hear next is Riley yelling, "BOSS FIGHT!!"

CHAPTER 17

The alpha wraith takes huge slow steps closer to us, snarling as its claws dig into the ground of the chamber. I draw my dagger and move slowly aside while keeping my eyes locked on the beast. This was bigger than the murkodile and the terrorghast, and we've only scratched the surface of what we're capable of. If this were a traditional gaming format, this thing may have a red skull over it, showing we weren't ready to fight it and could be killed in one or two strokes.

This thing opens its hazy mouth, the mist forming long, jagged teeth and stares us down like the predator it is. It raises one of its clawed limbs and brings it down in a fast-stabbing motion.

"Scatter!!" Mark yells out before jumping to the side. Everyone dashed or leapt to avoid the incoming attack before its strike cracks the floor and shakes the room. I grunt as I pick myself up off the ground and scan for the monster, seeing it was skulking and not immediately attacking. It's not like the other mistwraiths, which attack like pack animals and without thought. This thing seems smarter and more aware.

I scan the room for the others while trying to keep my distance from the alpha. "Guys, this thing is too big… we've gotta regroup."

Too late. Mark takes a running start from one of the pews and drew back his spear over his head like a Spartan, lunging forward to strike. The alpha doesn't attempt to move as he flew toward it. Like swiping your hand through smoke, he fell through the monster's bod and slammed into the wall with a loud thud.

"Mark!" The alpha wraith turns to him groaning in pain on the ground and roars out at him. It starts in toward him and brings its claw up to stab down at him. As it draws back for the attack, its hazy form suddenly becomes less hazy and see-through to a more solid form. The claw comes down swift and hard, but Mark gains enough of his strength back to roll to the side, barely dodging it. Its claw buries into the stone floor and the 'wraith struggles a little to bring it back up for another strike, but a black streak flashes by and hauls him out of the impact zone.

Danica rushes him behind a portion of the wall that was sticking out for cover to stay out of the monster's line of sight. She looks down at him and then to me in fear. *We can't dodge this thing forever.*

"How do we kill this thing?!" Krissy is ducking behind one of the still-standing pews for cover while Riley is pacing side to side staring the beast down. That catches its attention and roars before charging through the center pews, putting Krissy in its line of fire. Her yellow eyes go wide as she tries jumping out of the way, only to be met with its front limb swiping at the ground, throwing her into a wall and slamming on the ground.

I lose my shit and take off into a full sprint at its back legs with the intent to cut into them and cripple it. My dagger goes clean through its leg without inflicting any damage, causing me to go sailing into one of the broken pews and tumble. It feels like I shattered my arm as I roll onto my back. I look up through squinted eyes seeing blue bolts of lightning flying across the room toward the alpha wraith. I watch the monster snarl and charge at Riley, still firing magic bolts at it wildly. Before it reaches him, the bolts went from going through it to hitting and damaging it. The bolt attacks don't stop it but make it stagger a small bit before reaching him. He makes a jump to the side out of the way but tumbles to the ground with a loud thud.

I grab onto the broken pew to get myself up back on my feet, grunting at the sharp pain in my arm. Riley and Krissy were grounded while Danica stood huddled over Mark and shuffling through her satchel. *Fuck, we're in trouble here. Come on, think!* The alpha wraith turns its attention to them, grumbles lowly and creeps toward them like a shark in the water stalking its prey. Suddenly her cat eyes turn to me, then to the monster before taking one of her Trick Cards out.

She sprints into view the monster and stands in the open. The alpha wraith was about to swipe at her before she threw her card yelling *"To the Ground!"* The card magically changes into a purple bolt and hits the monster's claw, causing it to suddenly drop to the ground with a heavy thud

"Dani!" Mark yells out in a broken voice. She stands in front of the monster in shock, not moving a muscle.

It's as if time freezes all around me; Mark is gaping at the scene from the ground, Riley's leaning against the wall near where he fell, and Krissy is still grounded and unresponsive. I look to my dagger, then to the others. I have new blessings from Olagog that I haven't used yet, so something has to work. *I can't just sit back and be useless.* This thing is knocked out on the ground, but it could get up at any moment.

"Blessing of Olagog! War Mind!!"

I feel a strange crease in my forehead, then the whole room turns black and red. I feel blood pulsing to my head as I scan the room, seeing my friends as these white silhouettes and the alpha wraith as a bright red one. Distorted Orcish whispers are flooding my ears at rapid speed, but I start to understand some of them. They're telling me things about the monster.

"Mark! Riley! We can hurt it if we can make it solidify when it attacks! Aim for the body, not the limbs!"

Mark's eyes are still fixed on Danica before noticing the alpha wraith is now twitching, showing that its petrified state is starting to slip. His fins fan out angrily as he charges the monster, getting between its stiffened legs and directly for its torso lodging his spear right into it with a yell. The beast reacts to it with a small twitch, meaning whatever Danica hit it with it is keeping it down, but we don't know for how long.

"Keep hitting it!" I run in and join the attack. He and I stab and prod at the monster a few more times until one of my attacks suddenly pierces through it. Its body starts moving more.

"Get back!" I run to him and pull him away as the beast twitched and creaked. The alpha slowly got back up with groans and growls before glaring down at us. "We need it to become solid to damage it," I say through my teeth.

Riley stomps his front hooves, getting our attention and the monster's, "Hey, ugly!" He cocks back his enchanted bracer and threw a punch in the air, "*Storm Bolt!*" A ball of lightning fires at the alpha and goes right through it. He starts galloping around it, shooting bolts to get its attention focused on him. It screeches and roars loudly, jabbing its claws at the centaur, fading in and out of physical form quickly.

"It's too quick with its change. We need to get it to slow down."

I keep my War Mind focus on the alpha looking for any structural weaknesses. As it attacks Riley, its legs glow brighter than the rest of it, giving me an idea. "We get in close and try to cripple the legs! Target the joints and don't hold back!"

I think I see him smirk, because he fans his fins out again and looks for an opportunity. Riley keeps up his barrage, but his attacks start losing intensity. "Guys, my magic is running out! Do something, fast!"

Mark yells loudly and charges at the monster, running into a slide underneath of it and jab upwards with his spear into its belly. The monster swipes at Riley as he gallops in circles, causing it to solidify as the spear lodged into its stomach. It wails in pain and looks underneath of itself at Mark and quickly swipes at him with one of its claws, piercing his shoulder and throwing him against a far wall. Mark cries out in pain when he hits the ground with a gaping wound in his shoulder.

I freeze watching Mark hit the wall, then direct my attention to the alpha. It's staggering as vapor starts pouring from its gut where it was stabbed. A weak spot. My blessing shows the beast's red hue was getting dimmer around its body and brightest in the wound.

"Riley! It's almost finished! Let's hit it hard! Go for the wound on its stomach!"

He nods with a grimace and we both charge off into a full sprint at the monster's clawed legs with a huge shoulder check. With our combined strength, we manage to knock the legs off-balance and make it cripple down to the ground in surprise. It exposes its lower body where the wound is knowing it could close up and be mist-like any moment. I regain my footing, grip my dagger firmly, and charge in for a strike. With the loudest roar I could muster, I plunge it into the wound with a hard twist, causing it to wail and screech in pain.

"Connor, move back!" I look back to see both of Riley's hands covered in electrical energy.

I jump out of the way before he thrusts his hands forward, galloping at the monster while yelling, "*Thunder Grasp!*" His hands connect with its wound and send surges of electricity into the alpha wraith. I watch it wriggle and thrash before knocking Riley back and away from him. The beast inches forward trying to get at us, but the damage is done as it begins to steam away into the air little by little, until all that is left is a haze of mist that evaporates into nothing.

The boss fight is over. We won.

CHAPTER 18

I collapse into a sitting position on the floor breathing heavily and holding my stomach as it aches and in pain.

"Who's not dead?!" Riley stands up from the ground arching and popping his back. I stand up slowly with a groan and raise my hand. Danica sprints to Mark's side and held him in her lap, "Mark... babe, are you okay??"

He groans loudly, "Ugh... this game can kiss my ass..." She sighs in relief and holds him tight, which makes him wince in pain. His arm is still bleeding from getting slashed. While she tends to him, I make a count of everyone.

My eyes go wide remembering that Krissy was hurt somewhere. I run to where she landed and see her holding the gash in her side. "About damn time, Shrek..."

"Shut up and hold on," I growl as I rummage through her satchel, grabbing one of her vials of potions. I pull the cork open with my teeth and hold it to her lips, which she opens and starts to swallow. The wound on her side starts to glow lightly red, stopping the bleeding and reducing it to a scar, meaning the health vial probably didn't fill her health all the way. Still, she sighs in relief and puts her hand on mine, "Thank you."

I hesitate for a moment but nod in response. I let my hand linger with hers for a few moments before pulling her up to her feet. I look to the altar where the Keystone is resting on the altar in a dim glow. Walking towards it, I start to see its intricate details; it's a jagged blue stone almost like a geode except for a deep-carved symbol on one side of it. The symbol looks like the head of a trident with arrows forming on each line. I slowly reach out and grasp it gently in my hands, waiting for something to happen. Nothing. It's just glowing dimly blue. I turn to the others holding it up, "We got it... Level complete, I guess."

They all look at me puzzled, in pain, and exhausted. Riley trots forward and asks a question that chilled me to the core, "Does that mean we stopped the mistwraiths outside?"

I forgot about the creepy fog monsters circling the temple outside waiting for us to step out. I put the Keystone in my satchel and hold my dagger tightly, "Let's find out. Dani, help Mark up. Krissy, help me get the gear drops. Riley, go ahead of us and make sure none got in. We'll be right behind you."

Everyone looks to me with concern except for Mark. While he may be shaking off that last hit, he kept his cool in the moment, "Let's do it. I want a shot at that four-legged murderer back at the camp."

It was like the *300* speech because everyone suddenly remembers who almost got us killed and made us seriously pissed. Riley cracks his knuckles and heads off ahead. Krissy dusts herself off and recovers her axes before going to the alpha wraith remains to pick up the drop orbs. Danica kept Mark's arm around her neck to support him as best as possible. I go to his other side and take his other arm. No thank you or nods, he just grumbles.

"Hey, don't bitch. You kicked some serious ass, so let us help." Given his current state, he has no reason to argue, so he sighs and nods. The four of us climb the stairs of the temple to meet Riley at the entrance, praying we don't have to face anything else. We very well may get stuck here if those things are still out there.

We make it to the corner of the hall where we came from and see Riley standing at the doorway. "Guys... you need to see this..."

I don't want to see what he's seeing because he looks freaked out, but we join him at the door and look out of it into the swamp. The mist is still there, but something about it changed. There are shimmers of blue in the mist that's making the mist thin out and clear. The entrance starts to get clearer to see through as the mist fades. Riley cautiously walks ahead to the opening, much to our quiet protests. I watch him walk out of the entrance into the thinning mists and it moves out of his way with every step he took. He turns around and waves for us to come outside. Taking a huge breath, I walk forward with Mark hanging onto me and Danica, with Krissy at our backs. As we walk out, the mist moves away from us and sunlight is pouring through, giving light to the swamp. When we're not being chased by evil ghost fog, this place actually looks kind of beautiful. The sun reflects various colors of green from the moss and murk, while shining light off of the pools of water.

I feel a tap on my shoulder coming from Mark, "Dude... look."

I scan where he was looking to see the thinning mist taking form of silhouettes. At first I start to panic, but I look closer at them and notice that they look nothing like mistwraiths, but like Centaurs. They're standing in a row in front of us until one of them comes forward a little closer. This faceless creature brings its left hand to its chest then in the air in a kind of salute, then the others do the same.

"It's a tribal sign of respect," Riley explains. "I think these are the souls that were taken by the alpha. Their spirits must've been twisted by the Keystone. But now they're free." He steps ahead of the rest of us and returns the signal by putting his left hand to his chest then into the air. The spirits dissolve away softly into the air. He was right, and now they're at peace.

"We need to confront Andrysus," I say firmly. "He has to pay for this and tell us where he got the Keystone."

"Then let's go in prepared, in case he gets ballsy with us." Krissy scowls as she opens her logbook, takes out the gold vial and drinks it back. She is surrounded by the golden hue and emerges looking a little different from normal. Well, as far as normal goes in the game. Her long white hair is now braided in almost a Viking warrior style. The wound on her shoulder absolutely disappears, leaving no scar behind. The tone of her devil-red skin is now a little darker, the tip of one of her horns is decorated with a pointed gold cap, and her tail is now decorated with a leather warrior's band near the end.

"Whoa," Riley and I say at the same time.

"Leveling up must restore health completely."

"And give us a new look, apparently."

Mark takes his arm from around my neck and investigates his Logbook. His buffing potion is full, so he pulls the cork with his teeth and chugs it down. Danica and I move to the side, and he's engulfed in the same shimmer that Krissy had. When it's over, Mark doesn't look in pain or defeated anymore. His blue skin is now decorated with some tribal tattoos, one of his finned ears is pierced with a couple of brass rings, and his fish totem necklace is replaced with a totem of a claw.

"This feels... good." Mark looks at his new tattoos and totem, "I can't wait to get my hands on that fucking donkey."

"Easy there, killer. We can't just march into the encampment and rope the druid like a rodeo horse. He's a huge member of their council and we're outsiders to them. Not to mention that we don't have the magic they wanted to protect their people, because it was a curse made from the Keystone."

Mark grumbles and balls up his fists, "Then what? He got his people killed and he's herding them here like sheep to the fucking slaughter!"

"Mark!" Danica smacks his shoulder hard, "It's a game, you jackass! They weren't really alive!"

"Jesus, Danica. You really aren't a gamer," Riley says, offended by what she said. "Look, to these NPCs, they were alive and important to them. Have some damn empathy. How did you ever make it through a relationship before Mark?"

His comment appears to be a hard pill to swallow because everyone goes silent. Danica's ears folded back, and her eyes are huge and a bit watery. Mark's jaw clenches hard as he takes a deep breath, "Fine. Let's go back to their camp and get him to confess what he did. Maybe then, we'll be able to move on and get out of this place."

I sigh and nod, "Mark's right. We said we'd follow his lead on this, and that's what we're going to do. This side quest is almost done, so let's get this done and get closer to winning the game."

As the party moves back through the Ordowell Bowels, I finally see what Corene was talking about when she said this place used to be sacred to the Centaurs. The sun lights the swamp up in a way that made it less creepy, and more lush and more vibrant. It got me thinking about the Keystone and what it's capable of. If this thing could corrupt dead souls and turn them into monsters, what else could it do? Were the other Keystones capable of the same thing? Or could they do different and worse things? And if we need to rely on these things to get us out of the game, what if it does something worse? This train of thought is sending me spiraling down a road I don't know if I want to be on. Whatever Dawson had planned for this game, it needed some serious updating and debugging before people got hurt upon release, or, at the very least, stopped entirely. He can't be serious with this being for kids or anything. The realistic damage reception, the realism of the NPCs, the uncertain occurrence of player death and what it could do to the player. It's all too intense.

Our walk seems to take forever until we finally see the tree line of the ridge where Sebaros and his hunters set up shop to wait for us. Two of the hunters see us and wave us down, prompting him to turn and give an approving smile.

"I am pleased to see that you are alive," he greets. "Did you find the source of the magic in the Bowels? What about the mistwraiths?"

"It's... best if we tell everyone back at the encampment. Trust me."

With a small look of confusion, he nods and motions for us to follow him back. The way back with the centaurs is completely awkward, knowing what we do. I'm only hoping he and Corene understand what we were about to tell them. As we enter the forest camp, the centaurs are smiling and clapping with hopeful eyes and gratitude, following us to the council circle. This wasn't going to be an easy task. We're welcomed back with pats and tribal salutes all the way to there where Corene is standing, softly smiling as we walk up to the council circle, but Andrysus' brow is furrowed so hard, his eyes have almost disappeared.

"The adventurers have returned, alive and well," Corene announces with a proud tone in her voice. The centaurs all cheer and clap with approval. "What did you discover in the Ordowell Bowels?"

I turn my gaze to Mark, who is completely pissed but takes a breath and coolly steps forward. "The magic you were looking for isn't what you thought. There was no protective spell or weapon. Just mistwraiths and a lot of bodies."

The whole encampment goes quiet. The faces on the council and everyone around are appalled and confused. Sebaros unfolds his arms, "Explain yourselves..."

I'm about to take over, but Mark maintains control of the situation. "The Ordowell Bowels were cursed by the power of a Keystone to the Mortal Gate. Some misuse of the Keystone caused an alpha mistwraith to be created, which in turn made an army of mistwraiths from the dead souls of Centaurs."

This causes a huge stir in the *harras*. "You say it was misused? Meaning it was mishandled by one trying to control it. Who do you believe caused this curse?" Corene demands.

Mark looks to Andrysus intently, "It was caused by someone who, while they had the intentions of their people in mind, became drunk with ideas of what the Keystone could give him, risking the lives of dozens of his people in the process."

This blows Andrysus' lid right off, "Preposterous! You are suggesting that one of our people caused this?!"

Mark raises an eyebrow and folds his arms, "I am, and we have proof. Connor?"

I nod and take the Keystone out of my satchel, holding it in the air for everyone to see. Some stir with gasps of shock; others are baffled quiet at its sight. Sebaros, Corene and Andrysus are shocked the most.

"Why did you bring it here?! It could possibly cause another incident!" Andrysus yells out.

"And *that*," Mark points, "is our proof. Only you, the one who tried to use its power to overthrow Corene and Sebaros so that you could command the *harras* yourself, would be stupid enough to mess with something you don't understand. You gathered your druid followers and took them to the temple of Iroas because you are completely full of yourself and wanted an audience."

I put the Keystone back into my satchel, "He tried to unlock the power of the Keystone through his magic, which summoned a corrupted monster that he thought he could control. When it started attacking everyone inside, he ran away. The alpha wraith devoured their souls and created an army of mistwraiths that contained the swamp and the Keystone."

Sebaros and Corene look at Andrysus in disbelief and anger. "Explain yourself, Andrysus!"

He starts to back away from the council circle, "I-It wasn't my fault... I wanted to destroy the threat that *you* were making us run away from! The Archon is trying to leash us, and *you* won't allow us to fight back! That magic was supposed to be our answer!"

"Instead," Sebaros snarls through his teeth and draws his bow, "you sacrificed our people and disrupted their rest because you were desperate for power. Hunters!"

About a dozen centaur hunters draw their bows on Andrysus, who freezes in panic. Corene suddenly breaks through the line and stares him down, "Andrysus, for crimes against the *harras*, you are to be put to death."

"You can't do this! This *harras* will perish without my knowledge!"

"On the contrary," Riley chimes in, "Nara is a skilled and awesome healer, and works wonders with offensive tonics. I'm sure she can trump your weak-ass skills no problem."

Andrysus turns ruddy and is ready to protest harder until he is taken by the arms and escorted out of the circle by the hunters, yelling loudly all the way out. Corene and Sebaros look to us with somber faces, "We would not have made this discovery if not for you. You truly are the Vanguards of the Realm, as legends tell. Thank you for bringing peace to the lost souls. We will give them their proper last rites."

Mark walks toward Sebaros, "I'm sorry about how I acted when we first got here. But I'm glad we were able to put that mule in his place."

Corene steps to Mark, "We are grateful. To show our appreciation, we would like to present you with a gift. Nara?"

The young Centaur healer steps into the circle and holds out an amulet made of wood, carved into the shape of a runic branch. Corene takes it and presents it to Mark,

"This is a token of our people. It holds natural protective properties, as well as symbolizing the kinship between us."

Mark takes the amulet with a simple, "Thank you."

"One more thing," Sebaros adds, "we think we know where you can find another Keystone. Our scouts have reported that there has been quite a large disturbance in the direction of the Grave Expanse. There has been talk of the Crimson Order setting up a checkpoint to keep travelers away."

"Sounds ominous enough. Plus, the Archon's presence there could be a clue to our next objective."

They look to each other and nod in agreement. I look to Corene and Sebaros, "Thank you. We'll try to stop this nightmare."

"We trust in you and your abilities. For now, please allow us to celebrate you and your efforts by letting us throw a feast in your honor!" The Centaurs all yell in praise and approval, hoping it gets us to stay. I'm sure they didn't need to convince Riley, who's staring like a schoolboy at Nara, but my mind went straight to what could be happening in the real world if we don't finish this as quickly as we can. Either way, we can't afford to lose any time.

"Thank you for the invitation, Sebaros, and I hope you don't take offense to us not staying. But with how things are right now, we need to move on and find the other Keystones. If things all over Albistair are as bad as this, other people need help." I approach him with my hand out for him to take. At first, he looks a bit disappointed, but eventually he takes it with a smile of understanding.

"Then allow us to help you resupply and prepare for your journey. It is a long one to the Great Expanse."

That's one request I won't turn down. The whole encampment salutes us with their tribal gesture, giving me the goosebumps. I politely return it, gesturing the others to do the same. It was time for the next step of our quest to get out of this game.

CHAPTER 19

Before leaving the encampment, we are given a restock of a few healing flasks, courtesy of Nara. She and Riley had some heavy conversations and flirting off to the side, making me suppress my laughs as hard as I can. While we wait for him to finish hitting on an NPC, Krissy starts handing out the gear drops we got from the alpha wraith. She got herself a set of Outrider black leather leggings that have some sort of mount bonus, which she hasn't used since we started the game. Danica receives a brown, hooded cloak with holes for her ears that give her a +2 increase in stealth and +1 intuition. Mark receives a set of brass bracers for his wrists and ankles, which ironically increases his swimming speed as some sort of racial perk. My orb gives me a set of crude leather boots that award me +1 constitution.

Riley finally joins back up with us and gets his orb, containing a leather armor piece for his horse half that almost resembled a saddle but makes room for his mana flasks and adds a +1 to his overall vitality.

"How'd that go, Romeo?"

Riley chuckles in response, "Gotta say, the realism in this game is scary good. She kissed me."

A unanimous pause, followed by an "Oh damn!", comes from the whole group, along with some claps. Riley bows his human half with a huge smile on his face, "I love this game! Hey, do you think our characters can have sex here too?"

The mood goes from surprise to disgust and discomfort. "Ugh! Gross!" I believe Danica blurts out.

"What?! It's a legit question!"

That becomes an awkward walk as we follow Krissy and her map that's now updated with our new destination: The Grave Expanse. According to it and what Corene shared with us, this place is a wasteland of sand and heat that went for miles. The Expanse is also known for a massive canyon that separates two sides of the land from each other. What the Crimson Order and Archon could be doing there is a huge mystery, even to the Centaurs. The worst part is that the journey was going to take at least two days to get there, and walking was becoming a nightmare.

"Guys… if it takes us two days to get to the next spot, how long do you think that is in the real world?" I ask in the open.

Of course, that doesn't make things less awkward than what they already are. I accidentally brought everyone back to the reality, no pun intended, that we're still stuck in a simulated game with no clue as to what's happening outside of it.

"Maybe it's an hour," Riley guesses. "Time is completely messed up when you're gaming, video or tabletop. Days can pass in a campaign while players are spending just an hour describing or adventuring the journey."

"What about our bodies? Do you think we're dying out there or something?" Krissy puzzles. That question bothers me the most because she has a point. There's no telling what the Crests, gloves, or even game mat could be doing to us.

He stops and turns to face her, making us stop in response. "It can't do too much to us. The only real thing at risk is our brain activity. Depending on how long we're in this, it could do a little bit of brain damage, like when you stare at a screen for too long and you start to get a headache."

"How do we know that's all that's happening?" Danica asks uncomfortably with her arms hugging herself, "How do we know that we're not in some sort of coma?"

I see everyone's uneasy reactions to the question, and frankly I'm not too comfortable with it either. We really don't know how long we've been in this game, and we don't know what kind of state our bodies are in outside of it. I should've listened to Sebaros and taken his offer on the feast. We're tired, anxious, and in no shape to get into another fight without getting stuck in our own heads like this.

"Krissy? Let me see your map." After a moment, she shrugs and opens it in front of me. I run my finger along the road that would lead us to the Grave Expanse. Like most fantasy game logic, there's a town in the way with a tavern. I point to it intently, "There. We'll stop there and rest up, then we'll go after the next Keystone."

Mark raises an eyebrow, "Seriously? The last town we were at ran us out after we saved it from a terrorghast."

"I know, but we need to unload a bit. Think about it. We're heading into the next level of the game, which will probably be more difficult. We're exhausted and need a break, so why take a chance on a place where we may not have to fight for our lives?" I walk up to him and grip his shoulder, "Besides, you need to be celebrated. You ousted a murderous traitor back there and saved a whole tribe of centaurs. You led this group to a win. Let's have a little fun. Even if it's simulated fun."

He blinks his huge fish-man eyes a couple of times, then lets out a huge sigh, "Dude I swear you're in love with me. Fine, I'm in."

I chuckle and swat his shoulder before yelling out, "Huzzah!"

Everyone blinks at me, takes a step back away from me, and all at once yelled, "Nerd!" I give them a middle-finger salute in response.

"Alright, guess I'll take point," Krissy says as she grips her map into her fist and moves in the direction of the tavern.

CHAPTER 20

As we trudge our way towards the town, the landscape
starts to quickly change from the lush, green fields of grass
and forestry to a rough, warm, dry landscape. The grass is
getting less and less frequent as we start stepping on
crunching sand and stone of a new and unfamiliar terrain.
The next thing to come is the heat. The temperature and air
suddenly get dry and hot, which is not a pleasant change for
any of us. It's like a full-on scene change in a movie or
game that took you from one part of the world to the next.
The horizon gets brighter, and the sky starts changing into a
hazy orange and yellow color. I can see the heat rippling in
the air the further we walk.

"Well, not exactly a beach vacation," Krissy jokes.

I chuckle a bit to myself, but then I see Mark
holding his neck with both hands. His body looks weak like
it was losing color. "Shit… we've got to get Mark to some
water! Krissy, how far are we from the Tavern?"

She quickly unfolds the map and points to it, "It's a
few more miles… but that's probably not enough time…"

Danica is holding Mark up as he tries to stay upright
and begins to lose more color. Riley runs to the rescue by
taking him from her paws and hoist him onto the back of
his horse half. He then trots over to Krissy and takes the
map, "Follow my tracks. I'm getting Squidward to the

Tavern and to some water." Without another word, he gallops off into the blinding sunlight until they're out of sight.

"Mark! We've gotta help him!" Danica yells through tears. She's pulling at her tail in frustration, and I swear I can see her shedding.

"We are helping him, Dani. We'll get there as fast as we can," I promise her, holding her shoulders. "Listen to me, he's going to be fine. Mark is a stubborn ass hat; we both know that. He's too stubborn to let this get the better of him. Let's just keep going. Okay?"

Her large, watery cat eyes look up at me with worry, flattened ears, and all. But she takes a deep breath and nodded. "O-okay. Let's go."

I nod and let her go, looking down to the imprints in the ground of Riley's hooves. "We follow his trail and it'll take us straight to them. We need to be on our guard, because we can get attacked at any time between now and then."

"Don't worry," Krissy says as she takes her axes out, "I gotcha covered."

I nod and draw my dagger in agreement, and then we start walking. The trail that Riley left for us is as deeply rutted into the ground as he could've made it, but some of the prints are covered by wind-blown sands. It gets harder as we kept going, still having miles to cover until we reach the Tavern. If only we had horses or something.

I wipe some sweat from my eyes and look ahead to a dust cloud forming gradually. "Guys... look ahead." The girls look to the dust cloud and see figures coming through it on horseback. The figures came into view quickly in the form of four armored figures carrying a familiar banner, clad in red and black. The Crimson Order.

"Shit..." we all say at the same time. The horses kick up dirt and sand as they get closer. When they're close enough, they start circling us on their mounts. Three of the four riders are wearing these crude helmets that look rough and jagged instead of smooth and rounded. Their armor is different from the soldiers we met at the first Tavern; instead of being shiny red and clean, they're rough and scratched like they just came out of battle.

The one without a helmet on is an older human man with a bald head, white goatee, and a large scar going across his left cheek to the corner of his mouth. He must've been in charge because he raised his fist, causing the other soldiers to stop and face us.

"State your business," Baldy growls. His fist grips onto the sword at his waist while his eyes shoot daggers at us. These guys were not the "warm and friendly" type that we met before. They were enforcers, ready to throw down.

"We're going to the Great Expanse," I say with caution. I try to be subtle while standing in between him and the girls.

One of the other soldiers growls an echo in his helmet, "Hired mercenaries for the battle, no doubt."

"Silence," Baldy orders as he glares down from his horse. "Is that true? Have you been hired to fight in the Battle of the Gorge? Who hired you?"

Krissy looks at me in confusion, which I respond to with a shake of my head. I look back to Baldy, "We aren't mercenaries. We're just travelers trying to get to the Tavern near the Expanse."

"Lies!" one of the other soldiers yells out, taking up his spear and pointing it at me. "You do not lie in the face of the Crimson Order!"

These guys are just aching for a fight. They don't care if we're telling the truth because we're not human. Stereotypical foot soldiers to the main villain of any fantasy story, who think their rules are the only rules.

"Just leave us alone!" Danica yells from behind me. Apparently that's the last straw with these guys because they all draw their weapons at the same time.

"Put them in chains," Baldy barks. "The Archon will tolerate no resistance to his cause. We shall make examples of them all."

The soldier with a spear to my face presses it into my cheek, feeling it slice open my skin and looking like he really wants to shove it through my skull. I glare up to him with fiery eyes and grab the spear shaft, "Get that out of my face." I pull at the spear hard, making the rider fall off his horse to the ground.

"Kick their asses!" I yell as I draw my dagger.

Krissy didn't need to be told twice. She takes her axes and swings at the closest soldier, who parries with his sword. I focus on the soldier on the ground quickly getting up and drawing a dagger of his own. Krissy is fiercely yelling as she trades blows with her attacker, but I wasn't about to get distracted. My enemy looks at me through the small opening in his helmet with a rage I've never seen in another person before. It's like he truly hates me without ever having met me before now. Is this the real side of the authority figures in this game? Or are they some rogue operation outside of the Archon's knowledge?

"Die, you tainted beast!" He lunges forward with his weapon, which was a bit longer than my own dagger. I dash backwards, causing him to stumble while I back up into Danica, who's trying to stay out of the fight. The soldier regains his footing and slices at me. If I move out of the way she would get hit, so I stand my ground. Expecting to feel the stinging pain of a knife in my chest, I instead watch as he fell straight to the ground after Dani's cat tail swept his feet out from under him. It's like a switch flipped inside her because she hisses loudly before pouncing on him, slashing with her claws. I don't think I've ever been more scared of her in my life.

"Connor!"

Krissy is fending off two soldiers at once when I turn around, but it's not going so well. One of them grabs her tail to hold her in place while his buddy swings at her with his mace. She defends herself as much as she can, while the one holding her tail grabs her by the hair to throw her off.

"Get off her, you son of a bitch!" I roar and shoulder-check him, taking him to the ground, freeing Krissy's from his grips. He looks up at me with the same level of hatred as the other guy, just burning in his eyes as we fight for control. I flash my teeth at him as I gain control and start punching him as hard as I can. I forgot how different my strength in reality was from the Orc that I am in the game. His face starts splashing blood from the cuts I'm leaving with every swing. My knuckles are starting to hurt, but I don't stop. Something takes over me as I keep hurling my fists into his bloodied face.

"Connor, stop!"

The plea rings in my ears, but I don't stop. Another voice in my head tells me to keep going. To make him suffer.

I raise my fist up for another punch, but it gets caught and held mid-air. I whip my head around to see Krissy's hands holding mine back. "Enough!"

I breathe heavily at her with my teeth bared, but then I glance at my bloodied fist and down at the knight. His face is almost a pulp. He's breathing heavily and spitting up blood. I release my fist and unclench my jaw, staggering my breath as I stand up. I'm shaking as I stand up with Krissy's hands still clenching mine. I turn around to face her and Danica, who is standing behind her with blood matted on her fur. We turned the golden sand and dirt in blood of the knights. The only one untouched by the fight was Baldy, who's frozen in horror.

"Y-you beasts... we will eradicate you all!" He turns his horse away and takes off into the horizon.

I take deep, heavy breaths trying to calm myself down. I stare at my trembling, bloodied knuckles. I almost killed that guy. But this wasn't like killing a minion or henchman in a video game. It's like having a person's life in my hands. A real person.

"You okay?" I snap out of my trance and look to the girls. They seem just as scared as I feel. Krissy carefully lets my hand go after I nod in response.

"Dani? You okay?" I look at her in shock with how bloody she is. It was the first time I've seen her fully give into her character and fight against something.

She looks at me with flattened ears and huge eyes, "I… I think I killed him…" We all look to her victim and fall silent. His face is practically in ribbons, but I can still see his chest rising and falling.

"He's still breathing."

"What kind of fucking game is this?" Krissy is grabbing at her hair frantically. "We almost killed them!"

"I don't think we had a choice, Krissy." They both look at me in disbelief. "They hated us. I mean, *really* hated us. I saw it in their eyes. I thought it was the sun reflecting off their armor, but their eyes… they were literally burning."

"You had that look too!" Krissy yells at me. "You weren't gonna stop until I stepped in! What the hell were you thinking?!"

"I was trying to save you! What the hell was I supposed to do?!"

"How about *not be a monster*?!" She blinks rapidly after those words fly out of her mouth. We all stand in silence. The only sounds to be heard were the dry wind and the clopping of hooves of the horses the knights rode in on.

I glare at Krissy before I glance at the horses. "We can get to the Tavern faster now. Grab a horse and let's go."

"C-Connor, I'm sorry," Krissy calls after me. I ignore her and jump onto a nearby horse, kicking into its sides and ride away. I don't look back. I can't.

CHAPTER 21

I've never ridden a horse before. Probably something I should've thought about before suggesting the idea. But I'm too pissed off and shaken from what we went through against those soldiers and the argument with Krissy to care. Her words are still ringing in my head like a damn bell, "*Monster. Monster. Monster.*" It makes my skin crawl and my head pound. What the hell did she know? I was trying to help her when those knights were going to pound on her. I saved her. And I'm the monster?

I keep riding in the direction of the Tavern, trying to drown out these thoughts in my head. In the process, I go from being pissed, to being in doubt. I can't remember the last time, or any time, that I've ever been so angry that I hit someone. I've never been in a fight before. I've been hit a couple of times, but I've never fought back. Back there, I almost beat the life out of an NPC, but it bled and gushed like a living person. What kind of sick, twisted mind creates programs that can feel pain and bleed? Dawson and SnoWire are known for making games that have some sort of moral fortitude imbedded in their characters and story arcs, like decision-based consequences or alliance factions, but everything we've faced up till now has only been scared of or hated us without any context. The Crimson Order seems to hate all the non-human races the most in Albistair, despite being praised by human NPCs as saviors and just. The human bystanders and bandits blame non-humans for the terrorghasts and other magical occurrences that were explained to us by Merrin. Then there are the Centaurs, who live in constant fear of the Crimson Order to the point they are distrusting of others and even betray each other. What were the other races like? Are they just as afraid? Surely there has to be at least one out there that's different.

My train of thought ends as a new image takes form ahead of me. The closer I get, the more the image starts to look like a building. It looks like it has a few trees for shade and horses tethered next to troughs. I think it's the Tavern from the map.

I slow my horse down and look behind me for Krissy and Danica. They trot up to me silently as I point ahead, "That's the Tavern. Let's find Riley and Mark."

We approach at a slow trot with our mounts, still not another word to be uttered between us. The closer we got, the bigger the building becomes. It was bigger than the first Tavern we visited, coming fully equipped with a horse stable, an outhouse, and seating areas under the trees. The trees surround a small pool of bright blue water and looked super refreshing. I try getting a closer look at the pool and notice something swimming in it. Or rather, *someone*.

"Mark?!" Danica must've seen it too, because she jumps off of her horse and runs to the pool. Mark emerges from the pool quickly, only to be tackled by Danica as they both crash back into the water.

I hop down from my horse heavily, almost falling to the ground. I regain my balance and take my horse's reigns, hitching it to one of the stalls. Krissy hitches hers next to mine and glances at me, "Are we going to talk? Or is this silent treatment shit how we're going to be from now on?"

I flash an annoyed look at her and sigh, "We'll talk. Just not right now. Let's check in with the others and make sure we don't get run out of this tavern either."

I look at it curiously and hear very cheery music coming from inside. The flickering lights from inside suggested either candlelight or even a fire inside, as the sun creeps lower in the sky. I can smell smoking meat and brewing ale coming from the chimney. This place already seems like it's better than the last, no offense to Merrin or her help.

"I'm so happy you're okay," I hear Danica say to Mark. I turn my attention to the two of them and instantly regret it, because it turns into the weirdest make out session I've ever seen between a cat-girl and fish-man. I give an audible "UGH" and turn away from them. Riley probably took a chance to get away from this.

"Hey. Where's Riley?"

He takes a moment from sucking face and points at the tavern with a sly grin. "Go inside and check it out."

I raise an eyebrow, but he gives me a reassuring gesture to go inside. I walk up to the Tavern and approached the door, slowly taking the handle and pulling it open. The inside was nothing that I had thought to expect. There's a huge hearth fire in the middle of the main room, surrounded by drinking and singing people. The far right of the hearth holds the musical entertainment; four musicians with a lute, a drum, a pan flute, and a singer. Along the walls of the main room are tables filled with people, young and old, celebrating various things. Not a single frowning face in the whole place, but the one thing that gets me the most was that there were no humans. Everyone in here was of a different race, singing and dancing and drinking together.

Before I get the chance to appreciate it more, I hear a familiar voice singing loudly and horridly. I look back to the band and see that one more member had joined the ranks of the music: Riley with a full tankard in his hand.

"Riley!?"

His bearded face went into a huge smile when he sees me. He lifts his mug and shouts, "Connor! Get your green ass over here!"

I hesitantly walk over to him before he drapes his arm around my neck and pulls me close, "About time you got here! This place is amazing! We're singing *Ode to the Free!*"

His breath reeks! I struggle getting out from under his arm a bit before I freed myself, "Dude, are you drunk?"

He shrugs aggressively before drinking from his mug again, "M-maybe! This place shoved a drink in my hands after I got Mark into the pool outside! Wait… what happened to you?"

His eyes scan up and down my clothes noticing the splotches of blood. I look to myself then back up at him, "That's… hard to explain right now."

He immediately gets serious and grabs my shoulder, "Let's go to the room they gave me. Come on."

I follow him through the crowd of people who all smile and welcome me like I'm a distant cousin. We go inside a room that had a door that lets his tall frame pass through with no issues. Inside, the room is fit with a bedroll, mirror, shaving kit, table, and stash chest. It seems like this place is able to accommodate individual races and their needs.

Riley lays down on his bedroll and offers me a chair at the table, "Talk to me, man. You look spooked."

I take the chair and look down at my hands, shaking a little bit. Riley is the only one who can possibly help ease my mind about what I did. I begin to explain what happened between us and the Order knights in the desert, getting a huge mix of emotions from his face. By the time I finish, he and I were sitting in silence for a solid five minutes.

"Connor… are you okay?" It's all he could come up with.

"No, Riley, I'm not okay. I am the farthest thing from okay. This is a fucking video game. I'm not supposed to feel someone's bones breaking under my fists. I shouldn't be able to taste the iron of that guy's blood on my lips. I almost killed him."

Another moment of silence that could deafen a stadium. Riley runs a hand through his hair before letting out a strained breath of air. "Dude… I don't have the answers here. This is completely new to me, too. Every virtual reality experience I've had, never came close to this. The only thing I can say is that you are not a monster. You can't kill what's not real."

I sit back in the chair and clench my fists before admitting something to him that I couldn't say to Krissy or Danica. Not even Mark. "The worst part… is that I liked it. I didn't want to stop. I wanted to keep wailing on him until the burning in his eyes went out… every voice in my head told me to end it. To end him."

Riley's eyes blink rapidly. "Dude… that's not you. None of that is you! What the hell is going on with you?!"

"I don't know!" I shoot up from the chair and throw it against the wall. "I can't tell if it's the fact I'm an Orc and it's part of my race, or if this is just years of pent-up rage just coming out all at once! I keep having these voices telling me to do shit that I don't want to do!"

"Wait," Riley stops me, "Voices? How often are you hearing them?"

I'm instantly confused, "What? Why does that matter?"

"Think, man! How often are you hearing the voices??"

"When am I *not* hearing them," I spit. "Every fight, every moment that my blood boils, it keeps telling me things. I'm weak, I need to act, I need to kill."

Riley looks shocked, "Dude… I don't think that's the game…"

I raise an eyebrow at him. He quickly stands up, "Bear with me for a minute. These characters we're playing all follow some sort of patron god that gives us the perk traits that we need to be our specific class of player. I haven't heard anything in my head since the spider fight. The second I did what it told me, I stopped listening. I just started doing things how I thought I was supposed to. But it was like it knew exactly what I was going to. What if… what if SnoWire has moderators that are acting as these voices? People acting as the patron gods telling us to do these things?"

I can't even comprehend what he tries saying after that. Nothing in me wants to believe that I'm being *Puppet Master*-ed by some sicko from the company that made this game. "S-so you're telling me that some freak is whispering in my ear to make me do things in the game??"

"What else could it be?? No game is so developed to where actual entities are talking to us like we are in ancient fucking Greece."

Another point goes to him. There's no other way that this can be explained logically. "So, the Crests we put on to start the game, are somehow connected to SnoWire and there are game moderators, monitoring our movements and dictating what we do... This is some serious engineering to command brainwaves."

We nod in shock and disbelief all at once. One thing is clear at this point; we need to get out of this game, now more than ever.

"I say, for now, we keep this just between us and leave the others out of it."

"What? Why wouldn't we tell them??"

"Because they can't handle it," he argues. "Look, they could barely handle the fact that we're stuck in this place. There's no way they'd be able to handle this either. Especially since we don't have proof to back this up. Just keep this between us until we know for sure. Okay?"

"Dude, that's so fucked up. They should know so they can be careful."

"Connor, I'm begging you. We've done so well getting a handle on this thing to the point we can actually win and get out. If they think that we're being pushed around like chess pieces by the same dicks that put us into this mess, they'll start stumbling and could possibly get killed. And we don't know what happens if we die in the game. Please?"

I suck in some air through my teeth and clench my fists. After a few moments, I unclench and nod, "Fine, but the second things get too messed up, I'm spilling."

He lets out a sigh of relief, "Thank you. Now, let's check on everyone else and get moving."

I follow Riley out of the room and back into the main room of the Tavern. People are still smiling and celebrating and enjoying themselves. It's weird to see since everyone we've encountered up to this point has been either trying to kill us or were too afraid to talk to us. I take this chance to really look at all the different races there are in the Tavern. There are tables of intermingling races, mainly Dwarves, some Tabaxi and Tieflings. The band is playing a lighter tune to set a more relaxed tone in the

Tavern. We start mingling towards the bar, which is being tended by a Tabaxi male.

"Welcome to my Tavern, travelers. I am Steady Rock. What may I serve you?"

Tabaxi names have always confused me, but it's not my place to judge. "Two tankards of ale will do us. Thanks."

"You forget about us?" I turn to see Krissy, Mark, and Danica behind us.

Steady Rock looks past me to gaze at Danica, "Ah, a new face amongst the cat-folk. Welcome."

His gaze must've made Mark uneasy, because he steps in front of her to block them. Rock grumbles a bit before turning to pour the mugs. Once he pours them, he puts them on a tray and sets them on the bar for us. "Enjoy."

I take the tray and lead everyone to one of the open tables. We sit at the seats, sans Riley's horse ass, and take a tankard.

"Just so everyone knows, we can definitely feel the alcohol here," Riley says excitedly. We all laugh.

I raise a tankard and say, "Guys... here's to staying alive and getting out of the game. We can, and we will, get out of this game. I promise." A pause falls over the table before everyone raises their mugs to mine in agreement and then drinks. The ale is so stout it makes us all twist our faces and wretch a bit.

"Holy shit," Krissy says with a sour face. "This is strong."

I can't stop from laughing, "Thought you were a party girl! Too much for you to handle?"

Everyone else lets out a loud "Oooooooo" in response. Krissy glares at me, smirks, and then starts chugging the ale. Our table is shaking as we slap our hands on it to encourage her. She lets out a loud sigh after finishing and slams it on the table. Mark starts drinking right after she finishes, getting the same encouragement. Then Danica. Then me. Then Riley. We all cheer after we finish, finally having a little bit of fun.

The fun suddenly stops as the door of the Tavern flies open. In the doorway, a group of five men and women filed in. Strong stalky builds, wearing sleeveless leather vests, fur pants and heavy leather boots. They have red symbols decorating their greenish-brown skin. They snarl as their bottom teeth had two large fangs protruding from them. Full-blooded Orcs.

The whole tavern gawks at them as they skulk inside and march to one of the open tables. One of them, a large female with a long black braid draped over her shoulder, hollers to the tavern, "Five kobold whiskeys. Now!" They all sit down while slamming their weapons on the table.

"Holy shit… those are Orcs," I half-whisper in awe. This is the first time I've seen other ones, which shouldn't surprise me. In most role-playing games, Orcs are very solitary and battle-hardened, usually ready to pound anyone's face in that looks at them wrong.

Rock brings a tray of small glasses to the table of warriors and sets it down. All of them take one glass, spit on the ground and yelled, "*Ve gijak agh vurgh!*" They throw back the liquor and slam the glasses onto the table.

"What did they say?" Mark asks me. Everyone looks at me waiting for a translation.

"I think they said, 'To blood and victory'. I think it's a toast to battle…"

Something clicks with Danica, "Wait… those red knights? Didn't they say something about a battle happening?"

She's right. The knights mentioned something about the Battle of the Gorge. If this was a battle the Crimson Order was involved in, it could have something to do with the orcs, too.

"Wait here." I stand up and walk over to the table. Mark tries getting my attention, but I ignore him and keep walking to the orc table. One of them sees me coming and nudges the female. *She must be in charge.* Her eyes shoot up and glare at me.

"What do you want, whelp?" she barks. The others glare with her and grab their weapons. I need to talk with them. I take a closer look at their emblems and runes, noticing they're dedicated to another Orc god. While my patron is the god of vengeance and victory, they're worshipping a one-eyed god of war and sacrifice.

"Glory to Kogan the One-Eye," I pull out of the air. They all look at me with no emotion in their faces. A moment passes before the woman stands up to meet me at eye level. I think she is going to take a swing at me.

She then starts laughing out loud and punches my shoulder, "Glory to One-Eye!" The others shout, "Glory to One-Eye!"

"Sit," the leader demands. I look back at the others, who look at me like I'm nuts, before I turn and sit down. "I am called Yeskarra, and this is my clan. What are you called?"

"Zarimm, Warpriest of Olagog," I reply. They all smile and hold their fists up.

Yeskarra looks to my clothes and runes, "You do not carry a clan mark, Warpriest. Where do you hail from?"

"I don't belong to a clan," I explain. "I am traveling with my companions, looking for the Keystones to the Mortal Gate."

They all stare at me in silence. Yeskarra suddenly gets serious, "What do you know of the Keystones?"

"Enough to know that the Archon and his Order are interested in the power they hold. And the Gate could've caused the Violet Moon event that birthed the terrorghasts."

The Orcs start looking a little tense, which seems really out of character. "I've seen what a single Keystone can do, and it's not pretty," I add.

"You have not even begun to understand the terror that they hold," Yeskarra warns me. "We have witnessed it's power at the Battle of the Gorge."

I clench my jaw. *There's a Keystone in the Expanse, just like what Corene thought.* "Let me introduce you to my companions and buy the next round. I want to know everything you know." I turn around and wave them to join the table. It was going to be a long conversation.

CHAPTER 22

Once they joined the table and introductions were made, Yeskarra starts telling her story.

"My clan and I received a request from other clans to help join forces in a battle in the Great Expanse's most treacherous region; the Gorge of Vaduhs. This gorge is a maze of deep and winding tunnels and caverns that have caused many travelers to be lost forever. The letter we received spoke of a battle. A battle between Orcs and the Crimson Order. No other details had been given to us, but it was enough for us to pack our camp and rally to the call. After a few days' travel, we met our brothers and sisters in the Gorge. The battle was a bloodbath. Many orcs and humans littered the ground. By the time we reached the forward camp, something had happened we of which we were unaware of. The camp held the flags of five clans and tribes: the Broken Bone, the Ear Seekers, Clans Karuck, Skortchclaw and Blood Moon. My clan, Murkhaven, was to be the sixth clan to bring the fight to the Order. Within the camp, the Orcs began to tear each other apart. It was if a curse of blood rage took them over and caused them to attack and slaughter each other. We were able to defend ourselves long enough to get away from them and regroup. While we were making our escape out of the battlefield, my scout Askuld reported a hooded figure that had a scepter unlike any other. On top of the scepter, a red glowing stone sat on it. A stone that held unfamiliar symbols on it. The wielder of the scepter was deep in the ranks of the Order, but they were attacking each other, just like our kin. Something possessed them all into attacking anything and anyone that comes near. I believe that it is because of the scepter is attached to a Keystone."

I clench my jaw tightly after she finishes the story. This sounds exactly like what we dealt with in the Ordowell Bowels. These stones seem to hold some unnatural power, that affects everyone around them, but, instead of twisting souls into monster ghosts, this red stone is filling them with a rage that makes them fight anyone near them.

"Yeskarra, we need to get to the Gorge and find that scepter," I tell her.

The Orcs all burst into laughter. Yeskarra only lightly chuckles and shakes her head, "Trust me, Zarimm. This is no place for you and your companions to venture into."

"Look, we need that stone," Mark says sternly, backing me up. "We think it can set things right. If we can—"

"Did you not hear what she said?" One of the others growls at me. "That place will infect your minds and make you rip each other apart. Not to mention that there is a terrorghast nest in those caverns. So, if the humans or Orcs fail to kill you, those tainted beasts will."

That was what turned the tables on us. We've only faced one terrorghast since starting the game, and these things were supposed to be the reigning demonic force we needed to fight. If we struggled to fight only one of them, how could we face a whole nest of them? Everyone goes silent, it's almost cryptic, but we can't stop. After what Riley and I talked about, we need to do whatever it takes to try and get out of here. That means collecting the Keystones and activating the Mortal Gate.

I take a deep breath, "Yeskarra. The Keystones may be the only way to fight and stop the tyranny of the Crimson Order and Archon. Obviously, his rule is causing all of Albistair to become divided and afraid. If my friends and I can get the Keystones keep them from the Archon, it could save everyone. Maybe even the clans that are affected. Please?"

It seems so stupid to plead with an Orc. They're a race of battle-hardened warriors that don't take to charity or aid. It's war and coin above all else.

Yeskarra looks at me with a grit in her teeth. "Some of my blood-brothers were in those tribes... If there's a chance to free them of this blood rage, I want them to be of their own minds. We are not tools of magic or the gods. We are our own weavers of fate."

Her clansmen look to their leader with indifference, but then look at us. One of them stands up and takes his dagger out, "We will bleed with you, Zarimm. Though you are clanless, you will fight as one of us." He cut into his hand and holds it up. Another orc stands up and does the same. Then another. And another. And another.

Yeskarra looks to me before standing up and cutting her hand and holding it up. "Tomorrow, we fight. Tonight, we drink. To blood and glory!"

I stand up and use my dagger to cut into my hand, holding it up to them. It makes me question how seriously I'm taking this game, but it seems wrong and dishonorable not to reciprocate. "To blood and glory." I scan over the others, and they all nod together.

"To blood and glory."

CHAPTER 23

That night at the Tavern, we drank ourselves stupid.
Kobold whiskey tastes like blood and rubbing alcohol
mixed into the most horrid cocktail I've ever tasted in my
life. I don't know how we're able to feel drunk, but it
definitely worked on us. I wake up in Riley's room on the
ground, surrounded by my friends who are all equally
passed out. I groan loudly holding my head and sit up from
the floor, causing a stir from everyone else. Quietly as I
can, I make for the door and leave the room. The tavern is
now half empty, due to some patrons being drunk and
asleep either on the floor or in their chairs. Carefully, I step
over and around the tavern until I make it to the door and
step outside. The gleaming sun causes me to flinch, until
my eyes adjust to the light. The heat is the next thing to hit
me, but it's not a blistering heat, more of a comforting
warmth.

I walk to the oasis pool nearby, stop at the edge of
the water and kneel to the edge. I take a handful of water
and splash my face, feeling the cool beads of water waking
me up a little more. I take another handful and drink it to
fight the dry taste in my mouth.

"First hangover?"

I jump up a bit and turn around, seeing Krissy
leaning against one of the trees with her tail swaying
behind her.

"Huh? Oh, yeah, I guess so. Strange how I can feel drunk in a game."

She nods and approaches me gently. "Listen, I need to talk to you. It's about what happened yesterday."

"N-no, you don't need to—" She puts a finger on my lips to shut me up.

"Look, I'm sorry. I was freaked out by what happened. Not from you pounding on that guy, that I understand. But because of what I saw in your eyes. I was freaked out because you're such a nice guy that I couldn't believe you did what you did. You just didn't seem like the kind to beat someone to a pulp."

I blink in surprise. I don't think I've seen her be sorry about something before. "Y-yeah… that freaked me out too. I guess I was just in a moment of adrenaline…"

"No, that's not it. What you did was something only a guy that didn't like seeing a girl get beat would do. That, or you're a closet psychopath, which I don't believe."

Fuck! She's gonna be mad. She's a girl that can take care of herself. She doesn't need that 'Chivalry isn't dead' bullcrap.

"The truth is," she continues, "I don't like feeling vulnerable. Every time I've been in a situation that made me feel weak, I would project some stupid attitude. I've been in a lot of relationships and have had friendships that made me feel bad. Hell, I've even been in a foster home that made me feel like absolute shit. But being like this? I feel like I can actually dish out what I say. And that's all from watching you."

I'm at a loss for words. She just opened up to me in a way that I thought would make her puke, but she meant everything she said, I could tell.

"Krissy, I know you don't need some knight in shining armor to help you when you're in trouble. You're badass. But you're also my friend, and I'm not going to stand by and watch you get hurt. That's not what I'm about. I'm sorry you saw me Hulk out like that, but I'm not going to watch you get hurt. I've got your back if you got mine."

Krissy tilts her head a little before giving me a small smile from the corner of her mouth. A *smile*!

"Zarimm!"

We both whip around to the voice. Yeskarra and her clan are already on their horses, geared up and ready. It makes me feel like a wuss that they don't seem drunk or hung over at all. "Gather your companions," she calls. "We ride for the Gorge of Vaduhs."

Her interruption causes me and Krissy to look at each other awkwardly before going back inside for the others. It takes us a little effort to get the others to wake up

225

out of their drunken sleep. As groggy as they were, they began to rise, groan, complain, and gather their materials. After gathering everything up from the room, we head back outside to meet with the orcs, who are waiting impatiently. Mark and Danica share the same mount while Krissy and I take our own. Riley trots up to the Orcs to engage in conversation before we prepare to ride.

"Travelers!"

I look back to the tavern door. Steady Rock jogs up to us with a small pouch in his paws. "You face a perilous journey. Please, take this. May it provide you safety and good fortune on your journey." He holds it up to Danica for her to take. At first confused, she smiles in gratitude and opens it. Pouring the contents in her paw, she's holding small coins that look different from common gold coins.

"Those are Tribute Tokens from Tabaxi Idols," Rock explains. "In the right hands, they will bring fortune and luck."

Danica puts them back into the pouch and ties it to her belt. "Thank you, Rock."

"Let us ride!" Yeskarra kicks her horse into a gallop, followed by her clan, then the rest of us.

The ten of us kick up the dust as we ride into bright orange sun rising over the Great Expanse, losing sight of the Tavern. As the sun started slowly rising in the sky of the desert, more heat started beating down on us. Luckily for Mark, he was able to fill a canteen of the pool water to keep him hydrated and strong. He's going to need it if the Gorge didn't provide any water along the way. I'm not the best on horseback, but this is turning out to be a lot of fun. It reminds me of every western movie I watched as a kid: A gang of like-minded riders about to face their foes with determination and purpose. Yeskarra and her clan are riding with so much purpose, so gritted and ready for anything, like Viking raiders. It makes me grateful that I was welcomed to become part of their people, even if I'm not really an Orc. It just feels awesome to be part of something great.

Askuld motions for me to move up the convoy, so I kick my horse to move a little quicker, moving up the line until I met with him and Yeskarra.

"We'll be arriving after a few more miles," she tells me. "We need to find a safe route inside the Gorge to gain tactical advantage."

I nod in agreement, "Okay. Send Askuld ahead to see if he can spot anything. We need to know if things have gotten any different from when you were last there."

Suddenly her finger is in my face, "Let us be clear. These are my men. We may have bled you into our fold, but do not think yourself equal to my command."

That stings a little bit, but she's right. I'm in no position to try and take over. With that, she gives the order and tells him to scout ahead.

In the awkward air between us, she starts talking again. "You are not like your companions, Zarimm. You seem to have a stronger hold on the ways of the world, how destructive it is, yet you maintain your strength and resolve. I do not know if it is your faith as a Warpriest or if it just in your nature, but it is becoming of you. Why not let them be with their people so you can be with ours?"

That's a question I can't answer without sounding crazy to her. I try thinking of a logical answer that would fit the conversation and the game rules, "While that's a great offer, I'm afraid I can't. We... we have a mission, but, if it means helping innocent people from being hurt, we're going to help in any way we can. No one, regardless of their race, deserves to be treated like what the Order is doing to everyone in Albistair."

She chuckles and nods, "A purpose given by a greater force than the gods themselves. Without purpose to drive us forward, we become nothing but pawns in the game of gods."

Those words rattle in my head a little bit. These NPCs all have their gods and beliefs, but who were they really giving praise to? The moderators and creators? The people that buy the game? Or even Dominic Dawson himself.

I look ahead to the horizon before Yeskarra holds up her fist, causing the convoy to slow down to a stop. All eyes face forward to a horse that's coming at us quickly. As it comes closer, we recognize the rider as an orc, but it's not Askuld. This one is wearing dark iron armor that's covered in blood. The horse it's riding in on suddenly rears back and throws the rider to the ground before galloping off past us.

One of the Orcs jumps off their horse, runs to the downed rider and notices something horrible. The body thrown off their horse was shot with so many arrows, he looks like a pincushion.

"Fuck," Mark exclaims.

"This is the result of the war that is ahead of us." The one checking the body pulls an arrow out from its back and holds it up. "These arrows are Orc made. They're slaughtering their own kind because of the power that the scepter has over them."

The Orc kneels and begins praying. The rest of the clan dismounted their horses, knelt to the ground, and began praying with him. I recognize the prayers being given, not to Kogan, but to Olagog, swearing vengeance for their fallen brother. In all honesty, it was the most wholesome thing I've seen in this world. After they finish their prayer, they all stand up and get back onto their horses, except for the orc who started the prayer who took the fallen one's weapon and put it into his belt.

"Whoa, dude," Riley shouts in shock, "respect the dead!"

He scoffs and mounts his horse, "I just did. He's not using his weapon anymore, and I'm going to use it to make Kogan fucking proud."

On that cheery note, the convoy continues riding deeper into the Expanse. We finally catch up with Askuld, who flags us down from the path we're on. We bring our horses to a cliffside and hobble them before joining him. Askuld is overlooking a path that went down into a sort of canyon. In this canyon, it looks like a goddamn horror show. Small rivers of blood that were green and red, soiling the grounds of the canyon. Orcs and red-armored humans litter the ground, some freshly killed, others decaying from time spent in the sun or from being picked by vultures.

"Welcome to the Gorge of Vaduhs."

I almost can't stomach the look of this brutal sight as I turn away and look to the orcs, "This... this is a fucking nightmare. You didn't tell us it was this bad."

Yeskarra chuckles and shrugs, "This is what we do. Now, this part of the Gorge isn't the one we can enter safely. There were sentries posted up before, that had good sight of anyone that crossed that skyline there. We need to find one of these caverns, that can get us close enough to the epicenter of the battle, thereby bringing us closer to the wielder of the scepter."

"It can't be that easy," Krissy says as she studies her map. "My map shows that the caverns and tunnels all eventually lead to cave-ins and drop-offs in their systems."

"Not to mention we don't really know where the terrorghast nest is, or even how many of them there are," Riley adds.

One of the Orcs nods in agreement and joins Krissy looking at her map. "There can be two possible ways into the epicenter. To the east, there is a gap opened in the surface that leads down into an underground water cavern. To the west of the Gorge is more open but could also be too obvious for any outpost to be stationed by either side. They'll be too busy opposing each other to take too much notice, but that's a gamble."

I stroke my chin a bit and then realize where everyone was going with this observation. "You're suggesting we split up."

Yeskarra nods to me, "Yes. We split up, meet in the middle, attack from two sides, catch the wielder by surprise and end this quickly."

"Ever done a split-up mission before?" Mark asks in a bit of a sarcastic tone. Everyone looks at him with cocked eyebrows. "Splitting up normally leads to people dying and shit. You really want us to risk that?"

Askuld points a dagger at the epicenter in the map, "This point here is where the battle is the worst. The wielder isn't allowing his power to kill them but keep them alive and fighting like fucking toys. If we go in there without a plan, we will be enraptured by the same magic. We need to finish this as quickly as possible, or we all die."

A silence falls in a bit of a real melancholy vibe. Eyes scan all over the place looking for alternative answers, but I break the silence. "Mark, we don't have a choice. We have a mission, and they have a people to save. Somehow, this all leads up to the Keystones and how the Crimson Order fits in. They obviously want the power that they hold, and they don't care who gets hurt in the process. They may not be... our people, but they're people nonetheless."

That's when things got pretty tense, but I still stand by what I said. These NPCs may not be real, but they're still as real as our characters are. Maybe I'm reading too far into this game, but these guys are definitely real in their own sense.

"Here is how we should work," Yeskarra takes command of the situation. "I'll give Korr, Nargol and Hagu to work with your Triton and Tiefling companions. They'll take the water cavern entrance and meet the rest of us at the epicenter. We will take the open approach and deal with stragglers as they come along."

"Wait," Danica protests, "I'm not going anywhere without Mark. Anyone who tries, I'll claw your ass up."

"I'll switch places with Dani," Krissy offers.

Not gonna lie, that kind of made me surprised and glad at the same time. Danica has all the right perks and equipment to be a sneaky attacker, but she would be worrying about Mark the whole time if she went with us. Mark is a Triton, making him the best possible lead in the water cavern. Riley obviously won't be much help in a tight space like an underground cavern, so he would go with me and Krissy.

"Alright, so we've got a plan."

I nod, "Let me talk with my friends before we go." She nods in agreement, taking her men aside while the others came with me.

I rub the back of my neck and take a deep breath trying to think of what to say. They look nervous with what we were about to do. Mark and Danica are holding onto each other tightly, Riley's making an inventory list of what he has on his person, and Krissy is clenching her jaw and twisting her tail nervously.

I swing my arms up and smack them against my legs. "Go ahead, let me have it. Let me know how stupid of an idea this is. God knows, I think it's insane."

At first, there's nothing but the wind in the sands. Riley breaks it with a scoff and chuckle of his own, "Oh, it's pretty batshit. We all know it and we're all thinking it."

"But" Mark adds, "we also know that this is pretty much the only thing we can do to try to get out of this mess. We haven't done a lot to get this far, and we're getting that much closer to leaving the game. It also means shit's about to get tougher and there's really no safe way around it."

I knew those two would at least have my back a little bit, and it's kind of gratifying to know. On the other hand, I don't think I'm going to get anywhere with Danica or Krissy in this plan. I look to the two of them, "You two okay with this?"

Danica looks away from me, her tail twitching back and forth in irritation. She hugs herself a bit before looking back to me, "You're an asshole. But, we really don't have a way out without this Keystone thing. I don't like this… no, I *hate* it. But I can't stay back while everyone else risks themselves. As long as you can promise that Mark and I will be okay, I'm in."

Wow. This whole time she's been blaming me for everything that's happened to us. For the first time, we're on the same page. The same team. "I promise, we're gonna be okay."

"You morons aren't doing a damn thing without me," Krissy points out as she crosses her arms. "Let's get that stone."

I smile and reach out to take Mark's arm. Then another one to take Krissy's. Mark took my arm, then Danica's. She took his, then Riley's. He took hers, then Krissy's other arm. We came together as a team.

"To blood and glory?" Mark says with hesitation.

I chuckle and shake my head, "No, that's too gory for us… The game described the Vanguards having a certain motto… a mantra that detailed their name. It said, 'As Vanguards of the Realm, you will ensure that Albistair is forever free'."

They all look curiously at me, but eventually start smiling. We all say it together:

"Forever Free."

CHAPTER 24

One inventory and level-progression check later, we separate into our teams and make for opposite sides of the Gorge. Krissy, Yeskarra, Riley, Askuld and I lose sight of the others when we turn the corner of a mesa.

"At least this isn't the first time we've been separated," I mention jokingly, trying to be positive in what we were doing.

"Dude, the first time we got separated, we were almost ripped apart by mist monsters," Riley retorts in a heavily laid-on tone.

Askuld turns to us with a look of surprise, "Wait. You were the ones who rid the Ordowell Bowels of the mistwraiths? You??"

Krissy cocks an eyebrow, "You heard about that?"

Askuld looks to Yeskarra, who chuckles lightly. "What he means to say, is that we had heard rumor of a group of travelers that the non-humans believe to be part of the prophecy said to usher Albistair out of these dark times. By the sounds of it, they were talking about you and your lot, but we weren't expecting the rumors to hold any truth. Many adventurers have claimed these rumors to be true before but have been proven false."

"Well, apparently the Centaurs believe we can reassemble the Mortal Gate and stop the scourge of terrorghasts," I reply.

Askuld starts laughing loudly before Yeskarra punches him in the back of the head. Orcs are universally notorious for using violence for absolutely everything, like affection, irritation, hate, and kinship.

"You runts are supposed to face the legion of beasts that were spit from the bowels of the Abyss, collect each of the Keystones, *and* liberate the realm from the tyranny of the Archon? This will be entertaining," Askuld barks heartily while rubbing the back of his head.

I see an opportunity. "What is it about the Archon? Is he some guy that roped in some crazed fanatics? That's an overused villain trope. I've looked in various books to try and figure this guy out, and there's nothing."

Yeskarra stops and turns around, glaring at me with a fierce look in her eyes. "The Archon is not some religious zealot. He is not even a person. The Archon is a beast that despises anything and everything that is not human. His Crimson Order is made up of the worst humans to ever take up arms against any of the other races. No one knows who this monster is under his mask, but he single-handedly caused the entire human race to hate all others in a matter of months. That was over twenty years ago. We have been in constant war with the Order, and they have destroyed many of our kind. Why? For not being his view of 'pure'."

I look back at her sternly, holding one of my hands up in defense. "I'm sorry. We didn't know. We have only had a couple of run-ins with the Order and didn't know how extreme they were."

"Their extremity pales in comparison to their hate towards all that are not human," Askuld includes. "He once promised that all people of Albistair would work together to repair the damage caused by the events of the Violet Moon and the terrorghasts by bringing all of our most prominent delegates together for a strategy. That same night, those same sorry *bra'shros* were executed in front of the whole capitol, accused of stealing the Keystones and planning to eradicate humanity. All non-humans scattered in the wind to avoid humans, and now we are destroying each other for glowing rocks that somehow make things worse."

Things aren't adding up here. This game is like a fantasy version of Nazi Germany, right down to the genocide and freaking superior race. What kind of development went into this to force the players into roles of a hunted people? It's getting ridiculous to have all these questions and absolutely no answers. I'm beginning to question whether anything would be made clear or not. What if Riley and I truly got us all stuck in this game for nothing? No beta testing rights, no payment, nothing.

"Well, we'll try to do something about this," Riley promises them, resulting in confusing looks from everyone, even me.

"I don't know what kind of horrors you guys have been going through, but you're Orcs. You're strong, resilient, and war born. Whatever this crazy psycho has done to your people, it won't keep you down. And you have us to back you up. We can't lose."

Crickets should've chirped, because no one gave a rally cry or even the slightest care to what he said.

"Okay, let's just get moving. The others will need our help if they get there first," I suggest. Yeskarra nods and leads us back toward the path ahead. We walk until she holds up her fist for us to stop and kneels to the ground. Askuld took a knee next to her and pulled out his sword, causing me to grab my dagger quickly. He looks back at me and gestures to his ear before pointing ahead of Yeskarra. I turn my head to try and listen to what he was hearing. At first, all I hear is the whistling of the winds in the desert. Then I start picking up small rings and clangs being carried by those winds. There's a fight happening ahead of us. Askuld smirks and moves ahead of Yeskarra in a crouching walk.

"He will scout ahead and assess the danger, giving us time to prepare ourselves," she instructs. Krissy nods and pulls her axes from her belt, but Yeskarra shakes her head. "Your weapons are in poor condition. Whatever you did to them, they are finished."

She glances down and looks at them, noticing that the grips are splintered, and the blades are dull and chipped.

It makes a little sense to me in that most video games force the players to change their weapons because of higher level enemies or losing their effectiveness in certain enemy battles. Instinctively, I look at my dagger and notice that it has some sharpness left, but not much. I knew that with my character's class, most of my strength and effectiveness comes from blessings and spells from Olagog, whom I can't tell if they're computer programming or some freak speaking into my head.

"Well, great. What does that mean for me? I'm sidelined?"

The Orc leader chuckles and shakes her head, "No woman of war is going to be kept out of a good fight on my watch. Let myself and Zarimm take the front, and once you find a weapon, you unleash the fury of your fiendish gods. Shall we, Warpriest?"

With a grin, I furrow my brow and nod. She smirks at me and races ahead in the direction that Askuld went to scout with her sword in hand. I quickly follow with a firm grasp on my dagger, hearing sounds of battle getting louder and louder. We run at a downward slope that eventually leads to a large opening like what Yeskarra's men described. At the mouth of the opening, there are scattered bodies and weapons lying around on the ground, belonging to both humans and Orcs. That doesn't stop Yeskarra as she gives a large roar and takes a hard turn into the opening. I come to a skidding stop when I see her flying backwards onto the ground, cushioned by dead bodies. From the path's opening, a huge juggernaut of a red knight comes stomping out in the open, dragging a large cleaving greatsword across the ground. His armor is crimson red with forged spikes along the shoulders, knees, gloves, and boots. His helmet has three large curving spikes going up the center of it, and his eyes are obscured from the small opening it has, but it's bone-chilling. As the knight saunters towards Yeskarra, his head turns to me and stares. I brace myself and squeeze the dagger in my hand, realizing that it's going to be enough against this guy.

"Ve gijak agh vurgh!" Yeskarra roars loudly and leaps into the air with her sword raised. Midair, she brings her weapon down on the knight in a slicing motion at his shoulder. The knight grunts as the loud crash of her sword connects with his pauldron but doesn't seem to faze him too much. He turns his attention back to Yeskarra, gripping his weapon in both hands, and swings it into a circling motion with a deep bellowing roar. The blade of his weapon connects with her midsection, throwing her back into the air and onto the ground.

In a panic, I quickly pull out my Logbook and started flipping through the pages frantically, looking for the blessings or spells I can use. There are numerous blank pages after I reach level three abilities, meaning I haven't leveled any higher since the fight with the alpha mistwraith. I get more panicked because my weapon is too low to inflict any kind of damage. I look up and see the knight staring me down with his weapon gripped and shoulder pointing towards me. With another bellow, he charges at me with his shoulder looking to tackle me down. In the moment before he reaches me, Krissy runs ahead of me and meets him head on only to get shoulder checked into the ground with a scream.

"Krissy!" I run after her before getting slammed in the chest and thrown back by the knight. With a large grunt, I hit the ground hard. I look up at him as he raises his weapon preparing to bring it down on me.

"Devil's Due!"

The knight suddenly is engulfed in flames and starts flailing as his weapon falls from his hands. I lean up on my elbow and see Krissy with her clawed finger pointed at the knight, eyes glowing orange, and fumes coming from her hand.

The knight groans and wails as he's set ablaze, thrashing around trying to put it out. I groan as I get back up on my feet.

"Kris, you okay?"

She nods and gets back up on her feet, "I'm fine! I read the Logbook and saw that I could do some fire damage as a Tiefling, but only if I get hurt, which sucks. That's not going to last long so we need to do something here!"

"Leave it to me," Riley chimes and gallops in.

"Where the hell have you been?!"

Riley trots past Krissy and I, while balling up his fists, engulfing them in storm magic. "I'm about to bring the thunder of the gods down on this asshole," he says in a gruff voice.

The knight stops thrashing around as the flames are doused and he regains his composure. He stares us down through his helmet and picks his weapon back up, growling like a beast. Riley slowly trots towards him with his fists lit up. Krissy walks up on his left side, holding her waist in pain. I join his right side, gripping my dagger tightly.

"We're not strong enough to take him on alone," I tell them as we square off.

"Then we fight like we've been doing," Riley suggests. "Pick him off with the small stuff. Krissy barbecued him, so his health must be down enough to finish him the rest of the way. I'll hit him with some mosquito bites, like with the last one, and we'll take him down."

"I need a sword or something."

The knight grips his giant blade in both hands and takes a huge swing at us.

"Tuck and roll!" I yell out and jump to the side. Krissy hops down and rolls away. Riley rears up and kicks out with his horse legs to try and throw the knight off, but the blade came swinging and caught him in the saddle tossing him aside. Riley cries out in pain as he hits the ground.

I growl and grip my dagger, "Hey, asshole! Let's dance!" I run towards him with my dagger and slide on the ground, slashing at his leg. I hear a grunt come from him after my attack before he slowly turns back to me, picking up his weapon.

"That's his weakness... he's huge but the armor and weapon are heavy," I say to myself. "If we're quick enough, he won't be able to keep up."

"Then what are we waiting for?!"

I whip my head around to see Askuld joining the fight, holding his sword and axe with a snarling grin on his face. I nod to him, gripping my dagger firmly in my hand. "Kogan, Olagog... give us a strong hand and some swift feet," I pray aloud as the runes on my dagger glow lightly. I see a look in Askuld's eyes, which seems different from before, but I put it aside and put my attention the knight. He grunts and muscles his weapon into his hands, dragging it toward us. Askuld runs in quickly at the knight, who releases his sword with one hand and swings out for a punch, but the orc ducks under and slashes at his back. While his attention is drawn, I run in and slash behind his knee, causing him to stagger again. Askuld returns to his feet and jumps in the air, bringing both blades down on the knight's head. That turns out to be a mistake as the knight brings up a free hand and catches him by the neck, squeezing firmly.

"Askuld!"

The knight turns his attention to me, not uttering a single word, and continues to squeeze at his victim. I know if I try making a move, the knight will break Askuld's neck. I'm out of moves.

"Blessed are those cleansed by the blood of the righteous and smite the wicked," the knight growls lowly. He stares up at Askuld, whose eyes are rolling back.

Before the job can be finished, an arrow comes flying by and sticks the knight in the arm that's holding Askuld up. The knight groans loudly and drops him, looking in the direction the arrow came from. My eyes follow his to see Krissy holding a bow in one hand while the other draws another arrow back into a knock.

"Bless this, Clifford!" She snarls and fires her arrow. It flies fast and hit one of the soft parts of the armor, causing him to grunt hard.

"Outriders are weapons experts," I say to myself. "Krissy! Keep hitting him with as many arrows as you can!"

She smirks and nods, knocking back another arrow. The knight pulls the arrow out of his arm starts marching towards her.

I focus my attention to Riley, running over to him as he struggles to get up. "Riley! Get up, come on man!"

He groans and gets up on the joints of his horse legs, "Dude... I can't do this... I keep getting knocked down. I'm as useless here as I am out there. Just get him and leave me here."

Now I'm pissed off. I launch out and punch him in the face. He turned back to me in shock. "Riley, get up off your horse ass and help me fight. This is a game, and you are the expert. Remember when we had that campaign two years ago when I first moved to town? We got cornered in a cavern with all those kobolds, and one of them knocked your life down to ten points of life. What did you do?"

The bearded centaur looks at me with a snarl. "I... I cast 'rain of fire' and inflicted maximum damage."

"Because you didn't give a shit about your own health," I add. "You saved my noob ass, and we finished that dungeon as a team. This isn't a single player campaign, Riley. We win together. Now get up and show him the wrath of a pissed off Stormlord."

We both turn to see the knight looking like a practice dummy with arrows in the soft spots of his armor.

"Guys, I'm out of arrows!" Krissy starts backing up after tossing the bow aside, watching the knight slowly get closer to her.

"Riley, hit him with small stuff. Aim for the arrows that are still stuck in him, see if it can add some additional damage. He's strong, but he's slow and we've hit him a lot. I'm going to get Askuld and Yeskarra on their feet so they can help."

"Wait, why? You said we were in this together," he protests.

"I'm a Warpriest. A cleric. I have a role to play," I retort. He hesitates before nodding and gallops past me. He starts hurling off some storm bolts at the knight, taking the attention off Krissy.

I run towards Yeskarra, bleeding out from her wound. She grunts as she holds it tightly, "Don't worry about me! Kill that beast!"

"Not without you," I say as I take my dagger out and press the blade against her wound. "Okay, Olagog! She's one of yours, so quit being an asshole to me and help her! *Healing Touch!*" The dagger's runes glow and hum as her blood starts returning to her slowly. I feel the dagger's handle prick into the palm of my hand as her wound became more healed. Whatever is happening, it's taking part of my life away and going into her. The wound soon disappears, and her breathing calms. I sit back, feeling weak from the spell and investigate my palm. The dagger's handle had small spikes that dug into my skin, but immediately retract back into the weapon.

She shoots up and looks at me, "You are a damned fool." I was about to argue with her, but she grabs me by the shoulders and plants a kiss on me. It lingers a moment before she pulls away smirking and stands up from the ground grabbing her sword racing back into the fight. I blink rapidly and look to the fight. Riley is galloping circles around the knight, hitting him with bolts of shock magic. Krissy shuffles through the dead bodies on the field looking for a weapon to use, and Yeskarra runs in with a loud roar. The knight is starting to slow down more, but he's still holding strong. I look around for Askuld and see him lying on the ground passed out. I run over to him with what strength I can ring up to get to his side.

"Askuld! Wake up, you friggin' gremlin!" I slap his face around to try and wake him up. He starts coughing and shoots straight up, gasping for air. He looks at me in serious confusion, "Did you… did you save me? You maniac. I should be feasting with the gods right now!"

"Yeah? Well, they can save you a table," I retort and help him up to his feet. "That knight needs to go down. You want to leave your chieftain to take all the glory herself?"

His eyes snap to his revived chieftain and growls, "Over my dead body! Raahh!!" He gets back to his feet and charges into the fight. The knight is now being overwhelmed. He goes back and forth between swiping with his hand and crushing with his sword, but every hit against him is too quick for him to react. He groans and growls until he falls to his knees.

"Respite!" He roars. He drops his weapon and drops his hands to his sides, and all the attacks stop. The air is silent, and everyone is out of breath. I walk up join the others as they face the knight on the ground. His hands come up and grasp onto his helmet, slowly pulling it up and off. His face is that of an old, grizzled man with a square jaw, long white hair, and a blind eye. He glares up at us with blood dripping from his nose and lips, spitting some of it out onto the ground.

"You have defeated me," he groans. "This battle is yours. Allow me to die with honor and face my god."

Yeskarra smirks and flourishes her blade, ready to strike. "With pleasure."

"Wait!"

Everyone looks at me confused. I step in front of her and kneel in front of the knight, holding my dagger to him. "I have questions. You have answers. If you give them to me, I'll give you what you want. If not, you'll be left to suffer."

The knight grumbles and spits again, "You do not decide my fate. My god will bring me to the Horizon where I belong."

"And where exactly do you belong? Is this Horizon somewhere beyond the Mortal Gate?"

The knight smirks, "The Mortal Gate leads to the seat of your filthy, blood-thirsty gods. The Archon is our champion of glorious humanity, cast out into our realm by the gods of your impure kind. We will regain our rightful place as the masters of the realm, and right the wrongs of your filth."

I stare him down, "Is that why you're doing this? Why is all this carnage happening? Because you think you'll gain control of Albistair? You're insane. I've read this world's history. Humans lived with all the races in harmony way before the Archon came along."

The knight looks at me with a rage I recognized from those knights that attacked us when we entered the Expanse. "Do not speak blasphemy to me, you filthy heathen. The Archon brought us power from the gods. He will sit upon the throne of the Horizon and bring us to glory, and all of you to heel."

I stand up from the ground with balled-up fists, "So that's the payoff, right? Enslaving people that are different from you?"

"Not slavery," he says proudly with a smirk. "Liberation. Making the other races understand where their places are in this world. They may be strong, gifted with infernal magic by their gods, and determined to plant themselves into our civilizations. But we understand the ways of the world. The only peace that can be obtained is through order and control. Look into the Gorge and see just how 'peaceful' your kind has been."

I clench my teeth and look back at the others. They're a mixture of pissed and concerned. Askuld approaches me and pulls me aside, "He does not deserve the death he is asking for. Let him suffer and let us proceed to the epicenter."

Before I could give my answer, I hear Krissy scream my name. I turn around to the knight holding a dagger in his hand raised high. "Glory to the Archon!" he screams and brings it down into the soft part of his breastplate. He plunges it deep and twists the blade, causing him to twitch and writhe until his body slumped to the ground. I back away in shock. I've never seen such a thing like this in a game before. It's becoming too real, even more than before.

"Connor, look," Riley says as he approaches the body of the knight. Krissy comes up to my other side as we stare down at the now lifeless body. It doesn't combust, whither, or disappear like the other boss fights we've had. "No gear drops," Riley points out. "The body is still here. Why is he different?"

With everything that the knight told us, I have more questions fewer answers than before.

"I have no clue," was all I can come up with. "We need to go. Let's just hope that Mark and Danica aren't having the same problems as we are."

CHAPTER 25

Walking into the mouth of the Gorge of Vaduhs is gut wrenching, stepping over a sea of battle torn bodies of humans and Orcs alike. At the suggestion of our traveling companions, Krissy picks a couple of swords along the way that would have to suffice until she gets better weapons. Riley is looking and acting better than he was before, holding himself up higher and more confident. Yeskarra and Askuld look to the fallen Orcs that had been killed in this battle, muttering small whispers over them, and pointing out clan symbols.

"This... this is dishonorable," Yeskarra says lowly to herself. "Our kind is supposed to fight for expansion and survival. We are a proud and powerful race bound by blood and glory. Not for needless slaughter."

"Who's to say this was needless," Riley suggests. "You said that the Crimson Order had been goosestepping on the races for a long time. Maybe these clans finally had enough of it?"

"Impossible. Our clans would have to come to a unanimous vote in a Black Circle to agree to go to war against another army. Something else is afoot, and I intend to find out."

Yeskarra grabs his arm, "We will find out what became of our people, Askuld. We will restore their honor and be free once more." Askuld looks to his chieftain and takes her arm in response like a Roman handshake.

It's funny to me, because Orcs are always seen as monstrous and easy-to-blame bad guys in movies and video games. To see them acting like a tribe of proud and powerful, green-skinned Vikings is almost inspiring. It's incredible that such a race of people is being destroyed like this, no matter the reality of it.

"You gonna stand there staring, or are you gonna kiss her again?"

My head whips around to Riley who's smirking at me. "I saw that. Felt real, didn't it? Same thing happened to me with Nara."

I hush him and look over at Krissy, who has her arms crossed. "What? Didn't like a little in-game action?"

"K-Krissy it's not like that…"

"Why would I care? Not like it was real or anything."

Before anything else can be said to make this moment worse, an arrow comes flying down and wings me in the shoulder. I yell out in both surprise and pain as the force of it makes me stumble back.

"Archers! Take cover!" Askuld and Yeskarra duck behind a rock formation. Riley and Krissy pull me behind another one on the other side of the Gorge. I groan as the arrow was lodged in my shoulder. A whole volley of arrows comes flying at us, keeping us behind cover. As I huff through the pain, I look at the arrow and noticed a familiar style of craft.

"Riley… pull this thing out."

He looks at the arrow a bit hesitant. "I-I don't think I can…"

"Oh, for God's sake, cover us," Krissy growls and grabs my shoulder. "Put this in your mouth and bite hard," she orders, picking up a broken arrow shaft and shoving it between my teeth. I bite hard, but not enough for my orc teeth to break it between my jaws. I lock eyes with her as she smirks and pulls the arrow out of me with a swift yank. I clamp on the shaft so hard that it breaks in my jaw, making me taste the splinters in my mouth. I spit it out and look at Krissy with annoyance.

"You're welcome." We both look back at the battlefield, seeing the arrows coming to a stop. We all look at each other with adrenaline and pause, knowing it's too risky to peek out.

I take the arrow from Krissy's hand and look at the design. It has a blackthorn shaft with green stone shaped into a crude, triple-bladed arrowhead. The feathers at the knock are rugged and black like buzzard feathers.

"Yeskarra!" I yell out, holding the arrow up. "It's an Orcish arrow! They're Orcs!"

She and Askuld look to each other in confusion and then look at the volley of arrows that were stuck into the ground. Askuld stands up from the ground and put his weapons away, stepping out of cover.

"*Broavheruk! Koga! Kulknej ayh Ork! Leav uuk ukpeak.*"

Riley and Krissy both look to me for a translation. "He's saying, 'Brothers. Stop. We are Orc. Let us speak.'"

We all look back to Askuld and wait to see how the shooters would respond. He seems confident that he can get through to them. In a flash of a second, three arrows pierce and pin him to the ground.

"No!" Yeskarra yells and jumps into the line of fire after him.

"Cover her!" I yell and I run after her. Krissy and Riley jump out to return fire, her with arrows and him with his storm bolts. Yeskarra pulls at Askuld's limp body before I pick him up by the legs to help her. We move him behind cover and set him gently down on the ground.

"Askuld! Speak to me!" Yeskarra has angry tears streaming down her face as she holds his face in her hands. His dark blood is pouring from his mouth as he coughs and groans from the pain. I look back to Krissy and Riley, who retreat back into cover. I look back at Askuld, still clinging to life. His hands come up to grab one of hers and one of mine.

"D-do not let them destroy our people," he utters with short breaths. "For blood... and glory..." The lights go out in the scout's eyes.

Yeskarra muscles and chokes back her cries before looking up, grabbing a bow lying on the ground and runs out into the open, taking arrows from the ground to fire at the attackers with a monstrous battle cry. I run out after her with my dagger in hand, take her by the shoulder and raise it high.

"*Granav alnej ukavrengavh!*" My dagger hums as a halo of fighting prowess engulfs us both. I feel a wave of strength rush over us both before she loads three arrows into the same drawback and lets them fly. The arrows meet a couple of targets, causing the archers to fall from their shelf of the canyon onto the ground. The remaining archers scatter to opposite sides of the open-mouth canyon to flank us, one being successful in winging Yeskarra in the shoulder.

"Riley! Three o' clock! Krissy, ten 'o clock! Give us cover!" I call out while pulling her away from the fight. I set her leaning against the rocky wall before turning my gaze back to the fight.

Riley is galloping in a zigzagging motion around the battlefield while being fired at before skidding to a stop with his storm bangle lighting up his fist. He cocks back and thrusts upward at the canyon shelf yelling, *"Chain Strike!"* A single link of chain lightning strikes the shelf of the Gorge, causing it to explode and the archer perched on it to come tumbling down to the ground and gets impaled on a spear.

On the opposite end, Krissy throws her bow aside and picks up her axes, making a running start to the canyon wall. She's getting shot at rapidly, but her axe heads are parrying them almost perfectly besides one that winged her cheek. She jumps up and digs her axes into the canyon wall and starts scaling upward toward her attacker with inhuman agility. *'Friggin Tieflings,'* I think to myself. She makes it up to the shelf, where her attacker tosses their bow aside and brings out two daggers from their boots. The two of them exchange blows and swings back and forth before I watch what I can only assume was a new skill she got from her leveling. Her axe heads burst into dark red flames before she flurries them and strikes her attacker from the ledge, plummeting to the ground. Krissy leaps and slides down the side of the canyon from her weapons scraping all the way down. I'm terrified and turned on at the same time at her skill.

I turn my attention to Yeskarra and grasp the arrow in her shoulder. "On the count of three… One," I warn her before yanking it out swiftly. She barely reacts and leans her head back against the wall. "Keep this up, and I'll make you my personal cleric," she groans with a chuckle.

I shake my head and stand with my hand out, "Let's kick this battle in the ass before we talk alliances." She takes it with her good hand and hoists up onto her feet. Riley and Krissy meet back with us at the opening as we stand over Askuld's body. Even in death, he looks like he's smiling victoriously.

"He is now preparing to take on new life of battle and glory at the gates of Nishrek," Yeskarra says as she kneels and puts a blade on his chest, placing his hands on the hilt. I take out my Logbook and hold my dagger above the body before reciting, "Olagog, god of vengeance and victory. Take this soldier into your army of the Deathless. May his strength and devotion lend power to your forces and destroy your enemies."

Yeskarra stands up and clears her throat to mask her crying, "Enough of this. Let us get to the epicenter and ensure our companions have not joined Askuld in the afterlife." She marches down the path of death ahead of us. While she goes ahead, I take the time to look to my friends who have been my guardian angels through this whole thing.

"Guys, I'm not going to let us die in this place."

Riley nods intently, Krissy after him. We press on after Yeskarra further into the Gorge and away from the field of corpses. In the meantime, I'm able to reflect on the events that have happened over the course of this side quest, like how all these corpses are still here and not disappearing like any other defeated enemy in any game, and how their deaths are so real.

The further we go into the Gorge, the more and more frequent the bodies become. "We're getting closer to the epicenter," Yeskarra announces as she unsheathes her weapon. This prompts the rest of us to prepare the same. Riley chugs down a phial of mana to renew the magic he spent on the fight, and Krissy grips onto her weakened axes. We're all so close to leveling up after that encounter in the last fork, but we may not be able to if things get crazy again. Most games don't let players level up if they are in the middle of a fight, and if that happens in this one, we may all be screwed in the next big skirmish.

As we make our way towards the epicenter, I start to observe the bodies, taking notice of all the different injuries and fatal wounds that killed the warriors. The Crimson Order knights are covered in arrows and blade gashes, but not all from the orcs. Some daggers, spears and swords are either stuck in the bodies or laying on the ground belong to their own soldiers. The blades of the Order are blackened and always contain a single dark ruby in the hilts to symbolize their brood. Whatever is happening here is causing everyone to attack someone ruthlessly and without prejudice, regardless of race or faction.

"Riley? What's wrong?" I hear Krissy ask in concern. I whip my head around to see him holding his head with one hand.

"Something… something magical is happening…" His eyes fall to his storm bangle, which is giving off a reddened spark, different from the sapphire jewel in the center. "It's… it's hurting my head…"

Out of instinct, I reach out and take his arm with my hand. That's when it gets weird again because my head starts to tense up and burn. Whatever Riley's feeling is now happening to me. Call it magic or the science of the game, but this feels like some sort of warning.

CHAPTER 26

Despite our current physical and psychological pain, we press on through the Gorge to find the others. It's hard telling if the others made it or are even still alive, but I don't want to think about that. Yeskarra is still deadly silent after Askuld's death, and I don't blame her for a second. Sure, she may be an NPC, but death is felt as heavily here as it is on the Outside, as I'm starting to call the real world.

Yeskarra stops suddenly, prompting the rest of us to follow her lead and look ahead of her. The canyon opens up into a vast opening of adjacent canyons, like a great crossroads. We finally made it to the epicenter, but that isn't the part that has us all horrified. Dead center of the Gorge is a mountain of bodies; a large spire of death built from the bodies of both Orcs and knights, like a monument of war and death. Atop the spire of bodies stands a cloaked figure holding a staff close to itself, with a great stone of red radiating a soft hue around it. Just like the Keystone from the temple in the Bowels that glowed blue and created the alpha mistwraith.

"It's a Keystone." That's when Yeskarra growls and steps forward.

"You, up there! Atop this atrocity! You will pay for the deaths of my kin with your own blood! Descend from your perch and meet your end with some gods damned honor!"

Silence. Not a peep from the figure holding the staff. The Orc chieftain growls again and marches forward.

"Yeskarra, don't! We don't know what that Keystone is capable of. We need to be smart about this." My plea falls on deaf ears as she keeps marching towards the spire of corpses.

"S-stay away!" The figure on top of the spire calls down. All of us look up at the surprising response. "I-I can't stop this... I don't wanna kill anyone else... please!"

I'm taken off guard. The figure isn't talking like the other NPCs in the game. "Something doesn't feel right."

"What part? The mountain of dead bodies or the guy that *made* the mountain of dead bodies," Krissy asks deadpanned.

"I don't like this," Riley retorts. "If that mountain of bodies becomes the Mindflayer from *Stranger Things*, I'm gonna puke."

Yeskarra growls and tries to traverse up the bodies to claim her vengeance. The figure up top seems to be quivering as they raise the staff up high, "*Stay away!!*"

The spire begins to quake, causing the ground under our feet to crack. Yeskarra doesn't let this stop her as she continues to climb. Suddenly, she gets snared by something grabbing onto her ankle. She looks down and sees a knight

266

with a missing leg grab her ankle with both hands and give an unsettling groan. Three more hands of dead warriors reach out and hold her in place.

"Yeskarra!" I take my dagger out and run towards the spire with Krissy and Riley on my heels. The closer we get, the more we start to see bodies from the bottom, spawn out from the spire. Undead monsters in the form of knights and Orcs rise to their feet, at least the ones that still had feet to stand on and they face us with monstrous looks of hunger on their faces. The sun is starting to set on the Expanse, giving the situation a more terrifying feeling as their eyes start to glow an eerie red, resembling the color that the Keystone is emitting. That's when it dawns on me: Instead of twisting restless souls into monsters, this one makes those affected thirsty for blood, alive or dead.

"Guys... it's a horde fight." I don't know what I'm going to be able to do against an army of undead compared to the others, but we don't have a choice. It's us versus zombies.

"I fucking *hate* zombies," Krissy says with a shaky voice as she takes a stance.

Riley balls up his fists crackling with electricity, "We are massively outnumbered here..."

The wave of undead begins to saunter toward us, picking up weapons where they lie. My eyes shoot up to the spire, seeing Yeskarra struggle and fight against her captors, then up to the figure holding the staff.

"Forget about the zombies. The goal is to get the Keystone. We get that and everything else stops."

"How the hell do you know that'll work??"

"I don't," I admit in all honesty. "But it beats getting eaten alive. Riley, you won't be able to climb, so just take out as many of them as you can. Krissy, we need to get up there and get the Keystone. Spread out and don't let them corner you!"

I take off to the right of where the undead are marching from, drawing some of their attention as they break into a run.

Fuck, these are World War Z *undead!* I think to myself as I race as hard as I can. The corpses chase me with disturbing speed to the point I hear their raspy moans closing in. I sense that one is almost about to grab me, so I quickly dart aside and watch it tumble in front of me on the ground. I smirk and take off again to a side that I saw wasn't crawling, quickly drifting towards it, and jumping up to grab the nearest body. My hands latch onto a piece of armor with jagged spikes that cuts into my palms. I wince and suck air in through my teeth as I look down at my pursuers, watching as they crash into the wall of dead bodies and struggle to climb over each other to get to me.

My eyes scan out to try and find the others. Krissy is getting overwhelmed by undead, but she's cleaving left and right with her axes glowing as hot as embers. She rips through a few of them before she runs off towards the spire to climb. Riley, on the other hand, is galloping like his tail was on fire while getting chased by an army of undead. He fires as many Chain Strikes and Storm Bolts as he can muster, knocking over the undead like messed up dominos as they fall in groups.

I regain focus as I climb up the bodies, my hands dripping dark green blood from the punctures. If I were myself on the Outside, this would've been a huge struggle because of my lack of physical strength, but as an orc I am making serious gains. I climb a little higher before I hear sounds of struggle coming from near me. I look down, the undead are still struggling to reach me, but not as close as what I was hearing. I look to my left, and an orcish arm is sticking out of the spire wearing familiar leather braces.

"Yeskarra!" I shift my focus to try and grab her hand. Her arm starts sinking into the spire and adding to its structure. I grab her outstretched hand and pull as hard as I could, feeling the struggle on her end. As I'm pulling, I feel something grab my other hand I'm using to hold myself up. A second mangled Orcish hand is pulling my arm into the spire with equal strength to mine.

"Connor!" I turn my head as far as I'm able to see Krissy has gotten overwhelmed and is being pinned by the undead. Her weapons were thrown out of reach, and they began to drag her to the spire. I try to pull myself and Yeskarra free from the undead grasps, but more hands pushed through to grab and pull me in. I start sinking into the spire of bodies and become part of its construction, yelling out terrified.

From behind me, a thunderous cry rang and bounced off the canyon walls yelling, "Incoming!!" The call is followed by a loud crash of rock and dust.

Looking behind me, I suddenly seeing the flying forms of Mark, Danica, and their Orc companions coming from a gaping hole in the wall of the Gorge. They come crashing down into a roll and quickly start sprinting before looking behind them. A flood of terrorghasts suddenly comes pouring out in ear-piercing screeches and crashes into the base of the spire. The undead that was pawing at us shifts focus on the monsters and charges at them with inhuman groans. The two armies of monsters crash against each other, causing the spire to shift and sway. I feel my captured limbs being let go, giving me the chance to pull Yeskarra's hand. The orc comes out gasping as she latches onto my side with blood coming from her nose and cheek.

"You are possibly the maddest Warpriest I have ever had the honor of knowing."

"Don't thank me yet," I say and look back. "Hang tight."

Before she can get the chance to argue, I let go of the limb I'm hanging onto and freefall onto the sloping bodies, sliding us down back to the ground. We go into a roll as the sounds of tearing, screeching, and groaning surround us.

Riley comes galloping at us and skids to a halt, "Get up! We're in a friggin feeding ground!"

I take his outstretched hand to get on my feet before helping Yeskarra up to hers. My gaze goes to the top of the spire, seeing the figure struggling to keep his balance. "We need to get the Keystone before we get swarmed. Where are Danica and Mark?"

"Right here!" They, along with Korr, Nargol and Hagu, run up to us out of breath and filthy. "Where did the terrorghasts come from??"

"They were nesting in the underground cavern you sent us to," Mark explains. "They were sleeping like a giant hornet's nest, and we had to move around them. It wouldn't have been a problem if we weren't attacked by Order knights and Orcs with glowing red eyes. They started attacking and woke up those things, chasing us out of the cavern. We found that opening and prayed."

I point up at the top of the spire, "That guy has the Keystone. Those monsters are gonna make him fall, and we need to get his staff. But we can't get through this mess. We need to charge in fast and hard. Everything we've got."

"I'll climb up to get the staff," Danica volunteers, making my jaw drop in shock. "I'm faster and can climb with no problem. Get them out of my way and I'll do the rest."

After a brief pause, Korr picks up a greatsword and laughs out, "Then what in the Hells are we waiting for?! For blood and glory!" Nargol and Hagu roar in agreement with their weapons up high.

I breath in heavily and hold up my dagger, invoking an aura of strength that surrounded us all. I hold my dagger up and yell, "Forever free!!" We all charge at the massive sea of monsters as the tower started shaking and getting shorter from the undead coming from the base of it. Some of the undead and terrorghasts see us coming and direct their attention to us, racing to get to us first. Korr, Nargol and Hagu take point as they roar in unison and begin swinging their weapons, cleaving, and hacking right down the middle of the swarm.

"Danica, go! We'll cover you!" Mark yells out before leaping into the air and jabbing a terrorghast in the chest with his spear. She breaks into an all-out, four-legged sprint, jumping from body to body, making her way to the top. The rest of us fight through to the base of the spire to keep their focus on us. While armies of both are tearing each other apart, some stragglers turn their attention to us at the base.

"None of them get past us!" he yells out.

"Not a fucking chance!" Krissy growls through her teeth.

The monsters start swarming us in full force, not letting us get the chance to breathe. My blessing was holding, but it won't for much more of this. Riley's magic is starting to lose momentum, probably running low on mana.

Come on, Dani, hurry! Suddenly, the ground begins to shake more violently. The creatures don't let up as it starts to crack and quake. I start seeing some of the monsters in the back of the swarm fall and disappear suddenly out of sight.

"The ground is caving in!" Danica's voice rings out from above. I look up to see that she has the figure in a grapple as they tumble down from the spire.

"Break the line! Run!" We break and turn into a sprint. The cracking earth is getting closer, and more monsters fell into it. The spire suddenly starts to fall into the growing hole, toppling over and falling on the monsters chasing us. I look back and see Danica trying to wrestle the staff out of the figure's hands. *If she doesn't get that staff, she's a goner!*

"Danica, get the Keystone! We gotta go!"

"He won't let it go! It's like it's stuck to his hands!"

My eyes flutter and take a good look at the person death-gripping the staff. Their face belongs to a male elvish character with darkened skin, black hair, and eyes that had white irises surrounded by glistening black. The first elf I've seen in the game, and he's shaken. Inside of his pupils is a hue of deep red like the color that the stone was giving off. Even with all of the noise around me, I can hear him muttering and repeating something over and over. "I don't wanna play anymore. I don't wanna play anymore. I don't wanna play anymore." *What the hell does that mean?*

The ground is shaking more and starts to open, causing the elf to slip into the opening hole. He yells out as he falls back, but Danica and I grab the staff quickly and catch him still attached to it. We both struggle to pull him up from his impending death.

"Hold on! Don't let go!" I yell to him. His eyes look up at us and the red starts to fade from them. We pull up with all our strength and get him to the stable ground we were on. While the elf is huddled on the ground in a ball, I look to the giant hole that opened and swallowed countless undead and terrorghasts, while those still standing continue to tear each other apart.

My eyes dart back to the elf, who shuffles against the wall of the canyon still gripping the staff.

"Holy shit, he's loony," Danica blurts.

I ignore the comment and approach him carefully. He shudders and hugs the staff tightly. "Easy, pal. Just breathe."

The red leaves his eyes as he looks up at me from the ground, "Wh-who are you? Why did you help me?"

"My name is Connor, and we know that the Keystone is responsible for this. We really need it. Can you give it to me?"

His eyes nearly pop out of his head, "Connor... You... You're a player?"

My eyes go wide when I realize what he is. He's not a boss, not an enemy lieutenant, not even an NPC.

"You're a player, too."

Danica's ears fold back.

The elf nods standing up and removing his hood. "My name is Matt. Matt Bauer."

All I could do was stare in silence. He used a real name that didn't come out as some weird fantasy name. I thought we were the only players in the game, but clearly we're not.

Matt finally composes himself before taking off his cloak. His dark elf avatar is average height with dark gray skin, a mop of black hair in curls on his head, long pointy ears with two small earrings in each, and white faded dust paint along his exposed arms and face like a clan mark. He's wearing a dark red tunic that was slim fitting against his slender frame, along with leather boots and fingerless leather gloves. Attached to his belt is a sheathed falchion that looked like it was made of shining silver and a blue-jeweled hilt.

He's holding the staff that has the red Keystone like it's glued to his hands while staring at Danica and myself. "I can't believe there are other players…"

"Trust me, we're just as surprised as you are." I hear running footsteps coming up behind us. Mark, Krissy, and Riley come running up to meet us, but Yeskarra and her Orcs slow down to a stop at the sight of Matt.

"Dani!" Mark yells out and picks up his girlfriend in his arms, holding her tightly. I make the mistake of watching their reunion that I suddenly get tackled by surprise to the ground by Krissy, who wrestles me under her in a pin.

I look up and her axe in her hand pointed right at my face. "If you keep doing stupid shit like this, I swear I'll kill you myself!" I nod aggressively before she puts it away and picks me up off the ground, hugging me tightly. From behind me, another pair of arms picks us both up in a huge bear hug. Riley's scruffy beard scratches the back of my neck, but I can't do anything in this sandwiched hug.

He puts us back down, causing us to separate and look at Matt, who is staring right back.

"Who is this guy? And why does he have the Keystone?"

"Move away from him," Yeskarra growls. She and the other Orcs have bows and arrows knocked back, pointing straight at him. He stands frozen before I step between them in the line of fire.

"Wait! I need him!"

The chieftain gapes at me in shock. "This Drow is the reason that our brethren's blood is spilled along this Gorge! It wields dark magic, and you defend it?!"

"I-I didn't mean for it to happen," Matt tries defending himself. "I-I was just trying to find them all when I was being chased by the Order knights! When I found it, the Keystone just went red and blasted everyone. When they got up, they started killing each other! I didn't mean to hurt anyone! Now I can't let go of this thing!"

Hagu spits on the ground, not dropping his aim. "Elvish shite! They would rather see us all bend the knee to their kind! Step away, Warpriest, or fall with it!"

Mark pulls his spear out and steps next to me, "Give it your best shot, you green pig."

Both parties are now in a heated standoff as I fix my eyes on Yeskarra, who is piping mad. At the same time, she seems conflicted.

"Yeskarra, I need him alive. He may have answers we're looking for. We stopped the undead and lifted the curse. You should look to see if any of your clansmen are still alive, and we'll take care of him."

It grows quiet for what seems like forever with everyone staring each other down, ready to fight. Yeskarra finally breaks that silence by easing her grip on her bow and putting it away, with Hagu and Nargol following her lead. She steps toward us after we lay our weapons down in response.

"I hope you know what you are doing, Zarimm," she says cautiously. *In all honesty, so do I.* She reaches behind her and pulls out an intricately designed battle horn and hands it to me. "You aided me and my clan in stopping this nightmare, now my people and I are in your debt. Do not make me regret this decision."

I nod as I take the horn from her. We grasp each other's forearms in their traditional farewell before she and her men turn from us and head back into the Gorge to find survivors. I turn to the others, who look at me in confusion. I have a lot to explain. On the other hand, so does the mysterious new player, Matt Bauer.

CHAPTER 27

It takes some time and effort for me to convince the others about the decision to save Matt's life from the other Orcs, but when they finally accept the fact that he was another player like us, it was enough for them to accept. Unfortunately, that's also when a whole new rush of confusion and frustration settled in. We decide it was best to get out of the Gorge and find a place to set up camp, away from the corpses and any surviving terrorghasts. Thanks to Krissy's map, there's a small oasis outside of the Gorge we can rest up. Even though it seems like daybreak is close, we still need a rest after that whole showdown. What I find interesting is that the magic that we use can be easily revived and ready to use after a little cooldown time, like taking a short or long rest during a campaign. Everyone is very wary of Matt, mostly because he's still holding the staff in his hands with the Keystone sitting on top of it. When we finally reach the oasis, it's kind of a fun and beautiful setup: Three tall palm trees reaching towards the sky, a small crystal blue pool of water, all surrounded by soft vibrant grass. Finally making use of the adventuring gear in our packs, we pitch a small camp under the shadows of the palm trees with a couple of pitched tents, some knapsacks and a small firepit to last us until sunrise.

While setting up the camp, I watch Matt stay huddled against one of the palm trees, still hugging the staff to his body like it was going to run away from him.

"You can relax, dude. We're not gonna kill you."

He stops looking so scared and more suspicious towards us. I sit down at the fire where the others are sitting and gesture to an empty spot next to me, knowing the others weren't about to sit next to him. He brings the staff with him as he takes a seat, making the circle of awkwardness complete.

"So how did you get sucked into this game," Mark asks suspiciously.

He tenses up, "I-I don't really know if I should say... I haven't been able to trust a lot of things since I've been here."

"Matt, it's cool," I try calming him. "We're all freaked out. We had no clue what we were getting into either. You can talk to us."

Matt's eyes meet mine, and something weird about him was finally showing. "I-I didn't get stuck in here. I volunteered to be here."

We all gawk. "I am a programming analyzer and alpha tester that works for SnoWire Interactive. I volunteered to enter *The Mortal Gate* when it was first fully developed."

That lit the fuse on the powder keg that was Mark. He suddenly leaps over the fire and tackles Matt to the ground yelling, "You son of a bitch!"

When they hit the ground, Matt suddenly vaults him off and away with hardly any struggle, sending him onto his back before getting onto his own feet. I quickly jump up to my feet and get between them, "Guys stop!"

"Connor, he's the reason we're stuck in this place!" Danica hisses. Mark thrashes against my grip while Matt stands stone faced, pissing everyone off even more.

"I'm not the reason you are here. I'm not even sure why you're here at all. This product wasn't meant to be in the hands of consumers until all processes were completed, which shouldn't be for another year."

"Tell that to Dominic Dawson," Riley snarls with clenched fists.

Suddenly his stone-faced demeanor disappears and gets replaced with shock, "D-Dominic Dawson? How? When?"

Mark gives me enough pause so I can turn to Matt, "He sent a copy of the game to my friend's shop with a chance to get paid for beta testing it. I don't know how long it's been since we've been in here, but it feels like weeks."

If his skin pigment could let him, Matt's face would've been white. His whole reaction doesn't make me believe he could've done this on purpose, or even be part of a plot to trap people in a video game.

"That's impossible. Dominic Dawson has been comatose for two years." He takes the shock and silence we fell in as an invitation to explain. "He believed in personally testing all of his products and merchandise to get the most out of his creations. Dawson is a prideful man and holds a lot of it in his work. With the development of this new technology that dumps the human consciousness and synapses into a database of virtual coding, he felt it was his right to be the first to enter this place. When we tracked his brainwave activity inside the interface, it was a celebration of success for the whole company. But suddenly, his frequency disappeared. We tried everything to get him back from the virtual world he had built. After trying for a whole year, his body remained in a vegetative state, and we ran out of options."

This whole revelation knocks us all on our asses. Dominic Dawson, the head of SnoWire Interactive, is stuck in the game just like us. If that's true, then how did we get the game? How did we get a virtual message from him? And why were we picked?

"That still doesn't explain why you are here," Mark growls lowly.

Matt glares daggers at him, "I was part of the last attempt to try and get my employer out of this place. I and three other programmers were put into this game to try and find his conscious mind and get him out."

That results in us all asking the same question at the same time, "There's a way out?!"

Our unified voice makes Matt jump back a bit and become eerily silent. Not a good sign. Krissy shoots up from her spot on the ground and rushes the elf with her axe in hand, "We asked you a question, you fucking weasel!"

"Krissy!" Her yellow eyes dart back at me to the point that I think she'll hurl her axe at my head. I stand my ground, "We need him." She snarls before pulling the axe away from his face. He catches his breath as I approach him, "Answer the question."

"Yes, there's a way out. But it's not easy." We wait for his explanation.

"The game's main AI system is retrofitted with a certain failsafe; in case it became too immersive or caused an internal blackout while players were inside. It's a glitch, of sorts. The glitch acts as a back door that can remove a conscious mind from the game. But it risks possible brain damage from the overwhelming radiation that comes from the equipment to the point that it could put anyone into a vegetative state. Even become braindead."

I look to the others for their reactions, which doesn't make me feel better. They all look conflicted, as if being vegetables or even braindead was a better alternative to being in the game any longer. "So, the other way out is to beat the game, right?"

"Theoretically, yes."

"Wait, what?"

"We didn't initiate the final protocol to relieve players from the system. Dominic felt it necessary to do it himself from within to ensure the game's immersive capabilities."

"That makes absolutely no goddamn sense!" Mark is at his wit's end with Matt, but it can't get to that yet.

Riley stands from the ground and starts his own questioning, "You said you were in a group to try and find Dawson. What happened to them?"

"We got into trouble when we started. My party got ambushed by terrorghasts almost immediately, causing us to separate. I think… I think one of them was killed."

Regrettably, this brings up the question that we were all concerned with, "What happens if you die in the game?"

Silence falls, and all eyes are on him.

"We made it clear in the programming that players who die in the game get sent back to their first spawning site. So, I went back to our site where we started and waited for anyone to come back. But no one respawned. I have been on my own since, looking for anyone else I came in with. While I was searching, I ran into a group of NPCs who were talking about some magic stone that sounded like the objectives we made for the players to find. That's when I decided to try and find the Keystones myself, thinking that they may be what Dawson and my colleagues were doing as well. I arrived at the Great Expanse and went into the Gorge, scouring multiple caverns until I found the Keystone, sitting on the staff stuck in a carved boulder. When I tried to take it, the staff infused with my hands and sent waves of red throughout the Gorge. I was stuck there with monsters and knights killing each other until you found me."

I look at the Keystone on the staff in his hands before reaching into my satchel, pulling out the one from the Bowels. Matt's eyes widen, "You found one?"

I nod and hold it up, watching it suddenly pulse blue. The red one begins mimicking the pulses until they both start humming in unison. Matt's fingers start to wiggle free from the grip of the staff until his hands completely free themselves. The Keystone fell free from the staff and came to the one in my hand. I grab it from the air as they both stop pulsing and put them into my satchel.

"Wait, I need those," he tries protesting. Krissy and Mark stop him with their glares and stances in front of him. "Look, you don't want this fight. I need those to get my boss out."

"Try it and I'll stick you like a fish," Mark challenges, unironically. Krissy grasps her axes in anticipation.

Matt grumbles as he lays a hand on the hilt of his sword that's holstered to his waist. Eyeing us all down, he quickly flicks his wrist and disappears in a puff of smoke. We look around for him until the sound of unsheathing metal catches my attention too late. Mark's legs are suddenly kicked out from underneath of him, followed by a quick swipe against Krissy's axes that force them out of her hands. The silhouette of the dark elf flashes away quicker than it appears as he comes back and kicks me in the chest, sending me flying onto my back. Riley tries flashing him with a storm bolt, but Matt is too quick as he zips side to side and lands on Riley's horse back with the blade against his neck. I get back up slowly and glare at him holding my friend hostage, "Easy now."

"I'm a Shadow Stalker," he explains, pressing the blade close to Riley's neck. "I'll have your friend's head rolling on the ground before you have the chance to react."

"A rogue class," I guess. Riley grunts as his hair is yanked back and the blade is against his throat. Krissy growls softly as she stands back up, offering a hand to Mark.

"I want the Keystones," he demands. "Hand them over and I'll let this one go."

I hold my hand up as my other one reaches into my satchel, "No need to threaten us… I see we're in a bit of a gambit here…"

As if on cue, Danica soars through the air and knocks Matt from Riley's back and pins him to the ground, ears flat and teeth barred. He looked up in shock and struggles as the rest of us gather around them both, weapons and magic armed. He stops struggling and takes a big gulp, "Okay… you got me."

Danica doesn't loosen her grip on him, nor does she remove her glare from him.

"Danica, let him go."

She glares at me, "You've gotta be kidding me. He almost killed Riley!"

"If he wanted to kill him, he would have. He's obviously had more time to hone his skills and is clearly a threat, but he thinks we are a threat too," I point out. "Let him up."

Danica hisses loudly at me before she hops up, all too ready to pounce again. Matt sits up and glares at us. "So, you're not amateurs… That's good to know."

I unsheathe my dagger and kneel to the ground, pointing it at him. "Someone in your company sent us this game. I've been gaming my whole life, but I'm not looking to stay in this place. My friends aren't keen on dying in here, either. That makes us all one hell of a threat. If you want to live through this and find Dawson, you'll help us."

I flip my dagger and sheathe it before offering a hand to him. His creepy eyes look at my hand then back up to me before taking it, using it to lift himself up off the ground.

"Agreed... okay, I'll help. But the second we find my team, or Dawson, I'm out."

I nod in agreement.

"Hey nerds," Krissy calls out for our attention, "we don't know where the other Keystones are yet. So, we're gonna be going in circles if we don't update the map."

"Actually, I have something that can help." Matt reaches into his satchel and pulls out a piece of paper. "When I went back to our respawn site, I found this note stuck into the door with a knife. It mentions a place called the Daggertip Arena that's not far from the eastern border of the Grave Expanse."

Krissy rips the paper from his hands and hovers it over her map. Just like before, it starts to reveal a new location to us for our next objective. She looks at it closely, "The arena is in some place called Caldanet, the Iron Vale."

I look at the location and how it compares to the other places we've been to. From what I can tell, it seems as if it is in the mountains or by cliffs shown through intricately drawn rock walls of black and gray sitting beneath a valley of grass and trees with a singular path. One way in, one way out.

"Alright, we have our heading. Let's rest up and get ourselves ready before we head out. We may run into some more Order knights or monsters before we get there."

They all nod in agreement and separate before going to check their leveling status. Everyone gets the chance to level up after the nightmare in the Gorge. Danica gains an increase in agility and speed by +2, as well as a slight increase in overall health, but nothing new in her Trick cards. Riley receives a +3 in magic and a new spell called "Storm Javelin" where he can hurl a bolt of lightning at the cost of a huge chunk of his magic. Mark gets a boost in dexterity by +2 and a small increase of agility by +1, while also increasing his Totemist amulet's effectiveness by acquiring "Tame". Krissy gets an increase in attack by +3 and stamina by +2, as well as acquiring a new Outrider talent where she can summon mounts in nearby proximity. In my new level, I gain a small boost in magic by +1 and wisdom by +2, giving me a new blessing called "Sacred Armor" where I can get an armor buff from Olagog's blessing. I watch Matt reassemble himself with his gear and abilities. Apparently as a Shadow Stalker, he utilizes stealth and agility to act as an assassin class that uses smoke and shadows to overtake enemies. This concerns me, because he can easily turn on us at any moment and we wouldn't know until it's too late, but I have a feeling he needs us more than we need him. Once we all finish leveling up and do an equipment check, we snuff out the fire and follow Krissy as she leads us in the direction of Caldanet. The Great Expanse is living up to its name; a huge expanse of desert stretching for miles. I hate to think of how much time it'll take for us to make it across this wasteland. One thing is clear; we need a ride.

"This walk is fucking stupid," Mark complains. Of all of us, he has the most reason to complain because of his race. In most games I've played, Tritons have been able to withstand land conditions, but SnoWire must've made extreme heat a weakness of their kind here.

"Tiefling, why don't you try to use your Outrider skills to find us some mounts?" Matt asks.

Her yellow eyes narrow at him in a way that shook me, "My name is Krissy, you dick. And I don't know how. I need to be in proximity, and I sure as hell don't see any horses around."

Matt rolls his eyes and marches over to her, grabbing her satchel and digs around. She struggles against him a little bit before he pulls out her horn she got at the beginning of the game. "You're telling me you haven't used this from when you first awoke in the game? Your class is a master of mounted beasts and combat."

Krissy rolls her eyes as she purses her lips around the mouth of the horn and blows. It bellows like a raider's horn into the open air. We stand around and wait for something to happen until some whinnies and neighs come from behind us. We whip around in surprise, and I instantly feel stupid. The Crimson Order horses that we took to the Gorge have returned to us.

"Well... at least we weren't too far for them to hear," I shrug. The horses gallop up to us and settle as we take their reins. Riley is lucky enough to not need one, leaving the five of us with three mounts. Mark and Danica saddle up on one together and Krissy gets on one with me, refusing to pair up with Matt as he's given his own. Once we're mounted up, the horses take off in the direction of our next destination, and hopefully the next Keystone.

CHAPTER 28

The ride across the desert feels like a solid hour, maybe an hour and a half, through dusty and sandy wastes. Thank God we have the horses, otherwise this would've sucked worse for us. The air is thick with tension as we ride towards Caldanet, everyone remaining silent and casting glances at each other; mostly at Matt. After the standoff at camp, it's no wonder that he's getting most of the heat. No pun intended.

"Do you trust him not to try and kill us?" Krissy turns to ask me. My grip was on the side of the saddle, but I couldn't hear her at first. I lean in to hear her better, so my grip changes to the sides of her waist. *Please don't smack me.*

"Not at all, but it's the best chance we have right now. He gave us a lead on the next Keystone, so we'll see how far his word takes us after that."

Riley trots up next to us, "I hope you know what you're doing, Tusks. I don't like keeping someone around that had a blade to my neck."

I sigh in defeat. I'm not keen on being allies with a shifty guy like him, not to mention he was part of the team that got us stuck here in the first place, but I know I'm right. We really don't have a choice at the moment. The trek seems to be getting longer with no end in sight of the

Grave Expanse. Our journey starts to slow down as the horses start getting tired and the sun reached its highest point. Looking around, everyone's visibly sweating, and it makes me worried for Mark, hoping we won't have another incident like the last time. But luck finally turns in our favor as the landscape slowly begins to change. The cracked earth and sand soon start being replaced by stone and soil, and the road we're on starts to slope upwards towards some stony hills. We pull our horses back into a small trot as we approach an opening in the hills. Beyond that opening, we stop our horses and look down at a city that's been dug into a cliffside. There are at least four or five spires of shaped stone and earth with bridges connecting them. The sun is casting a jagged shadow over this eerie looking city that's loud with clamoring citizens, pounding rocks and metal, and loud machines. The smell of fumes and the taste of iron dust fill the air in a very unflattering way. No mistake: we found Caldanet, the Iron Vale of Albistair.

"Looks to be some sort of mining town," Matt infers. "It's dug deep into the hills, using them as shelter as they dig deeper."

"If it's a mining town, this won't be a friendly place," Mark adds, surprising me. "Any show, movie, or video game that has a mining town always has either death, slavery, or corruption."

"Probably explains their arena as well," Riley ponders.

I hop off my horse and step closer to the edge of the hill, looking down at the city. I can't make out any of the people in Caldanet, but if it's mostly human, we may have trouble brewing here. We got lucky with the last tavern being occupied by non-humans, but how long can our luck last?

"It may be a smart move to cover up until we get a sense of where we're at and where the Keystone is," I suggest.

Matt swats me on the shoulder, "I need to find my party. Don't forget our deal."

Before I can react, Mark yanks him back and stands between us. "It's because of *him* that you're not planted headfirst into a pit full of fucking monsters. I swear I'll plunge my spear right down your throat if you try anything that'll get us killed. Keep your goddamn hands to yourself."

Matt holds his hands up while keeping his jaw clenched and eyes locked on Mark. The two could start a fire with how much friction is between them.

"Look, we're going to get killed if we're at each other's throats like this. The game is getting tougher and it's pulling us deeper in. We need to keep our heads on straight if we are going to find the Keystone *and* find the SnoWire team. So, stow your crap and let's get in there. The only ones who have cover are Matt and Danica, so they

295

should scout ahead of us to let us know what kind of vibe this place has."

"No way," Mark protests. "He's not going anywhere near her."

"The rest of us stick out like sore thumbs, Mark. As rogue classes, they both stand a chance to get by unnoticed."

Matt and Danica look to each other distastefully but end up nodding in agreement. "Fine, we'll go."

"Mark, I'll be fine. He knows I'll smack his ass around if he tries anything," Danica assures. He just grumbles, knowing he won't win that argument.

"Meet us back here at this spot," Matt says as he throws his cloak on. "We'll find the Daggertip Arena and come back."

With a nod, the two of them start down the path that led to a bridge that would get them to the closest rock island. The rest of us take up a hidden position and sit in waiting. We wait here for a long time, sitting on the ground listening to the sounds of hammering and faint voices. The sun is inching lower as we wait for them to return.

"This is taking too long," Mark mumbles from his cover.

"She's fine, Mark," Krissy assures him. "Your girl is badass. She's been carrying a lot of the group's weight lately."

"I don't care! She shouldn't have gone off with that rat in the first place!"

I shuffle over to him while trying to stay in cover, "What's the problem, man? You trust her, right? She's been getting better at the game and even saved Riley. Have a little faith in her."

"My problem is that I've been fucking useless!" He yanks the totem chain off his neck and waves it in my face, "The most I've been able to do is throw a spear and talk to fish! She's gone off and done more for everyone than I have! Why did this game make me a useless part of this group?!"

I'm stunned. His problem isn't being possessive of his girlfriend. His problem is he doesn't like not being more active as a player. Coincidentally, Riley is the one that chimes in.

"So what?! Dude, you're a Triton Totemist that commands animals and breathes underwater. The only thing that has been holding you down is that we haven't been in your element. But that hasn't stopped you from being an important part of this party. You saved me and Connor with that first fight against the terrorghast. You warned us about the murkodile that almost killed Krissy.

You even navigated us through the Ordowell Bowels. So, stop being a bitch about her getting the chance to be the tough one."

As if a frying pan smacked him in the face, Mark gawks at Riley with wide fisheyes before shutting his mouth and sitting back down against a rock. I throw a thumbs-up at Riley, who smirks and kneels on the ground near the rest of us.

I sit back down near Krissy, who's shaking her head and rolling her eyes. "How is it that you're all such dorks and yet you always rise up to the moment?"

Riley chuckles and looks at me, "This is *our* element. Before we met, Connor was a shy introverted guy that stumbled in my shop looking at single-player stuff. I got him to play in one of my one-shot *D&D* campaigns, and he sprang to life. All I had after the accident was gaming, so I made it into my business and my life's calling. Being able to take on different lives and feel like a hero? It's amazing."

I shake my head and wave him off, "You're lying. I wasn't shy or introverted. You needed a sit-in because your fifth never showed up. I just happened to be in the store at the time." We both laugh a little, even getting a chuckle out of Krissy.

Since we had some time, I figure now is as good of a time as any. "So, Krissy? We never really got your story."

This was a look I've never seen from her before: a look of discomfort. "I-I'd rather not..."

She's normally so upfront and blunt, hardly ever showing weakness or discomfort. Clearly I struck a chord, and I was willing to let it go, but my friends aren't about to do that.

"Come on, Krissy, it can't be that bad," Riley insists.

"He's right," Mark added. "I'm adopted. My adoptive parents flat-out refused to tell me for the longest time where I came from or who my birth parents were. About three years ago when I was graduating high school, I did some digging of my own and found them. They were immigrants from Korea who struggled to keep their visa in the States. I confronted my parents about it, and they explained that my birth parents left me with their immigration lawyer so I could grow up in the country and have a life better than theirs. The lawyer found a home for me, and here I am."

We all sit in silence for a bit, but I lean over and pat him on the shoulder. "We're all the better for you being here, man. I don't think I'll ever regret having that programming class with you as my lab partner. We killed that debugging project, and we found out how awesome we were in team campaigns on *World of Warcraft*."

He chuckles and nods at me, giving me a pat on the shoulder in return. My focus goes back to Krissy, who is still looking very uncomfortable. The awkward silence is broken when her eyes look off to the path opening near us. Danica and Matt walk back into view just as the sun was closer to setting. All of us stand up from the ground and join them as they remove their hoods.

"What did you find?" Krissy asks, hugging her waist.

Danica's ears flatten back a bit, not a good sign. Matt was the one to debrief, "Good news first; it's not exclusive to humans. There are a lot of different races that occupy Caldanet. Bad news; it's most definitely a slave-powered mining city. They're mining out some sort of black mineral ores that look very similar to the weapons the Crimson Order uses. The city is run by a gang of bandits calling themselves the Iron Vipers, forcing others to mine the minerals out and forge them into their own weapons and tools."

That brings the mood right into a screeching halt. As if this world doesn't suck enough with racist, imperialistic knights led by a phantom usurper and flesh-eating monsters. Why not sprinkle a little bit of slavery and trafficking into this nightmare?

"Bauer, no offense, but your developing company is really fucked up," Riley states flatly.

"I had nothing to do with this part of the process, Seabiscuit. I was part of the team that did the coding and landscaping. This is my first time getting this far into the story of the game. I had nothing to do with the environmental habitation or NPC development..."

"Anyway!" Danica interrupts. "We also found out about the Daggertip Arena. It's some sort of gladiator arena that punishes workers by making them fight each other in death battles. Winners get sent back to the mines."

"Jesus H. Christ, what is wrong with this game?!"

I bring it back to the situation at hand, "What about the Keystone? Anything about it going around?"

Danica and Matt shake their heads. "The best bet is that it's in the hands of the head bandit here. Maybe we can find out who exactly the psycho is, beat the shit out of them, and get it from them."

"This head bandit may also know where my party is." He's still determined to find anyone from his party. Probably the only thing I admire about the guy

"Okay, so here's the plan. We go in and try to blend in as best as we can, scout the different islands to determine the authority of the city, then rendezvous back here to debrief," I suggest.

Crickets. Total crickets. No one said a thing. Everyone is just staring at me weird.

"You all follow this guy?" Matt asks around with zero irony. "You can't expect that to really be the plan? This is not going to end well. We're going to get caught and put in chains. We should go in hard and fast, find the Keystone and rescue my team."

Suddenly, I feel less bad about my plan because everyone's now glaring at him.

"Sounds like a plan to me!" Mark calls out with a dry laugh. "Let's storm a *city* where we have no idea what their security is like, kick in the doors of every building we pass, *eventually* find the head bandit and take the Keystone that they may not even have, and somehow miraculously find your team of drones! Piece of cake!"

"Okay, then you come up with something, you damn child! Because that is what you are: Children!"

The argument suddenly comes to a stop when we hear the unsheathing of weapons coming from around us. A bunch of men and women in leather armor with fur trimming on the neckline, the top of their gloves and boots, and along the cuirasses are now surrounding us. Their armor is outfitted with hooded faceguards with rounded eyeholes to protect their eyes while leaving an opening to show their bared teeth. On their leather breastplates, a dark colored coiled snake with its jaws opened wide, indicating that they're pare of the Iron Vipers. Each of them is holding weapons that look forged from the metal that was described by Danica and Matt.

"Looks like some fresh stock for the mines, fellas," one of the bandits chuckles. The others laugh at the idea.

One of the female bandits chimes in, "A couple of them may be perfect for Bryce's personal collection." That gets some uncomfortable coos and wolf calls from the others.

"Does not matter," a huge bandit with a warhammer in his hands spits as he ambles closer to us. This brute is the biggest Orc I've ever seen. Stone gray skin, large arms and legs that could crush boulders, a jaw full of jagged and broken teeth, and armor that looks slightly tougher than the others. With how the others shut up when he spoke, it's apparent that he's in charge of this little band of merry dicks. "We chain them and throw them in the mines. The ones that give you the most trouble, throw them in the arena."

Without another word, the bandits howl and charge in. The six of us quickly arm ourselves and circle up shoulder-to-shoulder. The closest bandits to me are a human with a flail and a Tiefling with two daggers, who rage in with no coordination towards me. I flourish my dagger and quickly move to my right, dodging a flail overhead attack, and parrying a dagger swipe. The parry makes me stumble back a little, giving me a chance to invoke my new blessing; *"Sacred Armor!"* My dagger lights up red after pricking my palm, and the aura swirls around me in a swift motion, making me feel slightly stronger. I smirk at my enemies spinning my dagger and gesture at them like I'm in a Bruce Lee movie, egging them on. The human roars at me and comes running with his flail swinging around his head until he spins and extends his arm to attack. In response, I run at him full-speed and do a baseball slide at his feet, connecting with his shin and causing him to fall onto the ground with his flail flying out of his hand. Quickly getting back up, I suddenly jerk forward after feeling something hit me in the back. I turn around to see the Tiefling looking at one of his daggers, now blunted at the tip, then back at me. My Sacred Armor blunted his dagger after he tried stabbing me in the back. Recovering from his shock, the Tiefling throws it aside and flourishes his second one at me. He and I lock eyes and circle each other slowly looking for an opening. My eyes shoot to other parts of the fight to see how my friends are doing, and my concentration was lost in an instant. I see Krissy fending off an Elf with two swords and a Tabaxi with a single sword against her two axes. She's fighting back with grace and precision that's a credit to her class and race, holding them off as best as she can. But, in the heat of the fight, she fails to notice the lead bandit taking his huge warhammer and connecting the pommel to the back of her neck, rendering her unconscious.

"Krissy!" That was all the time my opponent needs before bull-rushing me and driving his foot into my chest, knocking me back onto the ground. I grunt loudly as I look up at the Tiefling about to bring his dagger down on my head. I quickly bring my arms up in a cross over my face and feel the force of the dagger on them, pushing my arms in to my face and hearing a crunch in my nose. The Sacred Armor holds up enough for me not to get stabbed through my arms, but the Tiefling pushes as hard as he can to try and pierce my armor until he's thrust off me to the side by a rush of black smoke. I shoot up from the ground to see Matt standing over the Tiefling with his sword lodged into the bandit's chest, quickly pulling it out to walk over and offer me a hand off the ground.

"Come on, kid. We're not out of this yet," he urges as I take his hand and pull myself up. Scanning the battle, I see Mark and Danica tag-teaming against three bandits. Mark is pushing back with his spear shaft against a female Orc that's fighting with a two-handed mace. While they're locked in a struggle, Danica vaults over him and pounces on the Orc with a hiss and tackles her to the ground. Those two wrestle for dominance, leaving Mark to fend off against a human and a Dwarf. The human draws back an arrow pointed at the Triton and fires. Thanks to his racial traits, Mark is very flexible and quick as he darts and ducks aside before hurling his spear at the human and catching him in the shoulder. The Dwarf roars out and charges with his battle axe, giving a large sweeping swing at his target. Mark lunges backwards before getting his feet kicked out from under him and landing with a thud. The dwarf rears back an overhead slash but fails to see him yank his arm and having the axe met with the shaft of his spear. I never noticed before, but Mark has a wire attached to his arm to bring his spear back to him *Scorpion*-style, much to his luck.

"I'll give the fish a hand," Matt says as he flourishes his sword. "You better go help out your Stormlord friend."

My attention shifts over to Riley, who's getting horse-wrangled by a couple of bandits. One of them has a lasso around one of his arms while the other one tries roping his legs. Riley grunts loudly, rears up and kicks out with his front legs, connecting with a bandit's face and knocking him far back. With his hand held high in the air he shouts, "*Storm Javelin!*" A long bolt of lightning extends in his balled-up fist. He cocks back and hurls it at the bandit that roped his other arm. The bolt sails and pierces through his gut, sending him flying back until the bolt sticks him against a nearby tree. He stands straight and proud of himself, not noticing that the one he kicked down is about to lasso him again before I come running and dropkick him from the side. Both of us go down hard into the ground, but Riley hears what happened and gallops over, rearing up to bring his hooves down on the bandit. I hear the crunching of bones before I get back up.

"Jesus, that was brutal…"

Riley shakes his head while huffing, "No one tries to rope me down."

My head whips around to scan the battlefield and look for Krissy. The last thing I see is the large Orc holding her over his shoulder and running towards the city below.

"Stop him! He's got Krissy!" The bandit turns back to me and smirks, holding out his warhammer and muttering something. The head of the weapon starts to glow bright orange before a huge wave of fiery energy erupts from it straight at Riley and me. We don't react fast enough before the wave hits us and sends us flying backwards. It feels like being blasted by a jet engine, the heat and the force that came at us, searing and painful. I land hard on the ground, smacking my head on the ground and black out from the pain.

CHAPTER 29

My eyes flutter open to Danica pouring a health potion into my mouth. "Thank God, you're awake!"

I grunt and cough as I look at myself as best as I can, seeing that the magic fire broke through my Sacred armor and singed my arms badly. "Ahh, shit… what happened?"

"That Hulk blasted us with some sort of magic," Riley explains. I look at him and see patches of his horse half burnt like my arms. "He took Krissy. We didn't get to her in time."

My heart sinks. Krissy was kidnapped by psycho slavers. "W-we've gotta get her back!" I try getting up, but the searing pain knocks me back down.

"Easy, Romeo," Mark says as he kneels next to me. "Let that health potion do its thing first."

I grunt hard in protest, but the pain is too much. It feels like I fell into a bonfire.

"The Crest sensors definitely did their job," Matt observes, rolling his shoulder. He sees the look I gave him but shows no remorse. "Our engineers made sure that the Crests could map the brain's synapses that way it reacts to the sensations a player's avatar feels. To increase the interactive experience by approaching realism. It's incredible what we're able to accomplish these days."

"Sure, while also making us feel pain to the point of death, you dick," Danica spits at him.

The health potion starts to sooth the burning in my arms, giving me a chance to find the strength to stand back up. "We need to get Krissy back before it's too late."

"We thought of that," Mark says as he puts a hand on my shoulder, causing me to tense a bit. "Sorry. Anyway, the bandits we took down still have their armor on. We can sneak into the city with their armor on so we can go by unnoticed. We'll try to scour the city as best as we can, find out where she is and get her back. We're not leaving until she's back, man."

I nod. Everything in me just heats up. There's no way I'm about to lose her because of us not being careful and getting ambushed the way we did. I hold my side in pain before I help strip the bandits of their armor. The Iron Vipers may be psycho slavers, but they sure equip themselves well enough, as if they're up against an army. That won't stop me if they've done anything to Krissy. We finish removing the armor and move the bodies behind one of the groups of bushes nearby. After I put my armor on, feeling wrong and awkward, but it'll have to work for now. I look to everyone else's armor, all looking like fresh recruits except for Riley. Centaurs stick out like a sore thumb if there aren't any others around, and this made the next part hard.

"Riley, you may be sidelined for this one. There weren't any Centaurs down there... none that were free, at least. A few of them were pulling carts of that black iron ore around," Danica explains to him.

Riley groans and shakes his head, "No way. I'm not sitting this one out."

"There may be a way you can help," Matt chimes. "While I was looking around, there were a lot of netted loads of ore and some fragile equipment. We may need you to be ready with an escape plan. If you can use your abilities to create distractions or avenues out of that place, you'll be our best shot."

Riley still doesn't like that, but even I think it's the best move at this point. "Riley... remember how we were excited we got for *AC: Unity*? When we were able to play together and to our strengths? You created distractions and pulled attention away while I used it to clear a path to our target? Treat this the same. You're not out of the loop, you're the architect of their downfall."

He sighs a bit and nods, "I get it. It's a stealth mission. Okay. I'll try to scale the upper levels without raising suspicion. Give me some sort of sign if you guys get into trouble. A puff of smoke or sound or something?"

"You'll know when it happens. Good luck, man."
He takes my arm firmly before he trails off to find the paths
to the upper levels. I look back at the others and give them
a nod before we head towards the city. The closer we get to
Caldenet, the uglier my thoughts get about what could
possibly be happening with Krissy. I can taste salt and dry
dust in the air almost makes me choke with every step I
take on the path before coming to a rope bridge leading to
one of the stone-carved spires that's poking out of the earth
like the tip of a dagger. The rope bridge gets slightly
wobblier with each step we take, and the ringing of
pickaxes gets louder from beneath us. I look down slightly
to see assembly lines of people moving in and out of mine
caverns, all with their heads down low like they're on death
row. It's making me sick to watch. I return my gaze to the
spire ahead, seeing carved windows and doors lit up with
torches. Along some of the walls of the spire are fluttering
banners that bear the insignia of the Iron Vipers, a darkened
snake coiled up to look like chain links with its mouth wide
open and fangs showing. The clamoring of voices floods
the air and bounces off the cavern walls.

Suddenly ahead, a group of Vipers are making their
way to the bridge when they spot us. They wait for us to
finish crossing. They're each different races but are led by
a human bandit with more protection and a larger weapon.
*The Vipers must gain better equipment with every increase
of renown or promotion that they get, maybe even
magically fueled one like the one that blasted me and Riley.*
We reach the end of the bridge and pass by them when the
human grabs my arm.

"Did you finish the job?"

I look at him through the eyes of my helmet, feeling his rough hand grip my arm. I turn to the others, who are faced off with the other bandits. I look back at the human and nod, trying not to show any hesitation.

"Any left alive?"

I grunt in his grip and shake my arm loose. "They're dealt with. The horse-leg took off into the Grave Expanse, but he won't be much trouble."

The human smirks and chuckles, "Another band of heroes falls to the venom of the Vipers. Good work. Bryce will be pleased. Go get your earnings and head to the Arena. We've got some fresh entertainment down there."

I nod slightly in response before they step onto the bridge we came in on. Mark comes up next to me and leans in close, "They're fucking crazy. We need to be careful."

"I agree." I pull myself together and look around carefully, "There's gotta be a way to get Krissy and find the Keystone. With this many bandits, it's gonna be hard to get around and get Krissy out unnoticed."

"Not to mention that the Keystone may be more difficult to acquire if it's with this 'Bryce' character," Matt points out.

"Then we split up into pairs," Danica suggests. "Matt and Connor can make their way down to find Krissy and anyone else they can. Mark and I will go look for the Keystone in the upper levels. We'll meet back up at that far rock spire once we have everything. Okay?"

Mark groans and stares Matt down, "If you throw my friend into the shit, I'll stick you like a worm."

"Very intimidating, Gills," Matt retorts. I still think this guy is bad news, but in all honesty, it's better for him to try something on me than to try it on them.

"Be careful. Don't let these guys get the better of you." Mark nods and shakes my hand in response before he and Danica start making their way down to the upper levels.

I sigh and turn towards the bridge that leads down to the lower levels, followed closely by Matt. "Do you ever think you put too much faith in your friends? This isn't some fairy tale. You don't win this game by being a Boy Scout, but by being cunning and smart."

"Right! I should be calculating and cold like one of the ass hats that designed this hellhole," I spit as we walk lower, pointing down past the bridge we were walking on. I point to a bunch of men, women, and even children, mining into the cavern walls for the black iron with shackles around their necks and ankles, malnourished and in severe pain. As we continue, I can see that most of the miners have these large marks on their backs, some fresh some not so fresh. Lashes from a guard's whip. "You really must be proud of yourself."

"I told you, I had no hand in the world building or the NPC programming. The landscaping, like the build of these cliffs, *that's* what I did. In fact, this specific region was meant to be a mercenary encampment where players would challenge the head mercenary for command of the camp. Everyone loves a good underdog side quest."

I roll my eyes until we get to the end of the bridge and make it to a deep walkway that overlooks many of the miners toiling away at the walls of black iron. Some of the miners turn to us for a moment before flinching away, going back to mining for the ore. It makes my gut wrench. They're afraid of the armor we're wearing, the armor of their wardens. These bandit psychos have the miners mentally abused and trained to work in the presence of them without question. It's like some serious Greco-Roman imperialistic slavery. If Matt wasn't in charge of the character behaviors or the development of the social interactions, he's still part of the development of this hell.

We walk along the ridge passing the miners who hardly tear their eyes away from the ore they're chipping at. Suddenly, a loud cheer and roar of voices comes from the lower levels of the stone-carved city. Matt and I look to each other with realization that the cheers must be coming from the Daggertip Arena. We see several bandits making their way down to the lowest level while others start to herd the miners away from their stations into these dug-in tunnels like a flock of sheep.

"Must be sending them to their cells while the guards watch the fights," Matt guesses.

"Fucking savages," I whisper. Ahead of me is a line of bandits going down a dug-out staircase leading to the bottom.

Matt is sticking close by me as the bandits rush past us down the stairs. "Tell me about the team you came with? Who are they?"

"Jack, Robert, Annette, and Lorena. My closest friends and colleagues from SnoWire. We developed the game in its alpha stage. It was meant to be a small operation of very large minds working to reinvent RPG experiences that a largely advancing world has never seen before. Suck it, Elon Musk."

"Wait, you need five to operate the game. So how..." Then I remember. He said one of his team was killed in-game. I wonder what that means for them in the Outside.

"Robert," Matt says in a hushed breath. "I just hope he's okay in the labs."

"Is that where you guys set up the game mat?"

He nods but doesn't respond as we hit a wall of mercenaries that are trying to huddle around a large enclosure made of stone with iron bars. They were all cheering and clapping for something we couldn't see. I'm not quite ready to see how bad this was gonna be, but I push through the crowd ahead of me. The more I push through, the more I start to see of the enclosure. It has large pillars of stone wrapping all around in a large rectangular shape. The top of the pillars had been carved into large spikes pointing at a downward angle like spear tips into the arena. I push past more of the mercenaries to try and look down into the arena. Suddenly, the crowd goes silent and looks up to a balcony that was overlooking the arena. Atop of the balcony, a figure in heavy-clad leather armor with black iron pauldrons, chest plate, and shin guards, topped with a leather hood that covered their face stands near the edge and peers down into the arena.

A slow chant starts in the crowd. *"Bryce! Bryce! Bryce!"* I think we just found the leader of the Iron Vipers.

Bryce's arms lift up to quiet his subordinates, and the chanting dulls to a stop. He begins to speak in a menacingly playful voice, "Vipers! Today is a day of celebration and glory! Today, we sanctify Daggertip Arena with new blood!"

The bandits go absolutely nuts and roar in thunderous applause. They all suddenly look down into the arena where doors creak open loudly on the north side. In the now-open doors, two bandits emerge pulling on the arms of a red-skinned, white-haired, woman who's thrashing against their grip. They throw her onto the dusty ground of the arena and retreat inside of the doors they came from. The woman looks up after dusting herself off. It's Krissy!

The south doors suddenly pull open, and two more bandits come out with iron clasped rods attached to the necks of two of the ugliest humanoids I've ever seen. Tall, mangy spotted fur, standing on canine legs, clawed hands, slobbering muzzles and beady yellow eyes. I recognize them from *D&D*; Gnolls. Humanoid hyenas with wild looks in their eyes as they glare hungrily at Krissy. She looks back very nervously at them with her hands balled into fists while they were released from their collars and their guards close the doors behind them.

I'm about to pull my dagger out until Matt grabs my wrist and gestures back up in Bryce's direction. The bandit leader is holding one of his hands out towards the arena with a stone that fits snug in his gloved palm. The stone starts to shimmer in a soft green glimmer until it grows into a glowing ray of iridescent green that shines down on the arena. Krissy glances up and freezes, as do the two Gnolls, watching the green ray cast down on them. The stone dims back down in time for Bryce to yell, "We all know the rules! Only one has a weapon to defend themselves! Winner lives, loser feeds the murkodiles with their dead flesh! Let us see who has the strongest desire to live!"

Krissy and the Gnolls glare back at each other with a crazy glare of hunger I can't begin to understand. I wait to see if she's the one with the weapon, but she just crouches in a wrestling position waiting for an attack. The two Gnolls separate and crawl on all fours facing her down. It's an eerily long staring contest, and the bandits in the crowd start to howl at the three of them to do something. That's when one of the Gnolls snaps its jaws and pounces at Krissy, who's taken by surprise and tackled to the ground. Her attacker pins her to the ground and drools over her as it quickly reaches behind its back and pulls out a small black iron dagger, raising it up to stab down. My heart stops and I lose my ability to speak, thinking this was it for her and I can't do anything about it. But in an unexpected twist, the second Gnoll comes barreling into the first one, thrusting him off Krissy and wrestling him for dominance. The two bark and growl like hungry hounds to take control of the dagger.

"What... but they came in together," I whisper, finding my voice again. "They looked like a tag team. What the hell happened?"

"I think I know," Matt ponders. "Bryce's relic is a Keystone. It must irradiate some sort of influence to make its targets lose their inhibitions and act radically. Like the red one."

I think about his theory, then reflect back on the purple stone from the Bowels. Each stone we've collected has had a different effect on those exposed to their power.

The purple Keystone twisted and corrupted the Centaurs into pack monsters, while the red one caused everyone to attack each other in a blind fury in both life and death. So, what is it about this green one? I turn my focus back to the fight, and something even stranger happens. Krissy shoots up, looks to the Gnolls, and screams, "*Give me that dagger!*" Like a red blur, she darts at the hyena-men and jumps into the fray trying to wrestle the dagger away from them. The three of them rip and tug at the dagger with all their strength until it suddenly goes flying out and away from them. When it hits the ground, the three of them stare at it then glare at each other. One of the Gnolls snarls and clamps its jaws around Krissy's arm, making her yell out in pain. As it bites down hard, she starts punching it in the face repeatedly until it yelps out and lets go of her. She then darts after the dagger with a crazed hunger in her eyes only to be shoulder checked by Gnoll number two. She rolls onto her side until she's back up on her feet in a stare down with the beast, stealing glances back and forth at the dagger just a few feet away from them.

I glance back up at Bryce's balcony, watching him hold the stone out again, making it shine down on them. When I look back down to Krissy and the Gnoll, they both yell out like animals and crash into each other in a frenzy. It howls in a broken voice, snapping its jaws, and slashing at Krissy, but her strikes were quick and aggressive, and it seems that the beast didn't have a chance against her. With a winding of her fist, it catches on fire and shoots forward, connecting with its muzzle, blasting it back into the stone-carved wall. The Gnoll falls limp as its head began to smoke. Krissy huffs and walks to the dagger, picking it up and staring at it with intense hunger. Her head turns slowly to her final opponent, who starts skulking towards her on all fours with teeth baring at her. "You killed my brother you hell-spawned whore! Give me that dagger, now!"

"Come and get it, you flea-bitten dog!"

The Gnoll sprints at her in a fury and leapt into the air with claws extended. Krissy hardly has time to react before his full weight lands on her, making them both tumble to the ground. I yell out "No!" in response, but it's masked by the overwhelming cheer from the bandits. The cheers come to a sudden pause as the Gnoll's body starts to squirm as if to rise over her dead body, but his body slumps over with his tongue lolling out and eyes rolled back while Krissy rises to her feet and holds a bloody dagger in the air. "*Mine!*" she yells out in victory. The bandits yell out in approval as she cackles.

That's when I put two and two together; this was a mining slave camp where they mined a precious ore that is used for tools and weapons, the bandits were wild with their attacks like they would do anything for the armor and weapons they would get for bringing in captives or killing trespassers, and the fighters in the arena aren't fighting for their lives but for the weapon they can use.

"Greed. The Keystone's curse is inflicting greed."

CHAPTER 30

The crowd of bandits clap and cheer for the victorious Tiefling, who can't tear her eyes away from the dagger in her hands, still dripping with Gnoll blood.

"So," Bryce calls down, "our recent catch has an overwhelming will to survive? Or does she simply desire our most precious resource in the Vale?" That invokes whoops and boos from the bandits. "Perhaps this creature will be the new champion of Daggertip?" An even bigger ensemble of boos came from the crowd.

"We can't just let them throw gladiators at her," I growl under my breath.

"We can't expose ourselves in a sea of enemies," Matt argues back. "We need to be smart. Let them put her back into the cell they got her from, we'll search for her and bust her out."

The sound of another set of doors opening draws our attention back to the arena. "Let's see if we have ourselves a new champion by putting the Tiefling against our very own! You know who is coming, you filthy rats," Bryce calls out with glee in his voice.

From the doors in the arena, a single person walks out without a bandit escort. This one is a woman wearing a light blue silk outfit like an old-school belly dancer that leaves very little to the imagination in terms of her figure, her blond hair is tied back into a high ponytail with a blue ribbon, some strands of hair tucked back behind long pointed ears. Her outfit is made complete with brass bangles on her wrists, knee high boots, and a silk cloth that wraps around her stomach. This woman begins to strut around with her eyes focused on Krissy, gritting her teeth in response. Whoops and cat calls come from the bandits, which is sort of uncomfortable for me to hear but also has me thinking back the fight outside of the city, where a couple of them said that we'd make good "additions" for Bryce.

"Oh my god," Matt gasps out with his eyes fixed on the other one.

"Dude, keep it in your pants."

"No! I know who that is!"

The crowd falls silent again as the woman is now merely feet away from Krissy. Bryce chuckles and holds his arms out, "Behold! The Temptress of Terror! The Sinister Spelldancer! Orilana!"

"That's Lorena!" Matt hisses.

"Lorena?! Like 'SnoWire, partner in development' Lorena?"

Bryce chuckles from his perch and holds the stone up again, "Let's see which of these lovely warriors will be given the privilege of being the Champion of Daggertip and bring glory to the name of the Iron Vipers!"

"We have to stop them from killing each other," Matt urges.

"Well, *that's* the fucking understatement of the hour, isn't it? We need to get in there."

"What about the Keystone?"

Too many things are happening at once and too many things that can go wrong. *Where the hell are Mark and Danica?* I pull my attention back to the arena, seeing Krissy and Lorena walking circles around each other like a couple of predators fighting over territory. Krissy grips the dagger firmly with a snarling look on her face, but her opponent looks comfortable and confident in the moment. Lorena starts to slowly dance in place, twisting and spinning with her eyes locked onto Krissy. In the process, she starts to become surrounded in a rippling aura of air. Krissy must've gotten tired of this display because she flourishes the dagger in her hand and lunges for her. What happens next is like an illusion because Krissy seems to miss entirely and flies straight through Lorena, landing roughly on the ground. The bandits whistle and howl in approval towards the elf, who smiles and curtsies in response to her adoring fans.

"What the fuck was that?" I ask aloud. This time, one of the nearby bandits hears me and answers.

"What are you, new here? She's an elven Spelldancer. Her dances are enhanced with magic. The more she moves, the stronger she gets. That was her evasion dance, causing her enemies to literally pass through her. It is very alluring, know what I mean?"

I raise an eyebrow, both in confusion and wonder. I can only imagine the person that suggested that kind of a class for this game to create a virtual stripper. Gross.

Matt yanks my arm to pull me away, "They can't finish this fight. You wanted to get her out of the arena, we need to do it now. Your centaur friend is around somewhere waiting to create a distraction, I'm going to give him a sign. Get their attention in the meantime." In that instant, he disappears into the crowd and out of sight.

"That damn snake." I look back to the arena and watch the girls stand off against each other. Krissy recovers from her spill and bars her teeth at Lorena, who sways back and forth rhythmically. *The more she moves, the stronger her magic is.* Krissy needs to get her to stay still, but under the influence of the keystone, I know she wasn't going to stop trying to defend her prize. *They're fighting over the black iron like it's gold... and there's only one there. What if there's more?*

In a moment of daring, I make a dumb move and start swiping weapons and tools from the belts of the bandits, pushing them through the bars of the enclosure and into the arena. They start getting confused to the point of grabbing onto me to get me to stop. I struggle hard against them until they hold me still and rip my helmet off. I try to pull away from them as best as I can, but they start to usher me through the crowd into an opening that overlooks the arena.

"I see we have a party crasher," Bryce calls out from above. "Perhaps we are just given a gift from the gods that wish to see more blood spilled in the arena! Toss him in!"

I struggle more, but I'm seriously outnumbered. With a large heave, they pick me up and toss me into the arena, plummeting down hard and fast. The height from the top to the floor below must have been two floors up because I slam hard, and it hurt a lot. My health must've taken a huge beating because I felt incredibly weak as I leaned up from the ground holding my shoulder. My eyes flutter open to see both Krissy and Lorena glaring down at me. At ground level, I can now see the effects of the Keystone on them; their eyes are giving off a creepy green color. Krissy is white knuckling that friggin' dagger and Lorena is looking down at me like I was going to mug her.

"Ladies, you are given another opponent that wants to steal your prize and your title," Bryce taunts. "Show him your will to win!"

"W-wait... Krissy, don't let the Keystone mess with you. It's me, Connor."

"You are *not* getting my prize, you pig-faced freak!" Krissy snarls as she flourishes the blade.

"Both of you are going to fall," Lorena adds while removing the silk cloth from her belly and starts twirling it. It begins to shimmer like the end of a blade with the flexibility of a whip.

"Shit." I pull my dagger from my belt and wait for the attack. The air is calm and quiet as the bandits wait to see what would happen. "Krissy... I don't want to hurt you... snap out of it, please. Lorena, I know you're a player. I'm here with Matt Bauer, he's been looking everywhere for you."

Neither of them so much as blink. The only thing I hear is a small whistling sound. Their eyes travel upward, so I do the same to see a whistling line of smoke like a firework going straight into the air. It makes a *pop* sound in the air. Small crashes in the background follow, causing the bandits to murmur and shuffle around. One flash of lightning soars across the sky and connects with a nearby lifted wench holding a netted bundle of black iron ore, causing it to fall and crash on top of a group of bandits.

"Someone is attacking our compound!" Bryce yells out, holding up the keystone. It shimmers green over his army, "Find them and bring them to me! I will handle our entertainment!" The bandits spread out with weapons drawn, ready to destroy whoever was destroying their enterprise. My gaze goes up to the balcony to see Bryce leap and plummet towards the three of us with what looks like a long, pointed cape that flows behind him. We all back away from where he lands, realizing that it's not a cape, but a long, scaly tail that coils to support his fall. The tail is bronze with black diamonds that trail up under his leather armor, which looks much bulkier than it had before, now that it's up-close. His hands come up and pull the hood down to reveal a serpentine face like a real viper that shared the same color as his tail, but his slit eyes are iridescent green like the keystone he held in his hands. Bryce is a Yuan-Ti, a race of serpent folk that are known infamously for their aggression.

He grips the Keystone firmly in his hand, noticing it's not affecting me like it should. "I find it interesting that you do not feel the power of this stone. It has brought me great wealth and power since I dug it up in the Iron Vale. All who are in its presence fall to the most intense and hungering of emotions: Greed. Perhaps you have felt this power before, but from another stone? Give me your satchel."

"Let them go, you slimy shit," I sneer in return, gripping my dagger carefully.

Bryce smirks and snaps his clawed fingers, causing Krissy and Lorena to move to his side. "Your Elf and Tiefling friends want what I offer. If I tell them that your death would give them their deepest desires, they will destroy you and, from the sight of you, that will not take much effort."

I'm shaken. Both of them stood ready, sharing the same look in their eyes as he does. They're his slaves. "Whatever plan you have devised to bring my reign to an end will not work, orc. My men are numerous, and they are driven by their greed."

I clench my fists tightly and look to Krissy, who is itching to attack if it meant she could have more of whatever this snake was offering. Lorena has her hands propped on her hips in a scary confident way while Bryce's tail snakes and strokes her legs in an uncomfortable way.

"Fine… I'll give it to one of them to give to you. Do it this way, or I'll kill them both to get to you," I offer.

The snake man chuckles deeply, "Agreed. Orilana, retrieve my prize." Lorena nods with no hesitation and steps towards me, holding her hand out. I reach for my satchel and pull the red Keystone out.

"I hope you're as good as Matt, Lorena. You're gonna need it," I say softly as I hand it off. The second it leaves my hand I feel an overwhelming wave of greed and hunger wash over me. It cripples me to my knees and causes my brain to pound. I can hear Bryce laugh as he slithers towards me, coiling his snake tail around me tightly.

"It does not matter what race we are, or what status we hold ourselves to, Orc. We are all hungry for more. Power, wealth, love, lust, possessions, all of it. It only takes the right spark to allow us to give in," he hisses at me. "But you, I do not believe you deserve to feel the satisfaction of your desires." His tail squeezes harder around me, and his mouth opens wide, baring two large fangs. I see him preparing to bite me until a shimmering ribbon wrapped itself around his neck, causing him to release me and shoot his hands to the wrap around his neck, dropping the Keystone. I drop hard to the ground and look up, seeing Lorena with her ribbon around the Yuan-Ti's neck and pulling hard at it.

"You know what they say? Cut off the head of the snake... the body withers." With a forceful yank, his head pops off his body like a cork. His body twists and flops wildly as I rise to my feet, breathing heavily and looking in Lorena's direction. She wrangles her ribbon back like a lasso and ties it around her waist, "You gonna stand and stare, or help your friend?"

Krissy! Past Bryce's body, I see her holding her head in pain. I run past Lorena and jump over the body, holding Krissy's shoulders. "Kris! It's okay! You're okay! He's dead!"

I swear I can hear her grinding her teeth before she slowly came back to a full standing position. Her eyes began fading from the green color back to their original yellow. A brief pause passes between us before she pulls me into a tight hug, "Connor! You came for me! Thank you!" I hold her close and sigh deeply. My eyes shoot open and see the bandits from the stands aiming arrows at the three of us. "Goddammit," I sigh. We separate and look up at them. They may not be under the stone's influence anymore, but they're clearly pissed off. The bandits knock their arrows back and look ready to let loose.

"Some rescue," Lorena spits.

Before I can retort, a loud voice yells out, "Forever Free!"

Some of the archers are suddenly thrown over the edge and fall into the arena. A bunch of collared miners begin attacking the bandits with their pickaxes and shovels, being pummeled, and tossed over the edge. The doors on the north side of the arena open with a burst, and in gallops Riley with a bunch of miners behind him.

"Riley!"

He smirks and holds his arms out, "Who's the horse-man?! I am!" Behind him follows a big brute of a human miner with the same weapon of that Orc that took Krissy resting on his shoulder. This mountain of a man joins Riley's side as they approach us, "I am Djaren. This Centaur aided me and my people free ourselves from the mines of the Vale. We understand you are the Vanguards who are helping Albistair become free from our strife. For that, we are grateful."

From behind him, the miners surround Bryce's writhing body and raise their weapons. "The Viper is dead! The Viper is dead!" they chant together. The body wiggles one last time, causing some drop orbs to fall from his utility pouches. Riley quickly scoops them up and puts them into his satchel, giving me a slight nod in assurance.

The south doors swing open and four bandits with their hands tied behind their backs are being led out by Mark and Danica.

"How the hell?" I ask aloud. Mark chuckles proudly and points to his totem, "Did you know these idiots have a feeding pool with two murkodiles in it? I finally got to use this thing right. They were dangling a couple of the slaves over the pool and toying with them while we were trying to find the Keystone. I remember getting really pissed off and then my totem started shining. They spotted us, but one of the murkodiles jumped up and latched its jaws onto the closest one. The other one dropped his shit and ran."

"It was nasty but pretty neat at the same time," Danica adds. "We found these four messing around in the one of the spires that we went to after getting the slaves down. They were trying to get rid of some papers before we came and surprised them. Check this out."

She hands me a page and I notice it has a large red kite shield with a black sword in the middle. The sign of the Crimson Order. I begin to read the page:

Bryce,

Your continuous contribution to the cause of the Archon has been beneficial and fortuitous. However, it seems you have failed to inform the Order that you have come across the location of one of the five Keystones of the Mortal Gate. It is our duty to inform you that this is your one and only warning to deliver the treasure to our forward camp outside the capitol city. Upon delivery of the Keystone, the Archon will pay you handsomely for your cooperation and will allow the continuation of your operations within the Iron Vale of Caldenet.

Glory to the Archon

My eyes scan over the page a few times before looking back to the others. "We know where to go next. The Archon is trying to collect the Keystones and they've set up a forward camp near the capitol city."

"Lorena!" My head whips around to see Matt running in and hugging the latest addition to our party, who simply blinks rapidly before awkwardly returning it. "I thought you were lost or dead!"

She pulls away from him and adjusts her outfit, "Honestly, I thought the same about you. But I see you made up for your absence by finding some help. Who are they?"

"They're… they're players. The game got out to the public," Matt explains nervously.

Lorena's reaction isn't one of shock or surprise, but one of annoyance. "Great. Just another log to add to the current dumpster fire we're in. Thanks, Dad."

That last remark makes us all cock our heads to the side, but Matt's eyes shoot open as he tries to shush her.

"Wait. Who the hell are you?" Riley asks.

Matt's about to answer for her when she puts her hand in front of his face, "I can speak for myself. My name is Lorena Dawson. I'm Dominic Dawson's daughter."

CHAPTER 31

"You're Dawson's daughter?!"

Lorena rolls her eyes and puts her hands on her hips, "Did I stutter? Yes, I'm his daughter."

"For God's sakes, Lorena! Why would you do that?!" Matt yells at her.

That's where I lose my temper and punch Matt in the face. "You're telling me you knew this whole fucking time and didn't say anything?! You son of a bitch!"

Matt is holding his face before pulling his sword back out, "You want a rematch? I'm tired of putting up with you shit heads! This ends now!" He rushes me with a large slash of his sword, only to be met with the blade of my dagger. I hold fast against his attack, even when I hear my friends trying to get us to stop. We clash our blades back and forth trying to gain dominance in the fight, him with his swift kicks to my sides and my legs, and me with my slashes and punches where I could deliver them. But Matt is quick. Wicked quick. With his agility and stealth exceeding mine, he's able to get more hits in than me and my health is falling fast. The only thing I have on my side is that my armor rating is high enough to provide some protection while my Sacred Armor is on cooldown. I want to smack myself in the head for forgetting that I have more tricks, or blessings, up my sleeve. I drive my foot into Matt's chest to push him away from me as I shout out, *"Granav alnej ukavrengavh!"* The battle focus blessing is beginner level, but it's what can help me get ahead of his quick movements. His white elven eyes dart at me before he disappears in a puff of smoke. I can still hear the others either cheering me on or cussing at me to stop, but my battle focus kicks in for me to duck down. I feel the wind of a flat blade cutting through the air and trimming a few strands of my hair. Matt slides on his knees and twists around in a defensive position, baring his teeth at me. I flip my dagger in my hand and charge at him. We're both about to clash before a strong gust of wind blows us both back to the ground and away from each other.

Lorena is twirling like a ballerina in a stage performance between us while an aura of air spins and twists around her in a shimmer. Slowly, she brings herself to a stop and glares back and forth between us. "If you both are done with your little pissing contest, I'd like to get out of this hellhole."

I dust myself off and stand up, not taking my eyes off Matt. "Fine, let's go."

"Wait."

We all look to the miner, Djaren, as he approaches us with a stone look on his face. "You will not have a simple task of getting to the capitol city. The Crimson Order has it barricaded by large walls with checkpoints at every entrance, which is only open to humans. None of the other races of Albistair are welcome within its walls."

That makes a lot of sense. If it's the capitol city in this forsaken place, humans would feel safe and uplifted from the rest. Especially if they're being protected by the Order and the Archon. But that also means that we would be attacked on site and easily overwhelmed without an army to help us.

"Well, that's just perfect," Mark groans. This causes us all to groan with him.

"Not to mention we're short two Keystones," Riley adds to the mountain of bad news.

"Unless we take that shortcut out that Matt talked about before we came here," Danica suggests.

Lorena's eyes dart at Matt, who shrugs in response. I note the exchange but decide to shelf it for the moment. "Let's just get out of this place. Let the miners retake the Vale."

We take about an hour with the miners helping them gather weapons and free the slaves that are still chained up. It makes me sick to see how many children they have chained up of all races. Once we scour every tunnel of the Vale, we regroup back in the arena to look at the map. Djaren is able to point out the general direction we need to take to find the capitol city, called Sacredcrest. The border of the city was like a giant fortress with about five archer towers, eighteen oil cauldrons, thick stone walls, and a giant door supported with black iron bars. In addition to its build, the capitol itself is populated with legions of Crimson Order knights and families of humans in countless numbers. To top it all off, the way to the capitol is cut off by a large river like a barrier moat.

"So not only does this psycho have a personal army, but he's using innocent and scared people to be cannon fodder between us and him." Djaren nods disdainfully.

"We may have luck with that forward camp outside of Sacredcrest," Krissy says as she drags her finger down to a small circle under the city. "If we're lucky, they'll have something we can use to get in and find the keystone."

"*If* they have either of the last two," Mark points out.

Lorena lets out an amused whistle, "You're a fun bunch of nerds, aren't you?"

"Says the dancing elf witch in a fantasy video game," Riley blurts.

"My dad is stuck in this stupid game, you damn donkey. I don't have to explain myself to *you*. Or anyone, for that matter." With that, she storms off out of the arena with Matt hot on her heels.

My eyebrows shoot up. This girl has a serious attitude. More than what I thought was necessary for this situation. Despite that, we start off after them out of the Iron Vale. The miners gave us good wishes and thanks for aiding them, which puts a smile on my face for helping them. It may be a simulation, but it still felt amazing and fulfilling to help liberate them all from slavery. As we trail after Matt and Lorena, Riley starts handing out the gear drops from Bryce to everyone around. I receive probably the coolest weapon upgrade I could hope for; a stone-carved club staff that's decorated with inscribed runes of Orc origins. It's longer than my first staff and feels perfectly balanced in my hands. The grip is firm and fits in my hands nicely, the pommel is an engraved stone coated in red paint that was almost as thick as blood, and the top resembles a bladed mace head with a glowing red hue trapped in the middle like a caged wisp. At this point, I've never felt stronger or empowered in my life. I look around at what the others got, which are all equally impressive. Krissy's axes now look like raider's axes with hellish adornments decorated on the blades and hilts, which are curved to points. Mark's fishing spear is replaced with a bronzed trident that looks similar to how Aquaman's weapon looks in comic books, only the shaft is wrapped in a tight netting. Danica's cards are still the same, but her paws are now decorated with brass bracers that look like they would hurt getting hit by as much as they look protective. Riley's now has one Stormlord spell bangle on each wrist crackling with sparks and energy. In spite of being stuck here, we are all growing into our roles fairly well. There are two more spheres left, but they wouldn't show us anything. Each of us try to use them, but they remain their forms. My best guess is that each one was for each of the party members, whether we like them or not. I decide to hold onto them until we got more answers from our new "friends."

The walk is awkward and silent, as no one wants to spark up another fight between us. We may have the numbers, but these two were alphas with all the knowledge they need to take us down anytime they want. The smartest move, at least in my opinion, is to wait to see how this new alliance plays out.

Along the way, we come across another small oasis that looks comfortable for a resting spot. Lorena must have the same idea as she's the first to run towards it, with Matt trailing after like a lost puppy. We catch up with them as they start to drink from the water and lie down in the soft grass. I pick a nearby palm tree to lean up against as everyone takes the chance to rest.

"Thank God I can still feel hydration. This is heavenly," Lorena sighs happily as she lays back in the grass. I glance over as she stretches out on the ground, her outfit almost failing to keep her covered. She casts a glance at me and winks, but I immediately turn back and away from her gaze towards Danica and Mark. Mark was in the pool of the oasis getting hydrated while Danica is giggling at him and making faces, which is pretty entertaining since they both are becoming more comfortable.

Riley is on the nearest side of the pool to me, kneeling in the grass and taking handfuls of water into his mouth and into his hair to wring it out. Matt is opposite of Lorena staring daggers at my friends and I, but his gaze hardly stays longer than a moment. On the far side of the pool, Krissy's taken shade under some of the trees and sat against one. She sees me looking and gestures for me to come over to her. I pull myself from the tree and start walking over to her spot, feeling gazes on me from the others.

I take a seat at the tree adjacent from hers and lean back, "You doing okay?"

"No. I'm not," she sighs angrily. "I got mind-jacked by a friggin snake-man and tried to kill you over a stupid knife."

I lean forward with my elbows on my knees, "That wasn't you. That was the Keystone. It did the same thing to me. Made me feel—"

"Hungry?"

I nod, feeling chills run up my spine. "The Keystones… they make you feel very strong emotions. The red one made everyone it affected feel bloodlust and rage, alive or dead. The blue one twists your soul with fear and isolation until you become a monster. The green makes you want everything that someone else has, hungry and envious."

Her eyes shift to Lorena and Matt's spots with a serious hate. "It's their fault. This whole thing is their fault."

"I know, but they're also the ones who can help get us out. I don't like it any more than you, but we need those clowns."

I look over at Matt and Lorena, who look back at us in response. Matt's glare is one of pure disgust and distrust, probably because of the shiner I gave him. Lorena's, on the other hand, was hard to read. Her eyes dart back and forth between me and Krissy with only a slight change of emotion. When she looks at Krissy, it was what you would expect two girl friends would do when one of them spills a secret and the other finds out about it. But when she looks at me, it made me a bit uncomfortable because she's lightly biting her lip.

"I don't trust her at all," I say aloud.

"Well, looks like she trusts you, Casanova."

I groan and pinch the bridge of my nose. "Why do you do that?"

"Do what?"

"Give me shit. I've done nothing but stick my neck out to help you this whole time, and you just make cracks at every turn. I can't figure you out! First, you're super concerned and worried, then you turn around and rip into me with that passive-aggressive bullshit. Are you really that scared of being real with me?"

She shoots forward and smacks me hard in the face. "I'm in this piece of shit game because of *you!* I was just fine being out there on my own until you came around! I didn't need any of this shit!"

I look back at her as calmly as I can holding my face where she hit me. Tears were forming in her eyes. Angry tears?

"But you still said yes. You still agreed to join us in this game. Maybe ask yourself why you did before you take another swing at me."

She stands up and grabs me by the collar, cocking her arm back and holding it. "Because *you* asked me. I should've said *no!*"

"But you said *yes.* And apparently, it's because of me. So, you tell me what kept you from saying no and being back in whatever life you have Outside? What was it about me that made you say yes?"

She stares at me in frustration and lets go of my collar with a grunt. "You want to know why? Because I have nothing else. No one in that shitty city or that shitty school. I was dumped here with nothing and no one. I've worked my ass off to keep a roof over my head and too many people have taken advantage of me and my trust. I'm not letting that happen again. No one is going to use me ever again. When you came fumbling in like some rom-com dork… it was the first time I felt like I wasn't going to be lied to and used."

Her reaction to the stone, and even to the game, starts making more sense to me in that moment. The idea of having someone warp your trust and worm into your head to make you think, say, and do things that you don't want to. I can't begin to imagine what that must be like, but it's clear what it was like for her Outside.

She turns her back on me, tensing up her body so I don't see her break. She doesn't like to be seen as vulnerable, and I just pushed her to it.

"I'm sorry. You didn't want me to pry, and I dug in," I say with a grunt of aggravation and turn to leave.

"Connor."

I turn towards her and am met with a kiss. A deep, lingering kiss that lasts a few seconds. She pulls away and we stare at each other for a moment.

"I said yes because you haven't given me any reason not to trust you. Just… don't dig anymore. Please."

I nod and swallow hard. She turns towards the others and walks over to them. I'm lost in my head for a moment. I didn't think it was going to happen like that, but it was good.

"Jeez, you're all so full of drama."

I whip around to see Lorena leaning against a nearby tree with a hand on her hip.

"That was none of your business," I spit back.

She giggles and shakes her head, "No? Then why did everyone else see what happened?"

I don't know if Orcs can blush, but my face feels hot.

"Where's your pet?" I ask, looking for Matt to be skulking around behind her.

"I told him to take a breather. He's like a stress ball ready to break. I needed to talk to one of you, and you seem to be the head honcho of this band of merry nerds." She moves away from the tree towards me, so it was just the two of us in that moment.

"It's about the place we're going. Sacredcrest? We can't get in, and you know it. Right?"

I nod.

"And that 'shortcut' your friends were talking about? It's neck-deep in terrorghast territory. The way I see it, we're up shit creek without paddles. I need to find my dad and get the hell out of here. So why don't we call it a truce and help each other?" She holds out her hand.

I glance at it, then back to her. "Not yet. You need to answer some questions, and I need straight answers."

She rolls her eyes and drops her hand, "See? Full of drama. Well? Let's hear it."

"The game. What was your dad trying to do? I need to know everything."

Lorena groans, but shrugs in annoyance.

"My dad is the biggest developer of interactive games of this century. He's a damn genius. Everything he worked on and created was meant to give the best immersive experience he could think of. *Valhalla Arena, Arcane Academy Online, Demigod Exodus,* all of them he pushed to the limits of graphic interface and story immersion. But one thing he held onto the most was his first experience playing *Dungeons & Dragons.* He never shut up about it. Every convention he ever attended, he saw how real people took it with their cosplaying, live action role playing, immense tournaments, every fantasy nerd's wet dream. He saw how much people got into it with their games and stories that he wanted to give them what he thought they secretly all wanted; for fantasy to become reality. So, like the genius asshole he is, he spent years working on this very game to make it so real that he forged a living, breathing world. Everything here is alive."

My face must look like I had a stroke, because she cocks her eyebrow and waves her hand in front of my face.

"Th-that's impossible... we're too far behind from that kind of artificial intelligence technology. Dominic Dawson couldn't have developed a program that literally creates life in a digital world. This isn't *Tron*!"

"Think about it, numb nuts," she argues, "Every time we get hit, every time we attack, every sensation that we feel is all immersive augmented reality. Do you see health bars on anything or anyone? Subtitles or dialogue options? No."

I want to argue, but I think back to the human knight we fought outside of the Gorge. He bled and didn't disappear into dust. Those knights I beat down, the blood on my hands, everyone's injuries. None of this should be possible.

"So, your dad created a reality where magic, monsters, tyranny, slavery, torture and death are possible for everyone... Not just NPC's... but—"

"For players, too? Yes."

"Why in the actual fuck would he do that? He designed a game where players get stuck in this place with no fucking way to leave?!"

Lorena sucks air in through her teeth, "That there is the problem. He didn't mean for that to happen. It was some sort of malfunction or miscalculation. He guaranteed everyone that his design was flawless. To prove his point, he was the first one to go in. He hasn't come back out."

My head is spinning. Dominic Dawson got stuck in his own game because he was too proud. "Wait... if your character dies in the game... what happens to you Outside?"

Here's the creepy thing; she doesn't look concerned or scared to answer. She just hums to herself, "Well, most likely your brain fries and shuts down. Best case scenario, you just suffer from brain damage that makes you a vegetable."

"Best case scenario?!"

"Easy, Shrek. As far as I'm concerned, my dad's best people have already begun to work on that so we can safely leave. Until then, we stay alive and look for him. With luck, he'll be able to find us a safer back door out of here and we can all go home. So, let's just play this out."

I back away from her and lean against a tree, slowly sliding down to the ground. *I'm such an idiot. I got all my friends stuck in an augmented reality where they could actually die. For what? Paid off college debt?* That was probably a lie, too.

"The person that sent us this game," I say aloud, "why did they do it? Dawson was stuck in the game the whole time, so he couldn't have done this…"

Lorena shrugs, "Not a clue. Maybe it was the company's idea to test it on the public?"

"That makes no sense at all! They would've sent out beta testing copies to professional gamers. Not a group of college students."

She shrugs again. That was starting to piss me off. "I've been stuck in here for God knows how long. Your guess is as good as mine, Grumpy."

I lay the back of my head against the tree and turn to look at the others. I'm feeling so guilty about all of this. They're in more danger than I thought. And it's all my fault. We need to get out of here. Suddenly, the shortcut out doesn't seem so bad, despite the swarm of monsters that are supposedly lurking and nesting in there.

"The way I see it, your dad deserves to be stuck in the hellscape he created," I mumble.

I expect to get hit, kicked, blasted, something. But instead, she chuckles, "I kind of agree. But he's our only way out. We need him."

"So where is he?"

"My guess is in that forward camp the letter mentioned. The Crimson Order and Archon need knowledge on the keystones, and he's the one with all the knowledge."

That brings up my next question; "The Archon. Who is he? A player? An NPC? Why make a medieval fantasy Hitler?"

"That's out of my wheelhouse," she admits. "My guess is that it's a programmed baddie. The endgame boss battle."

Of course, it would be that simple. Why not?

"Fine. Krissy has the map. Let's find the forward camp and see if Overlord Dawson is there." I get back up to my feet, but Lorena takes my arm before I can get any further.

"Don't say anything to the others. Nothing about what we just discussed."

I raise my eyebrows, "They deserve to know."

"No, they don't. As far as they know, all we need to do is find my dad and get out. The less they know, the safer they are. Matt will keep his mouth shut and I want you to do the same."

"You're making it very hard to trust you."

"Cry me a river. Lips sealed, okay?"

I groan, feeling her grip tighten on my arm. She's not concerned with their safety. She's saving her own skin. Unfortunately, she is right about them not being able to handle the reality. I nod begrudgingly and pull myself away from her.

"Krissy, we need to find that forward camp. Does it show up on your map?"

Krissy shoots daggers from her eyes at Lorena, who's standing behind me, before she pulls out her map. "Looks like the river cuts off a large portion of the map. The capitol is on the other side, and the only opening is about forty miles around."

Everyone groans.

"That would take days. *Weeks* if we run into trouble, which we all know will happen," Riley groans.

"Wait, look here," Mark said as he points closer to mouth of the river. I follow his finger and see a single strip of land that bridges one side of the riverbank to the other. A red tower symbol with the Crimson Order flag on it.

"That must be the forward camp. It's a bridge," he guesses.

"Which could also mean that it's a large concentration of Order knights," I add.

"It's a shorter trek than going around the river," Krissy argues.

"If we approach it at night, we may be able to sneak through," Matt chimes in. No one was listening to him.

"It seems to be about four hours from where we are." Krissy rummages through her satchel and pulled out her logbook. Flipping through the pages, she lands on one and smiles. "Oh, perfect."

I raise an eyebrow as she put the logbook back and pulled out her mount horn, blowing it into the air.

"Krissy, the horses are gone."

"I'm not calling for horses. I'm calling something better."

We all wait until we hear noises coming from the east. Over the ridge, a group of strange figures quickly shuffle their way towards us. A few of us take up our weapons, unsure of what was coming, but Krissy is smirking. The creatures finally come into view quickly, and it makes me gasp aloud. The creatures reminding me of the chocobos. They're a flock of flightless giant bird-like creatures. They're all in different shades of brown, blue, and gray, standing taller than Riley with giant spurred legs like dinosaurs, small wings that flapped against the wind to help them stop, and long necks that supported large beaked heads. The top of their heads almost resembles helmets; crested hard heads that sport three forward-facing antlers.

"What the hell are these things?" Riley asks as he backs away a bit.

"My Logbook calls them ferodons. They're indigenous to the forest areas here. Herbivores, but vicious fighters when they're threatened. The horns on their heads are for defense and territorial marking. They're fast. Faster than horses," Krissy explains. She slowly approaches the head of the flock and holds out her hand to them. The lead ferodon squawks out this strange guttural caw and clacks its beak at her, but she doesn't flinch. It closed the distance curiously before leaning its beak into her outstretched hand. The creature becomes comfortable and nuzzles into her hand. She smiles and strokes its feathers with her free hand.

"Don't approach them too quickly," she instructs. "Let them come to you."

We all spread out, Riley excluded, and wait. One ferodon with a combination of dark and light gray feathers struts towards me a little aggressively. I stand warily as it approaches and uses the same intimidation technique Krissy's did. I keep my hands to myself as it struts closer. It tilts its head like a chicken as it looks at me curiously while I watch it carefully, trying not to instigate a fight or anything. It closes the gap and gently put its head against mine, fitting my head between its antlers, chirping lightly. I chuckle to myself and pet it, looking around to the others as they met their mounts. I watch Krissy mount her creature as it squats down on the ground. We all follow her example and mount the ferodons.

Krissy gently grips a few feathers in her hands, looks ahead of her and calls out, "*Veat!*" The ferodon rears back, squawks out loudly, and darts ahead. Our mounts all repeat the same action as we take off after them.

CHAPTER 32

Say what you will about riding horses, but this is friggin'
amazing! The ferodons are quick and agile in their sprint
across the terrain and through the trees. They're much
quicker than our horses from before, even Riley's having a
hard time keeping up. Danica and Mark look like they're
having fun, winding around each other like children racing
each other around a supermarket toy aisle. It's kind of
adorable. Matt looks tense for the whole ride, not afraid but
driven, which is a little more concerning. Lorena is silent
through the whole ride, but she's smiling. There are some
points where she's trying to pass Krissy, but the alpha
ferodon squawked angrily at Lorena's mount to make it fall
behind. The sun is slowly making its way down over the
horizon, shining a beautiful red and orange glow over the
land. It's easy to forget the kind of crazy place we're in
when there's so much natural beauty and wonder in it.
Even the ferodons helped to make this place more bearable
knowing that there are ambient and understanding forms of
life here.

Krissy's mount starts to slow down as we emerge
from a tree line into a clearing before it comes to a
complete stop, instructing our mounts to do the same.
Ahead of us, the earth broke and dropped. The sound of
loud, thunderous crashing can be heard coming from the
edge of the bank. I slide off the back of my ferodon and
drop onto the ground, stroking its feathers before walking
towards the edge. I reach the edge and look down to see a

river, furiously crashing its waters against the banks on either side. The gap is large, and the river water looks to be about ten feet from the top of it. I feel small drops of water hit my face as I peer down. This river is not as calm and relaxing as the one near the centaur village we were at. I look across the river gap and scanned around, looking for the forward camp. I see a large tower poking over a hill on the other side of the river to the right of where we stopped, maybe a couple of miles away.

"There's the camp. Must be." The others dismount and join me.

"Looks like we're a little far from our destination," Matt points out.

Krissy looks back to the ferodons, "They stopped for a reason. Must be a place they avoid."

"Smart birds," Mark and Danica say at the same time.

I take a moment to assess our situation. We don't know what to expect when we get to that camp, but I am hoping we find Dawson there. He has a lot to answer for.

"Let's leave the mounts here. Maybe if we clear a path, they can come with us."

Everyone nods in agreement. We grab our equipment while Krissy strokes the face of her mount before turning it away. The flock turns back toward the forest and strut off calmly, prompting us to start walking towards the tower.

"What do you think is waiting for us?"

"A legion of pissed off red knights?"

"More jacked up slavers?"

I sigh aloud. "Nothing is ever easy."

As we walk, my focus keeps returning to the river, raging below us like a storm. The wind is light and breezy, so the water's temperament makes no sense. The sun is starting to disappear behind the horizon of the world, and the tower starts to become lit with torches. The closer we get, the more intimidating this tower looks. Clearly it serves as a watchtower that sat at the end of the bridge, painted in crimson red with flags of the Order on all sides of it. The top of the tower has partly closed window openings where torches hung from while also sporting a couple of ballistae pointed at the bridge. Inviting.

"Let's go back towards the trees," I suggest. "Don't let them see us. We need to come up with a plan."

"You mean like back at the Iron Vale?" Matt spits sarcastically. "Why are we following you at all? You stick out like a bad smell."

"And you absolutely suck at insults," Riley quips.

"All of you shut up," Lorena demands. "Let's go to the trees. I don't feel like being skewered by big fucking arrows right now."

With that, we make back for the tree line, just far enough to where we can still see the tower but be covered by the trees. We set up a small area to camp and plan. Using a tree branch and some torn up cloth, we make a torch that's just lit enough for us to see each other but not give away our position.

"We don't know what kind of defense that tower has, other than those ballistae," I point out.

"I don't think we can sneak into this place like last time," Danica sighs worriedly.

"I probably could," Matt smirks with a little too much pride.

"They'd see you too easily with that stick up your ass," Riley spits. He clearly hates this guy, and I can't blame him. He did try to cut his throat before.

Before Matt can say anything else, I hear Mark grunt hard. His webbed hands clutch his head tightly with Danica caressing his shoulders.

"Babe, what's wrong?"

"Ugh... I-I don't know... It's like... ugh, it's like a hundred voices are in my head," he groans. I look to his totem around his neck, but it's not glowing like it did when he heard the murkodile coming.

"What kind of voices?"

"They're angry... rushed... I can't tell what they're saying..."

Suddenly, an ensemble of horns sounds off from the direction of the tower, joined by muffled yells. I quickly snuff out the torch. "Dani, stay with Mark!"

I run out of the tree line, holding my new weapon in my hands, towards the sounds. I hear Riley galloping behind me and a few other footsteps, but I stay focused ahead of me. When the tower comes into view, so do dozens of Crimson Order knights with bows firing off their arrows. But they're not aimed in our direction. They're firing... into the river? I quickly stop to get a better understanding of what was happening. As I watch them fire towards the river, a long brass spear shoots from the water and pierces one of the archers, causing them to fall and plummet to the ground. I inch closer to the edge of the cliff and look down to where the spear came from. Below, eight blue-skinned warriors jump out of the river and latch onto the cliffside, and five more in the water are hurling spears upwards at the Order knights.

"Tritons!"

I watch as the warriors on the cliffside climb up as quickly as possible, being covered by their support in the river. The knights above continue to fire at them with volleys of arrows. A couple of the arrows find their way into the shoulder of one of the climbers, causing them to lose their grip and fall back into the river. One of the ballista bolts pierces the adjacent cliff, causing rocks and soil to dislodge and fall into the river below. One of the tritons in the river fails to notice and gets pummeled by a falling stone.

"We need to help them!"

"We'll give away our position!" Matt argues.

I pull out my Logbook to see if I have any new blessings or Warpriest spells to help, but it gets pulled away by Lorena.

"What are you doing?!"

"They're dead, Connor. That tower has too much resistance. If we try to help, we'll get pin cushioned."

I shake my head trying to argue when I hear yelling from the river. I look back to see that the archers started using fire arrows, hitting the climbers, and sending them back down into the river. The ones below grab their bodies and submerge back into the water. I grip my hands into fists and turn back towards the forest, shoving my way past Lorena and Matt. I return to the campsite where Dani and

Krissy are comforting Mark, tears rolling down his blue face. His gaze comes up to me with a look of pure pain and confusion.

"They were Tritons, like you." I sit down across from him with my elbows resting on my knees. "They were attacking the tower from the river. There were too many knights. They had fire arrows and—"

"I heard them," Mark says in a broken voice. "I heard them in my head… their pain and fear… Why?"

"It must be a racial trait," Riley guesses. "Tritons can breathe underwater but can't speak. They must have some sort of telepathy to communicate that works above and below water. They're a super empathic species, like what happened with the murkodile."

"That's fucked up," Krissy murmurs.

"Why were they attacking the tower?" Danica asks, caressing Mark's back.

He answers, "They were trying to get revenge. I heard them talking about the knights poisoning the waters with the dead or something."

The camp is quiet for a moment. It's like taking a moment of silence for the ones that died trying to charge the forward camp. It keeps bringing me back to the conversation I had with Lorena about this virtual landscape being "alive". Realistic death, loss, pain, and anguish.

"We need to get into that camp," Lorena orders. "So, let's lay out a plan to lay waste to those defenses."

"Are you out of your damn mind?" Riley seems to have had enough of her. "Those ballistae and archers decimated that cliffside! And gods know what their defenses are like anywhere else around the damn camp!"

I want to face-palm after he used the term "gods", but he's right. Without any real intel on the camp's defenses, we would get slaughtered.

"We're not getting anything done tonight. Let's get further out of their range of sight and set up a better camp. We can take inventory and make a plan after," I suggest.

I swear I can feel and hear Matt's eyes roll, but he was outnumbered in the vote. Even with "Princess Lorena" backing him up. We gather up our materials and move further into the tree line until we can barely see the torchlight around the tower. Using the tools and materials provided in our satchels, we manage to make a solid camp in a small patch of level ground surrounded by tall trees. We start taking inventory of our health and mana vials, the state of our weapons and tools, and checking our level vials. Since our fight with the Iron Vipers, everyone in the camp besides myself was able to level up, which didn't make sense until I guessed it was because I didn't actually fight. Riley's mana level is increased for him to manage more frequent and stronger magics. Danica's stealth and cunning are raised by +2 after her tactics to free the slaves. Krissy's stamina is increased by +1, which must have pissed her off after hearing about Lorena's +3 magic and +1 agility increase. Matt, surprising me the most, gets an increase in stealth and charisma by +2, and I didn't even see him do a thing. Then again, he's a Shadow Stalker, so it kind of fits. I look for Mark to see if he got anything, but I watch him walk through the trees and away from the camp. I took this chance to follow him, letting the others stay in the awkward campfire circle. I can't tell where he could possibly be going until I start hearing the crashing of waves. The trees open back up to bring Albistair's ocean into full view. It's massive! Radiant blue, frequent whitecaps, spritz of ocean water sprinkling from the air. Mark sits down on the cliffside, his feet dangling from the edge as he stares out into the endless ocean. I softly approach his left side, leaving about four feet of space between the two of us and look out over the water with him.

"I'm fine, Connor."

"No, you're not."

"… no, I'm not."

I put a hand on his shoulder softly. "We're gonna get out of this, Mark. After that, you never have to do anything like this again. Just like you promised Dani."

His seafoam-green hair blew in the wind, masking his face from view. "Why do you think we were given these races? Why couldn't we have the races we wanted?"

"You got me. Maybe it's some sick joke to give Dawson his jollies."

He shakes his head unconvinced, "I don't believe that. Riley got his legs back, plus extra. Krissy became a badass warrior woman. Danica is a cat woman on her hind legs that has saved our asses a few times. You're a freaking Orc that is all of a sudden, some solid leader. I'm a fish man that can hear the agony and anger of animals and other fish men. We're none of these things out there."

He's right. Dammit, he's right. I'm an absolute follower on the Outside, always following the rules and staying to myself. Riley should've been leading this whole thing with his knowledge of roleplaying games, but he's been distracted by his ability to walk and gallop. Danica has always been so charismatic and sturdy, but she's been shaken to the core since being in here, only stepping up if Mark gets into danger. I don't know shit about Krissy or who she is Outside, but this version of her is terrifying and intimidating. Mark? He's the life of the party, always doing things that he wanted. But here? He didn't know what to do in the next moment and is flooded with voices of people and things he can't control.

"Maybe… maybe we're supposed to be these characters because we are now opposite of what we fear the most about ourselves? Or even what we really are and can't admit it to ourselves."

He turns his face to me in a combination of confusion and irritation.

"Think about it. Riley couldn't walk on the Outside, and that made him feel powerless. Now that he is a Centaur, he can walk, run, jump, and fight. Why give that to him? Any other race he could've given would be able to walk, right? So why a four-legged battle mage that can shoot lightning? Because he's Riley; the enthusiastic paraplegic that can light up a room with his jokes and personality."

Mark tilts his head to the side, "So the game is resembling us? How the hell would it know these things?"

I've gotta tell him. I need to tell him about the game's overdeveloped artificial intelligence software. It's the only logical explanation I could think of. I open my mouth to tell him, but his eyes suddenly dart behind us. "Shit! Run!"

What happens next is so quick I don't react fast enough as a net suddenly wraps around me and starts dragging me back into the trees. I hear Mark yelling for me, but I can't break free of the snare I was in. I hear more yelling from other voices as I'm suddenly tossed onto the ground with a loud thud. I struggle harder to try and to get out of the snare until I finally catch a glimpse of my captors. A small team of tritons with spears, tridents and knives surround me. We were back at the campground, where the others are being held captive by the same Tritons. They're all whispering in a language I don't understand, but they're not happy by the way it sounds.

"Connor. It looks like you met our new friends," Matt grumbles as he's being tied up.

I grumble back, "Yeah... what a welcome wagon."

One of them hits me in the head with the blunt of their trident to shut me up.

"I'm going to turn your asses into sushi when I get out of this," Krissy growls. The one tying her up yanks on her hair to shut her up.

"Stop!"

All eyes turn to see who spoke. Mark is standing there with his trident at the ready. "Let them go!"

"Put your weapon down, boy," one of the Tritons commands in English. "Report to your garrison and you will be dealt with accordingly."

"I said... Let. Them. Go." His totem and his eyes start to glow, and some low growling comes from the trees behind him. The tritons suddenly back away from us and hold their weapons up as a large beast emerges into view of the campfire. It's about nine feet tall with a bulging body and two large legs with three clawed toes on each side. On its torso, four long slithering tentacles wave in the air. Its face looks like a bullfrog's head, only with three bulbous eyes and a wide mouth with jagged sharp teeth under its lips, leaving room for its prehensile forked tongue to slither out.

The Tritons don't seem too afraid, but they look taken aback by the sight of this monster that seems to be mimicking Mark's movements as he steps in closer.

"A bogtroll," one of them gasps in shock.

"Boy... how did you learn this magic?"

"Doesn't matter," Mark growls, rolling his shoulders. The bogtroll rolls its shoulders at the same time, showing some sort of melding of movements from them both. "This is Wartpod, and he's itching for some fresh food. Give me a reason not to let him."

It's a monstrous standoff between the Tritons and this beast, but they stand down and sheathe their weapons, cutting us all loose allowing us to shuffle aside.

"Why did you capture us?"

Their eyes are glued on the monster the whole time. "We were trying to stop you from delivering our kin to the Order knights at the tower," the lead Triton reveals.

"You thought we were taking him to the Order?"

The leader nods, "Bounty hunters and slavers have been taking our kind to the tower for reward. The ones that go in return to the ocean in pieces."

Mark stands up straight with the bogtroll miming him. "They're not bounty hunters. Or slavers. They're my friends. We saw what happened when you tried to attack the tower."

The leader cocks an eyebrow. "You… you do not have a garrison? No chieftain? What clan do you hail from?"

"They're my clan," Mark says and points at us.

I take this opportunity to try and smooth the waters, no pun intended. "Listen… we don't support the Crimson Order, and we're not bounty hunters. We're trying to make it past the forward camp to find the keystones."

The Tritons all look dumbfounded as they exchange glances between each other. The leader steps forward, "I am called Rolgos. I lead this garrison. Perhaps we can speak… without the beast."

Mark thinks for a moment before turning to the bogtroll, silently staring before it growls and turns away towards the ocean and disappears out of sight. It takes a while for us all to get comfortable with each other after the kidnapping. Once things settle, we tell our story to the warriors, who listen very skeptically and unimpressed.

Once we finish, Rolgos scoffs at us. "Impossible. There is no such thing as the Vanguards. It's nothing but a story to give simple-minded land dwellers some semblance of hope that the Order and terrorghasts will one day end. They will never end."

"It's all true," Mark tries convincing him. "We have three of the Keystones. We just need two more and we could possibly end all of this."

"Konvos, no." Rolgos calls him by his Triton name, "We have been at war with the Order for decades. The only thing that those Keystones do is bring misery and death. There is nothing beyond the Mortal Gate. The gods have long abandoned us to fend ourselves against the human blight. They used the story and myth of the Gate and the Keystones to lure all non-human races into traps so that they can be decimated by the Order. This is a genocidal war that will not end until either we or the humans are dead."

Every time I've joined in one of the campaigns back at "The Cache", I would hear players that pick Tritons as their race talk about how honorable, militaristic, and strong they are. They devote their livelihood under and above water to their gods and always defend the lawful good. But these ones are driven by fear and hate of the Crimson Order, and they're not about to admit to that. They're aggressive in their attacks and are not easily convinced that things could in fact change.

"So, what? You're doing all of this just to take a few knights with you to the afterlife?" Lorena blurts. *What the hell was her problem?*

Rolgos grimaces at her, "We are fighting for the freedom of our people! So long as that tower stands, our people are going to be fished and slaughtered without reason or remorse."

"But with their defenses, our attempts have proven to be fruitless," the one called Zinis adds. "Their archers are on constant watch and the border of the camp is too much for our attacks."

From what I'm able to tell, Rolgos sees this war as over already and they're all simply heading to early graves, so long as they kill a few knights in the process.

"What about the rest of your people?" Riley asks. "Surely this isn't all of you. There have to be more tribes of tritons than just you."

Rolgos snarls, "They are scattered. The other chieftains have divided themselves in democratic process instead of taking action."

"So, you went rogue," I deduce. "You think you'll be able to do more than the leaders of your kind?"

"Very Spartan of you," Matt utters.

Rolgos stands up and grips his trident, "Mind your tone, Drow! Your kind retreated into the shadows and left the rest of us to fend for ourselves! Every support that the elves could have spared has retreated into the mountains to keep your pitiful existence just a little while longer!"

"What if you had support?"

All eyes suddenly fall on Mark.

"What if you had backup? Enough of a force to turn the tide of this battle with the Tower?"

The Tritons all look to each other in confusion. Zinis was the first to reply, "What is it you mean?"

Mark points to his totem, "What if you had an army that saw the ocean and land as their homes just as much as you do? If you and your garrison succeed, maybe the other tribes of tritons would follow."

"You put too much faith into your magic, whelp," Rolgos scoffs.

"What do we have to lose, Rolgos?" Zinis retorts. Rolgos looks at him steaming pissed, but he continues. "We have lost so many of our brothers and sisters to gain no progress or momentum with our enemies. The other clans have been tied up in the bureaucracy that they have refused to lend any support. Even if these adventurers *are* the Vanguards, they seem more than capable of lending us the additional strength we need."

Everyone looks to Rolgos to gauge his response. He's standing somber at best before he shakes his head, "No. I will not allow for us to be caught up in myths and unknowns when our kind are being slaughtered." He straightens his leather armor, "We are leaving. Now."

He begins to walk back towards the cliffside that overlooked the ocean, but then he turns to Zinis and the rest. "That is an order."

They look from him to us, hesitant and conflicted, but eventually get up and follow suit. Say what you will about Rolgos and his shitty attitude, the tritons were loyal and proud. They walk away and out of sight, leaving only distant sounds of splashing.

"Well, that was a waste of time." Lorena huffs and leans back on her satchel like a pillow.

"This doesn't change the fact that we have to get into that camp," I point out.

"How do you propose we do that?"

This time, I don't have an answer. The only way in is covered by archers and heavy weapons. We have no way of knowing how many knights are in the camp, or if the

Keystones or Dawson are even in there. It truly looks like we're screwed.

"There's a drowned dungeon cell down there," Mark blurts out.

"Come again?"

He stands up and gestures to his totem, "Wartpod is very loud with his thoughts. He gets a lot of food from the cavern base of the Tower."

I hate that I understand what he means by food. "That beast told you about a secret entrance? How did the tritons not know about it?"

"It was probably Rolgos' fault," Riley guesses. "He's so focused on trying to take down the archers that he didn't strategize looking for structural weaknesses."

"So, what do you suggest?"

"We infiltrate through the drowned cell and try to get that gate opened before the Order knows what's happening. They'll get confused to the point that we can create a distraction for them to focus on while everyone else gets in and finds Dawson." Mark looks absolutely confident in his plan as he waits for us to respond.

At first, there's complete silence amongst the party. That's when Matt bursts into laughter.

"That has to be the dumbest plan I've ever heard! Are you seriously brain damaged? We know absolutely nothing about what to expect in that camp or how much resistance there is inside! You are risking our lives for an impossible odd that we'll find Dominic inside? Or even a Keystone?"

"I'm in," Lorena says with a shrug. Matt's jaw practically hits the ground. "You'll need a distraction, and I think that I can provide one. I'll need the Stormlord's help."

Riley smirks and snaps his fingers, causing a small spark to ignite. "I'm always down for some aggro."

"Wait a minute!" Matt tries to interject.

"Krissy and I can take the gate once it's open," Danica volunteers. "I have a few Trick Cards that can help us get in."

Krissy smirks and fist-paw-bumps Danica with a nod. "Let's fuck it up with some girl power."

"*Hold on!*" Matt yells. In all honesty, his reaction is pretty entertaining. "This is a goddamn suicide mission! For what?!"

"Your goddamn boss that you came in to find, you dumbass," I remind him. "And you're going with me and

Mark. You're our only other rogue and we may need you to do some killing."

Matt stands up and shakes his head, "You do not order me around, you arrogant child!"

"No, but I do. And you're going," Lorena orders him. He's dumbfounded. "You'll dance naked for the knights if Connor tells you to, you understand? If my dad is in there, you're going to find him and make sure he makes it out so I can kick his ass myself."

Matt shuts his mouth at last.

"Alright," I breathe, "let's make a plan."

CHAPTER 33

The sun is starting to rise over the horizon, shining red and yellow on the now-calm ocean surface. The wind is calm and soothing, and the only unsettling sound that can be heard is the marching of metal boots behind the battlements of the tower's defended walls. The plan is made and none of us have a whole lot of confidence in this hair-brained scheme we cooked up; Matt most of all, but no one gave a shit.

I watch with him and Mark at my sides from the tree line as our horse-legged and elfish companions made their way to the bridge of the forward camp.

"Halt! Archers at the ready!"

The archers all appear from behind the battlements with arrows knocked back and aimed at them. The one who gave the order is now standing on a platform that gives us full view of his appearance; dull red armor, blackened tattered cape, a longsword sheathed on his hip, long black hair blowing in the wind.

"State your business!" The knight orders.

Riley steps forward cautiously, "Good day, brave knights of the Crimson Order! My companion and I are a traveling troupe that wish to gain passage to the capitol city!"

"Sacredcrest is closed to non-humans," the knight informs them. "Take your troupe elsewhere."

"Racist pukes," Mark utters under his breath. I don't react as I watch, praying to whoever's listening that this works.

"My lord," Lorena curtsies. "We have traveled far in hopes to mend the relations of humans and non-humans alike! My companion and I are performers of the mystical and exotic, hoping to share our gifts of entertainment!"

"Where the hell did she learn to talk like this?" I can't tell if I'm more impressed or disturbed.

"Perhaps we can offer a demonstration, free of charge?"

The knight atop of the battlements crosses his arms. Riley is now holding his hands out and forms three small, charged bolts, tosses them into the air and starts juggling them. Lorena starts to dance as the bolts crackle around, using her talents to create small whips of fire to dance around her. Not going to lie, it's pretty entertaining to see. The knight is now watching with his head cocked to the side before holding his hand out, motioning for his archers to lower their aim.

"Now's our chance, let's go," Mark says. We nod and jog within the tree line to stay out of view towards the cliffside. "Let's hope that hypnotizing dance holds. Friggin Spelldancers, man."

I glance back quick enough to see Riley bounce a bolt off of his horse end back into his hands. He's got a lot of explaining to do if we get out of this alive. We reach the cliffside and look down to the calmed waters.

"Mark, you'll take lead. Matt and I will try to keep up. We don't know if our air supply will run out by the time we get to the cell. I hope your monster friend was right," I say with crossed fingers.

Mark nods before taking a deep breath and jumping into the waters below like an Olympic diver leaving the smallest ripple behind him. I look to Matt, who looks just as nervous about this as me, and we nod together before jumping. I keep my body stiff before bringing my arms to my chest as I connect with the water and plunge down. I open my eyes, hoping that it was like a movie where every character can clearly see around them beneath water. Amazingly, I can! I look below me to see beautifully colored coral reefs and beautiful fish swimming about. A school of fish suddenly parts and reveals sunken bones and bodies clinging to the rocks and corals below. Bones and bodies that belong to so many Tritons and even a few human bodies.

Suddenly I feel myself being jerked upward, breaching the surface of the water. Behind me, Matt is holding the collar of my cuirass. "You done sightseeing? I don't wanna be down there any longer than I have to be."

Another body emerges from the water, showing Mark's fisheyes hiding behind his hair before he pushes it back. "It's pretty far, but I think you can make it. Try to follow my path as closely as you can, don't stray far. We don't know how long our 'distraction' will last."

We both nod and dive down with him, swimming hard in a straight line. The worst part about this is my armor; it's heavy. If I'm not careful, I could sink. Matt and Mark were lucky that their armor sets are leather and cloth. We swim down further towards the base of the opposite cliffside, watching for any debris or fish along the way. Suddenly, the water becomes less clear and gradually darker. I look above us and notice that something huge is swimming over us, almost the size of a whale. In my moment of observation, I watch as it suddenly dives downwards. As it gets closer, I notice that it's not solid at all. It looks like a school of fish that is swimming together, but they aren't fish. These things are tentacled, pushing through the water with ease, sporting arms that hold pincers like a crab, triangular heads with a single large eye and a mouth of small, jagged teeth.

I react too slowly trying to grab my scepter that I suddenly get swarmed by them. Their tentacles latch onto my arms, legs, and part of my face. My worst fucking nightmare. I'm struggling as hard as I can to try and rip them off me, managing to tear one from my legs. The ones on my arms use their pincers to cut into my arms, causing me to yelp underwater and swallow a gulp. More start to swarm me. The eye that's not covered darts around to find Mark and Matt. Matt is slashing in the water as best as he can, managing to cut down a couple of them before getting overtaken. I can't see Mark anywhere. I manage to get one of my arms free to grab my scepter, hoping that mental prayers work just as well as vocal prayers. I grip it tightly and invoke Olagog for any strength he could offer. I feel the scepter's hilt prick me with something sharp, causing the adornments and jewel to glow red after tasting my blood. The weapon suddenly grows warm in my hands and causes the water around the head of it to boil.

"Bring the fires of war to your enemies, Warpriest."

The creatures start to back off a bit as the boiling water spreads out. I hold on firmly and swing around my body as hard as I can against the water, causing a wave of boiling heat to spread around me. The wave connects with a group of the creatures and causes them to be slung back like tiny torpedoes. Matt grabs onto my arm to get my attention and points his sword toward a small opening in the rocky base. I nod and swim as hard as I can, not bothering to look back. The heat of my weapon fades away quickly, and the weight of my armor began to feel heavier. I need to get to solid ground before I become Wartpod's next meal! The opening gets closer when I feel a sudden tug at my leg. I look down to see two of those things grab my ankles and pull. I jab at them with my scepter, but these ones seem sturdier with their grip. My lungs are starting to hurt. I keep trying to get them off me, but I'm losing strength. Quick as a flash, a blue streak comes swimming by and skewers both creatures. The blur circles back around and yanks on my wrist, pulling me quickly to the opening in the cliff and up to breach the surface.

I let out a loud gasp of air and grab the brick wall closest to me. I turn around to see Matt clinging to the same wall and Mark calmly floating between us. "You guys okay??"

I nod calmly, but Matt is less than calm. "What the hell were those things?!"

"Trykolds," Mark explains. "Gremlins of the ocean. We were in their feeding grounds."

"I'm leaving that one alone," I say with a small gasp of air. I look up to see a small portal of light coming from above. "It looks like a well. A big one."

"Suddenly it makes sense. They drop their prisoners down here after they're done with them, let them drift out as food… or warnings," Matt figures.

The blood on the well walls is direct evidence to the fact. It smells rotten and dank in here. But we need to make the climb if we were to do our part.

"Let's start climbing." I dig my fingers into the brick of the wall and start climbing up. Matt and Mark follow my lead, only faster than me. The weight of my armor and body is causing me to struggle while the Elf and Triton climb up like spiders on a wall.

"Come on, Connor. We're on the clock."

"Shove it, Bauer."

The well is deep, and the climb is hard. The bricks and stone start to look bloodier the higher we climb up. The poor victims of these psychos, all because they were different? Racism runs deep, even in the game world. The higher we climb up to the mouth of the well, the louder the voices and noises from above became; muffled voices and metallic ringing like something out of a quarry or a forge. We climb up until we're barely at the mouth of the well when we hear a few of the knights arguing about what to do with the "intruders" outside of the gate. Matt is the first to climb out of the well, slinking over the edge like a snake until he was out of sight. The voices of the knights are quickly snuffed out and he comes back into view, waving us up. Mark climbs out first with me behind him, lunging over the well into a small tuft of tall grass. Looking around, the forward camp looks like more of a prison camp: Cells and cages all over the place, some empty and others not so empty. Red-clad knights patrolling the ground and upper levels of the camp, stoking at the prisoners, or managing their weapons stock. The scariest part in our view is the ramparts where the archers and ballistae are; rows upon rows of arrows and bolts that could last the army for weeks, showing that this place is more important than we first thought. I scan around until I find the tallest point of the tower, where five knights are circling in patrol around one cell that has no bars or windows, only a single black iron door.

"Up there," I whisper and point. "That must be where our man is being kept."

"With a damn army between us and him, I don't like our odds," Matt argues.

"We just need to give them time. Let's try to move as quietly as we can. Matt, you're the rogue here. See if you can find any advantages or weaknesses we can use," Mark suggests.

"What are you going to do?"

Mark points to the cells along the interior of the camp, "I'm gonna get us an army of our own."

I nod in agreement, "With any luck, we'll have another Iron Vale situation. I'm going to try and scout for Dawson or the Keystones. Remember, when the signal's given, unleash hell."

We all nod together and then separate. As we part, I make for the tower's tallest point to try and assess any possible ways inside. The tower is clearly the strongest controlled structure of the forward camp, being all stone aside from the door. No visible signs of structural weakness from what I can tell, and the knights circling it look like Palpatine's Imperial Guards, only more intimidating with their polearm weapons; they're the size of spears, but the blade extends down at least a third of the way from the top, blackened and double edged. I can't tell if they are more sinister than the juggernaut from the Gorge, but I don't want to test that theory. I hear some rustling coming from my left where a knight is finding a space to... relieve himself.

'There's no way it can be that simple,' I think to myself. I scan the area to see if there are any peering eyes before moving towards him. I try to keep my weapon as unseen as I can before getting a few feet away from him. The knight finishes up and turns away, giving me the chance to grab his shoulders and pull him into the bushes, delivering the hardest punch I can to knock him out. It works, but it hurt my hand like hell. I search him for any keys or anything that can help, finding only a poultice of health. I turn away and scan around again for any other possibilities. *The tower has to have something for those knights to be relieved from duty or switch patrols.* I sneak through the bushes to try and get to the back of the tower only to stop at an alarming sight. This forward camp isn't just housing an important prisoner, but it's also hosting an important guest. At the furthest wall, there's another gate that's being guarded by two rows of about eight knights per side, all standing at attention while the gate starts to rise and open. Once it's fully opened, a small patrol of four

giant-sized knights walks in while a fifth figure marches in the center of them. This figure is tall and hulking, wearing an adorned suit of blackened armor that sported red tapestries along the waist and across the chest until it became a menacing cape flapping behind them. Their face is covered by the scariest helmet I could think of seeing; black with four horns curving around the back of it and blade-sharpened like the Shredder, finished off with a deep red faceplate that covered the whole face like a death knight with black holes for eyes. The knights from inside the camp all kneel to one knee and raise their fists in a salute with their eyes down. There's only one character that this monstrosity could be to make the knights bow and look away like this.

The Archon.

CHAPTER 34

The Archon steps proudly into the camp, causing the gates to close behind him. The knights that knelt slowly come up into a stand simultaneously as he walks past them. One of them stands in front of the Archon and bows his head.

"My Lord, the prisoner is secured inside of the tower, as ordered."

He doesn't utter a word. Instead, he looks to one of his guards and nods, who turns to the knight that spoke. "He appreciates your report and loyalty. Glory to the Archon and his ascension."

"Glory be!" The other knights reply in unison.

"Now," the guard snaps, "take him to the Hermit."

The head knight nods nervously and barks orders for a few others to prepare "the climb". Some lesser-clad knights shuffle to grab something from their armory station, returning with a ladder-like structure. They move it towards the tower and unfold it, revealing it to be a collapsible metal staircase, with the knights above securing it into their walkway and those below securing it into the ground.

Before the staircase was completed, a small scout runs up to the captain of the camp and kneels to him.

"Captain! The Elf and Centaur are still at the bridge of the east entrance. They are performing strange magics and refuse to vacate until they are allowed passage through."

The captain looks terrified of how the Archon may respond, so he fumbles with his words. "Fire warning shots, you fool!"

"Wait." The captain's head whips around to the speaking guard, who is receiving silent orders from the Archon. "The Archon wants them destroyed. Fire the ballistae upon them and be done with it. No filth is to be given entrance to the capitol."

The captain nods and points for the scout to do what was ordered. The scout scrambles to his feet and runs back for the battlements.

Shit! This is gonna ruin the whole plan!

I watch as the Archon approaches the staircase and begins walking up. Once he makes it up, the patrol guards escort him to the door and out of sight. I take this chance to try and get closer to see if they would leave the staircase unmanned. I'm so hurried that I step on a branch that gave a loud *snap*.

Suddenly, I have ten pairs of eyes all fixed on my location with weapons drawn. I try staying as still as possible until an arrow from above pierces my shoulder. I let out a loud yell, bringing the knights straight to me in haste. I stand up and pull the arrow free from my shoulder, gripping my staff intensely. The knights all hold their blades at me, glaring at me in hatred.

"How did you breach our walls, beast!?"

"You know that kind of talk won't get you anything. Have you ever said 'please' before?"

They glower and step closer.

"I'll take that as a no." I hold my staff readily as two of them advance on me. I block them both with my staff and push them back, giving me a chance to swing at one of them and connecting with his head. He lands with a crash as two more advance on me, one of them being one of the large knights that came in with the Archon. His greatsword clashes with my staff and causes me to stagger to one knee, giving the other knight a chance to strike me with the pommel of his blade. It stuns me just enough for them to tackle me down and wrestle my weapon away. I struggle against them with everything I have, but the hulking one slams his foot onto my neck to keep me still while the others chain my wrists. With another blow to the head, they stun me to the point I start seeing stars. They drag me away and hold a large greatsword to my neck.

They start talking to me, barking things at me, but I'm so stunned that all I can hear are muffled hollow voices. The big one strikes me with the back of his hand and brings me back to reality. I scan around me, trying not to move my head so much that I cut my own throat on the blade. The knights suddenly go quiet and move out of my line of sight. I look up and see the Archon descending from the staircase, two of the tower guards bringing a cloaked prisoner behind him. This guy is taller than I first thought, or maybe it's just from me being on my knees.

Like some Vader wannabe, I hear raspy breathing coming from behind his faceplate as he looks me up and down.

"Is this a meet-and-greet?" I ask up at him. "Sorry I didn't bring a picture for you to sign. Would've made a lot of money off that one."

The Archon makes a sound that almost sounds like a chuckle.

"Arrogance," he says in a gruff, hoarse voice. "Masking your fear with humor and deflection. How primitive."

"So, he *does* speak," I reply. "Gotta say, not what I thought you'd sound like. I was imagining you to sound like a preacher or prince, not an aging smoker battling halitosis."

Another blow to my head, this one making me spit out blood.

"So, you are one of the fabled *Vanguards*. Not quite what I was envisioning when I read your legends," he says as he walks around me, sizing me up.

"Guess this meeting is disappointing for both of us. Want to reschedule so we're more prepared? I'm free on Tuesday."

The Archon returns in front of me and steps up next to the cloaked prisoner. "You must be searching for the Keystones. Your endeavors have made your legends somewhat believable: The mistwraiths of Ordowell, the undead legions of the Gorge, even the slavers of the Iron Vale. Impressive feats."

He snaps his fingers and two of the guards start rummaging through my satchel, dropping phials, my Logbook, and a gear drop orb.

"Clever. You do not hold any of the Keystones you have found. Possibly with your companions?"

I look up at him with a smirk, "If I was going to get caught, I wasn't about to hand them over to you. Tough luck, big guy."

The Archon kneels to face me eye to eye. The eyes behind his faceplate look human but reddened and piercing. My joking humor disappears in that moment. "You like to think yourself intelligent and mischievous. But you are a simple creature. You and all those who infest my lands are simple monsters who can speak. When I finally ascend to my place on the Horizon, you and all like you will learn your place beneath me."

He stands up and returns to the prisoner, grabbing them by the hood. "This Hermit, so evasive and unpredictable, is going to be all I need in order to find the Keystones and reassemble the Mortal Gate." He rips the hood down, revealing a young face hidden by medium length blond hair, light brown stubble, and light blue eyes. His face is smudged with dirt, but there's no denying that face. That human face that resembles the master of immersive RPG game developing. The face of the man that I suspected this whole time was the villain of this whole thing, but instead is simply a prisoner of the game like us.

"Dominic Dawson."

CHAPTER 35

His dirty face stares down to the ground with glassy absent eyes, not responding to his name. The Archon steps away from him and back towards me, waving for his guard to remove the sword from my neck.

"There was speculation that the Hermit was an oracle of sorts, cursed with knowledge of the Mortal Gate and the power it held, as well as having a magical connection to the keystones. It was quite a task tracking him down, especially with this in his possession."

He reaches into Dawson's cloak and pulls out a glowing yellow stone. A Keystone.

"This stone gave him excellent magic of displacement, duplication and evasion. My men have caught many of his echoes that were spread across the realm, but never the real one," the Archon explains. "However, it also has robbed him of his sense of self. Displacing his logical and reasoning mind with that of riddles and nonsensical muttering from spreading himself apart so far and so numerously."

That's so jacked up. It's like what happened with Matt when he had the red Keystone, affecting him strongly. But how did it not affect everyone around him like it did with the others?

"Dawson? Can you hear me? Lorena is with us. We're getting you out of here," I call to him. All I can hear from him is incoherent muttering under his breath.

"Now, now, young Orc. Do not give this treacherous man false hope. You will not be leaving this camp. At least not alive."

I'm suddenly jerked up from the ground and pushed towards a bloodied stump. It's a damn chopping block. A large foot pushes me forward to lean down on the block; my head nestled in a blood-soaked rut. I gaze up to see one of the knights holding up a broadsword on his shoulder. Receiving a nod from the Archon, pocketing the yellow Keystone, the knight lifts his sword over his head to bring down. Moments before he's ready to bring the blade down, a spear pierces him in the side of the head, jolting him over and dropping dead. I look up to see Mark on the battlements, side-by-side with a few of the imprisoned tritons that were wielding harpoons. "Forever Free!"

The Archon growls before his attention is captured by a small explosion on the east gates. The signal. I laugh out loud to get him to look at me. I look up with the best grin I can make, "Surprise, motherf--"

My curse is cut off by another explosion that causes one of the ballistae above to burst into flames. The Archon stumbles backwards a bit and looks towards the east gate. Lorena and Riley run through the smoke and start projecting magic bursts of electricity and fire at the archers above them. Behind them storms in Danica and Krissy, attacking some of the ground troops trying to arm themselves. Krissy flourishes her axes and parries every attack coming from those storming towards her, but Danica is the one I was most impressed with. I expect her to use a Trick Card like she said, but instead she pulls out one of the Tabaxi Tokens that Steady Rock gave her. Holding the coin in her fingers, she calls out *"Read Them Like a Book!"* She flips it in the air, making it erupt into sparkling dust, and suddenly she's looking to all her attackers with the quickest eyes I've ever seen. Two knights at either side of her run in and swing their swords, causing Danica to duck and split below the blades as they come while swiping out with her claws, bringing them to the ground. One behind her brings his spear up to jab down at her, but she ducks aside so quick that it pierces the ground, giving her the chance to look up and kick upwards in a single bound that knocks him flat on his ass.

The chains binding me suddenly break free and I turn to see Matt looking down at me with a smirk, "Your stupid plan actually worked. Nice job." He reaches out with his free hand, pulling me up onto my feet.

"Let me log that as the first compliment you've given me," I snort. I run over to my grounded staff and come back to Dawson, idly standing there in the battlefield. "Don't worry, Dawson. We're getting you out of this."

I start parrying off blade clashes that came at me with flurries. After I knock a couple of them back, I whip

411

my head around to try and find the Archon. I finally see him as he walks onto the west path, gesturing for the gate to be closed behind him. The knights all abruptly stop attacking, causing all of us to circle around Dawson. It's suddenly twelve of us against thirty archers and eighteen armed knights, including the five tower guards now leading the assault.

"This futile attempt to liberate the Hermit will be in vain, Vanguards," the Archon calls from behind the gate. He holds up the yellow Keystone victoriously, "I have what I came for. Soon, my Crimson Order will deliver me your Keystones and I will have the last one within days. You have lost. There will be no quarter for those who stand against the light of the Horizon." The Keystone begins to glow bright yellow, surrounding him and his men in swirling yellow dust that causes them all to vanish, leaving us to face the armada.

"Well, anything you want to say to your dad before we die?" Riley asks Lorena.

She stands strong without looking at him, "No. Let's finish this."

The archers knock back their arrows, all fixed on us, and prepare to release. The ground starts to thud, growing little by little beneath our feet. We look around until a large familiar figure comes rushing through the smoke of the east gate. Wartpod lets out a large roar and barrels through the line of ground soldiers. From behind him, a small army of Tritons breaks through led by Zinis. "For our fallen! Bring these murderers to their knees!" The tritons disperse and begin attacking the knights.

"Hold this circle!" I yell. "Don't let them get to Dawson!"

Some arrows let loose, making us jump and dodge but manage to strike Danica and Riley. Mark yells out like a Viking, making his totem glow brightly and spiritually connect with Wartpod. Every motion that Mark made to attack, the bogtroll mimics in perfect synchronization. I take this opportunity to invoke Sacred Armor from my staff, causing it to light up and have a red silhouette of armor hover around my body. The army of Tritons is fighting tooth and fin to avenge their fallen kin. The Order knights are fighting back ruthlessly with no signs of retreat or surrender. Every cut and swing rang loudly in the camp for what feels like hours of struggle until it came down to the last few knights. They're fighting with every breath they have left as the Tritons strike them down righteously, leaving the battle to be won by us. Exhausted and beaten down, I collapse onto the ground as my armor disappears. I'm joined by Krissy and Matt on the ground while the others huff vigorously on their feet.

"W-we did it," I say breathlessly.

Matt nudges me from the side, "Maybe... you're not so bad after all..."

I give him a half-hearted chuckle as I look up at Danica, offering me a paw. I take it and rise back to my feet. "You are a badass cat."

"You just now seeing that?" She punches my shoulder playfully, but it's the one that got shot in. Ignoring the pain, I help her to get Krissy and Matt up on their feet while Lorena approaches her father, still staring down blankly and mumbling nonsense.

"Is he okay?"

She shakes her head, "Hard telling. He's been in here a long time. No telling what kind of things he's seen and done before we came in."

"Why is he human?" Riley asks. I avoid this question, but it's a good point to bring up later when we're not in a Crimson Order camp. He's a player like us, but he's human while the rest of us are different races.

"Maybe he had more control of it since he made it," Lorena guesses.

"What happened in here?" Krissy asks.

"The Archon. He was here."

Everyone but Mark and Matt looks at me in shock. "That's who was behind the gate?"

I nod. "The big bad of *The Mortal Gate*. Clearly not Dawson, and scary as hell."

"This is insane," Riley says with his hand to his head.

"He's as crazy as we were told. He wants the total genocide of non-human races. Apparently, Dawson is a character called the Hermit, who is magically connected to the Keystones and can locate them. That's why the Archon wanted him."

"Well, he's not getting much now," Lorena says, gesturing to her father. "His brain is fried. I can't make heads or tails of anything he's saying."

"The Archon said the Keystone Dawson had possesses displacement magic, allowing him to jump around different places in Albistair and create echoes of himself. But it also made him lose himself in his own head."

"So, the yellow Keystone affects human sanity?" Matt theorizes.

"Perhaps the more he used it, the more of his mind he lost. Putting strain on his brain the more he moved and mirrored himself."

"They do warn you about prolonged exposure to video games and what it does to your brain," Mark blurts.

I sigh heavily and run a hand through my hair as Zinis approaches us holding his bleeding arm. "Thank you for your help, Zinis. It couldn't have been easy going against Rolgos like that."

He shakes his head firmly, "Rolgos was wrong to turn away your help. We are a proud race, this is true. But we cannot allow our pride to cloud our judgement in the face of oppression. You went out of your way to help our people who still drew breath, and for that we thank you."

Zinis approaches Mark and puts his uninjured arm on his shoulder, "You are a credit to our people, Konvos. You will always have a place among our garrison."

Mark mirrors Zinis's gesture by putting a hand on his shoulder, "Thank you. You may also want to thank Wartpod. He stayed within a good distance to offer his help."

Zinis chuckles and nods, "He did indeed. If only we were all so inclined to help those in need, no matter their differences. May the gods bless your path, Vanguards."

With that, Zinis commands his men to aid the prisoners left standing to leave the camp and return to the ocean waters. We regain our composure and collect our items, ushering Dominic towards the gate that the Archon left from, knowing it's our only path forward. As we walk away from the camp, I notice how weak I feel and reach for a poultice from my satchel only to remember they were both taken away, along with my Logbook. Why did he take my Logbook? Without it, I can't level up. But an NPC wouldn't know about that. Would he?

CHAPTER 36

We put as much distance from the forward camp behind us as we can, guiding the still delirious Dominic with us. Thankfully, the trip isn't as taxing as the desert or the mountains.

"Does anyone know where we're going?" Lorena complains.

Krissy has her map out as we walk, "We're in the direction of Sacredcrest. If that scary ass knight went anywhere, my guess is there."

"To plunge into the mouth of the beast is to learn the truth," Dawson mumbles aloud. It's the only thing he keeps saying since he started speaking louder after the battle at the camp.

"What the hell does that mean?" Danica groans.

"You'd think he would be coming back to sanity since he doesn't have the keystone anymore," Riley questions.

"Lorena said it may have been different for him since he's been stuck in here longer than us." I pat the back of Dawson's shoulder, making him shudder slightly. He keeps muttering the same phrase over and over.

"Which brings us to the bigger problem," Matt starts, "The Archon now has one of the Keystones, he could have the last one without us knowing, and we are being caught up in tougher situations. The game is adapting to our levels and it's only going to get tougher from here."

He's right. The Archon is a scarier villain than I gave him credit for. The amount of power and influence he has over his knights, who all fought to the death, means he either has a Keystone that allows him to maintain control over his followers, or he's just that damn scary that the human population won't go against him. Either way, it's looking like we're reaching the endgame.

"Let's find a place to relax and recover while we try to bring Dawson back to reality… no pun intended," Riley suggests. Aside from his stupid joke, we're all in agreement that we need to rest. After such a fight, we need to eat and recharge. Krissy finds a place on her map that shows a small settlement that could be just what we need. What would make it more helpful is if we were able to tell if the town was friendly towards non-humans. I still haven't told anyone that my Logbook was gone, but it doesn't seem like the most pressing concern at this time. We have no choice but to walk this distance since Krissy's mount summoning was on a cooldown from the last time. I watch as Matt and Lorena stay by Dawson's side, but something about the scene is really rubbing me the wrong way. Matt is trying so hard to make sense of Dawson's muttering, but Lorena is just pressing on with a hand on his arm and not saying anything to him. She must be one of the most callous people I've ever met in my life. Ever since we found her, she's been a spitfire of resentment and backhanded comments. I thought after she found her dad she may show a little sign of humanity in her, but there was nothing. What was her deal?

We walk for a long while until we come up to a hill that overlooks the settlement on Krissy's map. At first glance, it looks calm and quiet, but the closer we get, the more haunting and abandoned it reveals itself to be. The small cottages, the longhouse, even the square looks like they've been ravaged and ransacked.

"What the hell happened here?"

No one says a thing as we pass into the settlement's borders. There are clear signs of battle; scorched stone and burnt homes, weapons scattered along the ground, broken fences, and scattered belongings. The one thing that's really disturbing me about this scenario is that there are no bodies. There are clear signs of physical battle and patches of blood everywhere, but no bodies to show what might have happened here.

I watch as Riley runs his hands along a nearby wall that shows clear marks of scratches or cuts in the stone. "It's like people just got up and skipped town while a fight was happening."

"Kris, where are we?"

421

She shuffles to find our location. "Lodger's Rest. It's a small settlement with an inn, a couple of shops, farmhouses, and a small cluster of homes. Population... 914 settlers..."

"Then where is everyone? Shouldn't there be bodies at least?"

"Real nice, Bauer."

Matt shrugs defensively only for Lorena to step in and defend him. "He's got a point. This doesn't feel right. Maybe we should scope this place out before we take a breather."

Hard to argue that. We separate into different parts of the settlement. I make for the longhouse first, thinking it would be the best bet to find something or someone left behind. The longhouse is at the tallest point of the settlement, giving me flashbacks to playing *Skyrim* and taking in the landscapes. The building itself is huge in width, built like a long hut using straw, stone and clay. There's a wooden sign that reads "Shepherd's Inn", showing a carved mural of a farmer herding a flock of sheep beneath the lettering. Outside of the large double-door entrance is a small cooking pit with four knocked-over chairs surrounding it. A cast-iron pot laying on its side with the contents, spilled out and covered with flies, picking at the leftovers. Taking a deep breath, I grab the brass ring handles of both doors and pull them open. As the doors part and pull open, a rush of putrid and odorous stink hits me like a freight train, making me wretch and cover my mouth and nose. It smells like fresh roadkill and rotten eggs. After recovering from the smell, I peek inside to a horrid sight; leftover body parts and scraps of people littered all over the ground. The bodies all look like they've been torn apart and shredded by some sort of animal, but it can't have just been one. I walk in as far as I can inside without vomiting to inspect it a little closer. To the side of the doors sits a large beam that's laid out on the floor with a cleaved body lying on top of it. By the looks of it, the beam is supposed to bar the door so that nothing could get inside. I scan around more and notice a small portal of light beaming down from the roof; a hole in the thatched roof that has been broken inwards, not out. Whatever got inside was strong, in some sort of pack, able to climb up onto the roof and break right through to feed on and tear into all the settlers hiding inside.

"Terrorghasts." The only – logical? – thing I can think of. It couldn't have been the Crimson Order, seeing that the settlers are all human by the looks of it. It also rules out spiders, bandits, and murkodiles, seeing that the monsters would've struggled against the materials of the building and bandits wouldn't leave all the valuables lying around.

"Oh my—"

I whip around to see Danica's ears fold back and eyes widen, her paws covering her face quickly. I shuffle to

423

get her away from the longhouse. "Danica, go find Mark. Stay away from this building."

"Th-th-they're all dead," she stutters in a broken voice.

I hold her close and hurry her down the path away from the longhouse as far as I can. I hurry her towards the square of the settlement until I find a bench outside of one of the smaller buildings. Quickly, I sit her down and hold her to try and comfort her as best as I can.

"Dani! Babe, what happened?!"

Mark comes sprinting toward us, so I quickly get up to let him sit next to her and pull her into his arms. She completely comes undone and starts sobbing. The others soon come flocking to her cries, asking questions that fell on deaf ears. I gesture for Riley and Matt to follow me, taking them towards the longhouse. Their reactions to the house of rotting corpses are a mixture of horror and disgust.

"Looks like you were right, Matt."

"I... this isn't what I—"

"I know. Let's just close this up."

Without another word, Riley and I push the doors closed. We stand back and look at the building in silence.

Was it wrong to mourn the massacre of computer-generated people? To feel that they didn't deserve this kind of end?

"Connor? You're a Warpriest. Maybe say a few words?"

My eyebrows shoot up. "Are you serious, right now?"

"Well, I mean—"

"Stop, Riley. Just stop. I'm done. I'm done pretending that this is all just a stupid game. Did you smell the air? That death and decay? I did, and it was horrifying. What am I gonna say that will give any of this a sense of normality? I'm a college student inside of a hellscape. I'm not a real Orcish Warpriest, you're not a real Centaur, and Matt's not an Elf. If I even try to humanize this shit, I'll lose whatever grip on reality I have left."

I turn away from the longhouse and walk back towards the settlement, putting as much distance between me and everyone else as I can. I need to get away from it all. I've never seen so much carnage in my life, and I can't even come to terms that it's all a simulation. That's what is making this all worse. This simulation. This augmented reality. It's all fucked up and I can't handle it anymore. Any composure and grounding that I had left is gone. I mindlessly walk until I find a carved statue sitting in the center of a small cluster of homes. I walk around it until I see the face of it. The statue is in the likeness of the Archon

425

in his full set of menacing armor, holding a sword across his chest with his right hand while the left is held up high in a fist. The settlement looked up to this guy like a damn hero. Merrin's story came to mind about how the humans look up to him to protect them from non-humans and the terrorghasts. Where was he when they attacked this place and mauled the settlers? Where was this so-called god-king when his people needed him the most? Hunting down relics, imprisoning Dominic, selling people to slavers and ignoring the calls of his supporters. That's where.

I snap. Taking my staff from my back, I start striking the statue, roaring with each swing. Once, twice, thrice, repeatedly. The statue starts to crack after a few more strikes. Rearing back with one more swing, I throw what strength I have at it until it comes crashing down, breaking, and shattering on the ground. I stumble backwards until I fall into a sitting position in front of the pile of carved stone, huffing heavily. My eyes are burning with rage, two hot tears trickling down my face.

"Connor…"

I don't turn around. I rest my arms on my knees and stare down at the broken statue, seething in hatred and anger. Krissy's clawed hand rests on my shoulder gently.

"What happened?"

"The longhouse. Bodies torn to shreds. I… I can't take it anymore. I'm done."

426

She lets out a deep breath and sits down next to me. "You finally cracked."

I gesture to the broken statue with a dry scoff.

"You know we can't stop. We can't quit now."

"Why not? Who's to say we'll ever get out of this? There's no way out. Dominic's dome is fried, the Archon has one of the Keystones, and God only knows what our condition is like on the Outside. We could all be in comas right now, and not be aware of it. What in the absolute hell can we do at this point? I've done everything I can to stay positive about this, but I can't do it anymore."

I'm clenching my teeth so hard to the point I think they'll break right out of my gums. My hands are balled up into tight fists to the point I can feel my nails digging into the skin of my palms. I don't want to move, think, or talk anymore. I just want this to be over.

I half expect Krissy to smack me upside the head, punch my shoulder, or just start chewing me out on how I need to get my shit together. Instead, she's silent as she shifts closer to me and puts her arms around my neck in a gentle squeeze, resting her head on my shoulder. We sit there in silence, the kind of silence that drowns out the rest of the world. I don't even feel myself reaching up with my hands and grabbing onto one of her arms.

"It's okay," she whispers. The tough-skinned Krissy was gone, replaced by this warm and empathetic person that makes my anger and frustration start to melt.

The moment gets interrupted by soft, incoherent murmuring. We both look up to see Dominic shuffling towards the broken heap of stone. He looks from the stone to the two of us with glassy eyes, "The eyes of the enemy are the eyes of the ally... the eyes of the enemy are the eyes of the ally..."

"Looks like you're not the only one who cracked."

I stand up from the ground, gently releasing Krissy's arm, and walk up to him. "Dominic, we can't understand what you mean. How can we bring you back?"

"To plunge into the mouth of the beast is to learn the truth," he replies blankly.

Sigh.

"There you are." Lorena saunters over to her father. "You two done sulking?"

I stick my finger at her, "Fuck you, first of all. Second, if you saw what I saw, you wouldn't be so high on your fucking horse."

"Big talk, Greenie. The sun's setting. Let's make use of these houses and get some rest. We'll make a plan in the morning."

She can't be serious. "This town is the sight of a massacre, and you want to camp out??"

"It's better than settling out in the open when we have blood-thirsty knights hunting for us, isn't it? These houses have walls and actual beds, something that our camping tools can't provide. We'll get some actual rest and regroup in the morning."

"She's got a point, Connor." The last person I thought would defend her stands up next to me. "Dani's a mess and we've barely rested since that last tavern. We could all use the rest."

Truthfully, I forgot about Danica during my own little breakdown. Besides, they're also right about needing rest. I don't want to move on with all of this weighing down on us.

"Fine. We'll shack up in this cluster. There are enough for us to share."

They both agree. I ask Krissy to get the others while I stay behind with Lorena and Dominic.

"Do you hate your dad?"

429

Lorena raises an eyebrow at me and crosses her arms.

"The whole time you've been around, you've done nothing but rag on him and his work. When we finally find him, you don't change a bit. You're passive with him and don't even seem like you care that he's gone full *Cuckoo's Nest* on us. So, what's your deal?"

"Wow, a regular detective you are," she sighs in annoyance. "My dad is a genius. He's broken the barrier for what's possible in game development and creating technology that creates the best virtual worlds. But he's an absolute moron when it comes to having a family. He dumped himself into his work to the point my mom left him. He didn't even fight to get custody of me. I did everything I thought he wanted me to do. I graduated at the top of my class, got my master's in engineering in record time, even helped him develop a couple of his past games. But it was never enough for him to show he gave a damn. So, excuse me if I find his current situation a little satisfying."

"You're a damn sociopath," is all I can respond with.

"No, I'm a realist. Treat your family like they're nothing, karma comes."

The silence is no longer soothing. It's painful and awkward. Thankfully, it ended when Krissy ushered everyone towards us.

"We're camping out?"

"More like renting out. We'll split these houses up amongst us as best as we can," I suggest. "Dani and Mark will stay together in that far hut."

They both nod in agreement.

"I'll take the big one there," Lorena announces. "Keep an eye on my dad and have room to be away from everyone else."

"What about me?" Matt seems to be genuinely concerned to not be included with his boss and Lorena.

"You can crash with me." I blink at Riley in disbelief.

Even Matt was taken back, but Riley crosses his arms and shrugs. "If you try to kill me again, I won't make it easy on you. Besides, I don't trust you with Connor."

I hate him so much. I know what he's doing.

"So that leaves us, huh?"

Krissy and I look at each other. Before I can try to protest it, everyone seems to just part ways and go to their huts. The only one who seems turned off by the idea besides me is Lorena, who looks at me with annoyance before saying, "You know where I'll be." She grabs Dominic by the arm and walks towards the big hut she claimed. I feel my face get hot and I try thinking of anything that I can to not make this moment more awkward than I was already feeling. She doesn't give me the chance to come up with something witty before she starts walking into the hut we're expected to share. With that, I reluctantly follow. Inside, the hut is very old-fashioned with stone interior and little furniture, including a wooden dinner table, two tall shelves that have scattered ingredients and tools for a kitchen, a small fireplace, and a solitary bed.

Krissy looks at the scattered items along the floor, "Feels wrong to be squatting in a murdered family's home, doesn't it?"

"A little bit. Personally, I'd prefer if we weren't in this settlement at all."

"Well, we can at least light the fireplace. Wanna take care of that?"

I reach for my satchel before I remember that it's gone. "Yeah… about that…"

"Wait, I think I got it."

Krissy steps over to the fireplace and throws some of the discarded items in it, making some kindling. She takes out her tinder box and simply blows into it towards the fireplace, causing a breath of flame to shoot towards it and ignite the fire.

I'm impressed. "Being a Tiefling definitely has its perks."

She smiles then stands back up. "You know, I've been thinking about why we were put in these bodies."

"Oh?"

She nods and sits at the edge of the bed, "What if the game thinks this is what we are supposed to be? You know, like, inside?"

I have to stop myself from laughing. "I doubt that's what it is. We're way behind to be having personality-matching character algorithms."

"Okay, smart ass. You are telling me that we aren't made for these roles? Look at Riley. The guy is an absolute geek that lives for fantasy. So why not give him the role of a galloping wizard?"

"I don't know. But the only one who could give us answers is currently rambling nonsense while sharing a hut with an apathetic daughter and a questionably devoted employee."

She sighs deeply and pinches the bridge of her nose, "Why am I the one that's trying to make you forget about the shitty situation we are in? That's usually your job."

"Because I'm out of answers, Krissy. I don't want to be the one everyone goes to anymore." I lean against the edge of the dinner table facing the fireplace. I'm exhausted, beaten, and out of ideas. I thought it would be easy to try and figure out how to fix all of this. I live for video games and I'm damn good at them. But even with all the games I've played, there's one that I haven't mastered or beaten: the game of life. My social skills suck, my family situation is practically silent, and my only friends are in danger because of what I roped them into.

I feel a hand on my shoulder gently turn me around. Krissy crosses her arms at me, but not in an angry way. She looks concerned. "You've gotta stop putting all of this on your shoulders. Just because things are getting tougher, you're just going to roll over and let this whole thing beat you down? That's not why you're this orc thing."

"Then enlighten me. Why exactly do *you* think I'm an Orc?"

"That's easy. You're this because you're strong and face all of your challenges head-on. Not to mention you help others before yourself, and that alone explains your powers and spells. You've helped and led us all this way. It doesn't matter what you did before this, it matters what you do moving forward."

That's always been my anchor, worrying about what I did before and how it would affect me. That's what made video games so comforting and addicting, because I always knew what the outcome would be, but here, everything I do has a consequence. If I'm gonna beat real life, I need to start now.

"Okay… no more looking back."

I lean forward and kiss her. It lasts a couple of seconds before I pull away and wait to see what she would do.

"So… is that all you've got?"

I smirk, "Not by a long shot."

We embrace each other close and kiss each other deeply. She teases me a couple of times to watch my teeth, but I'm too lost in the moment. That moment has us tackling each other to the bed and testing the lengths of what we could do in the game.

CHAPTER 37

The sun peeking through the wooden door and the scent of fireplace smoke pulls me out of sleep. I groan a little as I wake up before noticing that my arm and chest are pinned. Looking down, I'm holding onto a sleeping and naked Krissy who lightly stirs in my arms.

Holy shit, holy shit, holy shit!

I guess we found the answer to Riley's question about having sex in an augmented reality game. I gently remove her arm from around me and maneuver out of the bed, picking up my pants to put back on.

"Not gonna put on a show for me?"

I look back at the bed and see her sitting up, covering her body with the bedding, and smiling.

I lightly chuckle, "Good morning to you, too."

"I'll say."

I can tell I'm blushing because she's giggling at me and patting the spot next to her. I sit down without question.

"Trying to sneak out? Didn't peg you for the type," she teases.

"Never. Thought you could use a little more rest."

She gives me a dry chuckle, "I think we both got what we needed."

I chuckle back and peck her lips. "Take your time. I'm going to see if anyone else is awake."

I put the rest of my clothes on and walk out of the hut, closing the door behind me. Outside, the sun is barely coming over the hillside, giving an amazing look at the landscape from here. I scan the other huts to see if anyone else had woken up, but it's quiet and calming. After what happened yesterday, it seems like things could become easier. I rid myself of all the negativity I'm feeling and now I'm ready to beat this game.

A sharp whistle pierces the air before something sharp pierces my shin. I fall with a loud yell of pain to see a bolt sticking out of the back of my left leg. The calm air is now replaced with the thunderous sound of hasty marching gradually getting louder. From behind the hut that Lorena and Dominic were sharing comes a large army of Crimson Order knights right my direction. Small groups of knights broke into the adjacent huts and dragged everyone out into the center of the cluster. I limp in front of my hut to try and keep them away from Krissy, holding my staff with purpose. Four of them march up to me with their blades drawn and pointing to me.

"Connor?? Are you okay?!"

I call back to the door, "Krissy! Stay inside!"

Too late. She opens the door behind and is immediately caught by a couple of knights that got the jump on us both. We struggle against them as much as we can, but they overpower us with numbers. The knights wrangle all of us until we're forced onto our knees in the middle of the army. We all struggle against our restraints, but there's something about them that seems to get tighter the more we try to break out of them. The knights in front of us suddenly part, leaving an aisle for a huge knight to walk down. His armor is too easy to recognize.

The Archon.

He steps forward and pauses in front of us a few feet away, hands behind his back and breathing creepily with raspy breath.

"The infamous Vanguards. The fabled warriors who will free Albistair of the terrorghasts and overthrow my reign."

I stay silent, looking down at the ground, not seeing if the others were acknowledging his build up to a villainous monologue.

"After our encounter at the forward camp, I felt it necessary to make myself known to all of you. It would be in your best interest to acknowledge my presence and power, seeing that I currently hold it all."

Riley gives a hearty scoff in response, "With a crooked, black iron fist, maybe."

"Ah, the Centaur speaks. Good."

Goddammit, Riley.

"So, you see my reign as tyrannical. Ruthless. Without remorse." He steps in front of Riley and looks down at him. "What is it you hope to accomplish? Liberate the realm from its only source of order and security?"

He stays silent this time.

I'm afraid it will result in him getting a leg or arm broken, so I break the silence and get the attention on me. "You're the only one who sees it as safe and secure. You got the humans to follow you because you made them see the rest of Albistair's people as monsters, not citizens and families who are just trying to live freely."

"Orcs? Living freely? Who is it exactly that you are trying to convince, boy? It matters not your intentions or feelings on the matter. The fact is that we are all destined to be at war and to crave for power. You and your kind are no different."

He must love hearing the sound of his own voice. "Is that your whole argument? That you war is inevitable and you're just trying to be the one who wins first? That's such a stupid motive to be an evil asshole."

The hilt of a sword comes down on the side of my head, knocking me to the ground before one of the other knights forces me back onto my knees.

"You do not seem to understand, boy. You think that I was selected to be the one who brings glory and control to this realm, but I was chosen by the old gods to continue their great work. I am merely a conduit of control and power."

He holds his hands up to the sky, making them ignite into dark purple flames. "I am the avatar of the new order! I am the—"

His head suddenly falls free from his body from a clean cut that came from nowhere. The rest of his body crumbled to the ground before disappearing in a whisp of air. My jaw drops, but none of the knights move a muscle to retaliate.

"Jeez, he never shuts up." Lorena wrangles her Spelldancer ribbon back around her waist as she stands up from where he disappeared.

My eyes would've popped out of they could, but I don't think I'm as surprised or shocked as Matt is. "Lorena?! What are you doing??"

"Aw, Matty. Like you didn't see this coming at all."

Lorena starts up a twirl, encasing herself in a magic haze. The haze disappears and reveals her in a suit of crimson and black chainmail armor with accessories that still compliment her Spelldancer class, but her elfish features disappear completely. She's a human now, but not just any human.

"You... you're the Archon?"

She smirks with her hands on her hips, giving a small shrug. "Expecting someone else? You honestly thought that a computer-generated character would be smart enough to pull all of this off? It takes a genius to pull off this kind of devious plot. Like me."

I can't handle the betrayal, even from her. I knew she was apathetic and rude, but I didn't take her to be a backstabbing bitch.

The others don't seem to understand or take it either.

"You crazy bitch! You put us through all of this?!" Danica hisses loudly and thrashes against her restraints.

She chuckles, kneeling in front of Danica with pouty lips. "Well, not all of it. After all, you did take the bait and join the beta test."

"But you're in here too!"

"Just like she wanted…"

We all look at Matt. "She insisted that we enter the game to go after her father… but she *wanted* him in here. And us. She planned this all out."

I try to piece some of this together and she could tell. "Come on, Connor. You know you want to guess why I did this. Use that cute nerd brain of yours."

"You told me he never noticed you. That with all his genius and accomplishments, he didn't see your accomplishments or anything. So… you're trying to get his attention?"

"No, dumbass. I'm giving him a taste of his own medicine. I'm destroying his precious empire and creating one of my own." She stepped in front of Dominic and lifted his chin for him to look at her with empty eyes. "He made this game, and so many others, to give people a chance to live different lives. He treated all his precious fans and players better than he treated his own daughter. So, I made my own alterations to the coding in his precious creation so that he would be forced to survive in his own creation that turned against him."

I can't believe this. She's taking out a vendetta on her father and didn't care who got in the way.

"What about us?! What did we have to do with your family drama?!"

"Oh, that." Lorena giggles and steps away from Dominic, "That's just something I theorized while getting dear-old Dad stuck in here. First, I had to get his closest workers and supporters out of the way. That took no effort, seeing that Matt was the son that Dominic never had. Matt was ready to jump into the game and save him by any means necessary." She saunters over to Matt tauntingly and scowls, "Did you know he was planning to retire after *Mortal Gate* was released? He was ready to sit back and sip margaritas in Oahu while giving his empire to the only person he trusted would keep SnoWire going strong with new and exciting games. You."

Matt's eyes flutter before darting over to Dominic, still glassy-eyed and absent.

"I wasn't about to let that happen, so I took measures to ensure you would be trapped here, just like him." Her attention shifts towards us, "Then, I got an idea after I watched one of our own get killed by a pack of terrorghasts. He didn't disappear or disintegrate, but just choked on his own blood. This led me to theorize that with the original program designs and my own tinkering has messed with the system to ensure the most realistic interactions that players can encounter: the pain, bleeding, sensations, all of it. I have helped to create an augmented reality where you live and die in this world. I became the very god that these stupid programs worship. I created a living, breathing, fully-immersive world where I rule."

"Oh my God... you killed Robert... on purpose," Matt can barely say without his voice cracking.

"Small sacrifices, sweetie. I didn't think you two were going to last, anyway. So, you're welcome."

I see the pain in his eyes and finally realize something. Matt didn't just lose a co-worker. He lost his partner.

"You're insane. You're legitimately insane!" Mark struggles against his restraints, which causes him to wince at their tightening.

"Don't be so dramatic. You all truly believed you were going to be paid for testing this thing? You? Absolute nothings and no ones who were unhappy with their own lives that you had to live in a virtual world to escape."

"That doesn't give you the right to ruin other people's lives, you crazy bitch!"

Lorena takes a deep breath before slapping Danica across the face. "You would be smart to thank me. If you weren't here, you wouldn't learn how to be strong and cunning. I give my people the new lives that they need. Don't you enjoy it? The thrill, the danger, the chance to be something more?"

"You can't justify enslaving people's minds, Lorena! You destroyed people's lives just to prove how smart you were, and now you're on this psychotic power trip! You need help!"

Lorena shook her head at me. "You just won't understand. I'm not doing this to get my father's respect or live in his world. I'm here to make my own." Her attention goes to her knights, "Get them up. It's time to finish this."

We're all hoisted to our feet and forced to walk at the point of swords. I'm still trying to fully understand Lorena's motives to become this crazed virtual dictator. I could understand if she was trying to get her father's attention, but to rob him of his mind and the rest of us of our freedom? It doesn't fit. Did she expect us to become willing citizens in a virtual world while our real bodies grew weak in defenseless states? Lorena's smart, maybe too smart for her own good. Being in this world that she helped to create gave her a false sense of godhood to the point she really thought she was doing us all a favor.

"Lorena, why did the program make us into races that weren't human? We chose human races with our classes, so why the Texas Switch?"

She continues to walk ahead of us, not turning to acknowledge me. "Because I made you better. Why do gamers choose races that aren't human? Because they want to be different. We always work and fight to become more than ordinary."

"And the humans in the game? The racist, elitist humans that either run from us or try to kill us?" Riley raises a good point, but it only makes Lorena laugh.

"Because it's fun to show just how xenophobic and self-important people actually are. You can't tell me they don't remind you of everyone on the Outside. Now shut up and keep walking."

The march is quiet and tense. Every time I try to get the others' attention, I get shoved or hit. We're being ushered and directed like a flock of sheep, and I got a feeling we were being led to some sort of slaughter. I notice that the landscape soon becomes less soft and grassy, and more tough and dry, to the point the ground under our feet becomes cracked and gray. It reminds me of the pictures I looked up of Giant's Causeway in Scotland, hexagonal shaped stone discolored and grim. Further ahead I can hear the faint sounds of screeching and wheezing that starts sounding more and more familiar, the louder it got. It starts to dawn on me where she was taking us, the shape and color of the landscape, the sudden feeling of dread and pain, the sounds of monstrous screeching.

She's taking us to the Chasm... the birthplace of the terrorghasts.

CHAPTER 38

"Lorena… don't do this."

The others don't understand why I'm suddenly scared. They don't know the danger we're about to be put in. Lorena ignores my plea and marches us on until the screeching got louder. The marching suddenly stops, and she orders her men to push us closer to her position. She stands in front of a ledge that spreads across for miles. She turns to us and gestures for us to move closer. The knights force us forward until we're standing at the edge of the chasm, and I wish I didn't looked down. It's a deep, creepy, crawling trench of nightmares, illuminated by a faint purple pulsing light and the screeching sounds of terrorghasts. God only knows how many are down there, but I'm pretty sure we were about to find out.

"You made this?"

She gives her infamous shrug as if she's proud of her monstrous masterpiece. "Hey, every game needs a good plot. These beasties were my dad's idea, I just made them bigger in numbers and scary enough to get the humans to hate your races, but agoraphobic so they only attack at night or in dark areas. It's also where I threw the last Keystone. Clever, eh?"

My heart drops in realization, "You're making sure players don't leave the game by putting the last keystone in the largest nest of Terrorghasts. You don't want anyone to win… or leave."

She snapped her fingers, "Bingo, Sherlock."

She may be crazy, but this was deviously smart. If she was going to rule her own world, she had to make sure no one got out to stop it in the real world.

Lorena gestures to her soldiers, making them pull everyone away from the ledge except for me and Dominic. They all struggle and yell as best as they can, but to no avail. Dominic and I are placed with our backs to the chasm, our heels lightly hanging from the edge.

"You're going to kill your own father?? What the fuck is wrong with you?!"

"I won't let him ruin what I have built. You both are the only real threats to what I have planned once the game goes live Outside. For that, you need to be dealt with." She holds out one of her hands towards a nearby knight, who puts a tattered satchel in it. My satchel.

"You're so close to leveling up again, sweetie. Maybe you'll get lucky and use it before the monsters have a chance to tear you to shreds." She holds it over the ledge and lets it fall from her fingers. "Too bad we didn't click. You would've been fun for me to play with. Boys?"

Two of her biggest knights point their blades at us, keeping us pinned against the edge of the Chasm.

"Connor!" Krissy's crying hard trying to get through. Mark and Danica stay close together as they watch with horror-filled looks. Matt stood silently, staring at Dominic with remorse and regret. Riley is pinned down, being the biggest one of us all.

I look behind me into the deep chasm, hearing the endless screeching of what's looking below.

"To plunge into the mouth of the beast is to learn the truth," Dominic says clear as day. Not in a crazed mumble, but a fortified statement.

Lorena steps up to him with victory and determination in her eyes. "Think of this as a mercy-killing, Dad." With that, she shoves him back with both hands, plunging him into the mouth of the Chasm.

"*No!*" I watch him fall, almost losing my balance. His form gets smaller and smaller until he disappears into the purple abyss. His final words haunt my mind. *To plunge into the mouth of the beast is to learn the truth.*

"Don't worry about your friends, sweetie. They have their uses still."

I turn around and glare at Lorena, hatred burning in my eyes. "When I get out of there, I'm going to make you pay for this. I promise you."

For a brief, satisfying moment, her smirk disappears. She gestures to the knight that was holding me at sword-point. He presses the point of his blade to my chest plate and pushes, causing me to fall. Over the rushing air, I hear the others yelling for me. My eyes look to the dimly pulsing purple light that got closer and closer. I close my eyes and wait for the end of my fall.

This is it. Game over.

CHAPTER 39

"Well, that must've been some fall."

My eyes flutter open, trying to adjust to the blinding white light. My back stings with a burning pain, my head throbbing, and my ears ringing.

"Well don't just lie there, boy. Come on, get up."

I blink rapidly to further adjust to the blinding lights around me before raising my hand up to block some of it out. My eyes adjust just enough to see the back of my hand as it blocks the light. It's not green anymore. My nails aren't elongated claws. I bring my hand to my face, feeling around. My face isn't rough, my teeth aren't sharp and jagged, my nose and jaw feel normal again. I run my hands through my hair, feeling the familiar length and shagginess.

"Am... am I me again?"

"Not quite, I'm afraid."

I look up to see a tall figure standing over me with their hands behind their back. It's a man's voice talking down at me, leaning over and offering me a hand. I take his hand and lift myself up off the ground. In contrast to the white surroundings, the man stood back with his hands behind his back. He's a little taller than me with blond hair combed back slick. He's wearing black slacks with a dark blue button-up business shirt, finished off with a black leather belt and shoes to match. I take in his facial features and recognize it quickly.

"Dominic? Is that you?"

"At your service." He's smiling strangely at me, almost excitedly.

"B-but... you're different." I look at my hands and body. I'm wearing exactly what I was wearing before the game started. "I'm not an Orc anymore."

"Ah! So that was *you!* I like that I can put a normal face to the one that rescued me."

"You remember all that? You were—"

"Incoherent? Babbling? Downright crazy? Yeah, it took me a while to understand what happened while I was in the game."

I scan our surroundings, seeing nothing but fuzzy, blinding white nothingness. "Where are we?"

"Ah, yes. Apologies for our current landscape. We are still in the mainframe of my virtual interface network that collects all my game's data. Think of it as a sort of purgatory existence between the game's environment and our subconscious minds. I call it the Hollow because it is empty. Well, it used to be."

I take a few steps, then turn and scan the Hollow, hearing nothing coming from my footsteps. He was right; there was absolutely nothing but the two of us.

"How did we get here?"

"That, my boy, is entirely my doing. You see, I created a small glitch in my game's makeup for my alpha testing in case I began to feel critical effects from overexposure to the game environment. It was meant to pull my mind out of *The Mortal Gate* and bring me back out there."

"The glitched back door that Matt talked about," I realize. "To get back Outside."

"Ah, Matthew. Bright young man. It's a pity about what happened with him and the Keystone he found. I can't imagine what he felt."

"Wait... you *saw* that??"

Dominic chuckles and snaps his fingers. Behind him a screen spontaneously appears, showing various shots of Albistair's landscape and settlements. I see the Centaur encampment, the Ordowell Bowels, the Gorge, everywhere we've been. It's like Dominic is a god watching his creations at all times.

"You… you watched everything happen. Everything that happened to me and my friends! To your employees! To your fucking daughter!"

"Well, I needed something to do while I was stuck in here. Not to mention part of my conscious mind roaming around with the keystone it held."

I'm dumbfounded. Pissed off. Scared out of my mind.

"Why didn't you stop any of this?! Lorena tried to kill us both! She's got my friends!"

He snaps his fingers again, making the screen project a new image. It shows Dominic in some sort of room where he is wearing one of the Crests and resting on a bed. "Because I'm trapped in here, just like you. All the events of my game happen as they do. While the part of me that fell with you was out there, the rest of my mind was here, watching everything happen. I never realized how ambitious my daughter was until she set these events in motion."

The screen goes into a fast rewind to the moment he initiated the game and became motionless. I watch until I see a young woman enter the room; a young blond that sauntered over the unaware Dominic creepily. She walked to the side of the bed and started tinkering with his Crest, making his body convulse lightly.

456

"Is that—"

"Lorena," he confirms. "Bright young woman. Too smart for her own good. She got all her worst traits from me. Never forgave me for what happened between her mother and me. Even went as far as to trap me in my own creation, twisting it into a virtual prison where she was the warden."

"So, you really didn't send out copies of your game for people to beta test?"

"Absolutely not. That's when I realized my daughter's ambitions became more devious." He makes the screen change again, showing Lorena crying to a small group of people all wearing name badges that had SnoWire's logo on it.

"Matt said he and a small group came together to try and get you out."

He nods, "Matt is my favorite. He always develops new and exciting ideas to make our company shine brighter than others. The Crests and glove interfaces were his idea. He worked tirelessly to develop more so that he could try and free me from this place."

The video speeds forward to show two members of the group hugging each other closely before exchanging a kiss. "Is that Matt with Robert?"

He says nothing at first. Just watches the feed. "The first death…" The video feed shows Robert's body shaking furiously, other workers trying to get him stable before he stops shaking entirely. It shifts to some in-game footage where Robert's Dwarven character is being attacked by a pack of terrorghasts. The angle pans out to show Lorena, as her elf Spelldancer character, holding a stone in her hands that pulsed purple. It was a Keystone.

"She has one of the keystones that can open the Mortal Gate," he explains. "This one gives her control over the beasts, commanding them to attack where she wants them to. Like the settlement where you found the denizens piled inside of the longhouse. The keystone is powered by fear, and the people of Albistair fear uncontrollable magic, hence the magic-borne monsters. With them all terrified, Lorena's 'Archon' persona was able to seize power and control."

I can't take it anymore. I sit back down on the white floor and pull my knees to my chest. I'm in a nightmare. I put my friends into an unescapable situation and it's all my fault.

"Connor, I've tried everything I could to try and help you and your friends succeed where I failed." His voice changes into the one that was in my head during my worst moments. The voice I thought was Olagog, "I have been with you this whole time."

My eyes shoot open and glare at him, "You? You were in my head this whole time?!"

"In all your heads, actually. A side effect of me spending so long here to configure little alterations. Helping you to translate languages, learn new skills. I had to maintain secrecy in my messages to you so that my daughter wouldn't react irrationally."

I shoot up to my feet and lash out, punching him in the face. He stumbles back, causing the screen to disappear. "You lunatic! This is all your fault! Why did you do this?! Why couldn't you just tell us how to get out of the game?!"

He wipes his nose as if it were bleeding before he straightens himself up. "Because there is only one way out. There is only one way to return to yourselves without any damage to yourselves. Beat the game and stop Lorena."

I'm still in a state of shock and anger that I can't process what he's saying to me.

"Connor, I've risked much to bring you this far. I tried to do the same with my people, but Lorena stopped them all. Even Matthew is caught in her snare once again. You and your friends have collected almost all the keystones needed to open the Gate and leave this place. I want to help you succeed, but you have to trust me."

"*Trust you?!* You created a hellscape that has almost killed me and my friends. Your game is elitist, racist, and your daughter is a sociopathic nutjob that fucking enslaves everyone in it! Why in the hell would I ever trust you??"

He slowly steps towards me and puts his hands behind his back, "Because your friends' lives depend on you trusting me to help you."

He snaps his fingers again. The screen reappears, showing my friends being dragged in chains through the doors of a large, walled-up city. As they walk in, humans are yelling and throwing things at them like an angry mob. Lorena is leading them towards a castle-like structure in the city.

"Sacredcrest?"

"Yes. I don't know what she has planned, but your friends need you."

I swallow hard. He's right, I have to do something.

"How? We're stuck in here. You've never left, so how can I leave?"

The screen disappears again. "True, I am stuck here. But you, on the other hand, will be able to leave."

He reaches into his pocket and pulls out a small object. A familiar looking object, shimmering yellow with an engraved symbol. It's shaped just like...

"The yellow Keystone?!"

He chuckles and tosses it in his hand, "I still have a few tricks up my sleeve. When she took over the system, she intended on the final Keystone either being destroyed or in an impossible place to retrieve it."

"The Chasm!"

"Right again. She found this one in that settlement where you all taken prisoner. I had initially put it there as the sight of a terrorghast ambush in my original plot. But she didn't want anyone to complete the game, so she searched high and low for it. That's how she captured my Hermit persona, but she took a fake. A replica made of simple stone with a teleportation enchantment without her knowledge. This one, the real one, is the only way to open the rift back up and leave here."

"Wait... I don't understand. You've had this the whole time you were here? Why didn't you use it to leave? You could've completed the game and stopped this, right?"

He looks at me with a sad expression on his face, gripping the Keystone firmly in his hand. "This was meant to be my last creation. My last gift to my fans and consumers. A world that adapted and grew with them as they journeyed. But you've seen what's become of it. It's filled with every horrible thing that people want to escape from using video games. Death, dismay, war, corruption. It's not what I wanted, and now I am imprisoned by my own daughter and designs. I can't face it. I can't face *her.* So, I've chosen to stay here, letting my punishment fit my crimes."

"So, you just want to die? In here? No, you can't. You need to help me fix this!"

Dominic shakes his head, turning away from me. "I can't fix this. I am powerless outside of here. My Hermit persona has no strengths or magic. Lorena saw to it that I would not be able to fight against any enemies. The only thing that has kept the Hermit alive is my whispering into his mind. If all of me is put back into the Hermit, I will be weak."

I can't believe this. He's completely broken.

"Dominic, you can't just sit back and watch people get tricked into this hell. If we don't stop her, Lorena will have the game mass produced and trap innocent people in here just so she can play God. Your company, your legacy, your name will all be scrapped. Don't let everything that you've worked for go down in flames because you're a shitty father."

He stares at me strangely, keeping the sad expression on his face. Walking closer to me, he pauses before holding up the keystone. It begins shining yellow before shooting a beam past my shoulder. I whip around to see that a rift has opened in the Hollow. From the rift, I could feel rushing air pouring in.

"Once through the rift, we'll be in the Chasm where we entered from. Lorena believes us both to be dead, so her pets won't be expecting us. Let's use that to our advantage."

I nod sternly. We both walk towards the rift, seeing distorted reflections appear as we got closer. The reflections became clearer, showing us the images of our characters.

I observe Zarimm, then the Hermit. Both of them look to be ready with purpose. Dominic and I lock eyes.

"Forever free."

"Forever free."

With a brief pause, we both pass through the rift.

CHAPTER 40

With my footsteps heavy, after stepping through the rift, I stand on a dusty and barren earth. I look and feel myself, seeing that I have returned to my character form. I looked to my left to see Dominic in his Hermit form, still wearing the dusty cloak and shaggy long hair. My attention turns to our surroundings where dim purple colors flash around. We are surrounded by rock walls on either side of us. Within the walls are cracks and veins that pulsate with purple color in slow intervals. I put my hand on one of the purple veins and felt goosebumps travel through my whole body like there was static in the air.

"What gave you the idea to make this?"

"Honestly? Playing *Diablo* in my youth. I could never get enough of those swarms of monsters that players could grind through to level up and become better before the endgame."

The idea of endless terrorghasts spawning everywhere gives me the creeps. We barely could make it past fighting one of those things back in the village at the start.

That's when it hit me, "Then why aren't they? We've only encountered them a couple of times. Once in the village before the centaurs, and another in the Gorge battle. Why aren't they spawning everywhere?"

"Lorena. When the game was first engineered and launched, the terrorghasts would come in packs of ten to twelve per area of Albistair. But, when she took away my avatar and came into possession of the Keystone, she sent them all away, save for a few that would attack her victims."

"Sent them all away? To—"

A low growl echoes around us. He and I slowly look up, along the walls of the Chasm. The purple light still humming slightly, but just enough for us to see pure horror nesting and hibernating within the walls above us. Legions of terrorghasts slumbering inside the crevices of the walls like a nest of hornets.

"Well, shit."

"This… is going to be difficult."

"You think? Tell me, how do you suggest we get out of this alive?"

Dominic scans the walls with an inquisitive look, not seeming to be freaked out by the monsters in the walls like I think he should. Could he not see the same danger I am? Or has his time in the Hollow really made him that passive?

"When I first thought of this, it was always my intention that players would find themselves down here to bring them a real challenge. Players would need to be as delicate with their actions as to not wake up the beasts and search for an exit, much like a classic dungeon level."

That's less than helpful. I scan around the walls above again before something catches my eye. Something that was dangling loosely off a rock from the wall. I softly walk towards it until I was directly beneath it. The object seems like it's swaying from side to side, but it's still too dark to see. Another pulse of purple light flows through the chasm, giving off just enough light to reveal it.

"My satchel!" I slap my hand over my mouth. *Too loud!*

The walls remain still and eerie. None of the monsters heard it. I hope.

"Dominic, I need to get my satchel. It has my logbook and healing potions. If we don't get it, we could get devoured down here before we ever find a way out."

He puzzles on the idea, seeing how high up it was and what was waiting up there. "You can't possibly be suggesting you climb up there? Your armor and weight alone will cause problems and could wake every terrorghast in the Chasm."

"You're right. Thanks for volunteering."

He blinks at me, but I stand my ground. "You are a wildcard, Dawson. You were stripped of your avatar and given a plain human role. No armor, no weapons, nothing. Lorena wanted you to be weak in your own creation, but you're invaluable. Your knowledge is your power here, so use it."

We share a silent stare-down.

"Do you work as a motivational speaker when you're not here?"

"No, I'm a poor college student. Now get your ass up there."

With a deep sigh, he removes his Hermit's cloak and handed it to me. Lorena really screwed him over with this character design, giving him only that cloak, ratty clothes and linen footwraps. But, with any luck, his lack of armor and weighted items will help him climb the wall with hardly any issues. I watch as he finds his footing on the wall and starts his climb. The first twelve feet or so didn't have any nests or crevices, so it was an easy start. My heart drops when he makes it past the safe zone and starts climbing around the nesting terrorghasts. Every small motion they make, every disgruntled groan and twitch, give me more anxiety the closer he got to them. He was a few feet below where my satchel is dangling. In my head, I'm making a mental checklist of what was inside and how it can be used to help us get out of the Chasm. My logbook has my leveling elixir, which was my top priority. I pray that my health potions survived the fall, then I remember that it was a pocket-dimension item that held the lore books and Orcish horn I received along the way.

Wait... Yeskarra's horn!

My train of thought is interrupted when a rock from above fell to the ground. I look up to see Dominic looking back at me with a pale face and wide eyes. A large thud lands behind me, followed by a chittering growl. I slowly turn around until I'm face-to-face with a small, yet still terrifying, terrorghast that is now awake. Its three eyes stared back at me, scanning me. The barbed fin along its back was flattened down, but it starts to slowly raise as its mouth began to open. It's about to ring the dinner bell.

Quickly, I take out my staff and smash it against the monster's head, stunning it for a moment.

I look up at Dominic and whisper as loud as I could, "Hurry up!"

He nods at me and continues while I look back at the monster trying to shake itself out of its daze. I quickly jump at its back, putting the grip of my staff against its bottom jaw and pull as hard as I can. It's struggling and writhing against my grip, but my weight and strength gave it a real struggle. Above, Dominic finally reached my satchel and started to climb back down, but not as delicately as on the way up.

One wrong step and he can wake up the whole damn Chasm!

"Jump!"

"What?!"

"Jump on it!"

This thing is bucking like a horse trying to free its jaws. I'm pulling my staff against it as hard as I can while trying to urge Dominic to jump on it, but I lose focus and get thrown to the ground. I roll right into the adjacent wall, hitting my back on a protruding rock. The pain is ignored, thanks to the adrenaline of the moment. I glare at the beast as it opens its jaws to call for the others before it's pounced on and smashed to the ground. Dominic lands on its neck before rolling onto the Chasm floor, holding my satchel close to his chest. The terrorghast writhes on the ground, trying to get back up on its feet. Quickly, I get to my feet and run over to the beast, pressing my foot on its neck as it struggles. Turning my staff around to where the club is hovering over its head, I raise it high and bring it down with all my strength. And again. And again. Grunting with every strike until it stops squirming. The head of my staff is covered in the monster's gray blood before its body shimmered purple and disappeared into the air. The chasm grows quiet before the walls begins to hum louder and the purple light is glowing brighter.

"Ah, shit... *run!*"

I quickly grab Dominic by the arm and hoist him up onto his feet and we both start running. Where? We have no idea, but we need to get away from here. I look behind me as we run, watching the terrorghasts awaken from their rest and investigate the spot where the dead one disappeared. They all whip their heads around in our direction and screech in unison before running at us.

"Pick up the pace!!"

We run as fast as we can, hearing the teeth-grinding screeches and footfalls behind us grow louder. I take my satchel from Dominic and wrap it around me, scanning our surroundings as we run. Without warning, he shoves me to the right, into an opening that's small enough for the two of us to fit in. We hunker down as the stampede from hell whisks right by our small refuge. I can't even begin to count the number of them that were running by us, but it scares the shit out of me.

"We need a way out fast," he whispers to me frantically.

"What about the Keystone?! Doesn't it teleport?? Can't we get out of here like that??"

"Did you not pay attention before? It affects the mind, Connor! One use, and your mind starts to blink and fade faster than you do. We can't risk that."

Dammit, he's right. Just like what happened to Matt, Krissy, Lorena, and I when we were affected by the Keystones. It's just too risky.

I grab my Logbook and flip it open to the level page. My elixir is shimmering gold and full; my next level is ready. I pull it and pop the cork, but suddenly remember that we shine gold when we drink it. Will it give away our position? We're in a dead-end crack in the wall with nowhere to go. At least, not both of us.

"What are you waiting for?"

I hold my hand up to him, thinking hard on the options.

"I think I have a plan… but it's really stupid." I put my Logbook back in my satchel and pull out Yeskarra's horn that she gave me after our encounter in the Gorge.

"You can't be serious! Every beast in this Chasm will be on us if you use that!"

"But you know what I'm thinking, right? If this is like any other game I've played, I can get us the backup we need to get out of here. Again, it's a stupid idea, but it's the only one we've got."

Dominic stammers and stumbles, trying to think of an argument against my plan. "There's no other way out, but you can make it. I'll lead them away, and you climb out of here. Make this right, or I swear I'll haunt your ass for the rest of existence."

I shift out of the crack we are hiding in and stand out in the open, elixir in one hand and horn in the other.

I look above me to the cloudy, dark skies that were peeking into the Chasm. My thoughts immediately turn to my friends. To Krissy. "Guys… If I don't make it out of this… I'm sorry."

With a deep breath, I put the horn to my lips and blow as hard as I can. The sound from it is deep, hollow, and loud. From the mouth of the horn, tendrils of pink erupt with the sound and travel upwards to the top of the chasm until they're out of sight. Sudden echoes of screeching and clawing fill the air. I put the horn away and quickly drink my elixir, shimmering gold after taking in the last drop. I feel the earth tremble little by little as the screeching and rumbling gets louder. Palms sweating, fingers twitching, knees shaking.

Now!

I turn heel and haul ass in the direction we originally came from earlier. The terrorghasts make sure I know that they're hot on my heels no matter how fast I run. Squeezing the grip of my staff, I invoked my strength spell. *"Granav alnej ukavrengavh!"* The white halo surrounds me as my blood, used to power the spell, begins making me feel stronger.

473

"Please work, please work, please work!" I come to a stop, turn around rearing back my staff, and swing into the left wall. A large crack forms above where I struck it, traveling upwards, and shaking the crevices.

Dammit, come on!

They were getting closer to the point I could start seeing them like an evil flood of snarling lizards. I quickly shift to the right wall, cock back, and swing again. Another crack travels upward, causing some rocks to fall from the wall. My heart pounds loudly in my ears as the monsters get closer. I cock back my staff one more time, let out a wickedly loud roar and strike the wall again. This time, the crack splinters out further and makes the wall creak loudly. That was my cue. I turn tail and hoof it down the path. Behind me I can hear crashing and cracking and screeching. I look back to see if my plan worked. From high above, large stones began to rain down where I struck the walls, falling on top of the terrorghasts, falling in their way, even crushing some of them. It's a brief distraction, but one that gives me time. I turn to keep running, watching for any turns or spaces to use. *How far does this go?! There must be a way out!* I become distracted that I miss something popping out of the ground and trip over it, tumbling to the ground.

"Shit!" I groan as I sit up from the ground quickly, to see what I tripped over. A white stone poking out of the ground, of all things. The chasm lights up again, revealing my surroundings more clearly. It's not a stone. It's a skull.

All around me are different litters of bones scattered on the floor and buried in the dirt. So many gathered around this spot. *But why?* Near me by the wall, the only thing that isn't bone was a tattered length of rope coiled on the ground. I look up the wall then back down at the rope. These are the bones of people, NPCs or not I can't tell, that had tried to climb out and escape this place. My heart sinks.

"Nonononono! This can't be it!" I run ahead a little bit then come to a stop. The path ended. Nothing but a third wall of stone in my way. Dead end. Literally. I look up the wall and see a destroyed rope ladder that's too high for me to reach. I try climbing the wall to reach it only to have a stone fall from the wall, making me lose my grip and fall to the ground. Behind me, the screeching returns and got closer.

Fuck!

My back is against the wall, nowhere to go, with only my staff and a few spells to fight a legion of flesh-eating monsters. One life. No respawns or restarts.

No… this isn't how I go down.

I hold my staff strongly in front of me, seeing the swarm get closer. I grit my teeth, stand tall with feet planted firmly and yell, *"Come on!"*

One of the closer terrorghasts leaps out with its jaws and claws ready, only to be met with a fiery arrow to the head. More flaming arrows start to rain down on the terrorghasts, making them stop and stumble and fall just before reaching me.

I have little time to question what was happening before a cord of rope hits me in the head, bringing my attention up to the mouth of the Chasm. A long rope is dangling from the wall closest to me. I sheath my staff, grab the rope, and start climbing up the wall as quickly as I can. The screams and screeches of the terrorghasts below me are a mix of quiet and loud. One tries to climb up the walls below me to swipe at my foot, but I push away from the wall and come back with a double kick to its head, causing it to plummet. The volley of arrows and fire keeps coming, but none of them get close to me. The climb is stressful and tiring, my frantic steps are getting slower the higher I climb. The rope in my hands starts to tug upward, helping me to ascend faster. The atmosphere of the Chasm gets thicker as if I was breaking through dark storm clouds, but I break through. A number of hands grab onto my shoulders and arms, pulling me up onto the grassy surface of the earth. I can hear voices all around me trying to get my attention before I fall limp on the ground and pass out.

CHAPTER 41

My head is pounding loudly, yet the rest of my body feels comfortably rested as if I'm lying in a soft bed. I reach up and hold my head, but it's grabbed gently and placed by my side. I look up and see the unkempt face of a familiar human.

"You've got to be the craziest gamer I've ever had the honor of meeting."

"Dominic! You made it!" I lunge up and hug the rugged Hermit tightly.

He chuckles and returns the hug, "It was you who made that possible. You have some very resourceful friends."

I part from him to see some familiar faces standing over us. Sebaros is standing proudly with his arms crossed next to Corene. Yeskarra and Nargol are wielding their bows with smirks of victory. Djaren is standing strong and stoic between the Orcs and a familiar Triton, Zinis.

"You… you're all here!"

"You sounded the Horn. Of course, we answered the call," Yeskarra says proudly. "It is good to see that you are well, Zarimm."

"It has been a long time. You have made quite the name for yourselves." Sebaros crosses his arms and chuckles like a proud uncle.

"I am glad you are well. We feared we may not be able to repay you for your actions at the forward camp." Zinis looks different, being in more adorned armor and sporting a brass circlet on his head.

"Get a promotion there, Zinis?"

He's beaming proudly, "After proving Rolgos's strategy false and aiding your efforts, my now-freed kin demanded I take his place. I accepted."

"Nice! Djaren, I thought you would've gone home after what happened at the Vale."

Djaren, being the hulking giant he is, stands stoic in the corner holding the burning weapon he won in the Vale. "The Iron Vipers destroyed what families we had before our enslavement. I now lead the freed slaves and the Vale as a new community that shares its resources and welcomes refugees."

"That's... that's amazing. I can't believe you're all here." Reality sets back in. "Wait... my friends! I've gotta save them!"

I try getting up out of the bed I'm in, but Dominic holds me down. "Easy, my boy. I informed your associates here of the situation."

Corene nods in agreement, "We have intelligence on the Archon's plans. Supposedly, the Mortal Gate will reappear on the anniversary of the Violet Moon, tonight when the moon is at its highest."

"Shit! Lorena's going to have access to the Gate. I thought the location was lost when it vanished?"

"Yes, but with the unearthing of the Keystones and the presence of the Vanguards, the Mortal Gate has started to manifest where it first arrived: Sacred Mountain."

Nice work with the naming, Dawson.

"Wait. *Sacred* Mountain? As in—"

"The mountain that the capitol city is built into? Yes, it is above Sacredcrest."

I flatten out on the bed gripping my face, "Son of a bitch! Can *anything* not work out easily??"

Dominic puts a hand on my leg to get my attention, "Not all is so bad. We know where Lorena will be, and your friends are in the same place. She plans to try and keep us here by giving the illusion that your friends have corrupted the Gate to the point it won't open, but she doesn't know we have the last one. We have that to our advantage."

"Excuse me?" We look to Nargol, "the Archon... is a *woman*?" Yeskarra slaps him upside the head.

"She was a companion we picked up," I explain. "We thought she was an ally, but she stabbed us in the back. Threw me and her father into the Chasm. We tried to escape, but our abilities weren't working."

"It must have been the black iron. After studying its properties in the Vale, my people discovered that the Crimson Order forges their weapons and restraints from it in order to cancel the natural magics of non-humans."

"Treachery is a powerful motivator amongst our enemies. We know that pain. Now that the Archon has been unmasked, we can use that to our advantage."

I twist myself around so I'm sitting on the bed rather than laying on it, facing everyone in the tent. "It won't be that easy. She has all my friends, and I don't know what she'll do to them when she realizes the Gate won't work with the fake keystone."

"Worry not, Zarimm. We will reunite the Vanguards," Yeskarra promises me. "If we are to take Albistair back, we need the strength and favor of you and your companions to stand against the Crimson Order."

"It's only us, though. Lorena has the entire Order between the gate and us. How are we supposed to match her?"

Dominic smirks at me before nodding to the others. They all slowly file out of the tent, holding the entrance flaps open. "You're gonna to wanna see this."

Arching my eyebrow, I take to my feet and follow him out of the tent. Outside, the light of the sun floods my vision for a brief minute, revealing an army camp surrounding us. Massive gatherings of everyone, I and the others met along the way: the *harras* from the forest stand proudly as they practice their archery and conduct their herbalism, banners from at least seven orc clans fly high as the clansmen spar and sharpen their weapons, warrior tritons gather in huddles to recite their magics and prepare for battle, and the largest army of mixed races in familiar tattered rags and shackle-broken bracers forging black iron weapons and distribute them amongst their ranks. Suddenly, everyone in view stops what they're doing and face me as I walk out.

Djaren leads the others in front of the army and me, "You and the Vanguards have given us hope, young one. Without your efforts, we would be shackled by fear and oppression. We are ready to follow you to war with the Archon for the freedom of all in Albistair."

He kneels in front of me and puts a fist over his chest. After he kneels, the army behind them mirrors the action. It's like every story-based, narrative RPG I've ever fallen in love with; the scene where the hero's companions and acquaintances gather in common cause to pledge their strength for the final showdown. I have goosebumps everywhere, but I'm frozen in place.

"I... I can't ask you and your people to fight for me. This is my fight. You and yours have risked enough..."

"You do not have to, Zarimm. We are in this together." Yeskarra steps in front of me, kneels and puts her fist over her heart. Then Nargol, Zinis, Corene, Sebaros, and finally, Dominic. The army looks to me for a response. They're putting their faith and livelihoods in my hands for the final boss fight. They may all be computer-generated, but they're real to me in this moment.

I take in a deep breath and step forward. "This world isn't what it should be. It has stolen your freedom, your safety, your homes, and families. The Archon thinks she can keep us down by making us feel afraid and alone. But she's wrong. Look around you! Humans, Orcs, Centaurs, Tritons, Tabaxi, Tieflings, Elves together, to free Albistair from her tyranny! With our cause, we can turn the tide of the future! Save your anger and fury for the Crimson Order, leave the innocents to watch their army's strength fade into the very fear they use on us! Become the Vanguards that this realm needs! Freedom for Albistair! Freedom for all! *Forever Free!*"

"*FOREVER FREE!*" Like a thundering roar, the army shouted in applause and approval.

It's time to end this game… one way or another.

CHAPTER 42

~ Lorena's POV ~

I did it. I finally did it! Everything I've worked towards, everything I laid out for my stupid dad and those dumbass players to fall into. I have everything I need to get the Mortal Gate open and leave here safely. I'm going to make *so many* adjustments to this piece of shit and make it *my* masterpiece. I'm on a timeclock, though. The copies I've instructed to be delivered will go live in twenty-four hours, and I need to be ready to activate the protocol.

I throw on my cloak and look into the mirror, scanning my eyes over my new Archon armor; dark red and black streaked armor, slim enough for my figure but strong enough to protect me, adorned with the symbol of *my* order on the chest. I've added my own modifications to it to maintain my Spelldancer traits, keeping myself flexible while having steady weight. I love what I've done with the black iron ore, making it sap out the magic of non-humans like the players when they're captured. I'm a pure evil genius and I love it.

The sound of pained screams disrupts my train of thought. "Ugh, I told them to wait for me." I grab my crested helmet before leaving my quarters and make for the sounds. I deserve a fucking Emmy for my performance, tricking those idiots the way I did. I hardly made any effort!

I pass by guards and soldiers all through the halls of my castle, even by a few indentured servants that are washing the floors and tidying up my belongings. I love having servants. Keeps me free to plan and organize while my men have their fun torturing and preying on the non-humans. Luckily for me, I shed my Elf moniker to separate myself from the others. All the little things I've done before getting into this game has paid off.

With a wave of my hand, the guards ahead of me open the door to my prison where the others are. I hear the cracking of a whip as it opens. It makes me smile.

"Speak, you filthy beasts!" *Crack.* "I will make you speak!" *Crack.*

"Enough." The bosun stops himself as I enter. "Leave us. Bring a garrison ready for our ascent."

He bows to me, giving me chills of delight, and leaves the prison. The centaur was the toughest one to keep still, so I broke one of his legs upon entering the city. Made for quite a show to my people. The fish-boy was put near one of the fire pits, drying him out just enough to keep him down. The cat was put in one of the open cells after she bit one of my soldiers. The she-devil and Matt are leaning on wooden blocks, their backs bleeding from the whip.

"Are we having fun yet?"

They all look at me angry and disgusted. Ha, like it bothers me at all. They're in *my* world.

"W-why are you doing this?" The one named Krissy looks up from her block at me.

"Aw, sweetie. Were you not paying attention before I pushed your boy toy into that pit?"

She yells and lunges out, dropping sharply from being chained to the ground.

"Don't strain yourself, Krissy. You'll need your strength." I walk over to the cage that Danica is stuck in. "How about you, kitten? Do you know why I'm doing this?" She hisses at me. Cute.

"You're playing God." My head whips around to Riley. "You're taking over your dad's world and making it your own."

"And we have a winner, folks!" I give him a mock clap. He squirms on the ground, grunting at the pain of his leg. "Tell me something; have your parents ever just ignored you? Refused to let you become your best self for the sake of the family name?"

No answer. Silence. I hate silence.

"I have. I'm a genius, just like dear-old Daddy. I have a 168 IQ, graduated my private school at 16, college at 19, even ran a branch of SnoWire alone at 21. All of this while my parents underwent a long-ass divorce, not taking my thoughts into consideration. I wanted to stay with Dominic so he would teach me how to take over his successful empire of nerds and worshippers. In a digital-obsessed world, any who command a large corporation of codes and electronics run the world. I wanted that. I *still* want that. But Dominic didn't even fight to get custody of me. Mom got me instead, pushed for me to become a business and economics major so I could start my own company. I don't want that. I want what's rightfully mine. So, I took measures into my own hands. Sure, I was working as a branch manager of my dad's company, but it served as the perfect cover for me to develop my own programs and designs for his 'secret project', *The Mortal Gate*. Days before alpha testing was slated to begin, I paid a visit to his office. I tore his ass a new one, raging about how mad I was. As expected, he didn't react at all. He only said he was sorry and that this was for the good of our relationship. While he fed me his bullshit excuse, I planted my thumb drive into his mainframe and uploaded all of my programs and began my takeover."

"That's how you knew I'd bring you in," Matt mumbled in disbelief. "I thought you reconciled with your father. You used that to ensure I would ask you to help bring him out of his state."

I stroke his face, making him pull away. "Such a smart little cookie, aren't you? That's why you were one of my favorites. Until I found out that he was going to give you the keys to *my* inheritance. So, I made sure you would suffer in here."

"What about the ones who will play the game when it goes live? You're going to subject them a lifetime of mental prisons as their bodies decay in the real world!"

I admit, that was a difficult obstacle to try and work around, but Matt was more than helpful without even realizing. "Remember the tests we made on the Crests and gloves for the interface? So long as the SnoWire servers are operational and connected to all of the gaming networks, their brains will survive while their bodies are in a state of comatose. I swear, for a smart guy, you're pretty dumb. You are just as responsible for all of this as I am."

Matt falls silent and hangs his head. Good, he feels guilty. I win.

"Don't worry, kiddos. You'll still be able to live after this. Once I've finished my work, you'll be joined by every other sap who plays this game. I'll be their living goddess that gives them the ultimate fantasy lives they've always wanted. A world without disappointment."

The doors open as my captains walk in with their weapons ready. "Get them ready. We're going to address the people."

My men prepare the others and get them to their feet, keeping them controlled even as they fight and struggle. I put my helmet on and lead the march out of the castle. My people are furious at my prisoners, and I can't help but smile under my helmet. They throw curses, vegetables, even stones as we march them out. I don't intend on them to die here, but they will know who's in charge by the time we reach the Mortal Gate. I never intend on opening the only exit out of this game until I am fully satisfied with my results. When I get more test subjects into my world and give them the experience of a lifetime, I'll leave here to continue building. Thinking of the countless expansions and design builds I plan to give this place, makes me feel warm inside. I have my prisoners moved to a high-built stage where they are forced onto their knees, facing the angry mob of humans.

The boos and curses fall silently as I raise my hands to silence them. "Great people of Albistair! Allow your Archon to speak!" I take center stage, "I bring you the fabled 'Vanguards', the filthy beasts that all non-humans believe will overthrow your great leader and turn the tide of control to them!"

Boos. Glorious angry boos.

I raise a small bag from my belt, "But I, the Archon, possess four of the five Keystones of the Mortal Gate! I possess the key to our ascension to power and control for a peaceful and just realm!"

Thunderous applause. All for me.

490

"Once these beasts reveal to me the location of the last Keystone, I shall take my place in the throne of the Gods and bring you all to glory! The Horizon is within our grasp, and it will belong to us! All of the non-human races will either bow to my greatness or be cleansed by the light of our glorious power!"

I feel ridiculous talking like this, but it was what I needed to make my people happy. *My people. My world.*

"Archon! Archon!" My attention is pulled to a rushing scout cutting through the crowd. He quickly approaches the stage, "There's an intruder in front of the gates! An Orc! He calls to challenge you!"

An Orc? One single… no. No, no, *no!* Impossible!

A loud, boisterous horn calls in the air, causing my admirers to fall silent and look towards the gates. I jump down from the stage and push through the crowd, heading towards the gates of the city. The horn grows louder the closer I get. My men make space for me to quickly approach the gates. I climb the stairs that lead to the battlements.

My heart pounds and blood rushes to my face. It's *him.*

"*Lorena!*"

My men all look at me, waiting for orders.

"Lorena! I see you, Lorena! Face me, you treacherous bitch!"

My blood is boiling. *How the fuck did he survive?? Is my dad alive, too?? No, he'd be with him here and now.*

"Prepare to open the gates," I order. "Clear the square in front of the stage. My people will be given a proper example of what happens when the Archon is challenged."

CHAPTER 43

Lorena disappears from the top of the battlements; her archers still aiming at me.

This is such a stupid idea.

The gates open. Large red lights have made an alley that leads directly into the city. *Well, no turning back now, Connor.*

I take a deep breath before I start walking towards the open gates. The knights stare me down in hatred and resentment, but they're not as bad as the humans that are watching me walk in. They're talking under their breaths, but they're terrified of me as I walk in. The way inside goes on for a while before a large stage comes into view, and so do my friends. The sight of them makes my stomach do backflips. They look beaten and broken. I step into a large circle of Crimson Order knights, the alley behind me closing quickly.

"Connor!" Krissy's voice is hoarse, and her eyes are flooding with tears. The others look up in disbelief and shock.

"Welcome back from the dead, Connor." Lorena walks behind my friends on the stage, looking down at me.

"Thanks. It wasn't easy. Your pets say hello, by the way."

I can see her tense up. Good, she's shaken.

"Oh, I'm sorry. Do your followers not know that you have a Keystone that controls the terrorghasts?"

"Typical of a non-human," she snarls, snuffing out the whispers around us. "Putting the blame of our feared enemies upon the humans who are fighting to free us from the beasts."

Some of her followers protest me and curse at me. "Of course, the typical bad-guy turnaround. You're just as cliché as your 'epic reveal', Lorena. I thought you were supposed to be smart."

That hit a nerve. She pulls a dagger from her belt and puts it at Krissy's throat. "Don't test me. You won't get out of this alive."

Krissy looks at me worried, but my eyes are fixed on Lorena. I pull my satchel from around my neck and reach inside, pulling out the yellow Keystone and holding it over my head. Gasps and murmurs come from the humans that are watching.

"I challenge the Archon of the Crimson Order!" I slowly turn in a circle, showing the Keystone to the crowd. "If I fall, the Keystone and the Mortal Gate are hers. If she

494

falls, I claim the Keystones and her prisoners." I turn my focus back to her, "Do you accept my challenge?"

Silence. Thousands of eyes look to Lorena, waiting for a response. She's frozen in place; cornered and pissed off. *Perfect.*

"I accept." She takes the dagger from Krissy's throat and sheaths it. Her eyes lock onto me as she hops down from the stage.

"You're no match for me, Connor. I'm more experienced and stronger than you are." She grabs two ribbons from her belt and holds them tightly.

I take my staff into my hands and begin to circle around. "True, but I've gotten smarter after fighting your pets. My wisdom and intelligence are higher, and that's all I need. *Sacred Armor!"*

I pound the pommel of my staff on the ground. A red flash envelops me, causing my armor to illuminate and strengthen. She barely chuckles before twisting her ribbons in a flourish, *"Haste!"* Her movements suddenly quicken as she rushes in and whips her ribbons, attacking my armor. The impact is quick, but the force is what throws me off my balance. She whips them out at me again, only to meet the grip of my staff and get yanked towards me. She loses her balance and stumbles forward, giving me a chance to kick out and hit her stomach.

"Your dad was very disappointed in you, Lorena. He thought you could do better than what he did. Be better than him."

"I *am* better than him!" She rushes forward and spins into the air, bringing a whip of fire down on me. I block to the best of my ability but get blasted to the ground. In a swift action, she wraps a ribbon around my neck and starts to pull. I strain against it and swing my elbow into her ribs, making her cough out and buckle forward. My hands reach up and grab her by the cloak, flipping her onto her back.

Stumbling to my feet, I laugh at her. "After all of your talk about being better than everyone else, you are the biggest walking joke I've ever seen. You say people are awful, so you turn into an Elf. You want to be loved and worshipped, you become a human. A textbook narcissist."

She rolls into a kneel and snarls. She begins to dance. It's not one I've seen before, and it starts to become confusing. What I don't see is a wave of magic is spiraling towards me and affecting my mind, making me lose focus. That's all she needs before she runs in a dashing zigzag motion and gets around me before swinging a dagger at my side. My Sacred Armor barely holds as I feel the force of it trying to penetrate my ribs. My head is still fuzzy from what she did, so I wildly swing my staff around trying to hit her. Every swing I make, she stabs at me again and again. My armor is getting weaker. The last stab she makes plunges upward into the soft parts under my arm, causing me to yell in pain and buckle to the ground. My Sacred Armor disappears from around me. I hear Lorena breathing and chuckling like a demon before she rips my staff away from me.

"You see?! I'm the best! I am the hero of this story! You... you're just a weak, useless, lonely reject. You're a reject here, you're a reject out there!"

She holds her hands in the air, expecting the people around to rally behind her, but all she will hear is my laughing. Every chuckle hurts as I breathe out, but it's worth it. She looks down at me with a confused look.

"Y-yeah... maybe I am a reject. But I'm not alone." I take my hand away from my wound, blood dripping from my fingers, hold it up to the sky and yell, *"Rally of War!"*

All around me, a red aura begins to swirl and move up into the sky. Soon, the whole border of Sacredcrest flashes with this red aura before returning to me. The city falls silent until distant roars and yells turn all heads towards the walls. I smile as I see the Vanguard Army pouring over the walls and into the city. The humans begin to scream and run as our army charges towards the Crimson Order knights. Clashes of swords and blasts of magic cause mass chaos around us all.

"No!! Impossible!!" Lorena rips her helmet off, showing a face of shock and disbelief. Her captains rally to surround and protect her. I quickly get to my feet and run to

497

the stage. I use the pommel of my staff to break the chains holding everyone hostage.

Krissy shoots straight up and holds me close. "I thought I lost you!"

I returned the hug tightly, "Who, me? I had it under control."

More hands and bodies surround me as everyone stands up and hugs me close.

"Embrace each other later, we have a war to win!" All eyes dart to Sebaros as he gallops up to the stage and drops a sack of weapons.

"Danica and I need our magic items!"

"I will accompany you!" Nargol grips his two axes in his hands with a huge grin.

"We need to get the Keystones to end this! Where's Lorena?"

"Look!" Mark points to a retreating Lorena, going up a path near the castle that traversed upwards to the mountain. "Where the hell is she going??"

"She's going to the Mortal Gate! We need to stop her!"

"Connor!" I turn at the sound of my name. Dominic runs through the warring crowds to meet us. Matt sees him alive and well, jumping to hug him tight. Although surprised, he smiles and returns the gesture.

"I can't believe you're alive!"

"Thank our friend here for that."

"You're not scrambled eggs anymore??"

"Long story! We've gotta move!" I shuffle around my satchel to give Riley my last health potion for him to heal his broken leg.

"Connor, stick to our plan. Okay?"

Shit. I look at Dominic sternly before nodding in agreement. "Let's go! Danica, Riley! Get your stuff and meet us up on the mountain. The army will try to keep the knights off our backs!"

Everyone picks up a weapon and starts fighting through the mass chaos. We were met with a wall of red knights trying to kill us or slow us down. Like avenging angels, Krissy, Matt, and Mark fight tooth and nail against their previous captors. Krissy is wielding two swords and uses her newly acquired skill, Heat Seeker, to flawlessly counter and attack. Matt's abilities as a Shadow Stalker aid him as he puffs in and out of sight like Nightcrawler, cutting down and evading his attackers. Mark's use of a spear is flawless and fluid with every strike. Being away from the water, his abilities as a Totemist are limited, but that isn't stopping him from skewering everyone in his path.

All around us, the war raged on. The sun starts to set, replacing the orange sky with a sudden shine of violet from the other side of the horizon. The Violet Moon is coming, and our window was closing.

"Push through! We need to get to the Gate!"

The path ahead is riddled with archers and swordsmen trying to stop us from going on. We run into a group of archers that pin us down, making us stop and dodge to avoid being hit. We don't have any arrows and there are too many of them.

"*Thunderous Blow!*"

The group of archers are suddenly blasted by a shockwave, throwing them off of the path and the mountain. I look back to see an electrified god of thunder with horse legs aiming his hands where the archers stood. On his back rides Danica, the two of them galloping up the path together towards three charging knights with blades held high. Danica pulls one of her Trick Cards out and primes it, "Have a *Familiar Taste of Poison*, assholes!" She chucks the card at the knights, creating a large green cloud of poisonous gas to surround them. The knights stop their charge and choke on the air trying to breathe. We wait until the cloud disappears and all that remains are the writhing bodies of the knights.

"I love that girl." Mark runs ahead to catch up with them, having us follow suit.

The Violet Moon slowly rises over Albistair, the war still raging below us. The climb is starting to take its toll on us, making us slow down our pursuit. A sudden ringing sound caught my attention. I whip my head around to find it only to realize it was coming from above.

"More! *More!* Put your backs into it, goddammit!"

"What the hell is going on up there?"

I push past the others further up the path. Even ground is finally within reach, and so is the sight of Lorena and her men around a stone arch. The arch is thick and made up of multiple types of sediments and stone. Along the face of the arch are five small empty slots, each with a symbol designed above it. The knights around the arch are swinging their weapons at it frantically and with great determination.

This is the Mortal Gate. And Lorena is trying to destroy it.

CHAPTER 44

"Lorena, stop!"

She whips around and faces us with wide, angry eyes. The six of us all stand before her, winded but ready to fight.

"You ruined everything I planned! You selfish shits ruined my world! Now, you'll never leave here!" She frantically shuffles in the sack on her waist and pulls out the purple Keystone. This one is bigger than the others with a star-like engraving on its face.

"Lorena... don't do this. Think for one damn minute! If you destroy the Gate, you'll destroy the only way to leave! *Your* only way to leave!"

"I'll find another way! I won't let you stand in my way anymore! Even if I have to rebuild from scratch!"

She holds the Keystone over her head and up at the Violet Moon. The Keystone starts to illuminate and hum before a purple beam of magic shoots over the horizon. The battle beneath us suddenly stops, and the only sound that can be heard is a large collective of screeches and howls. We all look to where the beam went and watch as a stampede of terrorghasts storms its way from the Chasm towards the city of Sacredcrest.

"Are you insane?! You're going to kill everyone here!!"

She only smiles maniacally as she holds the stone. "I will destroy everything unless you lay your weapons down and bow. I am the only one who can call them off before they rip apart every ally you've brought with you."

The terrorghasts are getting closer to the city. Suddenly, everyone diverts their attention to the sounds with their weapons shaking in their hands. The civilians are barricading themselves inside of their homes, but the Vanguard army stands as strongly as they can.

"Lorena. That's enough."

Her eyes shoot past me and widen at the sight of Dominic, calmly walking up behind us.

"No... you're dead... I killed you..."

"My daughter, look at what you've done. Look at the chaos you've created. Is this the world that you wanted to create?"

His hand points out to the horizon where the beasts were charging. The Violet Moon lit an ominous atmosphere over all of Albistair. Fear is fueling the power of the Keystone that controls the beasts.

"I made this fantasy into a reality. *ME.* You never would've achieved this kind of greatness without *my help!*"

Dominic sighs, taking small steps towards her. "Lorena, you've let your intelligence cloud your judgement. You think creating all of this gives you control, but the programming has corrupted your brilliance."

"Like you ever noticed! I did everything to get you to notice me! To give me what you were going to throw away! I will outshine your achievements and create something better! I beat you!"

The Violet Moon is now directly overhead at this point. The Mortal Gate began to shimmer under its light, the slots for the Keystones dimly lit.

"Lorena, I was going to give up my position to reconnect with you. It took me too long to realize that my passion for my work destroyed my relationship with you. I was going to give it all up for you."

Her angry eyes soften into confusion. He steps closer, almost at arm's length to her. "While I was trapped in here, I saw what you were doing. I began to understand your anger and frustration towards me. I want to make this right. Please. Let me make this right."

They stand still for a moment. The screeching of the terrorghasts were now louder. They're getting to the walls of the city.

Lorena's eyes fill with tears as Dominic reaches out and holds her arms gently in his hands. "Let's go home and make this right…"

A flash of rage glazes over her eyes before she shoves her dagger into his side.

"NO!" Matt lunges, but I hold him back.

Dominic gasps and kneels to the ground in front of his daughter. She breathes heavily before pulling the dagger out. "I *am* home. You have no power over me, here."

He coughs a gargled breath and looks up at her. "Th-there's… more of me in you… than I thought, Lorena… Your pride… your ego… is your blind spot."

She tilts her head to the side in confusion before he rips the Keystones from her belt and throws them back to me. I let go of Matt and grab the sack, "Get her Keystone!"

"*Destroy the Gate!*" Lorena screams and retreats behind her men. The knights continue to try and hack at the stone. Riley bullrushes one on the left side, pummeling him to the ground. Danica and Krissy double-team the one on the right, flying at him in a leaping kick. Mark and I fight off the remaining knights while Matt rushes to Dominic's side, holding him in his arms.

"Mark, match the stones to their slots!" I toss him the sack and turn my attention to Lorena. Her eyes are glowing purple as she grips the stone in one hand, her ribbon in the other. "It's over, Lorena! Give me the Keystone! Don't let it control you like it did with everyone else!"

"*I am in control!*"

Behind me, I hear the crashing of swords and the screaming of people from down below. The terrorghasts break through. I'm not going to let them all die for her insanity. I had one more spell use, but it was a big one.

"I'm sorry, Lorena... *Divine Strike of Olagog!*" The end of my staff extends a long red blade of magic. I raise it high and bring it down in a swift motion. The purple left Lorena's eyes, now filled with shock. We both look to her hand that was holding the Keystone, her whole arm cleaved from her body with the hand still gripping it. The Keystone stops glowing, but the battle below still rages on. She falls to her knees screaming in pain, trying to grab it frantically. I rush to grab it, prying it from her lifeless fingers and run to the Gate. The others have slotted the blue, red, green, and yellow Keystones and are waiting for the last one.

"Connor! They're coming up!"

Danica's cries bring my attention to the mountain path. A swarm of terrorghasts have broken through and are coming right for us. I turn back to the Gate and the final slot, take the Keystone, and lock it in place. The colors all join in unison, causing the Mortal Gate to illuminate and erupt in a blinding white light that blasts us all to the ground.

I groan in pain as I look up from the ground, seeing the blinding light disintegrate the pack of terrorghasts into purple dust. I hear the screeches become less and less frequent from below as I crawl to the edge of the mountain path. In the city, clouds of purple dust evaporate into the air. My eyes follow them all the way up before I notice the Violet Moon changing color, becoming its once radiant white.

"We did it…"

CHAPTER 45

I stand up to my feet and turn to the others. They all stand up in confusion, looking to the Gate. The keystones are giving off crackles of magic as the center of the archway begins to ripple and create an image in it. The stone archway is glowing in a shimmering image of the Outside. While it is nighttime in Albistair, it is bright and sunny on the other side.

"It's open... we won!"

Riley rears his legs back and shouts in excitement. Mark and Danica embrace each other in laughing tears. Before I can react, Krissy is smashing her lips into mine, wrapping her arms around my neck. I return her kiss eagerly until we part lips and just hug. We both hear shouting coming from below and look down. The Crimson Order has laid down their weapons and knelt in surrender. The entire city, human and non-human alike, are chanting one word over and over up at us.

"*Vanguards! Vanguards! Vanguards! Vanguards!*"

I smile with Krissy still in my arms and raise my fist high, receiving a thunderous applause in response.

"Dominic... Dominic please stay with me..."

I turn towards Matt and Dominic on the ground. He's bleeding from his knife wound into Matt's hands, who can't hold back his tears. "Somebody help him!"

"Let me try," I insist. I flip through my logbook to see if I have anything left. My major spells have been used up, but my "Spare the Dying" cantrip may be able to work. I exerted a lot of strength fighting to get up here, I just hope I have enough left.

"*Ukpare avhe Dyaumn.*" The red tendrils snake into the wound, but it isn't working. "Matt…"

"No, dammit! I'm not letting this happen!"

"Matthew, stop. It's okay." Dominic rests his hand on Matt's, smiling up at him. "You don't have to worry. I'll be okay. You all need to leave."

"What?"

"It was his idea," I explain. Everyone's eyes fall on me. "We needed to get the Keystones, and he knew she wasn't going to forgive him. He insisted on it. It was the only thing we could do."

Mark looks down at him, guilt starting to come over him. "You sacrificed yourself to help us?"

He keeps smiling and nods. "It is the ultimate lesson to be taken away from this adventure; strength comes from the many and overpowers the one. I want to thank you all for helping me. You will need to step through the Gate now if you wish to end the game."

We all look at the shimmering Gate and then back at him. He whispers something to Matt that only he can hear, something that floods him with tears and forces him to nod in response.

His eyes set on me, "Connor, remember what you promised me."

I nod. "Come on, guys. Game's over."

We all stand up and face the Mortal Gate. I can only guess their hearts are pounding as hard as mine is. "Who's first?"

"Get me the fuck out of here," Danica volunteers. She approaches the Gate, looks down at her cat-like body one last time, then pushes through. Like a smooth, watery curtain, her figure causes a ripple in the Gate before it smooths back out.

"Can't say I didn't see that coming."

"Don't worry, I'll go next." Mark steps forward before turning his back to the Gate. "See you on the other side!" With a smile, he backs into the Gate and disappears.

My eyes dart to Matt, who is lost in his own head. I rest my hand on his shoulder, "It's on you, man. You know what he wants, but it's your choice." He looks to me sadly and then to Dominic, who is leaning up and watching us.

"I know. Thank you for not killing me."

I chuckle and shrug, "It was tempting. Find us when you're out there, okay?" He agrees quietly before walking through.

Krissy steps up next and turns to me with a smile, "You and I have a lot to talk about after this."

"I know. I'll see you soon." With a wink, she walks through. "Okay, Riley. Your turn."

"Connor... I don't want to leave."

Fuck, I knew this was gonna happen. "Riley..."

"No. Don't you understand? I belong here. I understand the world here! I can walk! What do I have to go back to?"

"Riley, I'm not leaving without you."

"Then let's stay! We can turn this all around! Come on, Con-Man! You and me? We can run this place!"

"*No.*" He blinks in disbelief. "Riley, look at what happened here. Do you want to lose yourself like what *she* did?" I point to Lorena, but her body is gone. We both blink and look around. "Where did she go??"

A loud scream lets out as Lorena swings a sword with her remaining arm, striking Riley's horse half and crippling him to the ground.

"Riley!"

"You wanna stay, you piece of shit?! Fine! You'll stay in *pieces!*" She lifts her sword to swing again but is tossed to the ground when Dominic lunges up and tackles her.

"*Go!*"

I quickly pick up Riley as best as I can and walk him towards the Gate. "You can hate me for this later, Riley!" Much to his protest, I push him into the light of the Gate and watch him disappear.

The sounds of struggle continue behind me. Lorena wrestles with the wounded man, both too injured to overcome the other. I run into the fray and kick her away from him.

"Dominic! Come on, this is crazy! Come with me!"

"You *promised me! Go, now!*" Before I can protest, he picks up a sword and throws it at one of the Keystones, striking it and disrupting the Gate's stability. He was going to shut it. Lorena got back to her feet and snarled at me, prompting me to turn and run. I hear her screams getting closer to me as I leap towards the dwindling light of the Mortal Gate.

CHAPTER 46

With a loud gasp, I shoot up and suddenly see a group of paramedics surrounding me.

"This one's awake! Get a gurney! Kid, you okay? Can you hear me?"

I am breathing heavily and nod before looking to my hands and feet. I'm in the same clothes I wore when we started the game. We made it.

"Connor!"

My eyes dart around to find the voice before I'm tackled back to the ground. Krissy, in all her human beauty, is holding me tightly to the point I almost can't breathe.

"Jesus Christ, I could kill you right now! You didn't wake up!"

"I'm okay! I promise! Where is everyone else?"

"Right here!"

Krissy let me up to see Mark, Danica and Riley all wrapped in shiny aluminum emergency blankets. About eight paramedics were around us, along with some police officers.

"We made it… holy shit we made it!" I pull her back in for a hug, laughing hysterically. She pulls back a little to look me in the eyes before kissing me. This one beats the kiss in the game. Real and warm.

"Miss, we need you over here, please." Krissy was taken from me and sat down with a paramedic and a cop.

One of the cops and paramedics start asking me questions and checking my vitals. According to them, the worker that Riley paid for us to use this space found us attached to the game mat and unresponsive. He tried several things to get us out of our little immersive trance when he noticed our bodies reacting to some sort of shock, most likely while we were being attacked. He called 911 and they sent everyone they could to try and wake us up. In the game, weeks seemed to have passed by. Out here, it was nearly thirty-six hours of exposure to the technology. They checked us for long-term exposure effects like seizures, dizziness, and disorientation.

"I don't know what it is with you kids today and your video games, but this could've killed you or put you in a coma." The lecture isn't surprising.

"I'm fine, I promise. Trust me, we're not doing that again."

After all of the checkups and lectures are done, we're instructed to leave if we didn't want any more trouble. I nod in response and move over to the backpack I brought with me, slinging it over my shoulder.

My attention gets pulled to the game mat, flashing something on the face of it. "Guys?"

The rally to me and watch the flashing turn into words on the mat.

It reads: *"Campaign Successful! Start New Game?"*

My eyes meet the others', who all look back at me in concern. I reach to the mat, yank it up and throw it to the ground. "Let's go home."

~One month later~

I shake in my bed, unable to pull myself out of the dream. Giant insects and lizards, Lorena's rage-filled eyes, the red knights charging with swords, all flooding at me in endless waves. I can't get away from them. They're everywhere!

"Wake up!"

My eyes shoot open, the feeling of sweat running down my head and face, I'm breathing heavily and looking everywhere. The only thing to bring me back to calm is a pair of arms wrapped around my neck.

"Babe, you okay?" Krissy lightly strokes my face, wiping some sweat away from my head.

Swallowing hard, I nod in response. "Sorry... just another nightmare."

She kisses my temple, "It's okay. You're okay. I'm right here."

My breathing slows down, and I start to calm down, resting a hand on one of her arms. "Thank you..."

We kiss lightly before I go to the bathroom to wash my face, shutting the door behind me. Cool water fills into my cupped hands. I lean forward and wash it over my face, taking a deep breath as the drops fall back into the sink. I turn the faucet off and stare at myself in the mirror.

Fuck, they never stop.

It's been a whole month since we escaped the game, but it still haunts me. Riley hasn't talked to me since our argument at the Gate; he just pours himself into work at The Cache. He's ignored every call I've made to try and talk to him. He banned me from the store and refuses to see me at all. Mark and Danica were in a rough spot for a while, but they are doing better now. They got a new place together off-campus and have grown closer than before, which is great. Krissy and I talk a lot, even though we knew exactly what we wanted. We started dating the day after we came back from the game, and it's been amazing. But even so, I'm still getting haunted by dreams of the game. Was it guilt for leaving Dominic and Lorena behind? Was it the aftermath of so much exposure to the equipment? Whatever it is, it's been giving me nightmares for weeks.

A knock at the door brings me back to the moment, "Connor, don't take too long. We need to be at the café in an hour."

"Yeah, okay. I'll be out shortly."

A couple of days ago, I got a phone call from an unknown number. It was Matt, who finally reached out after dealing with the fallout of TMG's cancellation and criticism. The news was all over the place about both Dominic and Lorena's "mysterious illness" that landed them both in comas. At least that was the official story. He reached out to have me meet with him at a local café for something he wouldn't explain until we met. It's funny that I can't envision him as a normal person, only his Dark Elf persona.

I take a quick, cold shower to wake me out of my haze before handing the bathroom over to Krissy. I much prefer crashing at her place more than her at mine, seeing that I still haven't found a cheap enough place for myself. Plus, her place is cleaner than mine. We both gather our stuff, head out the door and make for the bus stop.

"So, we're meeting the new CEO of SnoWire live and in person. How does that make you feel?"

"Honestly, strange. We've never met him face to face, only seeing him in the news when he took over the company."

She nods. "Wonder if he reached out to anyone else..."

"You mean Riley?"

Another nod. "He has to come around eventually, right? He knows you couldn't leave him in the game."

"Right. Well, tell that to a guy whose whole life is games and roleplaying that got his legs back in an immersive experience. Honestly, I don't blame him for wanting to stay. But I wasn't about to lose my friend. Call me selfish."

She grabs my hand and interlocks our fingers, "It's not. He'll come around."

Giving a half-hearted smile, I turn my gaze to the window. The trip takes us about twenty minutes by the time we make our stop. The café comes into view while we walk down the street.

Once inside, we meet the hostess. "Hi, we're supposed to be meeting with someone. Matt Bauer?"

"Right this way." The hostess leads us towards the back of the café and to a private seating area. The area has a large table with four people at their seats, one in a wheelchair.

"Riley…"

Riley looks at me with disapproval and turns away.

"Connor! Krissy!" Mark shoots up from his seat and hugs me hard. I laugh and return it while Danica and Krissy hug each other lovingly. I part from Mark and look to the fourth person; a man in his early 30's wearing a navy-blue suit, sporting thin glasses on his nose, his black hair styled in a small fauxhawk. He smiles and holds out his hand, "Zarimm the Warpriest, I assume?"

I smile and take his hand, "Matt… it's great to meet you in person."

"Likewise. Please, take a seat."

Everyone sits back down after catching up, aside from Riley, and look to Matt. "So, what's this about?"

He clears his throat, pulls out a briefcase and opens it. Inside, he pulls out five envelopes and slides them to each of us. "While our company in its current state is unable to provide publicity for beta testing rights, we are able to compensate you for the testing of TMG."

I lift an eyebrow and open my envelope. Inside, a check for forty thousand dollars signed to me. Danica shrieks when she reads hers, Mark hugged her tightly after opening his, and Krissy grips my arm tightly in excitement. Even Riley couldn't hold back his surprise. "Dude… we can't take this. Not after—"

"I insist," Matt interjects. "Dominic insisted that all the assets be divided amongst you for everything you've done."

Dominic. Even when he's not here, he's still pulling strings. "And the promise he had us keep?"

Matt nods, removing his glasses. "At his request, the servers for the game have all been pulled and the entire system has been deleted. *The Mortal Gate* is no more."

An eerie silence falls over the table. This could only mean that Dominic and Lorena can't be pulled out of the game, and they're gone. Dominic insisted that the only way to make things right was to keep him and his daughter in the system to ensure that there were no other ways the game could trap anyone else in it.

I look to Riley and see the defeat in his eyes. His alternate life with legs is now destroyed.

"There's also one more thing I wanted to discuss." I return my gaze to Matt, who now is holding a single packet of forms up. "An offer." He puts it on the table and slides it my direction. "I spoke with your professor at the college, who informed me that you are creating a new game. *Soulscape*, I believe the name is."

I start reading through the packet. It's a contract for SnoWire Interactive to hire me on as a developer and give me creative control over my game's commission and development. "Holy shit…"

"You have a bright future in this industry, Connor. If you want it."

Flipping through page after page got me more excited. This is what I've wanted my entire college career, and Matt was going to make it happen for me. "I… I don't know what to say… After everything that happened."

"I understand. It's been a hard transition for us all. But I think you have what it takes to help me right the wrongs SnoWire has made. What do you say?"

I take a deep breath and look down the table to Riley. "Riles? What if you did this with me?"

His eyes shoot up at me in surprise, "What?"

"I mean it. You could help me with story development and mechanics. You're amazing at immersion… and I need my friend with me."

"What about Mark?"

I shake my head, "He's out. I promised him that I'd never involve him in games like this again."

Mark and Danica both nod. "Don't get me wrong, we'll support you when you're a big, bad game developer millionaire. But we're out of that scene."

"You know I'm ready to support and help you," Krissy assures me. I smile in response but return my gaze to Riley.

The silence was a little deafening as we all wait for his response. Riley takes a beat before backing his wheelchair from under the table, turning it and wheeling towards me. I stand up from my seat and face him, ready to take on whatever resentment he has.

To my surprise, he holds his hand out for me to shake. "Truce."

I smile in response and take his hand, shaking it. I look to all my friends, smiling and nodding in approval before setting my eyes on the patient Matt. I take a pen from the table and sign his contract. Whatever this future was about to hold, my friends, my girlfriend, and my new partner are going to be there with me on a new adventure. One that I have feared until now. The game of reality and living.

"Let's make some magic."

AFTERWORD

Thank you for reading *The Mortal Gate*!

I want to also thank my beta readers, without whom I wouldn't have been able to make this story possible.

Please leave a review!

This story is available on Amazon, where you can leave a review and tell me what you think!

Follow my links below to stay up to date on any and all of my current and future projects. Thank you for your support, and I'll see you on the next adventure!

Facebook Page: https://www.facebook.com/overtonbooks

My Official Website: www.overtonbooks.com

ABOUT THE AUTHOR

Seth Overton is the author of *The Mortal Gate*, his latest
GameLit novel that explores the idea of escaping reality versus
escaping from yourself.

Born and raised in Missouri, he has found enjoyment losing
himself in a good fantasy or science fiction book to feed his love
and appreciation for imagination and creativity. Taking his love
for books and writing, Seth became an English Language Arts
teacher graduating from the University of Central Missouri to
teach and inspire the next generation of writers.

Seth currently lives in Texas with his wife teaching high school
and also works to write enjoyable, relatable, and compelling
stories for his readers.

ABOUT PARTY UP PUBLISHING

Party Up Publishing LLC is an independent publishing group for authors, by authors. We specialize in LitRPG and GameLit. We party up independent authors together for the mutual benefit of marketing, editing, proofreading, graphic design, production, and branding of our titles. We are for authors, by authors because we are all stronger together.

Connect with Party Up Publishing:

Website: https://partyuppublishing.com

Facebook:

https://www.facebook.com/partyuppublishing/

Email: contact@partyuppublishing.com

Newsletter: http://eepurl.com/g92gi9

Street Team:

https://www.facebook.com/groups/PartyupPunlishing/